Freedom Street

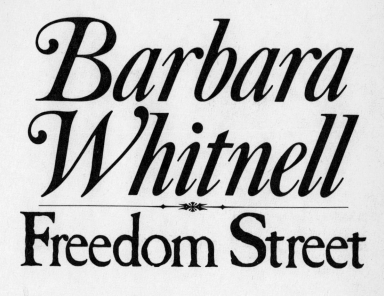

Barbara Whitnell

Freedom Street

Hodder & Stoughton

LONDON SYDNEY AUCKLAND TORONTO

British Library Cataloguing in Publication Data

Whitnell, Barbara
  Freedom Street.
  I. Title
  823'.914[F]

  ISBN 0-340-43034-6

First published in Great Britain 1989

Published by Hodder and Stoughton,
a division of Hodder and Stoughton Ltd,
Mill Road, Dunton Green, Sevenoaks, Kent TN13 2YA
Editorial Office: 47 Bedford Square, London WC1B 3DP

Photoset by Rowland Phototypesetting Ltd,
Bury St Edmunds, Suffolk

Printed in Great Britain by St Edmundsbury Press Ltd,
Bury St Edmunds, Suffolk

For my dear daughters
Lindsay and Judi
with much love

Book One

1

It was cold in the cellar; cold and dark, and the fear of those who waited hung in the air like a sea mist, damp and corrosive, seeping into bones and chilling hopes.

The waiting had gone on for ever. Charlotte Bonnet pressed close to her father for warmth and wondered if it would ever end. The home she had left seemed no more than a dream. Once she had walked in sunlit fields, had played in a courtyard where geraniums spilled from urns and the scent of roses mingled with those of herbs and hot bread, but here in the cellar under the crumbling auberge on the quayside at Nantes, such memories had no more reality than the gilt-framed pictures they had been forced to leave behind on the walls of the chateau.

The only light filtered through a small, high grating, and those who waited were no more than dark shapes, half-seen figures hunched beside bundles that contained what possessions they had been able to carry with them. Though weary beyond words, few could sleep. For the most part they waited in a tense, heart-quickened silence. Many had made long and arduous journeys, fraught with danger. In retrospect, even these seemed preferable to this endless waiting.

'If you value your lives, keep your voices down,' the landlord had said, as singly and in family groups they had taken their places in the cellar. 'The dragoons have been in town all day.'

They needed no further warning. Every soul in that place had good reason to fear the men who, they knew well, would fall upon them with all the glee and savagery of a hungry wolf pack, were they to be discovered. As Huguenots, their faith had sustained them through many trials, but there was not one among them who did not fear the dragoons. Caution had become second nature.

A baby cried and was instantly hushed. Pale, strained faces turned towards the sound, and there was an uneasy stirring.

'That child will be the death of us!'

Madame Bonnet spoke with suppressed savagery and this, to Charlotte, was the most terrifying thing of all, for though she knew her mother to be an austere woman who smiled seldom, still she was never less than kind, particularly towards the weak and helpless. Neither was she easily intimidated.

Even she is frightened, Charlotte thought, her panic rising. *Even she!* She would as soon have expected the chateau to step down from its eminence or the Loire to change its course.

'We must have courage, madame,' her father said mechanically.

'How much longer, m'sieu?' There was a note of anger in Madame Bonnet's voice, as if this whole enterprise had been bungled and someone should be held to account.

'Not long, not long, my dear.'

The whisper was subdued but there was undeniably a testy edge to it. Dr Bonnet's reply was precisely the same as that of an hour earlier and an hour before that, and it was impossible to escape the conclusion that he had no more idea than anyone else when the waiting would end.

Indeed, there was no real reason why he should. He was a refugee, just the same as all the others, but from the very beginning he had assumed leadership. For the most part the arrivals had appeared to be of the artisan class and the assumption had seemed natural; he was, after all, a doctor, a qualified physician, married to a de Sezy. In his view, those facts alone gave him the right to command.

He allocated places and issued instructions, and no one had questioned it. It was only when his wife had taken it upon herself to add her voice to his, reproving two of the families for occupying more space than she considered reasonable, that Charlotte had heard a few hostile whispers. She was uneasily conscious that these would have found an echo in their home village of Brissac l'Abbaye.

'She'll stick that long nose into my business once too often,' she had heard the tenants say; yet they hastened up to the chateau the moment they were sick or hungry or had a dispute with their neighbour, knowing that Madame would know exactly what to do.

The de Sezy family had always been in authority, but though they lived in the chateau they were never remote from their tenantry as some were. They were not grand or fashionable or wealthy. They never attended court, not even in the far-off days when they worshipped in the approved manner, but were themselves of the earth, part of the surrounding rural community. It was said that in the past they tilled the soil alongside the peasants but wore their swords as they did so to show their superiority.

From this stock had come Albertine de Sezy, now Bonnet. Dressed in her sober grey gown, she accepted the women's dutiful curtseys as her right, but still she would roll up her sleeves and gird up her skirt to help at a birthing or a laying out of the dead, and was known throughout the area as an able nurse. She would set a broken limb as readily as she dispensed bread and soup to the beggars who applied to the chateau for alms.

'Doubtless we are waiting for the evening tide,' her husband said, after a silence. Charlotte detected the note of irritation again, and she knew precisely what he was thinking. Someone should have *told* him something! What would others think now of his assumption of leadership? He was thinking that his ignorance made him look a fool, and she had long been aware that – perhaps as a result of his diminutive stature – of all things he hated to be the object of ridicule.

He must have been aware that in Brissac l'Abbaye he was the butt of many a ribald joke, for the villagers were not known for their delicacy; still, as in the case of Madame, those who were sick or in pain were thankful for his services. He had come to the chateau from Paris to attend the Seigneur in his last illness and had stayed to marry the old man's daughter once the funeral was over. He was small, fastidious, precise in his speech and immaculate in dress. Ever conscious of his lack of inches, he affected high heels and an over-extravagant full-bottomed wig to compensate, and this in itself was sufficient to make him the cause of amusement to the rude peasantry. However, the joke was enhanced by his marriage to Albertine de Sezy, for she was a big, raw-boned woman, awkward in manner and well past her first youth. Long resigned to the fact that she would die unwed, for there was no money in the family to provide a suitable *dot*, the proposal from Anton Bonnet, monsieur le docteur, had been a delightful surprise to her for he was as ardent a Huguenot as she, and a man whose undoubted skills made him a man she could respect.

When she knew that she was *enceinte*, her gratitude to God

11

knew no bounds and if the birth of a girl came as something of a disappointment, she was prepared to accept her lot dutifully and with submission, sadly aware of the fact that her age made it unlikely that she would ever produce a male heir for the de Sezy estate, such as it was.

Well, such considerations were unimportant now. Brissac and the chateau and the tenants were in the past. Ahead lay an uncertain future in a new country.

'The evening tide must surely be in and out again by this time,' she hissed tartly. Her husband drew a long and calming breath.

'Courage, my love,' he said. 'We are, after all, in God's hands.'

Charlotte, hearing this exchange, felt small comfort. Oh yes, they were in God's hands, no doubt. So, presumably, were all those who had been tortured or killed or sent to the galleys for their beliefs; so, too, the countless others whose livelihoods had been destroyed, who had been prevented from entering crafts or practising their profession. 'Perpetual and irrevocable' was said to be the shelter granted to the Huguenots by the Edict of Nantes in 1598. Less than a century later, on the twenty-second day of October 1685, that shelter had been swept away. Those who did not follow the Catholic faith were persecuted remorselessly and flight was the only option for those who refused to abjure.

The nudge in her ribs made Charlotte jump nervously. A boy had wriggled close to her. She recognised him as a member of the family grouped to her left, elder brother of the baby who had cried.

'What do *you* want?' She spoke almost rudely, in a way that would have been unthinkable in the old world she had left. He had startled her, caught her off balance.

'Look what I've found!' The whisper had a carefree, almost gleeful note to it that had no place in that cellar.

'We've been told to keep quiet.'

'I *am* being quiet! Look, isn't he beautiful?'

Her curiosity whetted, Charlotte craned her neck to see what he was holding, then recoiled with a gasp that in other circumstances would certainly have been a scream. She disliked spiders and beetles, was repelled by waving feelers and the slimy trail of slugs, so that the enormous insect held between the boy's cupped hands filled her not with admiration but with disgust. She had never seen such a huge cockroach and the sight of it made her shudder.

12

'Take it away,' she hissed. 'I hate such things!'

The boy removed himself and his friend, laughing at her. The meagre light from the grating glinted on his hair, thick and fair and abundant, and showed her that he was about her own age. But not at *all* of my class, thought the girl from the chateau, looking down her nose a little. He was dressed in a tunic of rough homespun, heavily soiled and stinking of the farmyard.

'You're as bad as my little sister,' he said. 'All girls are as bad as each other.'

'And all boys are monsters.'

'Is your brother a monster? Where is he?'

'I haven't got one.' Charlotte muttered the words defiantly, as if the lack diminished her.

'Then how do you know?'

The boy's voice had become progressively louder and was now sufficiently intrusive to call Dr Bonnet's wrath down upon his head, after which he kept his silence for a full ten seconds. When he next spoke, Charlotte found he had inched closer again and that his voice was no more than a murmur in her ear.

'How many sisters have you?'

'None.'

'You haven't *anyone*? There's only you?' His whisper soared up the scale in astonishment. 'I have two sisters and a brother. My sisters are Minette and Louise and my brother is called Jean, but he's only a baby yet so he's not much good for anything.'

'Take that horrid creature away.'

'Don't fret – he's shut safely away. He'll do you no harm. What's your name?'

Charlotte hesitated. In normal circumstances she was fully aware that her mother would not think this boy a suitable companion, for the pungent aroma that arose from his tunic, if for no other reason.

He saw the sideways, dubious glance and a hand went to his mouth as he stifled his laughter. Laughter! Here! Charlotte was impressed with his insouciance.

'You think I'm a peasant, don't you? Well, I'm not! My father is a silversmith and we come from Tours. We dressed as peasants to help in the escape. My sisters hid under sacks of grain in the cart my father drove, for you know what they do to girls when they're caught, don't you? They throw them into convents and they never see their families again.'

'I know all that.' Her reluctant admiration left her abruptly and she turned away from him. He was not discouraged, it seemed.

'My name is Paul – Paul Belamie. Shall we play a game to pass the time? I know lots and lots of riddles –'

'You talk too much.' Charlotte's voice was stiff and cold. 'And you smell horrible. Go back to your mother.'

For a moment he looked at the pale blur of her face in the darkness, chewing a finger as if in thought.

'Look,' he said. 'I'm sorry I spoke about what they do to girls. It's not going to happen, is it? We're safe now.'

She kept her eyes on her skirt, pleating and re-pleating the material with restless fingers, fear a cold, hard knot in her chest.

'Go away and be quiet.'

'I can't help the smell!' His voice sounded as if it were brimming with laughter again. 'I slept in a pigsty last night. The pigs had gone, but they left behind much to remember them by.'

'Just go away.' It was no more than a sullen mutter and she would not look at him.

'I didn't mean –' he hesitated a moment, then touched her arm. 'What's your name? You haven't told me.'

It took her a moment or two to decide to answer.

'Charlotte,' she said at last.

'Look, Charlotte, everything will be well. The worst is over now. Truly you mustn't be frightened.'

'Why not?' She raised her head suddenly and glared at him. 'Why shouldn't I be frightened when everyone else is? My father, my mother – yours, too, if they have any sense. If you're not frightened it's only because you're too much of a baby to understand the dangers.'

'I'm ten years old!' His voice soared indignantly and from all directions came whispers of protest.

'And I'm nearly twelve.' Eleven years, seven months to be exact, but she felt in need of all the status she could muster. 'So do as I say and go back to your mother.'

'I'm not a baby!' Indignation made him forget caution and his voice rose again. 'I tell you, mam'selle –'

The clanking of a door cut through the silence and his words broke off short as all around inert figures stiffened into attention, ears tuned to the noise that came from somewhere outside the cellar. Bold footsteps were coming closer, and Charlotte, like every other fugitive who heard them, could not draw breath for the fear that paralysed her. Instinctively she shrank back against her father and clutched at his hand. It was icy cold and she could feel that he trembled. More than one person approached, that much was clear, for they could hear the sound of voices.

The landlord had looked in on them once or twice during the day but always stealthily, unwilling to stay. Why, suddenly, was no concealment necessary? Immediately to Charlotte's mind came the picture of those first dragoons who had strode into the kitchen where her mother had been discussing household affairs with Bettine. They had been bold and confident too, hectoring and demanding and throwing everything into chaos.

The family had been forced to quarter them at the chateau. They had been abused, turned out of their beds, their furniture used for firewood, their food commandeered. Charlotte pressed her face against her father's shoulder, wanting to blot out the images that came to her mind; the gross faces, the unreasoned malevolence that seemed to motivate the men. There was one among them she hated more than any of the others. He was small and squat and swarthy, with broken teeth and foul-smelling breath, and he was forever seeking her out and finding occasions to touch her. There were many narrow passages in the chateau. If he should meet her in one of them, he would make great sport of pressing her flat against the wall as if he had no room to pass, while his hands explored her childish body.

Her revulsion to him was instinctive. She could not speak of it, not to her mother nor to anyone. She felt his touch to be sinful and abhorrent, yet in some strange way she felt guilty too and began to suffer nightmares.

Escape meant the abandoning of home and possessions. In Brissac l'Abbaye a blind eye had been turned to the edict preventing non-Catholics from practising medicine before the arrival of the dragoons, but once they were not only in the village but living at the chateau it was a different matter. Either Dr Bonnet would have to give up his profession or he would have to leave France.

The decision to leave was not taken lightly. If caught, the penalties for such fugitives were heavy, but after much thought and discussion the Bonnets decided that there were two freedoms without which life for them both was intolerable: freedom of

15

worship and freedom to practise medicine. Escape was the only answer.

Through a network of safe houses they had made their way to Nantes where they had been assured that, in return for payment, the innkeeper would arrange passage to England. There had been moments of grave peril on their journey to the port. For half a day they had been forced to lie silent in a cave while dragoons searched the area nearby. On another occasion they had watched others passing over a bridge being stopped and questioned, and with no alternative but to continue, they, too, had passed over, dry-mouthed and expecting instant arrest. However they had been unaccountably ignored and allowed to proceed freely. Surely, surely a merciful God could not allow their venture to fail at this late stage? Or had the innkeeper done no more than pocket his fee and hasten to betray them? Rigid with fear they listened to the steps coming nearer. Charlotte could hear her mother's laboured breathing, and in the shadows someone murmured a prayer.

The heavy door to the cellar was beginning to creak open.

'I trust I find all in good heart?' The words were spoken in a pleasant, relaxed, conversational tone as a man and a woman preceded the landlord over the threshold. 'Thank you, patron, for escorting us. Come, my dear, shall we join all these good people?'

Tension drained away slowly as everyone stared in astonishment at the newcomers who clearly were not dragoons, though the heedless way in which the man carried a lantern, lifting it to look around the cellar so that shadows leapt and danced, seemed reckless to the point of lunacy.

The innkeeper was bowing and making his exit backwards, almost as if his latest guest were a prince of the blood, yet at first sight there was nothing immediately impressive about the man except his height and his extraordinary thinness. All eyes were on him, the silence still so profound that it seemed the entire company had been struck dumb.

'God bless us all,' the man said. 'And to him be the glory for bringing us safely to this place.'

He had spoken in a voice not overloud, but vibrant, pitched to reach every corner of the cellar; and now, at last, there were stirrings of relief and mutters of 'Amen'.

'We've been told to keep quiet and show no lights.' A lone,

truculent voice came from the shadows behind the newcomer. The lantern swung around to find the speaker who wore the rough jerkin of an artisan.

'And rightly so, monsieur. You've done well to hide your presence all day. This town has played host to a troop of dragoons since dawn, as I well know having spent the day in hiding only yards away from them, but I can vouch for the fact that they have ridden away now, convinced that no Huguenots remain. Be of good cheer, my friends; your long vigil is almost over. God has led us to this place and will surely guard us until we reach a place of safety.'

By the light of his lantern Charlotte could see that his face was pale and gaunt, the eyes deep in their sockets as if he had suffered a grievous illness. His dark coat hung loosely upon his shoulders as if made for a much larger man, and for a moment she took him to be of her father's age, or even older, for he seemed to move with difficulty. Then he chanced to look in her direction and she saw that she had been mistaken. His face might be ravaged, but it blazed with a young man's eagerness and passion. She could not look away from him, so compelling were those sunken eyes and the sudden, unexpected beauty of his smile.

'I have good news for you,' he said. 'A fishing boat lies at the quayside not twenty yards from this place, and is ready to sail the moment the tide turns, which will be in something under forty minutes. I myself have spoken to the master of it and he seems a trusty fellow, sympathetic to our cause.' His voice continued above the expressions of relief that arose on all sides. 'Shall we join in prayer to ask God's blessing on what will undoubtedly be a hazardous journey?'

In common with the rest of the company she scrambled to her feet and bent her head, closing her eyes to join in prayer, but she was conscious throughout not so much of what he said but of the voice in which it was spoken. She had heard such a voice once before in her life. When she was no more than five or six a company of mummers had called at the chateau to perform a Passion play. There was one among them whose voice had caused her flesh to shiver with delight, child though she was. Afterwards she had heard Bettine remark to the other servants that a man like that could get a girl to lie on her back by doing no more than reciting the days of the week. The remark had seemed incomprehensible. Bettine must have lost her wits, Charlotte thought, for who would wish to sleep when such a voice could be heard?

The voice of this stranger was no less compelling. His words not only sounded like liquid gold but had the ring of true authority. Excitement grew in her, filled her, so that there was no room for fear any more, and she sensed the same elation all around her. He had given them all back the conviction that God was, after all, on their side, and as the prayer came to an end one would have thought all danger passed, so great was the sense of joy.

'May we know your name, monsieur?' Almost as soon as the stranger had fallen silent, Dr Bonnet bounded up and confronted him, giving a perfunctory bow. He reminded Charlotte of a terrier walking stiff-legged around an unfamiliar wolfhound, unsure of his reception but determined to relinquish none of his territorial rights. She loved her father dearly for he had always been more affectionate and approachable than her mother, but she was old enough now to see that there was something inherently laughable about his self-importance and was at times, secretly and much to her shame, a little embarrassed by him. 'Allow me to introduce myself,' he said now. 'I am Anton Bonnet, physician, at your service, monsieur.'

'Your servant, monsieur.' The stranger bowed in return. 'Gabriel Fabian, master silk-weaver of Nîmes.'

There was a gasp as he spoke the name and a murmur of excitement rose from every corner of the cellar as it was repeated from one to another. Charlotte moved closer to her mother across the gap her father had vacated and grasped her arm.

'Maman, maman, did you hear? It's Monsieur Fabian!'

It was a name everyone knew, a name that had been on the lips of every Huguenot in the region. Gabriel Fabian was a hero, a legend, a byword for fortitude and fidelity. He had been accused of attempting to convert his workpeople to the Huguenot faith and had been imprisoned and subjected to torture, but despite all that his persecutors had been able to do to him, he had steadfastly refused to abjure.

His story had been passed from one Huguenot community to another and had inspired them for, as they had all been quick to see, it had much in common with the experiences of St Paul. A fearful death had seemed inevitable, but one of his jailors had been so impressed by his spirit and his eloquence, that he had allowed Monsieur Fabian to escape.

From all directions men and women emerged from the shadows to shake his hand, even to touch his coat, until finally, with the greatest good humour, he begged them to return to their places.

'Please,' he said. 'Let us all rest while we have the chance. I regret my own strength is depleted, thanks to the hospitality of those in authority, and as for my wife, she has already undergone more today than anyone should ask of her. Come, my dear. Here is a place for you to sit.'

So dominant a figure was he that his wife, standing in his shadow, had passed almost unnoticed. Now, as he moved the light towards her, Charlotte saw that she was a small woman, barely reaching his shoulder, pale of face with a neck that drooped like the stem of a flower, her hair as shining as corn silk.

Longingly Charlotte drew in her breath. How she envied that hair! Hers was dark and thick, a mass of tangled curls, and it constantly refused to stay confined in the braids that hung to her waist. When she was small it had made her cry with pain to have a comb pulled through it, and she had prayed earnestly each night for many months that she would awake in the morning to find that it had become smooth and golden.

Beauty, to Charlotte, meant blue eyes and a pink and white complexion like delicately tinted china. She could see that the silk-weaver's wife was indeed beautiful. A dark cloak with the sheen of velvet enveloped her body, and as she moved it swung a little to reveal that she was heavy with child.

Monsieur le docteur, returning to his seat, murmured that in his view it was foolhardy to allow a woman to travel in that condition.

'Yet it may be they had no alternative,' he said. 'These are troubled times.'

His wife nodded in agreement.

'What can Monsieur Fabian do but leave the country for his own safety? Besides, they would not want the child born here.'

No one present would argue with that. Any child born in France since the Revocation was required by law to be baptised into the Catholic faith, with severe penalties enforced should the parents allow religious observances to lapse. However, there was no gainsaying that Madame Fabian looked dangerously close to her time. The doctor sighed and shook his head.

'Troubled times,' he repeated gloomily. 'We can only hope and pray.'

Despite his apparent doubt there seemed a different spirit now among the other fugitives. The buzz of conversation was kept low, but the fearful suspense was gone, replaced by a feeling of optimism, even excitement.

Paul Belamie appeared at Charlotte's side again.

'This time tomorrow we might be in England,' he said. 'I can speak English, you know. "Good morning good evening please thank you at your service sir."' He ran the words together, and Charlotte laughed at him, for her father had spent some years in London while he was studying medicine and had ensured that she knew better than that. A gleam of mischief appeared in her eyes.

'I know some English too,' she said. 'Shall I tell you the most polite thing to say to an Englishman? After all, you want them to think you respectful.'

The boy considered the question for a moment, chewing his lip, clearly undecided as to the propriety of taking advice from a girl. Finally he nodded.

'Tell me, then. What should I say?'

'You should bow like this.' Solemnly Charlotte dipped her head. 'Then you should say: "A thousand pardons, sir, for I stink like a pig."'

'A thousand pardons, for I stink like a pig.' Carefully he repeated the words and Charlotte bit her lip to suppress her laughter, though she had no real hope that he would remember her instructions – which was, she thought, a great pity, bearing in mind the fright he had given her with that horrid insect.

'Are you going to London?' he asked. She shook her head.

'No, to Canterbury. I have an aunt there, my father's sister. She has lived there for a long time. There are a great number of Huguenots in Canterbury, you know.'

'I know that.' She had imparted quite enough information for one day, his tone implied.

'Are *you* going to London?'

He drew his mouth down dolefully and shook his head.

'I wish that we were! It's a fine place, they say, the finest place in the whole world, but we are to go to Sandwich because that's where my uncle lives. He has a market garden and says there is work for my father – which I think is a *great* mistake! My father is a craftsman, not a farmer! He should go to London and work as a silversmith; that's what I think.'

'You've a lot to say for yourself, haven't you?'

He opened his mouth to reply to this but was called to his mother's side before he could speak. Everywhere bundles were being retied, possessions gathered together, children called to heel. Footsteps could be heard approaching the cellar but no one was afraid now. The silk-weaver had achieved a near-miracle, lifting spirits and renewing courage so that the future no longer threatened but beckoned enticingly. When the landlord opened the door and signalled for them to come, they picked up their burdens and pressed forward – stealthy, silent, but full of hope.

What had they to fear? God was on their side and ahead of them lay freedom. Gabriel Fabian had told them so; and that, for the moment, was quite enough.

The fishing boat was no more than thirty feet long. The smell was overpowering, the hold cramped and slimy, but so anxious were they to embark on this journey that no voice was raised in complaint, each group attempting once more to settle itself in as little discomfort as possible.

Charlotte tried with all her might to edge nearer to the silk-weaver, for it seemed to her that both he and his wife were brushed with magic – he so renowned a hero, she so beautiful – and she longed to hear that spellbinding voice once more. All her efforts were thwarted, however, as her mother made for a different part of the hold, quickly annexing some space against a bulkhead.

'This will do well enough,' she said, adding under her breath as she glanced to her left, 'It's to be hoped that baby keeps quiet. We're not out of danger yet.'

Charlotte looked over her shoulder and saw that the Belamie family were once again destined to be close neighbours. The baby was quiet enough now, peacefully asleep against his mother's breast, but there was scarcely enough time to register the fact before the ship's captain battened down the hatch, thus condemning them once more to darkness and silence. He had echoed Madame Bonnet's words, but more forcefully. They were still in grave peril, he told them. Many an escaping Huguenot had been recaptured on the high seas and it would be an hour or two yet before they could be allowed a light or a breath of air.

Madame Bonnet, in an unusual gesture of warmth, drew Charlotte close to her.

'The night will be long,' she warned. 'You must try to sleep.'

Though Charlotte protested that she could not possibly sleep, that she had never been further from it, she realised some time later that she must, after all, have lost consciousness for she opened her eyes to find that a light had been hung from a beam and was swinging like a pendulum. The sea had strengthened and the boat was rising and pitching, and all around people were groaning in distress. Someone was standing on the ladder that led to the hatch, hammering on it urgently with his clenched fists, demanding that it should be opened.

Many vomited where they sat; still others rose to their feet and stumbled over all obstacles, both human and inanimate, to reach the ladder and join their voices to those already standing there. All at once the hatch was lifted from above and a draught of pure, cold air flooded into the hold before once more the aperture was obstructed, this time by the press of bodies trying to get out.

Those who were left were a bedraggled and unhappy-looking band. The motion of the ship together with the stench of the fish was enough to turn anyone's stomach, and Charlotte was no exception though she could see as she looked around her that there were others in a far worse state. The Belamie family seemed to be withstanding the hardships better than many. The two families were positioned very close together, Madame Belamie's head resting against the bulkhead only inches from that of Madame Bonnet. Her husband was on her further side and her children were sleeping around her with all the abandon of young puppies, apparently quite untroubled by all that was going on around them.

'You and yours have strong stomachs, madame,' Charlotte heard her mother say, her approval of this fact apparently overcoming her qualms regarding the baby. Madame Bonnet approved of strong stomachs. They indicated strength of character, she considered. Weakness of any kind was regarded by her as only fractionally less despicable than indecency.

'I thank God for it,' Madame Belamie replied.

'You should sleep, madame.' Madame Bonnet was always ready with advice. 'Extreme fatigue could cause the loss of your milk, and what would your baby do then?'

22

Madame Belamie laughed softly. Charlotte liked the sound of it.

'There is little danger of that, madame. My children may have gone short of many things, but this, at least, has always been in abundant supply. I think I am beyond sleep! There will be time for rest later – and time to wash, too. I am ashamed of the figures we all cut. I have worn this dress and apron for a week now and it was in a filthy state before ever I bought it from a goose-girl who came past our house each day. I shall burn it at the first opportunity.'

'It has served its purpose.'

'Indeed it has, and I am not ungrateful. Have you travelled far, madame?'

Charlotte was conscious that her mother replied and that the conversation continued, but the voices were no more than a background murmur that lulled her to sleep.

When next she woke she was aware that something dramatic had happened. The silk-weaver and his wife had settled in a corner at the far end of the hold where he had spread a straw palliasse in an attempt to make her as comfortable as possible. Earlier they had appeared to be resting, but now the eyes of all those left below were directed towards them for Madame Fabian was half sitting, half lying, clinging to her husband and moaning piteously.

Charlotte sat up too and rubbed the sleep from her eyes.

'What is it? What has happened?' she asked her mother.

'It seems your father was right.' Madame Bonnet's voice was grim as she reached out and shook her husband's shoulder. 'Wake up, monsieur. Monsieur, wake up – your help is needed.'

'What? What?' Monsieur le docteur spluttered a little as he sat up and straightened the wig that had slipped sideways. 'What's afoot? Are we discovered?'

'It's Madame Fabian. It seems her time has come.'

Dr Bonnet looked towards the silk-weaver's wife, and as he looked the transformation took place that Charlotte had seen many times before. Her father's small and undeniably comical person was suddenly cloaked with dignity and consequence, his skill and knowledge investing him with a kind of nobility. He adjusted his cravat and brushed his coat with his fingers, and rising to his feet he went across to her.

'The poor soul – oh, the poor soul,' Madame Belamie said softly.

23

'No doubt I shall be needed too.' Madame Bonnet stood up. 'No, no, madame –' as Madame Belamie indicated her readiness to accompany her. 'Your family needs you and I have much experience in these matters. There are practicalities to consider. For instance, Madame Fabian must have privacy.'

'Privacy!' Madame Belamie echoed the word sceptically. 'How can such a thing be possible in these surroundings?'

The captain, hastily summoned, said much the same, but Charlotte could have told both of them that if privacy was what her mother decreed, then privacy would somehow be achieved. The captain was ordered to bring sail cloth, to rig up a screen across one corner of the hold, to fetch more light, and to the surprise of everyone except Charlotte, he did what he was told – or at least directed others to carry out Madame Bonnet's instructions.

Other passengers were herded to one side in still greater proximity, all except those who decided that the chill night air on deck would be the lesser evil. Monsieur Belamie was among those who vacated the hold, and he took Paul with him for the boy had woken and was groaning in distress, clearly not possessing the kind of stomach that Madame Bonnet found so admirable in the rest of his tribe. His father bore him away, but Charlotte was glad that Madame Belamie stayed below with the baby and the two small girls, who still slumbered peacefully. She neither wanted nor expected her parents to behave any differently in the face of Madame Fabian's need, but still she felt bereft now that both had left her and secretly would have liked nothing better than to curl up against Madame Belamie just as her own daughters had done. Naturally, she did not do so. She was, she reminded herself again, only five months away from her twelfth birthday and almost grown up.

Children woke and whimpered and, exhausted, slept again. Not Charlotte. The sudden drama had catapulted her into wakefulness and now she could not sleep at all, her attention caught and held by the shadows beyond the sail-cloth screen that appeared to be moving in some mystic, elemental rite that awoke all kinds of nameless terrors in her.

She had twice seen a horse drop a foal and had stroked the head of the kitchen cat as she had given birth to four kittens, but she had never connected those apparently pain-free events with the act of procreation itself or been close enough to anyone

24

in childbirth to realise that it was in any way different. Now, as harrowing gasps and groans came from behind the screen, she felt as if a dark and horrifying world was being revealed to her, and shuddering uncontrollably she curled herself into a ball, her head resting on her knees, her arms encircling them.

She felt a hand on her shoulder.

'*Ma petite*, do not distress yourself.' There was concern in Madame Belamie's voice, and a wealth of kindness. 'Madame Fabian is in good hands. Oh, how you shiver! Come, let me tuck your cloak around you.'

Such tenderness was unaccustomed and astonishing. Charlotte, quite used to her mother attending to the poor and sick, had never considered that she, as well as they, might be called needy.

After a time her father returned to his place, though the cries had in no way abated. He shook his head when Madame Belamie pressed him for news.

'She is well enough, but a long way from delivery,' he said. 'I propose to sleep while I may.'

He was snoring in no time and Charlotte marvelled at it for it was impossible to shut out the pitiful moans from behind the screen. They seemed to indicate a level of suffering that no living creature should be called upon to endure, least of all a fragile, beautiful woman such as Madame Fabian.

Madame Belamie saw her continued distress and responded to it.

'My dear child, try to sleep.'

'I cannot!' Charlotte trembled, her eyes still fixed trance-like on the makeshift screen. 'Madame, how long does it go on?'

Calmly Madame Belamie smiled and shrugged.

'Who can tell? For the first child, it is often many hours. We must thank *le bon Dieu* that Madame Fabian is so well attended – a qualified physician and a woman as practical and experienced as your mother! Why, I never had such care, believe me. You must not worry so.'

A particularly sharp cry made Charlotte wince and bite the side of her finger, stifling her own cry.

'Madame Fabian will think it all worth while when she holds the child in her arms,' Madame Belamie went on. 'Consider the reward of this travail! A tiny baby, each feature perfectly formed down to the last, smallest fingernail! I promise you, my dear,

25

there is no joy to compare as you will assuredly find out one day, God willing.'

'I did not know —' Charlotte paused and caught her breath as Madame Fabian cried out again. 'I did not know there was so much pain.'

'God wills it so. In his Word he tells us, in pain and suffering ye shall bring forth thy children. Now sleep, child. When you wake you may find there is yet another passenger on this old tub!'

Obediently Charlotte closed her eyes, but she could not sleep. Thoughts and questions chased themselves in her mind. She wanted to ask *why* God had deemed so much pain was necessary, and what of Monsieur Fabian who had suffered so much himself? Was he sorry that he had inflicted this awful agony on her? How could any man who loved his wife assent to it, especially a man such as he who knew what it was to undergo torture?

As for Madame Belamie's statement that there was no joy to compare with the joy of motherhood – well, for herself, Charlotte felt it was a joy she could well do without; in fact, it seemed astonishing to her that the human race had survived for so long, generation after generation of women being duped by such a fallacy.

Eventually she must have dozed a little. Suddenly she awoke with a start, aware that dawn was breaking and that her mother had come from behind the screen, her face putty-pale and creased with fatigue. The doctor was roused once more, and swiftly he crossed the hold and went behind the screen.

The swell had lessened and the boat no longer pitched with such violence. Some who had spent the night on deck came down again; others, desperate for fresh air, went up. Charlotte was hardly aware of any movement and gave no more than a passing thought to the fact that she was both hungry and thirsty. Her eyes were riveted on the screen and the dimly seen movements behind it. With deep thankfulness in her heart she realised suddenly that the moaning had ceased.

She turned to Madame Belamie to ask if she thought that the baby had come at last, but found that she, too, had fallen asleep. Close on her other side two peasant women, sisters by their appearance, slept in each other's arms, the low-pitched snore of one answered by the high whinny of the other. Beyond them was a man, some kind of artisan, who slept with a boy against one shoulder, his wife resting her head on the other. The stench of fish had been augmented by the sour smell of vomit, and Charlotte would have clambered out on deck to join those in the fresh air if she could have brought herself to abandon her vigil; but she could not.

The thin cry of a newborn baby came from the other side of the screen and she turned once more to Madame Belamie who in the same instant opened her eyes and smiled.

'God be thanked,' she said softly. 'The long night is over. Madame Fabian will suffer no more now.'

'God be thanked,' Charlotte echoed, and as she clasped the hand that Madame Belamie reached out to her it seemed suddenly that all those women down through the ages knew best after all and that she, Charlotte Bonnet, had been childish and stupid. There *was* no excitement like this!

Her mother appeared carrying the baby swathed in a shawl and she thrust it towards Madame Belamie.

'Take the child.' Unsmiling, abrupt, she clearly had no time for expressions of joy. Charlotte felt the beginnings of a small whisper of fear, and she craned to see what was revealed when Madame Belamie drew the shawl gently aside to look at the baby's face.

It was mottled and scaly, encrusted with blood, little whorls of dark hair stuck tightly to the pulsating scalp. It was, Charlotte thought, quite hideous. No wonder her mother had seemed so strange in her manner! There must be something horribly wrong with the child – but why, then, was Madame Belamie smiling like that?

'Is it all right?' Charlotte asked, looking from the baby up to the woman who held it in her arms. 'It looks so – so ugly!'

Madame Belamie laughed.

'They often are at first. This one is well enough. A little girl,' she added, having carried out a brief inspection. She rewrapped the baby and held her close. 'Believe me, she will look normal once she has been washed. How thankful Madame Fabian must be that your father was –'

A strange and unearthly groan caused her to falter in mid-sentence, and all around sleepers were shocked into wakefulness and turned to each other with startled eyes. Charlotte, a clutch of fear at her heart, stared at the screen. Despite the safe delivery of the baby there still seemed to be much activity behind it.

27

'What can be happening, madame?' she asked in a whisper.

Dumbly Madame Belamie shook her head, her face ashen.

The cry rose again, a sound so tortured that Charlotte felt the hairs rise on the back of her neck.

'No! Oh God, no!'

It was a cry wrenched from an anguished soul, uttered in the voice that only hours before had proved an inspiration.

'Is it – has she –?' Charlotte could not bring herself to speak the words.

Madame Belamie shook her head and her lips moved as if she were praying. I should do the same, Charlotte thought wildly, but somehow she could not think of the words. She could only sit there against the bulkhead, an uneven plank digging into her back, conscious that a frightful, unthinkable tragedy had taken place only a few feet away from her, and there was such a tumult of protest in her head that coherent thought was impossible.

She wanted her mother. She wanted her so desperately that for a brief moment nothing else mattered, and she rose and went towards the screen before common sense halted her.

Her mother would be angry if she intruded when there were important, adult things to be done. She would say that Charlotte was old enough to control herself and should have stayed in her place.

For a moment she paused, and in that second the corner of the screen was lifted to allow her father to leave the small, improvised chamber; he, in his turn, hesitated, startled by the sight of his daughter so unexpectedly close to him.

She looked at him and saw the desolation in his face; then, as if to seek the cause of it, she looked beyond him to where, since he still held the sail cloth aside, the scene was presented to her entire and unobstructed.

If she had thought Monsieur Fabian's face ravaged before, now he looked like a man who had looked into the depths of hell. He knelt beside the palliasse, crouched over the figure of his wife, whose golden hair was spread all about her.

There was time, too, to notice Madame Bonnet's expression of total exhaustion as she stood helplessly beside him; then her eyes went to the palliasse itself and the blanket that covered the figure that lay on it.

Both were stained dark red; and as she looked, the stain spread

28

wider until her father dropped the screen and the horror was hidden from her.

'The Lord giveth and the Lord taketh away,' he said. His voice sounded stiff and formal, but she could tell by the way his hand moved over his face that he was greatly affected. 'I regret that despite all our efforts, Madame Fabian did not survive her ordeal.'

The words seemed to come from an immense distance, and as Charlotte looked at him his image grew blurred and the world seemed to spin about her. It was the first time in her life that she had swooned, and as she fell she seemed to be drowning in crimson blood, an entire ocean of it, choking and suffocating.

She thought she was dying, and she was glad of it, yet when consciousness returned and she realised that she was, after all, still alive and that her mother was bent over her in an attitude of concern, she experienced a moment of joy and triumph. At last she had caught her attention!

Then she remembered, and the joy faded. Slow tears seeped beneath her closed eyelids. She cried for the beautiful Madame Fabian and for her poor, tragic husband who had already suffered so much. She cried for the motherless child, and though she could not have put it into words, did not even realise it, she cried for herself.

Was this – *this* – what life had in store for her?

2

Canterbury had long been accustomed to the arrival of refugees. For a century and more they had come, both French and Walloon, seeking freedom of worship. On the whole they had been greeted with sympathy, laced with a dash of wariness – for foreigners were foreigners, when all was said and done, and they had strange ways. They wore wooden shoes and ate snails and garlic. But they worked hard, these Huguenots; there could be no doubt about that.

'Not a lazy bone among the lot of them,' one of the city fathers remarked approvingly. 'Some of our Kentish craftsmen will have to look to their laurels.'

'You can hardly expect that to make them popular,' another answered dryly. 'Local people won't think much of that.'

In the event, some did and some did not. For those who found work in the silk industry that soon sprang up, the arrival of the Huguenots was the best thing that had ever happened to them. Papermills were established; a bookbinding business, a gunpowder mill. A clockmaker set up shop in the shadow of the cathedral walls. So did an apothecary and a bookseller. Most of them prospered through sheer hard work and initiative, but inevitably their very success caused resentment in some quarters.

A rising tide of anti-Catholicism softened attitudes towards them, nor was sympathy lacking for the persecutions suffered by more recent arrivals, accounts of which lost nothing in the telling.

'We shall feel at home in England,' Dr Bonnet had assured his wife prior to their departure. 'You will see, my dear. We shall be welcomed there.'

Albertine Bonnet had wasted little time in idle speculation concerning the future. She put her faith in God and hard work, and had no doubt that recourse to both would ensure that the transition to a new life was as smooth as possible.

She and her family, she soon realised, were more fortunate

than many, thanks to the foresight of her husband. A full year before the arrival of the dragoons he had seen the writing on the wall, and despite her passionate desire to remain on her family estate, he had arranged the transfer of funds to his sister in Canterbury against the day when he would be forced to join her.

His wife had been furiously, vocally angry, not believing that the persecutions could worsen. Didn't they have little enough money to plough back into the land? Now what they had was gone, and would likely never be seen again. They were ruined, without resources – and what, she asked icily, did monsieur imagine they would use for a *dot* for Charlotte? Would he, perhaps, have the goodness to tell her that?

She fell silent, however, when the government placed restriction upon restriction, and when finally the dragoons came, preventing not only the secret practice of their faith but of her husband's profession as well, she folded her lips in resignation and made plans to leave, thankful that they could support themselves in England until official recognition of Monsieur le docteur's qualifications was granted and he was able to work once more.

Anton Bonnet had always been something of an Anglophile. He had lived in London as a student and spoke the language well. His sister, Hortense, had married a second-generation Huguenot, born le Clerc but anglicised to Clark, who was a dominie at the King's School in Canterbury. Thus there had never been any doubt that they, too, would settle in the same place. If Madame Bonnet was disappointed by her first glimpse of the city – if the huddle of roofs around the cathedral seemed shabby and unimpressive – she gave no sign of it.

'At least there are gardens,' she said. 'I had not thought, somehow, that the English would care for gardens. You will ensure, monsieur, that we have a garden, will you not?'

'Hortense has found us the very place,' her husband replied.

Madame Bonnet had taken one look at her sister-in-law, and though her expression had not changed she had known at once that there were few things on which there was likely to be a meeting of minds.

The matter of the house was no exception. It was, in Madame Bonnet's view, as far from the very place as it was possible to imagine, being small and cramped and dark, squeezed up in the corner of a narrow alley with no room to grow so much as an onion. If a memory of the chateau – decayed and crumbling as it was – had flashed upon Madame Bonnet's inward eye, then stoically she gave no sign of it. No recollection of the wide vista of winding river or the scent of geraniums and lavender clouded her expression. This, at least, was a roof over their heads, a place where they could live economically for the time being. Better things would come later, for what might be considered the very place for a Clark was not necessarily so for a de Sezy; neither did she consider Marianne Clark a suitable companion for Charlotte – but *qu'est-ce qu'on va faire*? They were cousins, much of an age, and it was impossible to prevent the association.

Together the two girls attended classes at the home of Mademoiselle Lamont, who instructed them in English, drawing, reckoning and all types of needlework. Twice a week, on a Wednesday and a Friday, they presented themselves at the home of Madame Berthot to be taught the rudiments of dancing and deportment, and on a Sunday they sat side by side in the crypt of the cathedral where, by generous decree, the Dean and Chapter allowed the Huguenots to worship in their own way. Mademoiselle Lamont was also a regular attender, and confided to Madame Bonnet that her task would be a great deal easier if all her girls were like Charlotte.

'Such a good, well-mannered, *quiet* girl,' she said. 'Sometimes I think a little too quiet – overshadowed, perhaps, by her cousin? But of superior intellect,' she added hastily, feeling the full force of Madame Bonnet's formidable stare. 'And so talented! Why, I have known few girls of her age who can paint so well. And as for her needlework, her embroidery is quite exquisite!'

'It is gratifying that you should say so, mam'selle.'

It was true that Madame Bonnet liked to hear praise of her daughter, but equally true that she felt much could be improved even if she would die rather than admit it to an outsider. Charlotte *was* overshadowed by Marianne; Mademoiselle Lamont had been right about that. Marianne was larger, noisier, more sure of herself, and laughed a great deal more than was seemly. The two girls showed a distressing tendency to giggle together, a matter which Madame Bonnet could only deplore, and she was thankful when finally the cramped little house in the alley beside the cathedral was exchanged for far superior quarters just outside the city walls at some little distance from the Clarks' residence.

The girls still saw each other every day, of course, but were not able to live in each other's pockets to the same extent.

How much better it would have been if only she had brothers and sisters as companions! Though Madame Bonnet was not given to useless emotions such as regret or envy, there were times when she felt a pang of longing for the children she would never have, particularly when the Belamie family came to call.

That friendship, forged during the traumatic night at sea, had never faltered. Sandwich was not many miles away from Canterbury, and his brother's business frequently brought Phillipe Belamie into the city. It became the custom for him to bring his wife and children to spend the day at Providence House, where the Bonnets now lived.

These were red-letter days for Charlotte. From the beginning she had felt a special bond with Madame Belamie, and she enjoyed the company of the smaller children.

It was Paul, however, who became her real friend. It took several meetings before they stopped sizing each other up. Paul was determined to allow her no feelings of superiority because of the age difference; Charlotte was equally determined to give no ground to illusory feelings of masculine grandeur.

In view of her detestation of crawling things, perhaps it was strange that it was Paul's delight in nature that brought them together. He possessed an insatiable curiosity about woodland creatures, and about the birds that were so plentiful in the fields around them. Together they collaborated on producing a book; Charlotte drew the pictures, Paul wrote the descriptions – and because he wrote in English, Madame Bonnet beamed and approved, commending his industry.

'If I were doing this on my own, it would be considered a waste of valuable time,' Charlotte said. 'Why she thinks you are such a little angel, I can't imagine.'

'Because I *am* a little angel!' He rolled his eyes, flapped his arms as if they were wings, and beamed seraphically.

'A little idiot, perhaps!'

'You should try speaking up for yourself. Seriously, Lottie –'

'I hate that name!'

'A thousand pardons! Seriously, mam'selle, your mother is not the ogre you make her out to be.'

'Not to you, perhaps. Sometimes it seems to me that everything I do is wrong. If Marianne and I laugh together, then we are behaving in an unseemly way. If I sit straight-faced, then I am taken to task for looking miserable. If I am idle for two minutes together, then I am reproved for wasting time. Yet you can lie on your stomach for hours watching rabbits and receive nothing but praise for your industry! I wish I knew your secret.'

Whatever his secret was, it defied definition. The world appeared to smile upon Paul because he expected it to do so and was more than ready to smile back. It was all a result, Charlotte felt sure, of living in a family, with brothers and sisters and a mother like Madame Belamie who, at that time, represented her ideal of womanhood. It was a thousand pities, she thought many times, that the Belamies lived so far from Canterbury and Providence House.

The new house was set at a crossroads and had once been an inn. It was a long, low, timbered building with two eaves like eyebrows and a thatched roof which covered rooms of a size Madame Bonnet considered far more satisfactory than those she had had to make do with at first. More satisfactory still, it was surrounded on three sides by a large garden and orchard – wild when they first moved in, but soon to be tamed by her formidable industry. Tangled brambles and honeysuckle and dog roses; thistles five feet high and venomous nettles, all gave way before the onslaught she set in motion. By the time Charlotte was fifteen, the chateau at Brissac l'Abbaye only a blurred memory, the garden at Providence House was neat and tidy with lozenge-shaped beds bordered by tiny box hedges and filled with regimented tulips, pansies, gillyflowers and marigolds standing to attention. Roses bloomed in orderly rows. Only beyond them, where a gate led through to the kitchen garden and the orchard, did the lilac blow and the honeysuckle continue to climb with unbridled joy.

Charlotte spent far too much time dreaming down there by the honeysuckle. When she was sent to pick gooseberries or pluck a few herbs she would be gone for hours, and more often than not someone would have to go and find her. She had been thinking, she would say when questioned, her eyes wide and startled. Somehow the time had flown. Had she really been away that long?

'Thinking of what, may I ask?' her mother would demand.

There was never a satisfactory answer. Charlotte knew it was useless to speak of the tantalising beauty of a bird's song or the

34

scent of blossom, both of which were more than sufficient to waft her wayward attention far from the practical tasks confronting her. Her mother valued little that she could not see or touch or taste.

Useless, too, to speak of the phantoms which seemed to people the garden. Even Paul laughed at her if she spoke of them. Charlotte liked the thought that the house had once been an inn, a place of refuge for pilgrims to Canterbury, or drovers, or travellers on their way to the Channel ports. What dramas had been enacted there? What meetings and farewells? Once when she had been drowsing in the warm sunshine of early summer she had seen quite clearly a woman walking towards her dressed in dark red, with huge sleeves close gathered at the wrist, a tightly fitting cap and a white ruff at her neck, but as disbelievingly she sat up straight and blinked she saw that she had been mistaken. There was no one there. She had been dreaming again; unless, perhaps –? No, no! Of course it had been no ghost, and it was sinful even to think that it might have been. Her mother would certainly dismiss it as nonsense and would be even more angry. Charlotte was in quite enough trouble as it was.

'The child is sensitive to beauty,' the doctor said easily when his wife complained.

'She is no longer a child, monsieur. Sixteen next birthday, and she should surely have put away childish things by this time and should realise that life cannot be dreamed away. In another year she could be married, with a household of her own.'

'In God's good time, my dear. I'm in no hurry to be rid of her!'

'It's not that I'm in a hurry, merely that one must consider these things.'

'Let her be a child for a little longer.'

Madame Bonnet disapproved strongly of this sentiment, but did not argue. Her husband had become more authoritative since living in England, as if he had gained in stature since leaving de Sezy territory. In these more sophisticated surroundings he was, it seemed, valued more and ridiculed less. It had taken a full year for the Medical Council in London to recognise his qualifications, but once able to practise his profession he rapidly gained the respect of many citizens of importance, though not everyone agreed with his revolutionary theories regarding bleeding and purging, which he felt certain were in many cases useless, if not positively harmful.

Cleanliness, good food and fresh air were far more helpful, he believed – and would have been laughed out of existence had not his devotion to his patients and some undoubted cures made people think twice. Now he had his adherents both in and out of the Huguenot community, and his fashionable, fastidious little figure in its coat of good, dark cloth, the cuffs revealing a fall of finest lace, snowy bands at his neck, was a familiar sight in the streets of Canterbury as he titupped along on his high heels, rejoicing in the acknowledgments of those whom many would consider his betters. He even sat with them in the coffee house – the mark of final acceptance.

Charlotte was at one with her father over the matter of her marriage. She had no wish to discuss, or even to think, of such a ghastly fate. Marianne, however, was quite the opposite and sparkled in the company of the opposite sex. She talked often of marriage, cooing over babies as if they represented all she wanted from life.

'Oh, sometimes I feel I just can't wait to grow up,' she said to her cousin, who found such sentiments incomprehensible. To Charlotte, marriage had much in common with death. It was, she supposed, bound to happen one day – but, please God, later rather than sooner. For the moment she was more than content to paint her pictures or sit with her embroidery with her thoughts free to roam.

She had been just past her fifteenth birthday when she had started work on a bedspread, and it was finally finished in the spring following her seventeenth birthday. She could hardly believe that she had inserted her needle for the last time, put the last stitch in place, and as she looked at the completed pattern she knew, with a lift of the heart, that she had created something beautiful, something that even her mother must surely admire. She draped it across two chairs, the better to show off her artistry, and in that moment a pale and watery sun broke through the clouds and shone through the window so that the colours of the threads glowed like jewels against the blue background.

Madame Bonnet, called from pounding herbs for a tisane, stood pestle in hand and looked at it. Charlotte waited, longing for the commendation she felt sure was her due. Was there anyone – anyone in the world – who would not cry out with admiration at the sight of it?

'There,' her mother said. 'That's done. You see what can be

accomplished with a little industry? Far better to spend your time with your needle than your paints, for a bedspread like that will make a useful addition to your marriage chest.'

Charlotte waited hopefully for a little more. Would she say nothing about the colours? Make no comment about the intricacy of the design? It seemed not. Already she was half turned towards the kitchen again.

'I thought,' Charlotte said, 'that I would give it to Marianne as a wedding gift.'

'*What?*' This, at least, had caught her mother's attention. 'Give it to Marianne? Two years of work and you think of giving it to that – that –' Her tongue tripped a little. The words she could think of to describe Marianne Clark were not such as should be used by an aunt of a niece. 'No, Charlotte. I cannot and will not allow it. It would be in tatters within six months.'

'It would be a suitable gift.' Charlotte did not look at her mother, but gently caressed the raised stitches, lovingly outlining the leaves and flowers and lovers' knots.

'You'll be needing it yourself before too long.'

'There's no hurry.' Charlotte's voice was light, unemphatic. She began to talk breathlessly. 'Now that I have finished this, I thought I would design a tapestry to hang in the drawing room in that space between the fireplace and the sconces –'

'Charlotte, are you listening to me? I forbid you absolutely to give that bedspread to Marianne. After all, you are older than she by several months and must surely be betrothed soon. It is not as if her looks are superior to yours, or her *dot* any greater.'

It had become a competition, Charlotte recognised. Now that Marianne's wedding date had been announced it had become a matter of pride that she, too, should demonstrate her desirability as soon as possible. Even her father was beginning to look around him, to question friends and associates about suitable men of their acquaintance.

'I am perfectly happy as I am.' She sounded sullen, not happy at all.

'Take the bedspread upstairs and put it in the press,' her mother said, dismissing her happiness as irrelevant, one way or the other. 'Believe me, you will thank me one day for not allowing you to dispose of it.'

Charlotte lifted the bedspread from the chairs and began to fold it. She thought briefly of rebellion, but knew she would stand no chance – and truth to tell, on this occasion she was not sorry to be overruled. The colour of the silk on which she had worked the intricate pattern was of a slate blue with a hint of purple which she found particularly pleasing, and the composition of the design had absorbed and satisfied her like nothing she had known before. Marianne had admired the work on more occasions than she could count over the past two years, but at the time she had chosen the blue silk her cousin had urged her to take the red. It was, she said, so much richer and more vivid.

Charlotte hated red. Red was the colour of pain and suffering and death, and stubbornly she had shaken her head and held to the blue without explaining her preference. Such matters were not to be spoken of, not even to Marianne.

Upstairs she put it away in the press as instructed, standing lost in abstraction for a few moments before drifting to the window where she stared, unseeing, at the garden below. It was not only the thought of marriage that weighed on her spirits, nor the loss of Marianne, that most cheerful and uncomplicated of companions. A more general dissatisfaction with herself and her life filled her with unfocused gloom.

If only she were more like her mother, brisk and purposeful; or like Marianne, who was never plagued by doubts about her appointed role in life; or like Paul who had gone happily off to London in his usual carefree way, to be apprenticed to a goldsmith, even though he had no real interest in the craft.

'I go to please my mother and father,' he said to Charlotte, and she had laughed at him.

'You go to please yourself,' she said. 'You have always wanted to go to London.'

He had not denied it, but had grinned back at her, self-confident and unafraid. How wonderful to be like that!

Her gaze sharpened as swiftly she came back to more immediate concerns. Someone was approaching the house down the lane which led from the city. It was Tante Hortense, tottering along on her pattens, her mantle flying in the breeze, her head at its usual proud angle. Charlotte's heart sank a little. She was fond, even admiring, of her aunt, but had no doubt that she had come to gloat a little more about Marianne, and had no hope at all that she would be spared any of it. Indeed, only a few moments passed before she was summoned by Nan, her favourite among the servants, who informed her that she was wanted downstairs.

'Your auntie's come,' she said. 'And your ma's not best pleased.'

Her round, country face was brimming with laughter and Charlotte joined in with it, for the whole household was aware of the polite acrimony that existed between the sisters-in-law, and was enlivened by it.

On her way out of the room Charlotte paused by the looking glass to tidy her hair, and the face that looked back was transformed now that she was smiling, so different from that of the girl who had stared down so moodily into the garden that no stranger would have recognised it as the same person. Her clear, peaty-brown eyes with their fringes of deepest black sparkled with life, so that her small, fine-textured face was almost beautiful. Her hair was as untameable as ever, but it was confined now in a netted snood with only a few rebellious curls falling over her forehead. Her mouth alone revealed her essential childishness and vulnerability. It was delicately formed, with pale, rather flattened lips.

'Madame was planning to go through the linen press once she'd finished in the kitchen,' Nan went on. 'She'll not like having to put it off.'

Charlotte laughed again.

'Indeed she won't!' Madame Bonnet, everyone knew, did not adapt readily to any change of plan. It was not orderly.

Neither, her most ardent admirers would have to admit, was Tante Hortense, and if Madame Bonnet had said it once she had said it a thousand times, she would have died of shame had her own household been so mismanaged. As for Mr Clark, one would have thought he slept in his clothes, he looked so disreputable. Really, she was fond of saying, one could have been forgiven for thinking that the rats had ~~~~~ the ~~~~~ ~~~~~ ~~~~~ the state of Hortense's kitchen, she would add darkly, this was perhaps not so wide of the mark.

What seemed so unfair, so manifestly hard to forgive, was that Tante Hortense, despite the shaming dust and dirt that prevailed in her home, thought a great deal of herself. Her *fontange* of linen and lace might lack the pristine whiteness of Madame Bonnet's far less fashionable headgear of coif and lappets, but she wore it like a queen. Similarly the knots of ribbons at her shoulders or the fall of lace at her elbows were frequently in want of a stitch, yet she had a grand manner which Charlotte found immensely impressive.

Tante Hortense had literary pretensions, a mind above running her finger along table tops or inspecting the corners for cobwebs. She wrote poetry and frequently gave little soirées where she read her verses aloud, occasions at which Charlotte found herself half embarrassed, half admiring. The verses were not very good, she realised as the years passed and her taste became more cultivated, but the supreme self-confidence with which they were delivered was formidable and she could not help but marvel at it.

Her mother marvelled not at all.

'Better she should attend to her duties than strike such attitudes,' she complained regularly, particularly when she felt she discerned more than a trace of her sister-in-law's distaste for domesticity in her daughter's character. 'How poor Mr Clark endures it, I cannot imagine.'

However, despite this, when Charlotte went to the drawing room she found her mother dispensing chocolate to her aunt with every appearance of amity, mollified perhaps by the laudatory tones in which Tante Hortense was praising her work among the widows and the orphans of their community. Madame Bonnet might have abandoned the peasants of Brissac l'Abbaye, but she had by no means given up her charitable work and had made quite a name for herself in their adopted city.

'I am so very, very proud to claim you as a member of the family, my dear sister,' Tante Hortense was saying as Charlotte entered the room. 'How much poorer would the sick and needy be without you! Why, here is our Charlotte.' Tante Hortense, having paid lip service to the sick and needy, abandoned them at once. 'My dear child, how pretty you look! Does she not look pretty, Albertine? I was saying to Mr Clark only this morning, our little Charlotte won't be far behind Marianne, of that you may be sure – and on that head you will be so interested to know, my dear, that only yesterday Marianne went with Mr Standish to inspect the house that is being made ready for them. It is a farmhouse close to the largest of the hop gardens, disused for some time but exceedingly spacious and needing only the labours of a stone mason and carpenter to make it utterly delightful. She is quite enchanted with it! Really, I have never known her happier, and why shouldn't she be, indeed? There never was a kinder and more generous man than Mr Standish.'

'She has no doubts about marrying an Englishman?'

Tante Hortense raised her hands in horror.

'My dear sister, we are all English now! Besides, how can anyone object to a worthy man like Mr Standish? English he may be, but his family is more than respectable – why, they own mile upon mile of hops! Marianne will lack for nothing. Which reminds me, Charlotte, I have come to seek your advice. Look at these.'

She reached for a small drawstring bag and from it spilled upon the polished wood of a table a selection of silks, all of different colours.

'I have just collected these from Monsieur Herault, the mercer in New Street. Marianne begged me to ask you which colour would suit her best, for you have such a good eye. She would have come herself but is engaged with Mr Standish, choosing furnishings.'

Charlotte looked at the multi-hued pool on the table and with a pleasure that was almost sensuous began sorting one from the other.

'It's so difficult for me to say.' She spoke hesitantly. 'Marianne and I have different tastes.' Despite the difficulty, however, she was fascinated by the task her aunt had set her. She spread out the squares of silk and smoothed them with her fingertips. Some were plain, some patterned; some pale, some vivid. It made her feel happy, just looking at them, even though she was choosing not for herself but for someone else.

'Marianne always looks well in pink,' she said at last, picking up a square of deepest rose. 'This, I think, would be suitable for a bride. Suppose she wore it with a lighter chemise of the same tone –'

'And cream-coloured lace!' Tante Hortense clapped her hands in an extravagant gesture of delight of the kind that Madame Bonnet deplored so greatly. 'Oh yes, I can see it, Charlotte – a wide sleeve with a fall of lace at the elbow. It would be quite delightful, don't you agree, Albertine dear?'

Madame Bonnet's face wore the pinched look it always adopted when a show of frivolity offended her.

'I'm sure any of them would do very well,' she said. 'God, after all, looks on the heart –'

'But alas, the rest of us have to make do with the gown,' Tante Hortense retorted quickly with great good humour, laughing at her sister-in-law's shocked expression. Charlotte concentrated on fingering the silk, concealing her own smile. She could not help liking Tante Hortense for this reason; she found much to laugh at in life which compensated for those times when she caused embarrassment. There was not a great deal of laughter to be heard within the walls of Providence House and most of that was on the further side of the kitchen door.

Tante Hortense swept the pieces of silk back into the bag.

'I shall pass on your opinion to Marianne, Charlotte, and I am quite sure she will be grateful for it and will heartily agree. By the by, Albertine dear, I heard news at the mercers that might interest you. Monsieur Herault told me that he has been in correspondence with your Monsieur Fabian concerning some new process for dyeing silk –'

'Scarcely *my* Monsieur Fabian!'

Tante Hortense waved aside the objection.

'You know perfectly well what I mean. It seems there is the possibility of his visiting Canterbury later in the year so that they may exchange views.'

Charlotte's expression gave no sign of her sudden sharpening of interest. The story of the birth of Monsieur Fabian's daughter at sea and the death of his wife was common knowledge, and the Bonnets' part in these events was a matter of general interest and comment. Dr Bonnet had been much commended for his skill in saving the child; that Madame Fabian had lost her life was considered God's will, and therefore inevitable. Indeed, so great was Monsieur Fabian's reputation in the Huguenot community that the incident had played no small part in the ready acceptance of the doctor's credentials.

Charlotte's memory of the events of that night had become distorted over the years, as if it were a picture where the central figure had been cleaned and restored while the background was allowed to fade. Clearly she remembered Monsieur Fabian as he had appeared that night amid all the gloom and fear of that cellar, charming and bewitching all who looked upon him. As for the rest – the howl of anguish, that slow spreading stain – that was the stuff of nightmares. This she had pushed away, buried deep, did not allow to exist for her. No, she had said when Marianne had questioned her curiously on the matter, she had seen nothing. Her voice when she spoke of it was off-hand as if the matter was of little importance, and quickly she had turned the conversation to other things.

The truth was that Gabriel Fabian had a wholly secret fascination for her, as if for one brief moment she had caught a glimpse of someone more than human. Nothing would have induced her to utter the blasphemy, but in her mind, the image of his ravaged face was as Christ might have looked upon the cross.

She knew, of course, that he had suffered some kind of breakdown after the tragic loss of his wife and that Madame Belamie – dear Madame Belamie, of the serene nature and loving smile – had looked after the baby, nursing her along with her own small son until such time as Monsieur Fabian had recovered himself sufficiently to establish himself in London with a house-keeper and a wet-nurse for the child. The ensuing years had brought scraps of information her way, and these she had jealously hoarded.

Her main source had been Paul Belamie, who had much to thank Monsieur Fabian for.

Dr Bonnet had received a letter after Monsieur Fabian's recovery.

'What I owe both to you and your wife, my dear Monsieur le docteur, is equalled only by my debt to Madame Belamie,' Fabian had written. 'My thanks can never adequately be expressed. I pray God that the kindness and devotion which you showed me may be returned in equal measure throughout the days of a long and happy life, and beg that you will ever bear in mind that if the time comes when I may perform any act to help you or any member of your family you will instantly apprise me of it.'

Though none of the doctor's household had felt the need to solicit his help, in the matter of Paul's apprenticeship the Belamies had done so. It was the dearest wish of Monsieur Belamie's heart that Paul should follow the craft which his father had regretfully abandoned on his arrival in England. He had felt it expedient to do so since his brother already had a thriving business in Sandwich and was anxious for him to participate in it, but it was not a decision that he had made lightly.

Paul, he had decided long ago, should carry on the tradition in his stead, and he had approached the silk-weaver for advice. He had received more than advice. It was entirely through Monsieur Fabian's financial help and kindly influence that the boy had been apprenticed to the well-known gold and silversmith, Charpentier, who was both a friend to Monsieur Fabian and also a fellow member on the committee of La Soupe, the organisation that dispensed charity to newly arrived refugees in London.

He had been kindness itself to Paul ever since the boy had taken up residence in the capital. Indeed, said Madame Belamie, no member of his own family could have been treated with more generosity.

It was from this source that Charlotte had learned most about the silk-weaver's household. She knew that he lived in Freedom Street, in the district of Spitalfields to the east of London where so many Huguenot silk-weavers had settled. She had heard about the fine furnishings of his house, and the steady stream of sedan chairs bringing fashionable ladies to his door to choose their silks.

His housekeeper, she had learned, was a widow, an aunt of his late wife, without children of her own and devoted to the little girl who was called Elise, as pretty as a picture, the apple of her father's eye. All this she knew already, but she hoped to learn more as, with her face carefully blank, she sipped her chocolate and listened as her mother and aunt continued to talk of him.

'No doubt he is married again by this time,' Madame Bonnet said. 'It is, after all, six years –'

Tante Hortense was shaking her head vigorously.

'No, no – not so! The matter was wondered at by Monsieur Herault when he told me of the visit, for he said himself how strange it was that Monsieur Fabian had never taken another wife, and he with a young child to care for.'

Charlotte sensed rather than saw that her mother was looking at her speculatively and she knew precisely the direction of her thoughts. The mention of any single gentleman had the same effect on her these days.

Her mind is like a ledger, Charlotte thought rebelliously, with all the credits and debits neatly totted up. In the case of Monsieur Fabian she knew that the account was overwhelmingly in credit. He was not only French, but a hero and a Huguenot. He was well to do, by all accounts, with an established business. He was no more than fourteen or fifteen years her senior. Most of all, an alliance with such a man would mean unimaginable prestige for the Bonnet–de Sezy side of the family and a crushing defeat for Tante Hortense in the marriage stakes.

'Perhaps he cannot bear the thought of replacing the woman he loved,' she said. Her mother ignored this piece of foolish romanticism.

'I think,' she said carefully, 'that if he comes to Canterbury, it would be no more than civil to invite him to stay with us here once his business with Monsieur Herault is done. I know that my husband would be delighted to see him again, for the experiences of that night united us in a unique way. I shall ask Monsieur and Madame Belamie at the same time.'

Charlotte fought to calm the panic that rose at the thought. Did she want him to come? Part of her longed for it, but on the other hand she knew it would be the end of something that was inestimably precious to her if she found that her hero of the gaunt face and shining spirit had turned into a complacent businessman. She did not want to see him doing everyday things like eating or drinking, blowing his nose or taking snuff; yet on the other hand she thought sometimes of his voice and yearned to hear it once more, just to see if it was as thrilling as she remembered.

But as for her mother's ambitions regarding marriage – well, they were simply absurd! Apart from the fact that there was no reason why such a man should look twice in her direction, she could imagine nothing more terrifying than marrying a legend. It was quite unthinkable! She would as soon marry the Wizard Merlin.

Tante Hortense was preparing for departure, tying her mantle and collecting her parcels.

'Come and see Marianne, Charlotte. She has so much to show and tell you.'

'I should like nothing better.'

'Then come tomorrow – we shall depend upon it! You too, Albertine. Come for a dish of bohea tea.'

Bohea tea! How typically affected of Hortense!

'Charlotte may come, of course, but I have work at the orphanage.'

Up went Tante Hortense's hands once more.

'Really, one cannot *imagine* what they would do without you.'

Once the visitor had gone, Madame Bonnet belatedly turned her attention to the linen press, with Charlotte an abstracted and half-hearted assistant at her side. Together they sorted through sheets and table covers and towels, all feather stitched and embroidered by Madame Bonnet, but though the stocks seemed more than adequate, she could not avoid shaking her head mournfully over all that she had been forced to leave behind.

'It breaks my heart,' she said. 'I began my marriage chest when

I was but a girl. It is never too early to make a start, Charlotte.'

'Maman – please! I have no wish to be married yet.'

'No one is considering it yet! I merely remarked that it is as well to be prepared, though we must not delude ourselves that it will be easy to find a man prepared to overlook the fact that we can offer no *dot* worthy of the name.'

'Long may he conceal himself,' Charlotte said boldly, causing her mother to round angrily upon her.

'When will you learn to consider before you speak? Can you not see how we worry about such a lack, your father and I? After all, we are no longer in our first youth and it's the dearest wish of our hearts to see you comfortably settled with a suitable husband. It is thoughtless beyond words that you fail to see how troubled we are, solely because of our concern for you.'

Charlotte murmured an apology and for the moment her mother said no more, only the vigour with which she piled one folded sheet upon another evidence of her inward agitation.

'What is to become of you should you *not* marry, that's what I ask myself.' Her anxiety could not be contained for long. 'After all, even you will not be young for ever, mam'selle. Other girls have brothers and sisters who may offer a home, but you are alone – and if I may say so, Charlotte, you make little effort to help yourself in this regard. Heaven knows there is much I criticise in Marianne, but there is no gainsaying that in company she is lively and draws others towards her.'

'Whereas I am dull and tongue-tied.'

'You make no *effort*,' she repeated. 'Think to yourself, what do you want out of life? A home and husband of your own, with your own children about you? Or would you choose to be like Mam'selle Lamont, who teaches the children of others and is quite alone once they have gone home, with nothing but a lonely old age staring her in the face?'

Charlotte had no answer to this question, or at least none that would satisfy her mother. She did not consider that Mademoiselle Lamont had too unenviable a life; though on the other hand, there was something a little strange about her, a desperate girlish edge to her voice that made her the butt of jokes and mimicry among her pupils and seemed to say that she must hide at all costs her essential loneliness and frustration. It was generally agreed among the handful of girls who presented themselves at her house daily that she longed for children of her own; as indeed, was the implication, every woman must.

At this thought Charlotte became aware of a sensation of panic, a rising tide that she had suffered more and more recently and knew to be shameful, for surely this swimming of the senses and racing of the pulses at the thought of childbirth must mean that she was unnatural, some kind of freak of nature? No normal girl would feel so afraid, so repelled. How could she ever confess it? No one would understand, least of all her mother who would no doubt have been astonished at the number of times her daughter had considered the alternatives before her: marriage and childbirth – or celibacy and loneliness?

It was a ghastly, cruel choice and she found it impossible to reach any conclusion. The only result of her considerations was this paralysing fear which made her incapable of taking a breath or making a movement. Then there were the nightmares. They had plagued her in the past, she remembered, while they were still in France, but then had followed a period of tranquillity. Now they had returned once more – nightmares in which she was pursued by grotesque creatures with talons dripping with blood that sought to devour her flesh. Sometimes she was in a deep forest, at others in a dark, rat-infested cellar with no way of getting out except through the trap door where the creatures swarmed in, slimy and obscene.

She did not understand why she should suffer so, any more than she understood why the sound of the cathedral bells floating across an orchard bright with blossom could make her eyes fill with sudden, unexpected tears; or why colours seemed to have a life of their own when so many others of her acquaintance seemed unable to tell the difference between one shade and the next.

She even saw people in terms of colours. Her mother was a kind of dun brown, which seemed strange as she invariably wore grey. Madame Belamie, on the other hand, *was* grey, but not the dark grey worn by her mother. Charlotte saw her as a soft grey with tones of both blue and white, rather like the breast feathers of a dove. Tante Hortense was a majestic purple, Marianne either a deep rose pink or a pale shade of blue, Paul a clear yellow.

Charlotte had tried to explain this to Marianne, but not unexpectedly her cousin had looked at her as if she had gone off her head.

Monsieur Fabian, she had decided long ago, was a shade of

deep emerald green, rather the colour of an embroidered cloth her mother had just folded and placed on the chair. She concentrated on it fiercely, filling her mind with its colour so that there was no room left for the panic, and soon she felt the distressing physical symptoms ebbing away and found that she could breathe and swallow, turn her head and act quite normally.

'I'll try to be better,' she said contritely, and her mother looked at her, clearly knowing nothing of the byways through which her thoughts had been scurrying.

'I hope so,' she said, still unbending. 'For your own sake.'

The invitation to Monsieur Fabian was written and despatched, and though Charlotte could not decide in her own mind whether or not she wanted the visit to take place, in the event the matter was decided by forces outside the control of anyone in Canterbury. Monsieur Fabian wrote a cordial reply, but said that he had been forced by pressure of business in London to postpone his trip.

The blow to Madame Bonnet and her matchmaking activities was not so great as it might have been since another possibility had recently revealed itself. Dr Bonnet had, two years previously, become the medical adviser to a certain Mr Clouter (born Cloutier), a manufacturer of paper who was himself of Huguenot descent. His family had come to Canterbury two generations earlier and had prospered mightily, becoming so wealthy that the present Mr Clouter had purchased a large estate called Hinchcliffe Hall some five miles from the city, and now lived the life of a gentleman. As his health was far from good, he needed the services of a physician at frequent intervals and it was not long before the professional relationship between the two men developed into something akin to friendship, albeit a friendship heavily laced on the one side with patronage and on the other with gratified deference.

Mr Clouter was a widower, but as he was almost seventy years of age, even Madame Bonnet refrained from considering him as a possible suitor for her daughter – though regretfully, and only after much heart-searching. It was his son, also a widower, who aroused her interest. Hugo Clouter was a major in the army and lived in London – well thought of by King William, his father reported proudly, and in and out of the palace with as much familiarity as if it had been his own home. The recounting of this detail gave Dr Bonnet as much satisfaction as if he were the proud father himself.

'You say he lost his wife six months ago?' Madame Bonnet was anxious to get down to essentials.

'About that time. Poor fellow, he had many years of her indifferent health to contend with, his father tells me.'

'Are there children of the marriage?'

'Alas, no – the cause of much disappointment, I understand, both to the Major and his father. He is disposed to marry again without delay, and I do not think, my dear, that this is an opportunity we can afford to let slip.' He carefully arranged the lace that fell from his cuff, unable to hide the smile of satisfaction.

Madame Bonnet was less optimistic.

'Soldiers never have sufficient money. He will look for a woman with a sizeable *dot*, of that you may be sure.'

'The son of Mr Clouter?' The doctor looked amused. 'Well, money never comes amiss, I grant you that, but I hardly think that it will be the point at issue for the son of Mr Clouter. It is the old gentleman's dearest wish to see his son happily settled and to hold his grandchild upon his knee before he dies – which both I and he know may not be long delayed. Should Major Clouter look with favour on any young lady, just so long as she is healthy and ladylike, and preferably French, then I cannot believe that any lack of money would put the matter in jeopardy.'

'Have you spoken of Charlotte?'

'I had no need to. Mr Clouter has seen her at church and admires her looks. He makes no guarantees, of course, but thinks a meeting should be arranged. Say nothing to her for the moment, for he does not know yet when the Major will be next at Hinchcliffe.'

Fervently Madame Bonnet clasped her hands together.

'Oh, how I shall pray for a happy outcome! To see Charlotte mistress of Hinchcliffe Hall would be more than I had ever hoped. Not that she would find the task beyond her, for does not the blood of the de Sezys run in her veins? She would take to it as naturally as a bird to the air!'

'We must not build up our hopes, madame.'

Returning to earth, Madame Bonnet nodded.

'You are right, monsieur. There are many hurdles to cross.'

Charlotte's own attitude to marriage was not the least of them, she realised. When finally the date of the Major's arrival at Hinchcliffe Hall was known she went quietly into action with her usual efficiency. The pastor of the church in Canterbury was to achieve his eightieth birthday on 10 August. Marc le Brun was the elder statesman of the French and Walloon community in the area, and though he only preached occasionally these days he was still a dominating figure and was regarded by all with the utmost respect.

Some kind of celebration of the occasion had long been talked of; now Madame Bonnet took matters into her own hands. She and the doctor would give a supper party in Monsieur le Brun's honour, to be held, God willing, in the garden of Providence House, which should be looking its best at that time of the year. Musicians would be engaged, a buffet prepared.

'Oh, a *fête champêtre*!' cried Tante Hortense when she was told of it. 'It will be the talk of Canterbury. How *dashing* of you, Albertine!'

'I merely wish to mark the occasion in a suitable manner,' said her sister-in-law, for once less than forthright.

Mr Clouter was naturally invited, being himself a prominent member of the Huguenot community, and since his son was to be at Hinchcliffe at that time, his inclusion in the invitation was a matter of simple courtesy. So Madame Bonnet averred, and so Charlotte believed. It was Marianne, who had heard it from her mother who had heard it from the doctor, who told her differently.

'My dearest girl, the whole thing is arranged so that you can meet him,' Marianne giggled. She now was a bride of several weeks, but as far as Charlotte could see she had changed very little. 'Isn't it exciting? Imagine having the entrée at court and hobnobbing with the King and Queen! And then being mistress of Hinchcliffe Hall when the old man dies! It's a palace, they say, with all manner of treasures in it. Why, what's the matter, Charlotte? I declare, you have turned quite green.'

The nightmares redoubled their attacks on her, leaving her pale and unrefreshed at the end of each long night. Once or twice Madame Bonnet came to her in the night saying that she had heard her cry out. It was only a bad dream, Charlotte told her mother, aware of how inadequately these words described the horrors.

Not surprisingly, Madame Bonnet was brisk in her response. Charlotte had eaten too heavy a meal, she said; indulged in too many fanciful thoughts, read too many unsuitable books that had overheated her imagination, forgotten her prayers. In short, such foolishness was entirely Charlotte's own fault and could only be rectified by firmness of purpose.

Charlotte endured all such pronouncements in silence, despairing of ever finding the words to explain that these night-time obscenities were in some way connected with marriage and childbirth – least of all to her mother, who had at last, and with great joy, told her of the impending meeting with Major Clouter.

On the day of the supper party, Marianne and her husband, Tante Hortense, Uncle Clark, and Richard, eldest of the three Clark boys, sat down to dinner with the Bonnets at four o'clock. Other guests began to arrive at seven, and before long the summer evening was enlivened by the sound of voices and the sight of guests dressed in colourful finery.

There was applause and a few respectful cheers as the white-haired old pastor came into the garden in his black robes and white bands, supported on each side by his son and daughter-in-law. He stood for a moment smiling delightedly at his flock before lifting a hand, at which signal all stood silent with bent heads while he pronounced a blessing. Once this was done, he was escorted to a high-backed, carved chair where he sat with great dignity, holding court, while around him others were sitting in chairs that had been set in groups, or promenading, drifting from one knot of friends to the next. The musicians, stationed in the rose garden, played the works of Mr Purcell, and on all sides was heard praise for the weather, the flowers and the felicity of the occasion.

There was as yet no sign of the Clouters, and Charlotte began to hope that something had delayed the Major in London and that perhaps he would not come at all.

She had been given a new gown of cream silk for the occasion, with a tiered skirt and a stomacher of yellow and cream trimmed with echelles. Earlier, Marianne had dressed her hair for her in a new and becoming style, but as Charlotte had sat before the mirror undergoing this transformation, she had been less than satisfied with the face that looked back at her. Her colour was never high, but on this day when from the hour of her waking she had been haunted by the night's terrors, she had a pallor which even Marianne remarked on, occupied though she was by an almost unbroken account of the blisses of married life.

Comb in hand, she had broken off to look at her cousin more closely.

'Does something ail you, Charlotte?' she asked. 'You are prodigiously pale!'

'I slept poorly last night.'

'Thinking too much about Major Clouter, I'll wager!'

'Oh, Marianne!' Charlotte turned and looked at her appealingly. 'Surely you can understand how I feel, how apprehensive I am. My parents have set their hearts on this match, I can sense it, and from what I can gather old Mr Clouter is happy to connive at it too. He told Papa that he has seen me in church and thinks me a docile, pretty little creature. Those were his very words. Docile! In other words, a nobody, meekly accepting my fate whatever it may be.'

'Well, your papa told my mama that he would not allow you to be coerced in any way, however good the match. You would have to be agreeable to it, he said.'

Charlotte gave a short and sceptical laugh.

'It's true that I should not be beaten, or fed on bread and water, but there are other, more subtle ways of coercion, Marianne. Docile, indeed!' She turned back to the mirror once more and stared at herself. 'Is that how I seem to others? I suppose I do, yet I feel quite different inside.'

'I beg you to keep still!' Marianne was concerned with more practical matters. 'You are far too sensitive. What does it matter what people say? There!' She stood back, head on one side to study the effect of her labours. 'You look very well, even if I do say it myself.' Her voice took on a note of surprise. 'Yes, really, you look quite lovely – and would look even better if you would smile a little and allow me to apply some rouge.'

Charlotte did neither, but scowled ferociously instead.

'Pale of face I am, and pale of face is how he will see me,' she said. 'Though I have never ceased praying that he will be prevented from coming at all.'

Now it seemed that her prayers had been answered for there was still no sign of him. She began to relax, but just as she was engaged in conversation with Richard Clark who read a great deal and, rather like his mother, could always be relied upon to have some new bee in his bonnet, she became aware of a change in the atmosphere. Conversations were stilled, all interest directed towards the side of the house from where, direct from his carriage, had appeared Mr Clouter, dressed in black and leaning heavily on a cane, and the Major, resplendent in his uniform of a cavalry officer.

Dr Bonnet bustled across to meet them. He was most splendidly attired in a coat of blue velvet, pale breeches and stockings to match the coat. He looked like an exotic little humming bird beside his soberly clad wife who was not without a certain distinction in her dress of black silk and its lace-edged shoulder cape. None could compare with the Major, however, who had come in full uniform. The bright blue of his jacket, its quantity of gold braid, even the shine of his boots, all were dazzling.

He was a stocky man of average height, dark and somewhat florid of face, with a strong, down-curved nose and full lips.

'Oh, *how* I love a uniform,' Marianne breathed ecstatically in her cousin's ear. 'He is not at all ill-looking, Charlotte.'

'He's old,' Charlotte said.

'Not more than five and thirty.'

'Forty, if a day – and he has no neck, no neck at all. I cannot abide a man with no neck.'

Marianne giggled at that and dug Charlotte in the ribs with her elbow, for now the initial greetings were over, the daughter of the house was being beckoned to make her curtsey. This done, old Mr Clouter was escorted to another chair, the twin of the pastor's, and to her horror she found she was left alone with the Major. She was too shy to look at him directly and for a moment stood in confused silence, toying with her fan until she remembered that this was a gambit that once Marianne had recommended as being highly provocative to a watching male. Hastily she snapped it shut.

'May I get you a glass of punch, sir?' she asked.

'There is no need.' Smiling, blandly sure of himself, he waved Nan towards him and helped himself to a glass from the tray she carried, all without taking his eyes from the girl who stood so uncomfortably before him. She swallowed with difficulty and forced herself to smile at him politely, wishing he would not stare at her so intently. His eyes were small and a strange reddish-brown in colour, and they seemed to glow as if he were amused at some private joke. Charlotte suspected that she was the joke.

'Such a delightful garden you have here, Miss Bonnet – a small piece of France, no less! And such a glorious evening on which to enjoy it! I swear I wonder how any man can prefer to live in London.'

'Yet you choose to stay there.'

'Needs must, Miss Bonnet, at least for the time being. I long for the time when I can retire to my acres in the country.'

'There must be advantages. I hear you are much at court.'

'The court of King William is not renowned for its liveliness! I shall gladly relinquish my duties there once the King allows me to resign my commission. For the moment he seems to believe that I am too valuable to be allowed to leave his service.'

'Then you must certainly stay.' Nervously she smiled again, wishing he would stop studying her so intently. She looked away from him and in desperation brought her fan into play once more. 'Oh,' she cried, a note of hysterical relief in her voice. 'There is my uncle! I know he would be so interested to meet you, Major, for he is an historian with a particular knowledge of wars and battles – and – and –' She faltered, unable to think of Uncle Clark's further claims to attention. 'And all manner of military matters,' she finished lamely. 'Uncle Clark, Uncle Clark, do come and meet Major Clouter.'

Introductions were effected, and the men bowed.

'You were at the Boyne I believe, sir –'

Oh, *blessed* Uncle Clark! She had known he would not fail her.

'Gentlemen, pray excuse me. I believe my mother needs me.'

Charlotte bobbed a curtsey and made her escape, thankful she was no longer the target of that penetrating stare, but she had gone no more than a few steps before she encountered old Madame le Clerc, her uncle's mother. She was a vague, amorphous woman who had surprised everyone by the vigour with which she had resisted the anglicisation of her name. Now she clutched at Charlotte and implored her to go inside and find the shawl which she had earlier left upstairs. It was not, she said, that she felt cold *yet*, but she was quite sure that she might do so before long.

Charlotte, not in the least averse to putting a few more yards between herself and Major Clouter, did as she was asked, though as she searched for the shawl she told herself she was foolish to worry. What possible interest could a man like Major Clouter have in a simple country girl such as herself, when he was surrounded day by day with the ladies of the court? It was not as if her looks were outstanding, after all, and he could assuredly not have been overwhelmed by the brilliance of her conversation.

She found the shawl at last, hidden under several others, and felt almost light-hearted as she ran down the stairs. With her mind on other things, she found herself startled suddenly by the sight of a beautiful, unknown woman facing her at the foot of the stairs – then laughed, for it was nothing more than her own reflection, mirrored in the old, gilt-framed looking glass that hung on the wall.

She halted and stared, not recognising the reflection as the girl she saw every day of her life. For some inexplicable reason she had not realised until this moment how the new coiffure had changed her, made her seem older and a little fuller in the face. The new gown, too. It was, she saw now, vastly becoming.

Her first reaction was one of delighted surprise, for who does not like to look better than she imagined? But then she felt a small, cold, warning breath of fear. This was how Major Clouter had seen her. For a moment she studied herself with an intensity equal to his as he had stared at her in the garden; then with a last, astonished look she went to take the shawl to Madame le Clerc.

Even as she bent to hand it to the old lady, she found the Major had come to her side.

'I must insist that you show me the entire garden,' he said, offering his arm. 'We have a formal garden at Hinchcliffe, you know, and I am thinking of enlarging it. You must come and give me the benefit of your advice.'

'It is my mother who could advise, not I,' Charlotte said quickly.

'But you must come anyway.' His hot, eager little eyes were on her again. 'Say that you will, Miss Bonnet. There are many flowers in bloom there, but none, I swear, as lovely as you. I shall petition your mother, and both of you must come.'

They went, of course; and later in the week they journeyed to Faversham in his company to take tea with his sister. Two days later he called unexpectedly and stayed to drink coffee, and a week later the Bonnet family were invited to join the Clouter party at a Municipal Ball.

He was attentive and full of flattering speeches. He and Charlotte discussed nothing of importance and spoke only plati-tudes – in fact Charlotte was required to speak very little for the

Major was content to talk of his doings in London and his feats of derring-do in battle, and did not care to be interrupted, a circumstance that was entirely to her liking as she had known from the first that she had nothing to say to him.

She also knew that suddenly her mother was delighted with her and that her father's face was wreathed in smiles whenever he looked in her direction; that the most succulent strawberries, the best cuts of meat, the breast of chicken, were all put upon her plate, and that an unprecedented interest was taken in her wardrobe, no fewer than three new gowns being pressed upon her.

By the end of the summer her betrothal to Major Clouter had been announced.

Afterwards she could not explain the wild recklessness that made her agree to it. She did not succumb immediately. The nightmare attacked her night after night until she grew afraid to sleep. After a while, it simply ceased to matter; she was able, it seemed, to function without sleep, but everything around her had an air of unreality about it, as if she had stepped into a topsy-turvy world of pure fantasy, where nothing was as it seemed.

Her parents told her unceasingly during this time that they cared only for her good. Was it the age difference that concerned her? Then she should cease worrying forthwith! A man of forty was in his prime. Far better to marry such a one who knew how to look after a woman and was well-established in life, rather than struggle in poverty with some young man who still had his way to make in the world.

Did she, perhaps, dislike the prospect of becoming a soldier's wife? Why, she need have no fears on that score, for Major Clouter had made no secret of the fact that he was determined to come home to Hinchcliffe Hall as soon as possible now that his father's health was so precarious – and think then, her mother urged her, of all the comforts she would enjoy! To be mistress of such a house was beyond anything she could have reasonably expected, given the regrettable fact that her parents could only offer a small dowry. She surely was the most fortunate, most honoured girl in the whole of Canterbury – nay, in the whole country! – to be singled out by such a man.

It was only when Charlotte was with Major Clouter that the pressure ceased. Then she was able to sit and smile, withdrawn into her own private world where none of these clamouring voices reached her. The Major did not badger her. He was content, it seemed, to continue his monologue, devouring her with his eyes, watching and waiting.

At the end of one night when she had scarcely closed her eyes for fear of what her dreams might hold, she found she no longer cared what was to become of her. All she wanted was peace. If marrying Major Clouter brought this about, then she would marry him. If bearing his children killed her, then so be it. She had, it seemed, to marry at some time. Perhaps Major Clouter would prove no worse than anyone else.

3

Freedom Street began life importantly enough at its junction with the main thoroughfare where the traffic never ceased and the air was constantly filled with the cries of itinerant vendors and warring coachmen whose wheels had become locked, competing with the calls of the footmen clearing a way for their noble masters and the farmer driving a flock of sheep to market.

There was often a ballad-singer at the corner, too, as well as beggars and pickpockets and barkers drumming up business for the latest fantastical attraction – a contortionist or rope-walker or fire-eater.

Freedom Street was less congested, for it led nowhere but to the teasel ground once cultivated by the clothworkers, and the substantial houses, huddled cheek by jowl at the top end of the street, gave way to humble cottage dwellings.

The house where Gabriel Fabian had hung his sign – a large wooden spool to denote his trade – was one of three, quite close to the corner, set up and back a little from the street, like three gaunt old maids withdrawing their skirts from the mud.

They were not grand houses, not to be compared with those being built in the new squares and crescents to the west, still less to those mansions whose gardens fronted the river, but they were solid and modestly prosperous – the respectable face of Spitalfields behind which lurked crowded courts and alleys and cocklofts crammed with pale-faced humanity, thieves and beggars and prostitutes fighting for existence alongside those more fortunate who had found work in the clothing industry in one form or another.

More French than English could be heard spoken in the streets, for Spitalfields had acted like a magnet to generations of refugees, always a haven for religious dissenters. Now it had become the most important centre for silk manufacture in the country. From Lyons and Nîmes, from Tours and Bas-Poitou they had come – merchants, master weavers, journeymen, dyers, throwsters, designers. France's lack of toleration had resulted in infinite benefit to England.

Gabriel Fabian's speciality was patterned silk and he had built up an enviable reputation since his arrival in England. Like Dr Bonnet, he had possessed sufficient foresight to transfer funds, knowing even before his imprisonment that he would be forced to leave France eventually.

He was one of the fortunate ones, he told himself frequently, for many had arrived with nothing but what they stood up in. Yes, God had been good. There were times, mainly when he was in the company of his small daughter, when he almost convinced himself.

'You should take a wife, Fabian,' his friends at the coffee house would say. Even the pastor at the French Church in Threadneedle Street where he was a member of the Consistory had been moved on more than one occasion to make the same suggestion, at which Fabian would smile pleasantly and agree – without, however, showing the slightest sign of following their well-meant advice. His name had never been linked with that of any woman since the tragic death of his wife, though many had gazed languishingly upon him. He had been left with a limp after the torture he had suffered at the hands of the dragoons, but this was seen as a badge of courage and merely added to his undoubted attractions. The pain he still suffered was something he kept to himself.

It was in merciful abeyance on the warm August night when he sat in the yard at the back of the house, idly throwing a ball for Elise to catch – or, more often, to miss with crows of laughter.

The looms that were housed in the loft of the house were silent now and the bustle of traffic was largely stilled. The hard blue sky had paled, and the shadow of the mulberry tree, planted by his predecessor, had spread its blessing over the yard. Elise, tiring at last of chasing the ball, climbed on his knee and wound her arms about his neck, and at the feel and scent of her he felt the hard knot of bitterness within him melt with love.

'Tell me a story, Papa,' she begged. 'Tell me about the boy David and the giant.'

It was a favourite of hers, heard many times over, and she did not hesitate to correct him if he deviated even minutely from the form of words she had grown to love.

In that moment, he was conscious of contentment; and when

young Paul Belamie was announced and shown to the courtyard, this feeling was enhanced for he felt warmly affectionate towards the youth, almost as if Paul were the son he would now never have.

'My dear boy, what a pleasant surprise,' he said, signalling to the maid to bring a second chair.

'Pray do not trouble yourself! I'm happy enough here.'

Paul hunkered down on the small stone wall surrounding the mulberry tree and Elise scrambled from her father's knee to embrace him.

'You haven't been here for a long, long time,' she said accusingly.

'I know, and I'm sorry for it.' The apology was directed over her head towards Fabian. 'An apprentice has little leisure.'

'Tantine says they are idle and good for nothing.'

The two men exchanged the glimmer of a smile.

'Tantine,' her father said, 'occasionally exaggerates.'

'If you please, sir –' Another maidservant had arrived to present herself diffidently before her master. 'Madame says the little one must come to bed.'

'Oh, *no*, Papa!' Elise clung to Paul's arm. 'Tell Tantine I cannot come yet! Paul has only just come.'

'But the hour is late, sweeting.'

'*Please*, Papa! You tell Tantine. She must do as you say.'

'Wicked one!' With pursed lips he shook his head as if in despair, yet she recognised the play-acting and knew that she had won. 'Very well. Tell Madame Colbert Elise may have ten more minutes.'

As the nursemaid withdrew to follow these instructions, Elise, with a squeal of joy, flung herself upon him.

'What news have you from home, Paul?' Fabian asked, stroking his daughter's silken hair. 'I trust your parents are well?'

'Very well, I thank you, monsieur. My mother's last letter was full of Charlotte Bonnet's betrothal.'

'Really?' Fabian raised his eyebrows. 'Dr Bonnet was kind enough to ask me to stay with them when I contemplated visiting Canterbury recently. I wish his daughter happy, though try as I might I cannot remember her. Of course, she can only have been a child when I last saw them.'

'And you had other things on your mind,' Paul pointed out gently. 'I must say I find it hard myself to believe that she is of an age for marriage. Of course, I've not seen her for some time, but there was always a sort of childish innocence about her, as if she were younger than her years.'

'Well, no doubt she is delighted at the thought of becoming a wife,' Fabian said easily. 'I must send a gift. When I think what I owe Dr Bonnet – and your mother, of course –' He smiled down at Elise, and had no need to say more.

'Monsieur –' The stern voice of Madame Colbert sounded an intrusive note in the peace of the courtyard. Politely Paul rose to his feet, and bowed slightly.

'Good evening, madame,' he said, but received no more than a curt nod in reply. Madame Colbert, it seemed, was not in the best of moods.

'Monsieur, it is the child's bedtime,' she said.

'Oh, *Tantine!*' Elise wailed.

'I granted her an extra few minutes in honour of our visitor –'

'Nevertheless, she must come now.' The grim face that this plain and dumpy little woman had turned upon Fabian softened as she approached the child, and her voice took on a playful, doting tone.

'Come along with Tantine, little treasure. There is bread and milk for you inside.'

'I don't want bread and milk!'

'You will take a little chocolate then, of that I'm sure.'

'Papa –' Elise turned away from the woman and clung to her father. 'Papa, let me stay.'

'Tantine knows best, sweetheart.'

There was a distinct lack of conviction in Fabian's voice which communicated itself to Elise. Paul thought, not for the first time, that these two were laying up trouble for themselves.

His brother, Jean, was now seven years old, just a little older than Elise, and there was also another small girl in the nursery. It would be exaggeration to say that there was no dissension in the Belamie household, but he had certainly never heard so much as he had been a witness to in Freedom Street. His parents loved their children greatly, but provided discipline and firmness too.

Not so here. He could barely remember a time when a visit had taken place without tears and pleadings for one reason or another, the present disagreement merely a minor incident compared to some he had seen. Elise was a bright and engaging child of exceptional beauty, but the concentrated devotion of these two adoring adults would, he considered with all the sagacity of the elder brother, be the ruin of her – which was strange when one considered Fabian's deserved reputation for wisdom, even saintliness. Was it possible to be *too* long-suffering?

If so, it was not a defect that was likely to affect him, Paul thought sardonically. It was, in fact, a sense of dissatisfaction that had brought him to see Fabian that night, and he had every intention of voicing it as soon as the opportunity occurred.

With Elise gone, protesting to the last, Fabian contemplated the youth before him.

'You look well,' he said. 'As if the Lord has only now done making you. What it is to be sixteen and strong as an ox, with all your life ahead of you! How goes life *chez* Charpentier? It's a long time since I heard your news.'

'I'm sorry, monsieur. I should have come –'

'Not at all, my boy – it was not said in reproach. You have little enough time to call your own, I'm well aware of that. I assumed that no news was good news.' He looked at Paul apprais-ingly, narrowing his eyes a little as he did not answer immediately. 'Was I not right?' he asked.

Paul hung his head and fidgeted with a few pebbles that lay on the ground, balancing one upon another. For a moment he did not answer, then he looked up at Fabian with a self-conscious grin.

'You put me in a dilemma,' he said. 'If I say "No, you are not right", you will think I only come to see you when beset by troubles, which isn't true. I have missed coming here, seeing you and Elise, but as you say there's little time to call my own and the weeks pass quickly. Yet I would be lying if I said that all was well.'

'Charpentier is satisfied with your work. I saw him not a week ago when we met at a meeting of the committee of La Soupe.'

'Did he say that?' Again the upward look. 'I suspect he had no wish to offend you.'

'Not at all! He would tell me the truth no matter what it might be.'

Paul hurled one of the pebbles to the far corner of the yard.

'Well, he may be satisfied with my work, but I am not! I shall never make more than a mediocre goldsmith, monsieur. I have no real talent for it. No imagination, no ability to make things of beauty. I shall never be more than competent.'

'And that is not sufficient?'

Paul shook his head.

'No, it is not. You see, monsieur –' Eagerly he bent towards Fabian, his face alight with earnestness. 'I am determined to succeed at something, though I am not at all sure at what. You of all people must understand that! Whenever people speak of high-quality silk, they speak of you. In under six years you have taken this city into your two hands and forced it to acknowledge you as the best.'

'And you look at me and think what a happy man I must be?'

'I know that without silk you would not be happy! Everyone knows you have two passions, your daughter and your craft.'

'At least you put them in the correct order.' Slowly, thoughtfully, Fabian reached into his pocket and took out his snuff box, his eyes on the boy before him. In silence, he took a pinch.

'Are you saying,' he said at last, 'that after two years' apprenticeship you have decided to abandon the craft?'

'I am saying it will never be for me what silk is to you. Oh, at the end of seven years I should no doubt be able to mend a ladle or engrave a coat of arms – but never, never will people speak of gold and Belamie in the same breath, for I have no real talent.'

Slowly Fabian nodded, acknowledging the validity of Paul's opinion, and the boy felt a glow of gratitude for his understanding. Had he tried to explain himself to his father, there would have been voices raised and fur flying by this time.

'What would your father say?' One would think, Paul thought, that the silk-weaver had been reading his mind.

'He would be angry, I think. Ever since he abandoned his own craft he has wanted me to carry on where he left off, as if my work would compensate for the loss of his.'

'I suppose a son to follow in one's own footsteps seems, somehow, the ultimate achievement.'

'Your father was a silk-weaver before you, wasn't he?'

Fabian nodded again.

'A good one,' he said. 'If I am half as good, then I have reason to be proud.'

'He must have been pleased with you.'

'He died when I was but a boy.'

'Then your mother – she was pleased, I am sure.'

It was as if a shutter had come down over the silk-weaver's face, as if memories had stirred, muddying the clear water of his contentment. He stood suddenly.

'Come, my boy – let us go inside and take a glass of wine, for the light is going so fast I can hardly see you. We shall light the candles and talk of you, not of me. I feel sure that you must have some plan at the back of that head of yours. Does the business of banking interest you?'

Paul, in the act of standing up, straightened and stared at Fabian.

'How did you guess?' he asked. 'I have often wished that Monsieur Charpentier was a banker as well as goldsmith, for many are –'

'His brother is.'

'I know – but in Amsterdam!'

'Let us talk of this a little.'

Together they went inside, Paul marvelling at this man's perception and sensitivity. It seemed altogether typical that he had not even had to voice the dreams that others might find incomprehensible. Why, when he had mentioned banking to Harry Porter, one of his fellow apprentices, he had looked at him as if he were mad, as if no one in their right mind could see that there could be excitement in it. Here was Monsieur Fabian, however, behaving as if it were the most normal thing in the world.

He poured a glass of wine and handed it to Paul.

'You know, of course, that there is talk of constituting a Bank of England to finance King William's fight against France? Many goldsmiths are afraid that all the money in England will come into its hands and they will be out of business.'

'I have heard it argued that its effect will be quite the opposite, monsieur. It will generate credit which will increase trade and the circulation of money. Oh, the Tories are against it, I know, but I incline to the Whig view – as you do, I feel sure.'

'Hmm.' Fabian took a thoughtful sip of his wine, and looked at him, saying nothing. What would I advise, he thought, if this was my own son? The Belamies trust me. I must tread carefully.

'I think you should complete your apprenticeship,' he said.

'Believe me, monsieur, I have no intention of doing anything else. I wondered –' He broke off awkwardly, conscious of how much he already owed this man.

64

'Yes?' Fabian prompted.

'Is there not some other master who would take me? Someone who is banker as well as goldsmith, so that at least I can gain some knowledge of financial matters.'

'It interests you that much?'

'It fascinates me, monsieur. Oh, I am grateful to you for arranging my apprenticeship with Monsieur Charpentier, I should hate you to think otherwise, but from the beginning I had no real enthusiasm for the craft. This is different! Money is the most powerful thing on earth –'

'And the love of it, we are told, the root of all evil.'

'I know that, monsieur, but still it is all-important. The conduct of the war, the rebuilding of the city, all the new houses in the west – none of them would be possible without money.'

'Have you mentioned any of this to Monsieur Charpentier?'

Paul shook his head.

'I thought I would speak to you first – ask your advice.'

'Perhaps his brother would take you.'

'In Amsterdam?' Paul looked at him in some dismay. 'I had not thought of leaving London.'

Fabian looked at him with mild amusement in his eyes. This young man wants it all, he thought, yet he was impressive all the same. There was an eagerness, a firmness of purpose about him that was no common thing.

'The city is, I understand, quite civilised.'

'But – *Amsterdam*, monsieur! I have had enough trouble learning to speak English.'

'A knowledge of Dutch would be useful in the world of finance.'

'I suppose it would.' There was a marked lack of enthusiasm in Paul's voice. He liked London. He had good friends here, and his family was not too far away.

'You would not necessarily be exiled for ever.'

'No, of course not.' The idea was taking root, growing in his mind. Amsterdam would not be so bad, perhaps. In fact it might be exciting.

'Shall I mention it to Monsieur Charpentier on your behalf?'

'Would you, monsieur? Oh, would you?' His imagination had caught fire now and his eyes were bright. 'I'd be eternally grateful –'

'Wait, wait! The place is hardly within my gift, but the matter

65

can at least be discussed. I will put your case to him and it may be that something can be arranged.'

'Monsieur –' Paul spoke softly. 'I don't know why you should be so good to me.'

'No?' Fabian smiled at him. 'You know full well the debt I owe your mother.'

'You have discharged that long ago.'

'Add to that the fact that I feel you are a young man worth helping, so much as it is in my power to do so.'

'Thank you.' For a moment Paul was almost tongue-tied with emotion, but his natural exuberance won the day and he smiled broadly and slapped his knee. 'By all that's holy, monsieur, you won't regret it! I'll make you proud of me, I swear it. There's just one more thing –' He sobered a little. 'There's the question of my father. I suppose that you wouldn't – I mean, would it be asking too much –?'

'If I were to write and put your case? No, Paul. He would feel hurt. Whatever is said to him must be said by you – but remember, nothing is agreed yet. I hardly think that either of us should say anything at this point. Wait until we see the way a little more clearly.'

'You're right, of course. I hope to go home for Christmas, so perhaps that will be the time to discuss my future.' He paused in thought and gave a short laugh. 'Strange to think that Charlotte will be a bride by that time!'

'The girl is clearly on your mind.'

'She is a good friend.'

'You're not happy about this match?'

'I know nothing of the man, except that he is an army officer and not only of Huguenot descent, but also wealthy. The Bonnets are delighted. It's just that –' He paused, and screwed up his eyes as if he were trying to get Charlotte into focus. 'She's somehow defenceless, more vulnerable than most.' He laughed again, with affection. 'Poor Charlotte! She was always in trouble for going off into daydreams. More than once she was beaten for it, for nothing angered her mother more.'

'Well,' Fabian said. 'It's her husband she will have to answer to now.'

The dinner party was a family affair, attended by aunts and uncles and cousins, all unknown to Charlotte, but for the most part

66

instantly recognisable as belonging to the Clouter clan by the dark, fleshy features. The jewels worn by the ladies sparkled in the late afternoon sun that streamed through the dining room windows, and more silver and gold gleamed on the table than she had ever seen brought together in one place. It seemed hardly credible that she would be mistress of all this splendour one day. Why me? she asked herself.

She was fully aware that the same question was in the mind of many of those who sat around the table. Though she was wearing the cream-coloured gown she had worn the night she first met Major Clouter, since it was by far the finest she possessed and was now made even finer by the addition of the pearl and ruby pendant and the ring that were his gift, she knew that she fell far short in the eyes of all these relatives. She could see it clearly in the eyes of his sister, Mrs Matthews, who looked at her with unmistakable derision. She was an intimidating woman, no less so because this was the second meeting that Charlotte had endured. It was to his sister's house in Faversham that Major Clouter had taken Charlotte to tea in the early days of his courtship. Mrs Matthews had terrified Charlotte then and she did so now, staring at her smoulderingly beneath her heavy lids. She uttered conventional politenesses, but they were stilted and a fool could see she meant none of them.

Mr Matthews, so Major Clouter had informed his bride-to-be, would inherit a baronetcy on the death of his father, and was a pale, etiolated man who reminded Charlotte of nothing more than rhubarb grown under a barrel. He had pale yellow hair and prominent teeth, and a foolish look in his round blue eyes. Baronetcy or no baronetcy, it looked to Charlotte as if his formidable wife had made a bad bargain.

Dr Bonnet was in his element. He sat on Mrs Matthews' right hand and sparkled with animation; but Madame Bonnet was, like her daughter, largely silent throughout the meal, for the conversation was concerned for the most part with people and events of which they had no knowledge. However, towards the end of the meal, Mrs Matthews turned towards Charlotte and addressed her down the length of the table.

'It's hoped you speak English, Miss Bonnet,' she said. 'Hugo don't care to speak French, you know.'

Nothing would have pleased Charlotte more than to reply tartly that had Mrs Matthews taken the trouble to engage her in conversation on the opportunities offered to her, then she might know how good was her command of the language; however, she naturally said no such thing, but forced herself to smile politely.

'I think I speak English tolerably well,' she said. Indeed, she knew that her vocabulary and grammar could scarcely have been bettered and was unprepared for the loud, braying laugh that emerged from Mr Matthews' lips. He made a grab for her hand, as if to kiss it.

'Mam'selle, I've never heard anything so exotic in my whole life,' he chortled. 'No bird ever trilled so sweetly! I could sit at your feet for ever.'

'Charles!' There was more boredom than annoyance in his wife's voice.

'Charles likes a joke,' Major Clouter said, heavily and without humour. Charles, he had previously told Charlotte, also liked cards and gambling and had never done a day's work in his life. Major Clouter did not, it had been made obvious, think a great deal of his brother-in-law.

Charlotte looked towards the Major and saw that he gazed at her with that particularly brooding expression that always made her feel awkward. She had no idea what it portended, whether she was being blamed for Mr Matthews' flirtatiousness or whether he despised her lack of confidence. Nervously she sipped her wine, wishing he would watch her less. She had spoken of it to Marianne, whom she regarded as an authority on all things pertaining to the opposite sex, but she had only laughed and told Charlotte not to be a goose. He looked at her because he loved her, Marianne said. Why else?

Charlotte could not answer her, but when after a few moments she stole another look in his direction and saw that his eyes were still on her, she felt a small trickle of distaste and foreboding chill her spine. He *gloats*, she thought, and hastily took some more wine. Perhaps all men were the same. How was she to know?

The salon to which Mrs Matthews led the ladies, leaving the men to their port, ran the length of the house, with long windows giving on to a terrace. Charlotte looked about it curiously, for on the only other occasion she had visited Hinchcliffe Hall she had been entertained in a smaller sitting room in which old Mr Clouter spent most of his days. There was a tapestry of heroic proportions on the wall at the near end of the salon, and she looked at it closely, partly to disguise her unease and partly because such things were always of interest to her. Somewhat to her surprise, since she felt quite sure she intended to ignore her brother's future bride as far as it was possible, Mrs Matthews came and stood beside her.

'Do you admire the tapestry?' she asked.

Charlotte hesitated for a moment, in something of a quandary, for she felt it to be heavy and overpowering and not much to her taste – yet such an opinion could hardly be uttered in this company. After a moment she compromised and said that it was, indeed, a remarkable piece of work. Mrs Matthews looked at her sideways with a knowing smile, as if aware that she had not spoken the entire truth.

'Shall I show you something you might prefer?' she asked. She put her arm through Charlotte's with every appearance of cordiality and led her down the room, stopping halfway where a smaller tapestry hung between two wall sconces.

Charlotte agreed readily that this was more pleasing to her, being lighter and more delicate, and Mrs Matthews said she was entirely in agreement. Perhaps she had misjudged her, Charlotte thought. She seemed, after all, to be putting herself out to be pleasant.

'Has Hugo shown you our family portraits yet?' she asked. 'Yours, of course, will be among them soon, for it is the custom in our family for the men to commission a painting of their wives. See, here is my mother.' They had progressed further down the room and had now almost reached the far end where several large oil paintings were framed in heavy gilt. 'Of course, she changed a good deal towards the end. Her health was never good following Hugo's birth.'

'You have sons yourself, I believe?'

'Three, to be exact.' Her smile exuded pride and self-satisfaction. Charlotte was certain she also detected a note of defiance, as if she were saying 'There – beat that, you little upstart!' 'Two of my sons are still at home, but my eldest boy, Edmund, is at Winchester. He is a brilliant boy, Miss Bonnet. No parents could wish for a better, more lovable son.' She looked around her, a long survey which took in the whole of the room. 'Edmund is attached to Hinchcliffe, just as he is attached to his uncle. He has always thought of this as his home.'

'I hope he always will.' Charlotte spoke quickly, believing that she had at last divined the reason for Mrs Matthews' thinly veiled hostility. No doubt she thought that her sons would be excluded from Hinchcliffe, once it had a new mistress. 'I hope all your sons will continue to feel at home here. I long to meet them.'

'Hugo so wants a son and heir.'

'Of course. What man does not?' She spoke lightly, fighting to ignore the fluttering panic that was beginning to stir within her. Hoping to change the subject, she progressed to the next picture.

They stood together and looked up at the portrait of a young girl. 'A pretty child, is she not?' Mrs Matthews remarked.

Naturally Charlotte assented, though privately she thought it a vapid, empty face, its main feature a lack of any sign of intelligence. Pretty enough, she supposed. It struck her suddenly that there seemed a vague likeness to Mr Charles Matthews.

'Can this be your daughter?' she asked in some bewilderment. She had not heard of any daughter, but that did not mean that none existed. Mrs Matthews laughed scornfully.

'My daughter? By heaven, I should hope not! No, I had no liking for the girl, though I was sorry for her, I have to admit that.'

'You speak as if she is no more.'

'She died six months ago.'

'Oh, how sad! She is so very young.'

'Hugo likes them young.'

The significance of her words took a moment or two to strike home, and when it did, Charlotte gasped in astonishment.

'This – this is Major Clouter's first wife?'

'Your predecessor. Yes, this is Diana. Did I not tell you that all the Clouter brides have their portraits painted? I always thought her name singularly inappropriate, for she was more of a timid mouse than a huntress.'

'But – but she is so *young*!' Charlotte said again.

'Fifteen at the time the portrait was painted. She was married on her sixteenth birthday. Tell me –' She stepped back from Charlotte a little and regarded her narrowly, her head on one side. 'How well do you know my brother?'

'I –' Charlotte paused uncomfortably. 'I know that he is a generous man.' Indeed, he had showered her with gifts during his courtship. She was the luckiest girl in Christendom, her mother had assured her. 'My parents think highly of him.'

'And you? Do you think highly of him?'

'Of course.'

She answered quickly, and saw Mrs Matthews' lips tighten in a brief and mirthless smile.

'I promise I will do my best to make him a good wife,' Charlotte continued breathlessly. 'I am aware of the honour he does me.'

Even as she spoke she felt astonishment that one half of her could be uttering these dutiful platitudes when the other half was shrieking in panic. It was as if she had no will in the matter at all; as if she opened her mouth and the time-honoured responses emerged of their own volition.

'Honour!' Mrs Matthews laughed derisively, and looked once again at the portrait. 'Diana did her best. She was a brainless little fool, but one has to allow that she did her best. Still, it was never enough.' She paused for a moment, then turned to peer into the face of the girl by her side. 'You do realise, of course, that he killed her?' she said.

'What in heaven's name can you mean?' Charlotte stared at her in horror.

'He killed her. Oh, not with poison or blunderbuss, but with something equally lethal. He wanted an heir, as I told you. Poor Diana.' She spoke lightly, as if the matter was, after all, of little consequence. 'While I was producing my fine, healthy boys, she had nothing but miscarriage after miscarriage. Hugo was quite sick with fury. It became an obsession with him, this need to produce a son – no matter that his wife lost her health and her looks and even her reason, in the end. She carried only two children to full term, but the first was stillborn and the second lived only a few hours. Even so, he outlived his mother –'

The panic was now a roaring torrent in Charlotte's ears. She felt faint and groped for the support of a chair that stood nearby. It was as if all her nightmares had come to life, here in this elegant room.

'I expect you are thinking it would be different for you.' She was aware that even though her face was turned away from Mrs Matthews, still she was being watched closely. 'You are young and strong and no doubt imagine that such a fate could not be yours. Well, pray God you are right, for believe me, if you are not, you may expect no mercy from Hugo. He was told by more than one physician in London that any further attempt to have a child would almost certainly end in Diana's death, but it counted for nothing. No matter what the danger, he forced himself upon her –'

'You cannot know that! You cannot know he forced himself.'

'She told me, poor dazed creature that she was by that time. And now, six months after her death, he is taking another young bride. Have you any idea what is in store for you, Miss Bonnet?'

Charlotte stared at her, her mouth so dry she could hardly speak, her heart pounding so rapidly that it seemed to fill her whole body.

'You hate him, don't you?' she said at last.

'I *know* him! Shall I tell you what he said of you when I questioned him? He said you were just such another – just as docile and meek as Diana, but with the advantage of a more robust physique. French countrywomen, he said, were in general good breeders. He said he wanted you, not for your wit or charm or wealth – which were all non-existent, so he told me – but because you were a blank canvas on which he could paint whatsoever he wanted, that you lacked the spirit to be other than his creature.' She had come close and with her head thrust forward into Charlotte's face was speaking softly and rapidly with a kind of gleeful relish. 'He said he would take you and mould you, and that you would obey him without question and fulfil all his needs –'

'Stop it, stop it!' Charlotte pressed her hands to her ears to block out the hateful sound of her voice.

'Run, Miss Bonnet, while you still have the chance.'

'But we are betrothed! I can do nothing now.'

'Betrothed you may be, but you have yet to take your marriage vows. I speak for your own good –'

Charlotte saw the expression of annoyance on her face. She had fallen silent as she looked beyond Charlotte's shoulder, and the girl knew they were no longer alone. She turned to find that Charles Matthews had approached and was urging them to return to the other end of the room where the gentlemen had now joined the ladies.

'Enough of these girlish secrets,' he said playfully. 'Come, Mam'selle Charlotte, take my arm. I long to hear more of your delightful conversation.'

Charlotte could only stare at him in reply, unable to think coherently or form words, so loud was the tumult of her emotions.

'Miss Bonnet has been looking at poor Diana's portrait,' his wife said, as if in explanation, and his face took on a suitable gravity.

'Ah yes, poor Diana. Poor, poor child. But allow me to say, mam'selle, that your fate will be far different. I can tell you will produce a quiverful of healthy infants.'

He was grinning again by this time, and to Charlotte's tortured imagination it seemed that his face had taken on the likeness of a death's head. Still he proffered his arm, but so ghastly did his aspect seem that she could not bring herself to touch him.

Instead, his wife took a firm grip on her elbow and led her to the other end of the room. The walls seemed to be swaying, the floor undulating, and the other guests congregated there seemed to Charlotte grotesque and unreal. The heavy features of the Clouter relations seemed exaggerated, their short necks now non-existent, their lips thick and misshapen. She felt as if their eyes were on her and her alone, and to her horror, she saw Hugo Clouter, her betrothed husband, making his way towards her.

It was as if she had never seen him clearly until that moment. Even across the expanse of carpet that separated them it seemed to her that the gloating look in his eyes had become more sinister, more threatening, as if here at last, seen face to face, was the original of the obscene creatures from which she had taken flight in so many nightmares.

She could feel the clamminess of sweat on her brow and body, and it was impossible to breathe. Mr Matthews had taken his place beside her once more and was braying on about her voice and the way she trilled her Rs, but none of it was more than a senseless background to the roaring in her head. The only words that had any meaning for her were the four that had formed themselves in her mind and seemed to tremble on her lips as if longing to be spoken – four words which, if uttered, would bring disgrace not only to her but also to her blameless parents. She would be dishonoured for ever, she felt sure, and though she was beguiled by the sweetness of those words, she was conscious of terror.

In the frightening clangour that filled her head, all the other occupants of the room seemed to retreat, losing substance and reality. Only he was there, growing larger and more menacing with every second, smiling and smiling and devouring her with his eyes.

She became aware that he was speaking, his brows drawn together questioningly as he bent towards her.

'Is something wrong, Charlotte?'

She nodded, unable to speak, her teeth chattering.

'What is it? Are you unwell?'

He reached out to take her arm, and it was his touch that finally unloosed her tongue and released the words that filled her head.

'I cannot marry you,' she said clearly.

For a moment it seemed as if the house itself was holding its breath, for the bald statement had emerged in a far louder voice than she had intended and had sliced through the gentle buzz of conversation so that all faces turned towards her, eyes rounded, jaws hanging open.

There was a silence during which Major Clouter's already florid face became suffused with angry colour.

'I *beg* your pardon?'

Charlotte's trembling fingers were busy with the catch of the pendant which was hung around her neck, and fumblingly she unfastened it and thrust it towards him, at the same time trying desperately to pull the ring from her finger.

'There you are, Major.' Breathlessly she pressed them into his palm. 'I cannot marry you. It was a mistake. I am sorry, so very sorry.'

The frantic, fruitless apology was meant as much for her parents as for him. She repeated it, looking wildly round the room as she tried to locate them, but her panic-stricken gaze seemed unable to focus and she could not distinguish individual faces, conscious only of universal shock and condemnation.

'*Je regrette* –' she whispered, retreating into the language of her childhood. '*Je regrette* –'

Desperately she looked from face to face, but nowhere could she see any hint of sympathy or understanding. Gasps and mutters of disgust seemed to swell and swell until the noise of them filled her head and made her senses swim, and with one last despairing look, she picked up her skirts and ran from the room.

4

Charlotte had always gloried in the colours of autumn, but in the months that followed her flight from marriage she felt chilled as if by a premature winter, so cold was the wind of disapproval that blew on her from all directions.

The story had gone round the city like wildfire, and she was conscious of curious stares and whispers whenever she ventured abroad, for each version of the events at Hinchcliffe Hall seemed to be more colourful than the last. One account, she learned from Marianne, reported that she had flung Major Clouter's ring at him across the dinner table; another that she had screamed vile abuse at him in language no lady should be aware of, causing so much distress to his father that the old man had suffered a seizure on the spot.

The doctor and Madame Bonnet treated her, not harshly, but with cold politeness as if she had suddenly become a stranger to them – or at least, they did so once the initial shock had worn away. At first they had been all but incoherent with anger and shame.

'Did we not say a thousand times we would not coerce you?' Madame Bonnet demanded angrily. 'Did we not say that the decision must be yours and yours alone?'

Miserably, silently, Charlotte nodded.

'Then why did you disgrace us and insult the Major? Why accept his offer and then treat him so, before so great a company! Can you not see how you insulted the entire Clouter family, as well as disgracing us.'

'I'm sorry,' Charlotte whispered.

The set of her mother's lips said all too clearly what she thought of the apology.

The doctor's face wore its mask of tragedy for weeks. Charlotte had made him a laughing stock, he said. How could anyone now take his word seriously – he, who had been befriended by the most powerful men in the city, but had now been humiliated by a slip of a girl?

Vainly she had tried to explain.

'Papa, Mrs Matthews told me what manner of man he is – how cruel he was to his wife, and how she died. I could not bear it!'

'Pooh!' He would listen to none of it. 'Of course Mrs Matthews has no wish for her brother to marry, still less father an heir. Her precious son Edmund would inherit Hinchcliffe Hall were Major Clouter to die without issue, and with such a wastrel for a husband the woman will stop at nothing to see that he does so. Shame upon you for being taken in by her lies.'

'Perhaps they were not lies.'

'In any event, it's too late to mend matters now. He'll not have you after making such an exhibition of yourself.'

'I do not want him to have me.'

He paid no attention to her distress, as stern-faced and unrelenting he went from the room. Kind though he could be, in his view she had made him look a fool in the eyes of his fellow citizens, and this was not something he could forgive easily.

As the weeks went by she could feel her mother's worried gaze resting on her. All too clearly, she was asking herself who would have her daughter now? What man of stature would risk being made a laughing stock at the eleventh hour – and all for a girl whose looks were fast deteriorating and with no dowry worthy of the name?

Charlotte knew as she stared into her mirror that she was growing plainer by the day. Her self-esteem was diminished to the point where it barely existed, and she strove to efface herself altogether, moving silently on the periphery of the household in the hope that no one would notice her, haunted by the words that Mrs Matthews had quoted – that she had neither wit nor charm. Was that really true? Oh, how she would love to believe that her father was right when he said that Mrs Matthews had lied to her, about this matter if about no other. But she could not convince herself.

November and December passed, bringing the bleakest of winters to a part of the country noted for its snow and bitter weather. Charlotte was almost totally deprived of Marianne's company now for she was by this time expecting a child and was not unnaturally wrapped up in her own concerns, as well as being confined to her isolated farmhouse by the bad weather. If it had not been for the cheerful Nan who resolutely set herself to the task of lifting Charlotte's spirits, the girl would hardly ever have seen a smiling face.

'You must put it all behind you, mam'selle,' Nan said to her one day, seeing how pale and thin Charlotte had become, and how bleak was her expression as she stared out at the colourless landscape beyond the window. 'What's done is done. There's no sense brooding.'

'What's to become of me, Nan?' Charlotte asked the question softly, not turning from the window. 'What can any woman hope for, who neither wishes to marry nor to remain alone?'

'Oh, come on, now!' Briskly Nan turned her from the window and pushed her into a chair. 'I'll put another log on the fire and fetch you some chocolate. You'd like that, wouldn't you? You've had little enough all day, heaven knows, and must be famished.'

She bustled away and returned with the chocolate, but though Charlotte took it from her gratefully and began to sip it, she continued to stand and look at her anxiously, twisting her hands.

'Miss Charlotte,' she said at last. 'Do you listen to what I say! The Major wasn't the one for you, no matter that he had a big house and plenty of money. He had a way of looking at a girl that scared the daylights out of me, never mind what it did to you. You're better off without him, and that's the truth.'

'I wish my parents felt the same.'

'They'll get over it, and so will you.'

'Everything's so gloomy! I thought perhaps the Belamie family would come at Christmas to cheer us, but it seems they are all to go to London instead, to be the guests of Monsieur Fabian, the silk-weaver.'

'Well, I'm sure that's very nice for them.' Nan was drawing the curtains across the window.

'I wish I could go too. I wish I could go almost anywhere, away from here – Paul is to go to Holland, did you hear? It has all been arranged by Monsieur Fabian.'

'He must be an important man.'

Charlotte, staring into the depths of her chocolate, said nothing, and Nan sighed as she looked at her.

'Look, lovey,' Nan said, kneeling beside her. 'Nothing's so bad as can't be mended. That's what my ma always says. You'll feel better come the spring. Everything looks better when the sun shines.'

'You're a dear, Nan,' Charlotte said, doing her best to smile. 'I can't imagine how I would live without you.'

Somewhat to Charlotte's surprise she found that Nan spoke nothing but the truth, for the spring brought relief in the shape of Madame Belamie who had come to Canterbury with her husband, leaving the children behind in Sandwich with her sister-in-law. Some legal wrangle over the leasing of land had brought them and they were to stay for several days.

Charlotte could, at that moment, think of no one she would rather have seen. She had always felt a special bond with Madame Belamie ever since their vigil together on the boat and was aware that the older woman regarded her with fondness. However, on the first evening, it was a look of concern she saw in Madame Belamie's eyes across the dining table, and she knew that her changed appearance was not passing without notice.

Madame Belamie would know the reason for it, of course, for who within the Huguenot community would not? The story would have reached far beyond the confines of Canterbury; but naturally no one mentioned it that first night. The conversation instead centred mainly on the doings of the church in Sandwich, which did not interest Charlotte greatly. Her thoughts wandered, as they had been more and more inclined to do lately, until mention of Paul and the Belamies' recent visit to London attracted her attention.

'What takes the boy to Amsterdam?' the doctor asked. 'I had thought him so well settled with Monsieur Charpentier in London.'

'So he was – and I confess I did not take kindly to the change,' Monsieur Belamie replied. 'But he and Monsieur Fabian between them convinced me he was right to go. He'll gain greater breadth of experience, there is no doubt of it, and since his new master is brother to his old and all has been amicably settled, we can raise no valid objection.'

'We hate the thought of him being so far away,' Madame Belamie said sadly. 'But he was set on the plan and it was endorsed by Monsieur Fabian, in whom we have great faith. Truly, I do not think I have ever known anyone so kind. His goodness to Paul has been beyond all things. He has treated him as a member of his family ever since his arrival in London and speaks most fondly of the boy – and as for our stay with him, we were treated right royally.'

'A spell in Amsterdam will enlarge his world right enough.'
The doctor smiled reminiscently. 'I have never ceased to be
grateful for the opportunity I had to study in England, and
the feeling of freedom and emancipation I enjoyed. He will
come back the better for the experience, there's no doubt of
that.'

'If he comes back at all.' Monsieur Belamie lifted his hand to
quell the cry that sprang to his wife's lips. 'No, no, my dear, we
must be prepared for him to stay. Amsterdam has become an
important centre for silver and gold and Paul might well think
his future lies there. Of all our children, he is the one who has
never hesitated to see what lies around the next bend. He is fond
of his home, but he'll never be tied to it.'

'But surely he'll come back once he's completed his indentures.'

'Perhaps he will. We can only pray that the good Lord will
watch over him and guide him into the paths that he has ordained
for him.'

'You are right, of course. His future is not for us to determine.'

Charlotte intercepted the look that passed between them. It
was full of warmth and sustenance and seemed, in that moment,
to show that marriage could have its advantages.

An end to loneliness – but only, surely, if one married the
right person? Under other circumstances it represented a life
sentence with a jailor who could act as brutally as he saw fit.
And even with the best of men, there were the duties of a wife,
demands that would be made –

She could feel her hand begin to tremble and was forced to lay
down her knife for a moment, fiercely concentrating her attention
on the pattern which was chased round the rim of her plate. The
blue of it was deep, the blue of gentians, the blue of the frothy
flowers that Maman grew around the edge of her flowerbeds.
Lobelia, was their name? She filled her mind with the thought
of their blueness until the wave of panic retreated and she was
able to pick up her knife again.

No one appeared to have noticed anything amiss. They were
still talking of Monsieur Fabian. His daughter Elise, the baby
who had first seen the light of day in the dark and stinking hold
of that ship, had suffered an illness during the latter part of the
previous summer and even by Christmas had barely recovered.

'It must have been a most severe fever,' Madame Belamie said.
'I thank God that she recovered, for Monsieur Fabian dotes on

her, as one might expect, and what the poor man would do were he to lose her cannot be imagined.'

Dr Bonnet shook his head.

'One cannot wonder at her illness,' he said. 'The foul miasma that rises from the river, all those overcrowded courts of Spitalfields –'

'Oh, it must be a vile place indeed,' Madame Bonnet agreed, though she had never seen it. 'Of course we all know that les Anglais have little use for cleanliness, that goes without saying, but I have been told that the stench of the streets passes belief.'

'There are places where that is true,' Madame Belamie conceded. 'But oh, madame, the new buildings that are rising now are quite magnificent, with squares and crescents set out in a manner that is elegance itself. And the parks! Oh, I would not have missed any of it for the world. As for the city – why, no one would dream that it is less than thirty years since the whole was razed to the ground. You must certainly go there yourself some time.'

'I have always considered Canterbury good enough for me,' Madame Bonnet replied dourly.

Charlotte almost choked upon her ragoût, for she could remember many occasions when Canterbury had been far from good enough for her mother and had suffered greatly in comparison with France. However she made no comment, wishing only that she had been born a boy, like Paul, and was able to leave home to see the world, or at least a small part of it. Paul was bound in his apprenticeship, of course, and no doubt worked hard, but despite that he was the eventual captain of his own fate. Why, she raged inwardly, had fate decreed that she should be a woman? And why, having done so, had it made her so fearful of what was in store? She felt ashamed and thought that if she could speak of it at all, she might be able to do so to Madame Belamie.

Though even she, Charlotte thought inwardly, would undoubtedly consider me mad. Perhaps I *am* mad!

She almost brought herself to speak of it one day when she walked towards the city with Madame Belamie, but somehow the words would not come. It seemed safer to talk of Monsieur Fabian.

'Is he much changed?' she asked Madame Belamie. 'Do you remember how he seemed so – so magical when he appeared in that cellar?'

Madame Belamie smiled at the thought.

'How could I forget it? There is a kind of magic about him still. He attracts attention wherever he goes, and people look up to him. Yet there is something about him –' She stopped short, and Charlotte looked at her enquiringly. Helplessly she shook her head. 'I cannot help myself feeling sorry for the man,' she said. 'It's not simply that he has lost his wife. There is something else that troubles him, some deep sadness. Oh –' She shrugged her shoulders and lifted her hands. 'Perhaps I am fanciful. There were times, though, when I surprised him with such a look of melancholy on his face that almost I could have wept for him.'

'He dotes on his daughter, you say.'

'Yes.' Madame Belamie's expression lightened, and she laughed. 'And a regular little minx she is! Not yet six years old, and she has not only her papa but the poor unfortunate Tantine wrapped around her little finger!'

'Tantine?'

'Madame Colbert, Monsieur Fabian's housekeeper. It seems she is childless herself and was devoted to Celestine, Monsieur Fabian's wife who died so tragically. She escaped from France herself shortly afterwards, and it seemed only natural that Monsieur Fabian should take her in. It was an arrangement of advantage to both of them, but I detected that there is little love lost between them. He should marry, of course, and I told him so.'

'And what did he reply?'

Madame Belamie was silent for a moment, remembering.

'Poor man,' she said softly after a moment. 'He said such a thing was impossible.'

'He must have loved Celestine very much.'

There was something in Charlotte's voice that caused Madame Belamie to look at her, her expression troubled.

'Pray don't brood so, my dear,' she said, taking her arm. 'You are young and your life is before you.'

Her sympathy was Charlotte's undoing, and she felt the tears spill over, and for a time the two women stood clasped in the country lane while Charlotte sobbed, releasing much of the misery that had paralysed her over the past months.

At no time during the visit did she bring herself to speak of her secret terrors, but Madame Belamie's presence and friendly interest did a great deal to cheer her, allowing her to feel for the first time since the Clouter débâcle that she was not entirely worthless.

Higher spirits ignited a spark of determination. Somehow she would get away. Tante Hortense had spoken often of a friend of hers who had opened a school for young ladies in Hammersmith, a village a few miles out of London close to the river, where she instructed her pupils in writing and reckoning, painting, needlework and all kinds of domestic craft. It seemed to Charlotte that she would be more than capable of teaching every one of these skills. Or, given her knowledge of both the French and English languages, perhaps it might be possible for her to be taken into the household of a respectable family as governess, or even as companion to some high-born lady of good reputation.

Monsieur Fabian had helped Paul. Perhaps he would do the same for her. There was, after all, the oft-quoted letter still in existence, in which he had sworn to do all in his power to assist Dr Bonnet or any of his family, should such assistance be necessary. She would write to him, she resolved.

It sounded a simple enough proposition, but when it came to the point she found the wording of such a letter far from easy and spent a great deal of time turning the matter over in her mind. One afternoon, as she sat at her embroidery frame, it became clear that she was not the only member of the family whose thoughts had been in Spitalfields.

'I have been thinking,' her mother announced, using an introductory phrase that normally struck terror into her family. 'I cannot get that poor child out of my thoughts.'

'Which child?' Charlotte asked.

'Why, Monsieur Fabian's daughter, of course. There she is in London, assailed on all sides by those foul miasmas your father spoke of. She survived last summer, but what of this? We must renew the invitation to Monsieur Fabian to come and stay with us and to bring *la petite* Elise with him so that she might benefit from the country air. You must write to him, m'sieu. Do you hear me?'

Dr Bonnet, deep in his account books, had not heard. He shook his head and sighed dolefully.

'No sign of any settlement from Mr Carver,' he said. 'And he was the man who professed himself so grateful for my ministrations that he would be for ever in my debt. I must confess I did not suspect he meant it quite so literally.'

'M'sieur, I beg you to listen to me.' Madame Bonnet went to sit at the table beside him, laying her hand flat across the page so that in some annoyance he was forced to look up at her. 'We must write to Monsieur Fabian and invite him to stay, for the benefit of the child. With the weather turning so warm, London is no place for her, you must surely agree with me.'

'I have no doubt that Monsieur Fabian has any number of acquaintances in the country, should he wish to leave town.'

'Perhaps the matter has not occurred to him. As a medical man, you should point it out.'

'I have invited him before and he has not come. I have no wish to importune him. Now, madame, if you will allow me to proceed –'

'But m'sieu, think of the child!'

And think of your daughter! Charlotte could read her mother's mind so easily. She bent her head over her needlework and hid a cynical smile. Though no one could doubt Madame Bonnet's charitable impulses that called down the blessings of the orphans and widows of Canterbury upon her head, her daughter had not the slightest doubt that on this occasion, her concern for little Elise Fabian was no more than a ruse to entice her father to Providence House, where Charlotte could be dangled before him as a possible bride.

Well, there was no ambivalence now in her attitude. Even in the unlikely event of his making an offer for her – and from what Madame Belamie had said, it sounded an impossible dream on her mother's part – Charlotte had no intention of marrying him; not he, nor any other. However, it would, perhaps, provide her with an opportunity of speaking to him regarding employment in London. If she could recruit him to her side, her parents would find it difficult to deny her, so great was his influence in the Huguenot community.

Dr Bonnet was at last badgered into writing the required letter of invitation, and somewhat to everyone's astonishment, a rapid reply was received. Monsieur Fabian was, on this occasion, delighted to accept the invitation so kindly offered. He had been worried about the sickness in town as the warmer weather approached – so much so that he had been considering the possibility of acquiring a house in the country for the entire summer, so that his daughter could be taken to a place of safety. Perhaps, he wrote, it might be possible to find suitable accommodation close to Canterbury which was a city he had long wished to visit in the way of business. He would be most grateful if he and Elise, together with Madame Colbert, could stay at Providence House until such time as other arrangements could be made.

Charlotte had never seen her mother more pleased and animated.

'May God be praised,' she said, hands clasped and eyes shining with earnest excitement. 'How truly it is written that all things work together for good to them that love the Lord! Surely this must be a sign –'

She shot a look in her daughter's direction and broke off hastily, rising to busy herself quite unnecessarily with the straightening of a chair. 'Such an honour,' she went on. 'Charlotte, we shall prepare the blue room. Everything must be taken out.'

In vain did Charlotte object to this on the grounds that it was only a matter of weeks since the room had been thoroughly spring cleaned. Nothing would satisfy Madame Bonnet except that the whole process was carried out all over again.

'We must make sure everything is as it should be. The furniture, the hangings – praise God the weather is fine and the mattress can have the sun on it!' For a moment she paused, biting her lip. 'The bedspread is shamefully threadbare. I have it!' Her brow cleared. 'We can use the one you made, Charlotte. Praise the Lord I prevented you from giving it to Marianne, as you had in mind.'

Altogether there was a great deal of praising the Lord at that time, and even more polishing and dusting and scrubbing. The cover destined for Charlotte's marriage bed was smoothed over that in the guest bedroom, and she had to admit that it looked very fine against the velvet hangings.

The trap is being well baited, she thought grimly. Monsieur Fabian would be left in no doubt that her skill with the needle was without question – but what of her behaviour towards Major Clouter? Did her mother hope that Monsieur Fabian would be unaware of it? It seemed a vain hope, given the almost supernatural way in which gossip was transmitted from one band of Huguenots to another in a quite different part of the country. But perhaps Monsieur Fabian had a mind above idle gossip.

A smaller room was prepared for Elise and Madame Colbert.

It seemed hardly fair, Charlotte pointed out, that two people should be expected to occupy a smaller area than one, but her tongue was firmly in her cheek as she spoke, for she knew quite well that Monsieur Fabian was to have the best of everything. She feared a little for her mother when she considered the disappointment that must surely be in store when her plans came to nothing.

To welcome him, the Belamies had been invited to join the meal on his first evening, but since Providence House was to be full they had arranged to stay with another member of the community lately come from Sandwich to Canterbury. The entire household became involved in the preparation of a prodigious banquet; snails, cooked as only Madame Bonnet knew how; a whole turbot; a gigot of mutton, peas and asparagus from the garden and potatoes stewed with butter and herbs, followed by syllabubs and jellies made from the soft fruit now coming into season.

'Are we to ask Tante Hortense and Uncle Clark?' Charlotte asked, seeing the amount that was to be provided. Vigorously Madame Bonnet shook her head.

'No, no, that would not do at all! There is a bond that unites those of us who were together in that time of tragedy. This, do you realise, is the first time we shall all be together.'

'Will Monsieur Fabian wish to be reminded of it?' Charlotte asked. 'It was, after all, a time of great grief for him.'

'Grief in which we shared! Think of the letter he wrote – how he expressed his undying friendship and gratitude!'

Ah, the letter! Charlotte hoped sincerely that he set as much store by it as her mother clearly did.

On the day he was due to arrive, Nan helped her to dress in the blue muslin gown that had been made for her during her betrothal to Major Clouter. It hung loose on her now, but Nan tightened the cream-coloured stomacher and tied a Steinkirk around her neck, which disguised its shortcomings and ensured that she was in the height of fashion.

'How clever you are, Nan,' she said, looking at her reflection. 'How is it you know what fashion dictates and how to twist it to advantage?'

'I keep my eyes open.' Nan smiled, well pleased with the compliment. 'If you sit down, Miss Charlotte, I'll arrange your hair.'

'As my cousin did it when we had the party last year? Can you manage that?'

'I can try. I think I know how.'

Charlotte sat and looked at herself as the transformation took place, wondering why, when she had no wish to attract Monsieur Fabian in the way her mother hoped, she was causing Nan so much trouble. The answer lay in one word: pride. She had no wish to marry him, but she could not forget the glamour of his appearance and disliked the thought that his eyes might rest on her, however kindly, only to dismiss her as someone of no importance. She longed to make some kind of impact, to prove that she was not a creature without wit or charm. After all, she had to convince him not only that she needed employment but that she was worthy of it.

Dr Bonnet took the carriage into Canterbury to meet the London Mail, leaving a house shining from roof to foundations. Did Monsieur Fabian care to inspect its furthest corner with a spy glass, he would not detect the smallest speck of dust; nor was the garden any less a reflection of Madame Bonnet's love of order. Not a weed was to be seen among the beds of roses and pansies and pink geraniums. The kitchen hummed with activity, but for Charlotte and her mother, suddenly there was little to do but sit with folded hands and wait for the arrival of their visitors. Madame Bonnet took the opportunity to give Charlotte some good advice.

'Try not to go off into a daydream, Charlotte. I beg you to look bright and interested, should Monsieur Fabian converse with you – but without putting yourself forward in any way, of course.'

'I cannot believe that will require a great effort on my part.'

'Indeed not. I look forward greatly to what he has to say, and feel sure it is bound to be of the most inspiring nature. I suggest you devote yourself to the child.'

'Naturally I shall do my best to make her feel at ease.'

'Naturally! If it can be shown that the child feels some affection for you –' Awkwardly she hesitated as if she were uneasily aware that she was showing her hand too plainly. 'What I wish to say is that Monsieur Fabian is said to be excessively fond of the child, and must surely therefore take her preferences into consideration.'

She was looking earnestly at Charlotte with her face creased with unease, full of good intentions but clearly doubtful of her

86

daughter's ability to bring her plans to fruition. Any further exhortations were cut short, however, by the sound of carriage wheels.

Madame Bonnet rose and smoothed her skirt, at the same time smoothing the doubts and worries from her face, ready to greet the silk-weaver.

'Come, Charlotte,' she said; and together mother and daughter went out to meet the honoured guest.

Would he have become sleek and complacent? Madame Belamie had not said so – but then she had said very little. The questions buzzed in Charlotte's head as she walked behind her mother to the front door where, at the foot of the steps that led to it, her father's carriage was drawn up. She craned a little, unable to see round her mother's bulk, but she was aware, almost instantaneously, that something was wrong, that matters were not going according to plan. Madame Bonnet's breath was suddenly indrawn with a hiss and after only a moment's hesitation, she picked up her skirts and ran down the steps.

The whole scene was then clearly visible to Charlotte. Far from being sleek and complacent, the man emerging from the carriage looked instead more feverishly haggard than she remembered him, his eyes deep in their sockets and his face as grey as her mother's gown.

Madame Bonnet clasped her husband's arm.

'M'sieu, what is amiss? The poor man is ill! Come, let us get him inside. If you please, madame –' this to the plump, pallid lady, presumably Madame Colbert, who had stepped out of the carriage behind the silk-weaver and now supported him on one side. 'Allow me to take hold of him. I have some skill in such matters.'

Madame Colbert seemed only too pleased to relinquish her hold, turning at once at the sound of a child's voice. Elise, close to tears, was waiting to be lifted down.

'Poor little one,' Madame Colbert crooned, holding her close. 'Poor, motherless little one, come to Tantine.'

'Papa is so ill!'

Charlotte went swiftly to join them.

'He is in the house of a doctor. There is nowhere he would be better cared for,' she said comfortingly, and was unprepared for the look of anger that Madame Colbert turned upon her.

'He should never have come,' she snapped, as if she laid the blame for the decision at Charlotte's door. 'I told him! I warned him! But he paid no heed.'

There seemed little Charlotte could reply to this, but she smiled placatingly and attempted to usher them into the house where the others had now disappeared.

'Madame,' she said, 'you are most welcome, you and the child. I am Charlotte Bonnet, and I can assure you that whatever ails monsieur, he can be in no better hands than those of my father.' She smiled at the tearful little girl and touched her cheek. 'You must be Elise,' she said. 'We have all so longed to meet you.'

'I want to go home.' Elise buried her face in Madame Colbert's neck. 'I don't like it here.'

'It's been a long journey and you must be tired,' Charlotte said diplomatically.

'She should never have come,' Madame Colbert repeated.

'But since you are here, pray come inside. You must need refreshment.'

'A little warm milk for the child, perhaps.'

'Of course! She shall have it at once.'

There was no answering smile on Madame Colbert's face. Her lips were tightly pursed as she glanced towards Charlotte, but how different her expression when she looked at Elise! It was clear, Charlotte thought, that she idolised the child.

It was not until they were in the kitchen where, at the long scrubbed table, Elise's attention was distracted with milk and honey cakes and the chatter of Nan and the other servants, that there was an opportunity for Charlotte to make friendly overtures towards the woman.

'I wish you would take something yourself, madame. Some tea, perhaps? Though, of course, it will be served later in the drawing room.'

'I shall wait.'

'As you wish. How long has monsieur been ill like this?'

'Since this morning, though for some days he has seemed pale and tired. He suffers much pain from old wounds and refused to admit this illness was anything more, though it was clear to me he was in no state to travel, so anxious was he to bring Elise to the country.' Her eyes still snapped with anger. 'As if there was need to come this far! I have good friends in Richmond where we could have stayed all summer. Mesdemoiselles Bouverie asked – nay, *implored* us to go there, but he had given his word, he said, and his precious Canterbury friends must not be disappointed.'

It was hard, in the face of such hostility, to remain serene, but Charlotte did her best – though to say that she had not exactly taken to Madame Colbert was stating the case mildly.

'The journey must have been a nightmare for you,' she said.

'All yesterday he sat in the coach with his head resting on his hand and said nothing, and when we stopped at Rochester I made him go at once to bed. Then, this morning, he awoke with a fever which has become worse throughout the day until he is as you see him. He should never have come!'

Charlotte was growing annoyed at this parrot cry, but struggled to conceal it in the name of politeness. She looked to where Elise, her tears dried, was smiling at some finger play of Nan's.

'How like her mother she is,' she said. The golden, silky hair, the delicate complexion. How could she ever forget it?

For once Madame Colbert was silent, and glancing at her, Charlotte saw that her face had softened once more.

'You knew Celestine?' she asked.

'I saw her once, no more.'

'I was her aunt. Sister to her mother. I cared for her from the day she was born, and a lovelier creature never walked the earth. I shall never recover from her loss; never, never!'

Grief was understandable, but such intensity after six years seemed excessive, Charlotte thought. She murmured words of sympathy, but Madame Colbert said nothing, the flinty expression back on her face as if she considered she had revealed more than enough about herself.

'Does monsieur suffer from the same fever that struck Elise down last summer?' Charlotte asked. 'Papa believes strongly that the foul air of London is harmful.'

'That may be so. But Richmond is quite far enough to travel, and we had no need to come so far for the air there is every bit as pure.' Frowning, she watched the by-play between Elise and Nan. 'The child must go to bed. She grows over-excited with too much play. That slut has no idea of decorum.'

Charlotte was so astonished by this attack on the good-natured Nan that she could barely find words to speak; but in any case they would have been wasted, for Madame Colbert had already moved decisively to sweep Elise off to the room that had been set aside for her and the child, as if she could not bear to see someone other than herself occupying Elise's attention. Charlotte looked at Nan, and hid a smile as she saw her roll her eyes expressively towards the ceiling.

She saw them safely installed in their room and ensured that they were provided with warm water, and came downstairs again to find that the Belamies had arrived and were sitting alone in the drawing room looking concerned and subdued. Madame Belamie rose impulsively and embraced Charlotte as she came into the room.

'Oh my dear, what a shock for us all! Have you word of monsieur?'

'I know nothing. I have been seeing to the needs of Elise and her keeper.'

'Keeper?'

'Well, perhaps I am unkind, but she is not the most pleasant of persons! I gained the distinct impression that Madame Colbert holds us entirely responsible for Monsieur Fabian's illness by enticing him into the wilds of Kent.'

'It is those miasmas that your father spoke of that are to blame, you may depend upon it.'

Dr Bonnet confirmed this when at last he put in an appearance. He looked grave and shook his head as the others questioned him eagerly.

'It seems he has been suffering from headaches this past week but thought them unimportant. Now I find he has a rash on his abdomen and a fever so high he is almost out of his senses. He says himself there is already much pestilence in London although it is early in the year, and insists that we put him directly into the fever hospital lest we become infected ourselves.'

'How is such pestilence spread?'

Dr Bonnet put the back of his hand to his lips and coughed delicately.

'By the waste products of the body, madame – or that, anyway, is my own belief. Little is known for certain. Typhus is thought to be spread by infected vermin, but this, in my opinion, is the bloody flux, or cesspit fever.'

'Then surely,' Monsieur Belamie said, 'in all conscience you should take him to the hospital as he suggests.'

The doctor sighed heavily.

'I confess I recommended it to my wife,' he admitted, 'but she will not hear of it. Charlotte, where is the child?'

'By this time in bed, I imagine. She ate in the kitchen, and

Madame Colbert insisted that she should retire at once. She barely slept last night, she said, and is worn out with the journey and all that has happened.'

'She must be kept from her father. He was insistent on that. She is delicate, and suffered so greatly last year that he all but lost her.'

'Monsieur, I beg you!' From his far greater height Monsieur Belamie placed a hand on the doctor's shoulder. 'I yield to none in my respect of Monsieur Fabian, and I understand the feeling of duty that impels your wife to insist on his staying here, but I beg you to consider the possible results for your own household. Is it fair to endanger your own family, your own daughter? There are the servants to consider too.'

'Oh, Phillipe!' Madame Belamie's voice was reproachful. 'I can understand exactly how Madame Bonnet feels. How could she turn such a man from her house, no matter how sick he is? He has suffered so much!'

'The doctor must think of his own.'

'My wife is quite unafraid and assures me she will nurse Monsieur Fabian herself.'

Monsieur Belamie looked astonished, silenced by this demonstration of Madame Bonnet's formidable will.

'I hope the task will not prove too much for her,' said Madame [*la mie*] Bonnet, adding hesitantly, 'perhaps I –'

'With five little ones at home?' Dr Bonnet shook his head decisively. 'No, no, madame, it would be unthinkable.'

Monsieur Belamie looked relieved at the doctor's words.

'Of course you could not dream of staying here, my dear. There are women who can be employed for such work.'

Dr Bonnet rubbed his nose unhappily.

'My wife says that no such woman could be entrusted to wash with sufficient care and frequency and that very soon the whole town would be infected. For the same reason she will allow no servant near him.'

'But my dear doctor, even Madame Bonnet is not superhuman! She cannot perform this task alone, skilled though she is.'

Clearly ill at ease, Dr Bonnet cleared his throat.

'She says that Charlotte will assist. No, no, my dear,' he went on, lifting a hand to still his daughter's horrified gasp. 'Your mother is quite right, though I might not have thought of the matter myself. So long as strict attention is paid to cleanliness, none of us should take harm. If you wash in vinegar before and after attending to our poor patient, I am convinced you will be spared any taint of this pestilence. Besides –' Briskly he rubbed his hands together and attempted to smile brightly at his unresponsive daughter. 'Your mother is convinced that the time has come for you to be instructed in the care of the sick. It is a priceless skill for a woman, which she has proved many times over.'

'Monsieur, I cannot believe in the wisdom of this.' Monsieur Belamie looked outraged on Charlotte's behalf. 'Have you truly considered the matter carefully?'

'Perhaps Charlotte should speak for herself,' suggested Madame Belamie.

The three pairs of eyes turned to look at her and for a moment there was silence as Charlotte stared back at them. Suddenly she gave a short, bitter little laugh.

'All things work together for good to them that love the Lord,' she said. 'I heard my mother saying so only yesterday.'

Her father looked puzzled.

'I don't understand you, my dear.'

'Don't you, Papa? Maman would. In fact,' she went on, 'I wouldn't put it past her to have arranged the whole thing. Oh, never mind, never mind!' She waved a hand dismissively as she saw his bewilderment increase. 'I will help her, of course. It's not as if I had any other occupation.'

'You are not afraid?' Madame Belamie asked.

Charlotte shook her head.

'No, I'm not afraid.'

It was the truth, she realised. It was life that frightened her, not the prospect of death.

5

Madame Bonnet was too busy in the sickroom to enjoy the meal she had ordered so meticulously. Monsieur and Madame Belamie, Dr Bonnet, Madame Colbert and Charlotte sat down together, and the matter of Elise was discussed. Madame Colbert had much to say, most of it in the shape of recriminations, but finally it was agreed that she and Elise would return to Sandwich with the Belamies who, as soon as possible, would arrange their transportation to Madame Colbert's friends in Richmond.

'Where we should be at this moment, had my wishes been taken into account,' said Madame Colbert.

'And where would Monsieur Fabian be?' asked Madame Belamie gently. 'Kind as your friends may be, I doubt if they would have welcomed such a sick man or been able to care for him so expertly.'

To this Madame Colbert had nothing to say, but her dewlaps quivered a little with annoyance and her small mouth wore its pinched look of disapproval once more. However, the following morning Charlotte happened to overhear her in happier mood.

She and Elise were waiting in the drawing room to be collected by the Belamies in the coach that was to take them all to Sandwich, and as Charlotte entered the room she heard Madame Colbert say gloatingly:

'Just the two of us, *ma petite*. You and I will have a fine time together.'

Elise, wriggling within the confine of the arm that pressed her to Madame Colbert's side, seemed close to tears.

'I don't want to leave Papa!'

'Tantine will care for you, my treasure. Who loves you best? Why, who else but your Tantine?'

'I'm sure your papa will be better quite soon, Elise,' Charlotte said comfortingly. Madame Colbert looked round quickly at the sound of her voice. Charlotte saw that she had been taken unawares by her entrance.

'So it is you, mam'selle,' she said.

'Elise need have no fears about going to Madame Belamie's house. She is the kindest person I know. She has a little girl of much the same age.'

'I am all the company Elise wants or needs.'

Madame Colbert must have seen the scepticism in Charlotte's expression for her mouth tightened and her eyes narrowed. 'And as for you, mam'selle,' she went on. 'You will have monsieur to yourself, you and your mother. Do not think it will do you any good. He will not have you.'

Charlotte flushed scarlet.

'I can assure you our only thought is to care for him.'

'Of course, mam'selle.' Her green eyes gleamed maliciously. 'I understand perfectly.'

Charlotte seethed with impotent anger at the sly smile that played about Madame Colbert's lips.

'I believe I hear the carriage,' she said coldly. 'I wish you *bon voyage*, madame.'

And may I never have the misfortune to see you again, she thought.

Monsieur Fabian became very ill. If at times Charlotte had thought the prospect of death would not be unwelcome, she soon saw that this was not the death that anyone in their right mind would choose.

Madame Bonnet was calm and impersonal, frowning with disapproval if Charlotte showed any delicacy of feeling or squeamishness in dealing with some of the more unpleasant tasks.

'You must steel yourself,' she said hardily.

'But the stench, Maman! It turns my stomach.'

'You must summon all your resolve. It is our duty to tend this man, as the Good Book exhorts us.'

For some days Charlotte contrived not to see his unclothed body, though her mother sponged him as tenderly as any baby. She dreaded looking on him, as indeed she would have done any man, yet when the moment could be avoided no longer she found it was not horror but pity that swept over her, and the expected wave of panic was shocked into stillness. His flesh still bore the scars of the cruel tortures inflicted in prison, and the bones of his left hip were set in a strange and sickening way, so that the tears rose in her eyes as she looked at him.

'Oh, the poor man,' she whispered. 'The poor man.'

'Enough of that. There is work to be done.' Madame Bonnet's voice sounded hard, but Charlotte knew that her mother's pity and admiration for this man were as great as her own. Surely he must have been a saint to withstand such agony. No ordinary man could have borne it, no matter how great his faith.

With each day his fever rose until he was insensible, gasping through dry, cracked lips, uttering half sentences and incomprehensible sounds. His stomach became bloated, his bowels loosened, and Charlotte's heart bled for him, that such a proud man should suffer such indignities, and she was thankful that he was so far gone in fever that he was unaware of who was attending him.

She was so involved now in his care that the risk of catching the sickness never entered her head. It had become a personal battle and one that she was determined should not be lost. She followed her father's instructions to the letter regarding washing in vinegar, and both she and her mother breathed through vinegar-soaked rags; but even if she had not done so she felt sure she would be quite safe, for surely God would not strike either her or her mother while they ministered to such a man.

'Can he possibly live through this?' she asked her father one evening, after a day in which it seemed that Monsieur Fabian hovered dangerously close to death. 'He is so very weak.'

'I confess I am fearful of intestinal damage. If only the fever would break!'

'He cannot endure much more.'

'He has a strong constitution despite his injuries.'

There was little change the following day, but on the afternoon of the day after that Madame Bonnet gave it as her opinion that the crisis could well occur that night. The doctor, hastily summoned, endorsed her view.

'There must be something we can do,' Charlotte said desperately, but he shook his head.

'There is nothing to be done, but to wait.'

'And pray,' Madame Bonnet added.

Charlotte did both, after she had washed and gone to her room. The house was quiet. Soft summer rain had been falling all day, shrouding the garden in a fine mist, but now it had stopped and as she leaned from her window the freshness of the air and the scent of the garden were as balm to her spirits. She could hear the cooing of doves and a thrush trilling in the orchard. How strange, she thought, that the summer continued so full of loveliness when such a grim battle was being fought within the house.

The doctor stayed with Monsieur Fabian as Charlotte and her mother ate a silent meal. They were both tired and strained. Charlotte could think of nothing but the patient upstairs, but she had no wish to speak of him, for her feelings were as confused as ever. She knew that only by closing her eyes to his essential maleness could she continue to minister to him – yet she also knew that if he did not survive this illness it would be a mortal blow to her, too.

Her mother's thoughts were with him also, she knew. They had grown closer during this ordeal. Charlotte appreciated her qualities more, and was aware of the fact that she, too, had gained respect in her mother's eyes.

It was much later that night when Madame Bonnet kept vigil alone that the fever at last broke, and Charlotte was greeted in the morning with the news that Monsieur Fabian slept peacefully at last.

'So he will recover?' she asked her father eagerly.

'There is every chance now, God be thanked, but there will be weeks of illness yet, even if no serious damage has been done internally. The danger is not entirely over, but in my opinion the tide has turned.'

Charlotte had a few moments of real joy at the prospect until she remembered that a Monsieur Fabian restored to health constituted something of a threat. Once again he would be the object of her mother's machinations – not immediately, of course. No doubt she would allow a little time for him to recover his health and spirits. But eventually, without a doubt, she would be baiting her hook.

Suppose gratitude for his care made him feel it his duty to offer marriage?

The thought made Charlotte catch her breath, and she clutched the sill until her fingers hurt as she leaned out of the window to take in great gulps of air. And as she did so, she felt the tears slip down her cheeks, and she knew she was weeping because here was a man she might love, were she capable of it.

*　　*　　*

The tide had turned, as the doctor had said, and though the fever diminished only slowly, he was clearly on the mend. He slept a good deal, managed to take only liquids, and said little. One afternoon, Charlotte was sitting on the window embrasure of his room, a jar of buttercups on the sill before her, half turned away from him as she bent over a sheet of paper, paintbrush in hand. She had thought him asleep, but suddenly she heard his voice.

'What are you doing?' he asked.

Startled, she turned and saw that his eyes were on her, sunk into their sockets by illness but as bright in colour as ever and clearer than she had seen them since the day of his arrival.

'I am painting buttercups,' she answered him.

'May I see?' He lifted a thin, veined hand from the coverlet, and embarrassed she looked down at her work, dissatisfied with it and reluctant for anyone to see it.

'It's not finished yet,' she said.

'Then I will wait.'

He smiled at her as he spoke. It was as if a lamp had been lit behind his eyes, Charlotte thought, and for a moment could not look away but stared at him, fascinated. This was the smile that she remembered, and memory had in no way exaggerated its beauty. Coming to her senses, she put down her brush and got to her feet.

'You look much better,' she said. 'My mother said I was to let her know when you wakened as she has some broth for you.'

'I feel hungry. I would like that.'

'Then you are indeed better!'

'Tell me –' his voice arrested her as she was on the way to the door. 'I have been very ill, have I not?'

'Very, monsieur.'

'Is there news of my daughter? Where is she?'

'With Madame Colbert in Richmond. She writes they are both well.'

'Thank God.'

He closed his eyes as if exhausted by this brief conversation, and though Charlotte waited for a moment, he said no more.

For days he drifted in and out of sleep. Now that he was out of danger Madame Bonnet found excellent reasons why she should attend to other aspects of her household, so that the care of the patient was almost entirely left to Charlotte. Nan was allowed to help her now, for which she was thankful, but she was disquieted when the maid remarked that it was quite clear that Monsieur Fabian could not keep his eyes away from Charlotte.

'They follow you around the room,' she observed with relish.

'Nan, such nonsense! He barely speaks to me.'

'Did I say "speak"? "Watches", I said, and you mark my words, I know what I'm talking about. You think he's asleep, but half the time he's looking at you.'

'Don't say such things unless you wish to anger me.' Discomfort made Charlotte unusually brusque with her. The two of them were good friends, but the thought that she was being watched brought many disturbing memories of Major Clouter that she would prefer to forget.

However, she was once again painting, this time a mixture of flowers and trailing ivies, when she looked up suddenly and saw that instead of sleeping as she had imagined, he was indeed watching her, just as Nan had said.

'Oh monsieur, you are awake,' she said, flustered. 'I brought you chocolate earlier, but you were asleep and now it has gone cold. I'll go now and bring more.'

'No, don't go.' He lifted his hand as if to make a gesture of supplication, then let it fall heavily on the bed. There was no smile today, nothing but pain and bitterness in his expression.

'Do you feel worse, monsieur?' Charlotte looked at him anxiously.

'No, no, no.' Almost angrily he rolled his head from side to side. 'Stay and talk to me. I need some cheer.'

Charlotte swallowed nervously, unable to think of anything to say, cheering or otherwise. In desperation and as a last resort, no more satisfied with her work than she ever was, she held up the picture she had been engaged upon.

'Would you care to see my latest attempt?'

Without speaking he held out his hand and she gave him the paper. For a long time he studied it without speaking while Charlotte stood by and suffered agonies at the thought that he would almost certainly think it worthless. Would he criticise it? Even worse, would he utter some kindly, meaningless phrase – the equivalent of a pat on the head, given to a harmless, reasonably engaging dog? His expression gave nothing away. At last he handed it back to her.

'You have captured the delicacy,' he said at last. 'As for the colour –'

'It was the colour that attracted me – or rather, the combination of colours. Colours are very important to me.' Shyness was making her babble, and realising it, she fell suddenly silent.

'To me, also. What would a silk-weaver be, if he had no feeling for colour?'

Thankfully Charlotte grasped the conversational lead he had given her.

'Pray tell me about silk, Monsieur Fabian.'

His expression lightened and he laughed at that.

'You should be wary of allowing me such licence, mam'selle, for I can talk for hours on the subject.'

His voice had warmed, become more resonant, the voice she had heard so long ago and never forgotten.

'What type of silk do you produce?'

'I am a member of the Lustring Company,' he said. 'Lustring and alamodes are my bread and butter, but it's the patterned silk that interests me most and I venture to say I am becoming known for it in London. At present I am trying to perfect a method of refining the colours so that perhaps one day I might be able to reproduce a shade just as subtle as the flowers you have painted. Silk is a miraculous medium in which to work, mam'selle – and all produced by a humble worm! It stretches credulity to the limit, do you not agree?'

'I confess I have not thought of it.'

'Then think of it now, mam'selle!' He was sitting forward, the pillows at his back, his lean face with its strong features transformed now that his interest was engaged. 'All nature is our copy book. See the shape and the colour of that spray of ivy you have there. Can you not imagine such a spray traced against heavy ivory silk –' He broke off, shook his head, and laughed a little, leaning against the pillows. 'Forgive me! A man so single-minded grows tedious.'

'Not at all, monsieur.' As he had sketched the spray in the air with his hand, Charlotte had seen it, just as he described. 'A spray of that colour green with a background of ivory would look magnificent.'

'You think so? One day I shall weave it and send it to you.' For a moment he seemed to be contemplating her through narrowed eyelids. 'No, not ivory,' he said slowly. 'Not for you.

A soft shade of apricot would suit you better. That's it!' Eager once more, he smiled brilliantly. 'Apricot is without doubt the colour. Not pink nor yellow nor beige, but a subtle combination of all three – which at the moment I have to confess is quite beyond me, but which I can see in my mind's eye as clearly as I can see the blue of your gown. You *are* apricot, mam'selle, and there's no one shall say me nay.'

'And you are emerald.'

Charlotte's reply was instinctive and brought an astonished glance and a bark of laughter from him.

'*You* see people as colours?'

'I always have done.'

'So have I – though those I've confided the matter to are quite sure I'm mad! Do you know, I have never found anyone else who has the smallest idea of my meaning? Tell me, how do you see your mother?'

'Brown,' Charlotte said unhesitatingly. 'And Madame Belamie is dove grey.'

'So she is! Yes, of course, she could be no other. I am not so sure about brown, however. Do you mean dark brown?'

'Dun brown.'

'Yes, yes, I see that.' His face was alight with amusement and interest. 'Your father, I believe, is a very dark blue.'

'What of Madame Colbert?'

'Like snow when it has lain a day or two in city streets.'

'That's unkind!'

'I know, and I'm ashamed.' They laughed in happy conspiracy, until his laughter died and he laid back against the pillows. 'What children we are,' he said. 'Well, you have a right to be.'

He looked weary suddenly, all the life drained from his face.

'I've tired you,' Charlotte said penitently.

'Perhaps you are right.'

He did not meet her eyes but turned his face away from her as if he had lost all interest in her and her childish games. The sudden change of mood felt like a rebuff, even though Charlotte reminded herself how ill he had been, and blamed herself for allowing him to talk too much.

However, as the days went by and she got to know him more, she found that this was the pattern of their relationship. There were times when they could speak as if they were friends who had known each other for years; times when they played the

100

'colour game' as he called it, and he would laugh, carefree as any boy. Then, with no warning, his mood would change and he would become cold towards her, even hurtful.

It left her unsure of herself and more confused than ever. Sometimes it seemed that everything she did was wrong. If she spoke, then she disturbed his peace; if she moved quietly about the sickroom, then her very silence irritated him and he accused her of being over-submissive.

She began to think there were at least two Gabriel Fabians; the hero, who by the charm of his personality could draw others towards him when he so chose, and the misanthrope who cared nothing for the feelings of others.

Her parents saw none of it. Towards them he always showed his captivating side and there was scant sympathy shown towards Charlotte when she hinted it was not always so.

'He is an invalid still,' her mother said defensively. 'How can you show such lack of patience and understanding? Heaven help your children if you are fortunate enough to have any! Why, the man is the nearest thing to a saint that we shall meet in this life, and it behoves you to remember it.'

Thereafter Charlotte kept her own counsel. Gabriel Fabian was many things, she was beginning to realise, but a saint was not one of them – in fact there were times when she thought he must surely be the devil incarnate, the fallen angel, for he seemed to gain pleasure in tormenting her.

'Go back to the door and walk towards me again,' he would command from his chair by the window. 'Has no one ever told you that you plod like a farm boy? Hold your head high and swing your legs from the hip – don't push out your lip at me. I'm instructing you in how to be beautiful!'

'I shall never be that.'

'You could be. You *are*, when you smile; which, I may say, is so seldom one might be forgiven for thinking there has been a death in the house.'

'Sometimes I wish there had been.'

'Oh, capital!' Her waspish replies only served to amuse him. 'What a little vixen it can be when it tries.'

But then, just when she had decided that he was an impossible man to please and that she disliked him thoroughly, he would smile his enchanting smile at her and speak softly, reading portions of poetry that caught his fancy, exerting such magnetism that her hostility would fade as if it had never been, dissipated completely by the warmth of his charm.

One evening, when he was particularly thoughtful and had spoken little to her all day, he called her name as she was about to leave the room.

'Charlotte,' he said, and lifted his hand towards her. 'Come here one moment.'

She did as he asked, and he took her hand in his.

'Bear with me,' he said softly. 'I can be such a brute when the black mood is on me.'

Charlotte looked down, embarrassed.

'Monsieur, I know how you have suffered,' she said awkwardly, remembering his nakedness and the deformities it had revealed.

'It is not so much my own sufferings that beset me but those of the countless others who suffer still. There are many in prison *now*, Charlotte – now, at this moment. Someone who even as we speak is being broken upon the wheel. Can you see how guilty and helpless that makes me feel?'

Charlotte raised her eyes to his face, frowning with the effort of entering into his feelings.

'Helpless, yes! I can understand that. But why should you feel guilt, monsieur?'

He did not answer, but turned to look at the garden outside the window and his expression grew bleaker still as if at the contrast it presented to the conditions he had known. He let go her hand, but she had no feeling of being dismissed; indeed, she felt he wanted to speak of the spectres that haunted him. She sat on the window seat beside his chair, and waited.

'I was little more than a boy when my father died,' he said. He was speaking quietly without looking at her, almost as if he spoke to himself. 'He died of smallpox. It had naught to do with the persecutions. He was a silk-weaver, he and his brother, and they had a thriving business which I was destined to follow.

'When he died, I went to live with my uncle, Gregoire Fabian, and his wife Marie, so that I could learn the craft. No parents could have treated me with more love, more kindness. I think, perhaps, they are the finest people I have ever known, or am likely to know.'

'What became of them?' Charlotte asked. He turned to look at her, and his face was set in lines of suffering. For a moment he did not answer.

'My uncle refused to renounce his faith and he was broken on the wheel,' he said. 'He was accused, as I was, of attempting to proselytise his workpeople. He was an old man, Charlotte. White-haired, bent of shoulder, but with the kind of spirit that could never be broken.'

'What of your aunt?'

He looked sharply away from her and bit his lip as he struggled to master his emotion.

'She was taken to a nunnery,' he said. 'Beaten, and forced to do menial tasks, though she, too, was old and frail. I had news only months after I arrived in England that she had died – and I tell you, Charlotte, I thanked God for it, for I knew then that she was at peace, with her sufferings over.'

Charlotte laid a hand on his arm.

'I am so sorry, monsieur. So very sorry. What became of your mother?'

'My mother?' He gave a short laugh, but there was a bitter twist to his mouth. 'Oh, my mother is well enough! She found no difficulty in abjuring, and married a papist – a wine merchant of Nîmes where she lives still, no doubt thriving mightily. I give no thought to my mother, or she to me –'

'I doubt if that is true.'

He shrugged.

'I cannot speak for her, of course, but to me she is dead; as dead as my innocent Celestine, as dead as my saintly aunt and uncle. You frown, Charlotte. Do you condemn me?'

She shook her head.

'How could I? You have suffered more than I could imagine. You have every reason to feel bitter – but still I cannot understand the guilt.'

'Perhaps not. It makes little sense, I suppose, but one's emotions are not always ruled by good sense.'

'With that I can only agree,' Charlotte said, remembering her own dilemma.

She was thankful to see that he looked calmer now, as if the very act of speaking his thoughts had removed some of the hurt. He even smiled as he looked at her, though there seemed to be a trace of sadness in his expression still. He studied her without speaking for a moment, his gaze moving over her face. Then he shook his head.

'No,' he said. 'One's emotions are not ruled by good sense.'

'I shall bring you some bohea tea,' Charlotte said briskly, rising from the seat. 'There is nothing like it for restoring the spirits.'

'Dear, apricot Charlotte,' he said, and his smile was almost as normal.

The weather continued warm and soon he was coming down to sit in the garden for a few hours each day. Charlotte told herself that she was pleased he was now no longer in need of so much attention, and began to distance herself from him, leaving much of the fetching and carrying to Nan.

Though she had not yet judged the moment ripe, she had by no means given up the idea of asking for Monsieur Fabian's help in leaving Canterbury. Knowing him as she did by this time, she was aware that catching him in the right frame of mind was essential to her cause. As she carried out a tankard of small ale to him as he sat in the garden one morning in early August, she looked at him warily to gauge his mood, hoping that it would be receptive, knowing that she must speak soon if she were to speak at all. He would not be at Providence House for ever. He was already talking of finding a house in the area and sending for Elise, saying that he had been without her far too long and could not impose on the Bonnets' hospitality much longer.

He had a book open on his lap but was not reading it. Instead he was looking up into the beech tree that sheltered him, but he transferred his gaze to Charlotte as he became aware of her approach. He smiled, the full-bodied, brilliant smile. Good, she thought. He seems in excellent spirits.

'How pretty you are, Charlotte,' he said.

The compliment startled her, for he was not over-generous with them. She remembered Bettine, the servant from the chateau, who had said of the strolling player that he need only recite the days of the week to be rewarded with all manner of favours by a girl. She should hear him deliver such a phrase as this, Charlotte thought. Even a strange, unnatural, frozen creature as she believed herself to be could not fail to be warmed by it.

'See the colour of those leaves with the sun on them?' he asked her, ignoring her stuttered thanks. 'Have you ever tried painting them?'

She admitted that she had, but had never managed to achieve the colour to her satisfaction.

104

'Do you paint nothing but plants?'

'Not successfully. Well, even the flowers I paint are hardly successful, but they please me more than anything –'

'Do me the favour of being less *humble*, mam'selle! There is no need for it, I assure you. Your paintings are very pleasing. You should try your hand at design.'

Charlotte looked at him in astonishment.

'I shouldn't have the first idea how to set about it!'

'There are mathematical considerations, of course. The common width is half an ell, and the length of the repeat somewhere about half as much again. Then you are restricted in your use of colours, of course. You may use as many as eight in one design, but no more than three at any one time.'

'My head spins already! It would be beyond me, I am sure.'

He smiled and shrugged, and she could see that already his attention was drifting away from the subject.

'Well,' he said. 'It's your affair, of course, but it would not surprise me if your talent did not lend itself to design.'

It was not until she was on her way back to the house, her head swirling with delight at the thought that he considered her both pretty and talented, that she realised with annoyance that she had not mentioned the possibility of employment in London. She flirted a little with the idea of designing silk for a living and even tried a few sketches. The mathematical aspect was one that, though it seemed restrictive at first, began to intrigue her and she saw how there could be satisfaction in designing leaf and flower patterns within its confines; however, she drew nothing that she considered remotely good enough to be shown to Monsieur Fabian and finally abandoned the task as too technical for her.

The following day, Dr Bonnet spent much time in conversation with him and she had no chance to speak with him alone, then the next day Tante Hortense dropped in and took chocolate with him, Madame Bonnet sitting in stolid and disapproving silence as the two of them talked and laughed together as if they had known each other for years.

Charlotte walked to the gate with her aunt when she left.

'I had no idea,' Tante Hortense said, 'that saints could be so charming!'

'He is quite human, I assure you.'

'Oho!' She raised her eyebrows meaningfully. 'So you have

found that out, have you? Little Charlotte is not such an innocent after all!'

'I didn't mean –' Charlotte was covered with confusion. 'I mean only that he has his faults, along with the rest of mankind.'

'Would that the rest of mankind was so charming! Well, I wish you the best of luck, my dear.'

It was not worth protesting her lack of interest in Gabriel Fabian as a marriage prospect; after all, Charlotte thought, her mother had designs sufficient for both of them. When she returned to where Monsieur Fabian still sat in her company, she found them discussing a house that was available in a hamlet called Flewett's Cross, no more than a mile distant through the woods or three miles by the lanes. It would, according to Madame Bonnet, suit him admirably as a country retreat.

'I shall make the effort to see it within a day or two,' he said. 'I have presumed on your hospitality and kindness quite long enough, madame.'

'I am sure you are wise to think of spending the rest of the summer away from London.'

'Oh, that is not my intention! I shall have a week or two with Elise, but must return to my work as soon as I am able. I shall leave her here with Madame Colbert in the safety of the country, but though I have the best of men in charge of my looms, I must get back soon.'

It was clear to Charlotte that if she were to seek his help it would be best done within the next few days, and she resolved that she would do it the day following, no matter what his mood.

It was Madame Bonnet's day for going into Canterbury. She had matters to attend to at the orphanage, and she had not returned by the time Monsieur Fabian was due to take his usual measure of ale. Charlotte intercepted Nan, who was about to take his tankard to the garden, and took it from her, ignoring the girl's knowing grin.

''Twouldn't do to miss any chances,' she said.

Charlotte hated the thought of all the sniggers and speculations that she knew were current in the kitchen and elsewhere, and longed to leave it all behind. Heaven send, she said to herself as she left the house, tankard in hand, that he understood her point of view. Somehow she felt sure he would. For all his contradictory moods and his occasional sharpness, he was capable of intense and concentrated attention on another's concerns.

106

He was not in his usual chair beneath the beech tree. Charlotte did not immediately feel any disquiet for he had long since taken to walking for short intervals in the orchard or the kitchen garden. However, a brief search in both areas assured her that his lanky, lopsided frame was nowhere in sight.

Beyond the gate which led from the far end of the orchard were meadows, flat and open. She scanned them anxiously, beginning to fear that he might have gone too far for his own strength. There was no sign of him anywhere.

Well, he was a grown man and she was hardly his jailor. She took the ale back into the house, but when another thirty minutes or more had passed without his return, she began to feel the kind of anxiety that a mother must feel for a mysteriously absent child. Suppose he had gone for what he intended to be a short walk and had lost his way? Suppose even now he had collapsed with exhaustion somewhere in the wood, where a network of paths had been made by farmworkers walking from one hamlet to another? She chewed her lip anxiously. He was still far too weak for any prolonged physical effort.

For five minutes longer she hesitated, wishing that her mother would come home so that she could share her agitation, yet guiltily conscious that she would be blamed for failing to care for her charge adequately. Madame Bonnet, however, remained obstinately absent. Finally Charlotte hesitated no longer, and picking up her skirts she ran across the orchard, through the gate and across the meadow towards the wood.

Thank God for the silence, he thought. Wearily he sat down and leaned his head against the trunk of a tree, closing his eyes, so still that the rabbits he had disturbed came back to feed once more in the glade where he rested.

The wood was dim after the bright sunlight of the open pasture, scented with ferns and leaf mould, a silent sanctuary where, for a few moments, not even a bird sang. The peace was absolute, and he was grateful for it. Silently he prayed that it would enter into him and suffuse his spirit, calming the fret and confusion and the bitter, bitter regrets that had bedevilled him from the moment he had, as it seemed to him, been restored to life under the Bonnets' sheltering roof.

He uttered a sigh that was almost a groan, and drawing up his knees sank his head down on his folded arms.

'Thy will,' he whispered under his breath. '*Thy* will, O God. Forgive my rebellious spirit and make me a channel for thy purposes. Subdue my insubordinate flesh –'

The sound of the snapping of a twig somewhere behind him caused him to lift his head abruptly and look to his left. He caught the glimpse of a blue dress and knew that she had come in search of him, and the stab of painful delight he felt was a sure and certain sign that his prayer had not yet been answered. A thicket of holly bushes hid her from sight for a moment, but so great was the stillness that, though she trod lightly, he could hear that she approached nearer and nearer. Still he neither moved nor called out to her, but instead sat as if he had been carved into stone, waiting for the moment when she must appear through the trees at the far side of the glade.

It was, he thought, a pale shadow of what he had once known in his wife's arms; joy, enhanced by conscious delay. But here there could be no satisfactory culmination, no release of tension, no scaling of the heights – nothing but the bitter-sweet pleasure of seeing her approach, of witnessing her face light in the smile that appeared once she caught sight of him beneath the tree.

'Oh monsieur, *there* you are,' she said. He was conscious of her faint, flowery scent as in a billow of blue muslin she sank down beside him. She looked at him closely, and the smile died. 'You have exhausted yourself,' she went on chidingly. 'And very near exhausted me! I have searched everywhere. You should have told me that you wished to walk abroad, and I would have gone with you. I was afraid when I found you gone that you would have come here and mistaken your path, and I see I was right.'

'I wanted to be alone,' he said, and knew at once that, as all too often, the strength of his feeling for her and the need to conceal it had made his words sound far more abrupt than he had intended. He saw the wounded expression that she tried to hide with a lift of the chin, and railed at himself at his inability to be natural with this girl. Why, when he knew – had known all his life – that he had the power to charm any number of strangers, did he fail so frequently with this vulnerable child? Hurting her was the last thing he intended.

'I'm sorry,' he said, his tone softer. 'It was thoughtless of me. Forgive me for causing you such trouble.'

'When do you do anything else?' Her mischievous smile robbed the words of any sharpness. She was not one to nurse her hurt, and had learned to respond with a tartness equal to his own. 'Truly, I sometimes think you have no more wit than a child! I suppose you did not pause to consider what Maman would say to me when she returned to find you gone, and me with no idea where to find you?'

'I would have defended you.'

She was so close, and he longed to touch her. There was something vital, almost feral, in her thick, tangled hair, and his right hand clenched involuntarily as he imagined its texture, how it would feel to hold it. Her skin was pale, but fine as any he had seen, and her exertion had created a faint wild-rose flush across her cheekbones. The urge to wipe away the tiny beads of perspiration on her upper lip was almost irresistible. Instead he picked up a dry stick from the ground and broke it into small, meticulous pieces, forcing himself to look away from her.

'You frightened the rabbits,' he said. 'I sat so still that they took no more notice of me than if I had been that bush.'

'Never mind the rabbits. Are you rested enough to return home now?'

'I suppose so.' Still he made no move to get up. 'It's so peaceful here. I needed peace, Charlotte – craved it! I meant no slight to you, believe me. It was merely that I had matters to think over.'

He looked at her once more and she saw the troubled look in his eyes, the deep furrows that ran from his strong nose, bracketing his mouth.

'What is it, monsieur?' she asked softly. 'You cannot take on your shoulders the suffering of all Huguenots.'

For a moment he did not answer. Slowly, almost painfully as if he would have prevented the movement if it had been within his power, his hand reached out to grasp a fold of her dress.

'Such a pretty colour,' he said. 'The colour of summer.'

'Monsieur, what makes you so sad?'

'I must talk to you, Charlotte. Now is as good a moment as any, for soon I shall be gone.'

'I know. There is something I want to ask of you, too.'

She thought he had not heard her. He leant his head back once more against the tree and stared at a point beyond her.

'I scarcely know where to begin,' he said.

Puzzled, she waited.

'Charlotte,' he said at last. 'I have been made aware over the past few weeks by certain things your father has said, and by the very fact that we have been alone so often in each other's company, that your parents are hopeful of a match between us.'

'Oh monsieur, *please!*' The force of her response made him look at her directly and he saw that her face had flushed scarlet. 'Believe me, monsieur, whatever hopes they may have, I would never presume to think such a thing.'

'Charlotte!' His voice was gentle and he took her hand in his. 'I should like nothing more than to marry you. The presumption would be on my part, not on yours, for you are little more than a child and I am three and thirty. To me you are lovely in an artless and innocent way – yet there are depths in you that intrigue me, that I long to explore.' He reached to touch her cheek lingeringly. 'Please believe me, Charlotte. If ever I spoke harshly or unfeelingly to you the words were born of the bitterness that is within me. There have been times when I felt I would sacrifice ten years of my life to hold you close to me for one minute. Marriage, however, is out of the question, and if it were not for my accursed pride I should have found a way of telling your father so a long time ago.'

'Monsieur –'

'Hush, let me finish.' His finger moved to her lips, as if to prevent her from saying more. 'Who knows, I may not find the courage to speak again, and I should not forgive myself if ever you thought it was some lack in you that invited rejection. Charlotte –' He paused, as if selecting his words carefully. 'Charlotte, I was tortured.'

'I know that.'

'I was maimed.'

'I know that, too.'

'Aye, I forgot! My body holds few secrets for you. It has this one, though. I am unable to be a husband to you or to any woman. Elise is the only child I will ever father, for she was conceived before I was captured, while I was yet a man, a real man. And that is why there can be no marriage between us.' He picked up a stone and hurled it away from him angrily. 'Far better if I had died in prison. If death had come to me then, I should have been prepared for it – but no, I was allowed to escape it, just as a cat allows a mouse to run from between its paws, only to pounce again.' She saw the muscles tighten along the side of his jaw. 'Had I died in prison, Charlotte, my wife would have stayed in the comfort of her home to bear the child and would

110

likely have survived. Instead it was *her* death that our God of love exacted.'

Charlotte drew in her breath, looking at his face, knowing with certainty that it was unlikely that she would see such pain again. Eyes closed in his agony, he lifted his face and pounded the earth with his clenched fist.

'God forgive me,' he whispered passionately. 'God forgive me, that I should speak so. Show me thy purpose.'

'What purpose could there be?' Charlotte's voice trembled as the horror came back to her; the quenching of life, the spreading stain, the anguished cry. 'How could a merciful God order such things?'

Slowly Fabian shook his head and expelled his breath in a long sigh.

'His ways are not ours to know,' he said. He spoke as if exhausted – as if the journey away from faith and back again had been a long one. 'I cling to the thought that perhaps he has some other purpose for me. My story is not over yet.' He managed to smile, and picking up her hand once more, stroked it with his fingers. 'So long as you understand the reason why I cannot marry you, and from time to time think of me with kindness, then I must be content. I must wrestle with my own demons in my own way, and with God's help may one day defeat them. I think, perhaps, we should go back to the house, don't you?'

He would not take the hand she offered him, but struggled unaided to his feet.

'Pray lean on me, monsieur,' Charlotte said, watching him anxiously. 'You are tired, I can tell.'

He shook his head and took a few steps, then stopped abruptly.

'Wait,' he said. 'Did I not hear you say there was something you wanted to ask me? I gave you no chance! What was it you wished to say?'

'It will keep until tomorrow,' Charlotte said, and resolutely led him homeward.

6

They returned from the wood to find that Madame Bonnet had come home, and she was quite as angry as Charlotte had expected – chiefly with her daughter for not watching over the patient, but only marginally less with Fabian who had behaved, she considered, quite as irresponsibly as most ordinary men, which was not at all what she expected as she did not hesitate to tell him.

'I had thought better of you, monsieur,' she had reproached him, and had sent him at once to bed. 'And as for you,' she continued to Charlotte, 'if monsieur relapses once more into a fever, then I shall lay the fault at your door. Can I leave nothing to others? Do I have to remain in charge every moment of the day?'

Fortunately for everyone, Fabian's exertions seemed to have no ill effects, and he even came downstairs to supper in as charming and entertaining a mood as Charlotte had ever been witness to. It seemed as if his anguished confession of earlier in the day had somehow purged him of bitterness, and as she sat listening to him, smiling in response to his tales of the exploits of apprentices and of life in London generally, the magic of his personality enchanted her as it had done before. There is, she thought, no man like him.

And he cannot harm me!

The full realisation came to her as she prepared for bed, and so sudden and forceful was it that, half undressed, she sank down on the bed with her mouth open. Why had she not thought of it before?

If he, as he insisted, was not a real man, then certainly she was not a real woman. Surely they would suit each other very well? Even she, she thought, might prove a better companion than Madame Colbert – for whom he seemed to have no great affection.

Begetting children was part of a normal marriage, that she

112

understood, but surely other things mattered too? Friendship, for example. Respect. The ability to make a comfortable home. Oh, it must be possible to persuade him that she would be a good stepmother to Elise, a sympathetic companion, a competent housekeeper. Her mother's tuition had ensured the latter, if nothing more.

Breathlessly she pressed her fingers to her lips. It could mean the best of both worlds, she thought; the status of a wife without the hazards of motherhood. The prospect seemed too good to be true.

And so it appeared to prove when she voiced it the next day, nerving herself to do so at the first opportunity.

'My dear child, such an arrangement is out of the question!'

Fabian's response to her faltering proposition was like a blow in the face. They were walking in the orchard, out of sight and sound of the house. Charlotte had taken care with her dress and appearance and had noted with pleasure that Fabian himself was in good spirits. The sun continued to shine, which seemed a good omen.

It had taken considerable determination to utter the suggestion that as a matter of convenience they should become husband and wife, and to be rejected so forcibly made tears of humiliation come to her eyes. She turned her head from him to hide them.

'Come, Charlotte!' Fabian's voice was more gentle as he halted and took her by the shoulders, forcing her to face him. 'It would put both of us in an impossible position. You say you have no wish to bear children – but my dear child, you seem to have no conception of nature's urges, the body's needs. They are quite as strong for women as for men, I understand.'

'Not for me.' Charlotte looked at him angrily. 'And I am not a child! I wish you would stop calling me one! Why, I could have been a married woman by now, could have had a child of my own, if I had followed my parents' plans for me.'

'I had heard something of that.'

Charlotte laughed shortly.

'So the gossip reached as far as London! I am not surprised.'

'Paul Belamie told me that you were betrothed and later that the marriage was not to take place. He gave no details and I asked for none.'

'So you see I am not a child.'

113

'No.' His grip on her shoulders tightened. 'I know you are not. At least, not in some ways – but in others I am not so sure. Oh my dear Charlotte, how could I add to my many sins by marrying you? You may not be a child, but you are young and could change. In a year or two or three you may yearn for children, for physical expression of love –'

'I will not.' Charlotte moved his hands from her shoulders and walked away from him, tears springing to her eyes again. 'Oh, what's to become of me?'

He longed to go to her, to hold and comfort her, and his expression as he looked after her said so as clearly as any words, but her back was towards him and she was conscious only of his rejection. She wiped the tears from her eyes, straightened her shoulders, struggled for composure and turned to face him.

'Very well,' she said. 'You will not marry me. Then help me in another way.' There was an edge of desperation in her voice. 'I must get away from here. I am educated, more than many women. I can speak both French and English with fluency, as you know. I am skilled in painting and needlework. Surely there must be a lady in London who would wish to have me for a companion or as a governess for her child. Or perhaps I could teach in a school for young ladies –'

'Charlotte, Charlotte, such a life is not for you! Your parents would never allow it.'

'Oh!' Furiously she stamped her foot. 'You think *this* is the life for me? Living at home, being pushed into the arms of every eligible man between sixteen and sixty who appears on the horizon, hating the thought of marriage, hating being single, disappointing my parents, becoming the laughing stock of all their friends, the object of scorn and pity –'

'Charlotte, stop –'

Fists clenched by her sides, desperation contorting her face, she took a step closer to him.

'No, I will not stop! All I ask is that you support my endeavours to leave home. They will listen to you.'

Fabian lifted his hands helplessly and let them fall again.

'How can I? If you were my own daughter, I would feel as they would.'

The fight drained out of her. She gave a long and tremulous sigh and turned away from him.

'I see.' There was a world of hopelessness in her voice. 'There is no hope for me, then. I shall be thrown to the next Major Clouter who comes along –'

'Clouter? Hugo Clouter?' She made no response, and he took her by the shoulder again, turning her to face him. 'What has Clouter to do with any of this?'

'He was the man I was betrothed to. Why? Do you know him?'

'However on God's earth did you come to be involved with him?'

'His father lives hereabouts. He's a friend of my father. He is also a very wealthy man, which of course is all that matters. It grieved my parents greatly when I finally refused to go through with the marriage. I disgraced them in the eyes of the whole city, they said.'

'Thank heaven that you did! The man's a scoundrel.'

'Then you do know him!'

'I knew his wife – his late wife – better. She was a kinswoman of a close friend of mine in London and I heard much of their life together. He treated her abominably. God forgive me for speaking ill of any man, but Clouter is a brute, a depraved monster. I cannot believe that your parents were taken in by him.'

Charlotte laughed bitterly.

'Oh, he was all sweetness to them and they were only too eager to believe that I had made a good match. It will happen again, no doubt.'

'There can be few men as despicable as Major Clouter.'

His words were intended to encourage and console her, but it was clear that he himself was little calmed by them. His brows were drawn together and his face mirrored the pain he felt at the mere thought of Clouter's hands touching her innocent, unwilling flesh. The silence lengthened between them.

'Charlotte,' he said at last, his voice husky. 'Let me consider this matter. Marriage was a door I thought for ever closed against me –'

'Oh, monsieur!' Sensing he was weakening she would not let him finish. 'I would be a good wife to you, if only you would think again. My mother has taught me to cook the dishes you like so much, and I can sew and embroider –'

'Hush, Charlotte.' He reached out and touched her hair gently, feeling its life beneath his fingers, conscious of a deep sadness within him – sadness for her, sadness for him.

'And we are friends, monsieur, are we not?' She would not let him silence her. 'You know we are friends, though sometimes you can be unkind –'

'I doubt that I would change.'

'I should not want you to change! I tell you, monsieur –' She stepped closer to him and smiled up at him beguilingly. 'I admired you when I was a child, and I admire you still, even if you are not the saint my mother thinks.'

'A girl should always take note of what her mother says.' He was smiling now.

'No saint had a tongue as sharp as yours.'

'No saint had a nurse like you to plague him.'

There was a comfortable familiarity about this gentle sparring, for it was typical of many of the exchanges that had taken place between them during the past weeks. Perhaps it would not be a sin, Fabian thought. Perhaps God had ordained his meeting with such a one as Charlotte.

'Let me consider,' he said again. 'We should both pray for guidance. We must do nothing in haste.'

Nevertheless there was a small core of happiness beginning to glow somewhere inside him. Her nearness would bring pain, he knew. Desire for her would bring one more turn of the rack. But in spite of all the objections, the happiness was there and no cold breath of reason seemed sufficient to extinguish its glow.

It was only later when he sat alone in the garden after Charlotte had been summoned to other duties by her mother that he watched the butterflies hovering over the flower border and was reminded of his boyhood in France. For a season it had been the fashion among his friends to collect such creatures. They had competed to find the biggest and the brightest, impaling them upon pins, until suddenly he had sickened of it and repented his cruelty. Would Charlotte, he wondered uneasily, prove to be the biggest and brightest butterfly of all?

'Happiness becomes you, Charlotte,' Tante Hortense said. 'I have never seen you in better looks.'

'Thank you, Tante.'

Charlotte's mirror confirmed that she spoke no more than the truth. From the moment that Gabriel Fabian had offered formally for her hand and had been just as formally accepted, all her nightmares, all her horrors and fears, were banished just as surely as if they had been nailed into a coffin and buried beneath the earth.

Her mother's delight and relief had been evident, if controlled, but Dr Bonnet had been so moved as he shook his future son-in-law's hand that tears had come to his eyes.

'There is no man on this earth to whom I would rather entrust her,' he said, husky with emotion. 'We are deeply honoured –'

'It is I who am honoured, monsieur,' Fabian said. He had turned to look at Charlotte then, and she had basked in the warmth of his smile. Once it had illumined a dark cellar; now it seemed to light the entire world, so that the grass was greener, the colours of the flowers brighter, the sky a more cerulean blue.

'We will be happy, won't we?' Charlotte had asked him childishly when they were alone together. 'I'll try my best to be a good wife to you, and a mother to Elise. I hope you won't be angry if I make mistakes at first.'

'Dearest Charlotte!' Fabian took her hand in his. 'If I am angry at all, it is never with you but with my own private demons. I'm not always as sanguine as I should be.'

'Still,' she insisted. 'I know we will be happy. There is just one thing, monsieur –'

'I should not object too strenuously if, just once, you were to call me by my given name.'

'Gabriel?' Charlotte looked as if the suggestion alarmed her. 'It seems strange, but I shall try.'

'What is the one thing?' Charlotte hesitated unhappily. 'Well?' he prompted her.

'It's Madame Colbert,' she admitted, looking up at him guiltily. 'How will she accept me? She seems so very attached to Elise that I feel she will resent my presence.'

'Ah!' Gabriel laughed dryly. '*Notre* Tantine! Yes, I daresay she will be a discordant voice in this paean of joy that surrounds us! I shall have to consider carefully the matter of Tantine. To be honest I should not be sorry to have her influence over my daughter –' he hesitated a moment over his choice of words. 'Diluted,' he went on finally. 'Yet I owe her a good deal – more than I can repay – for she came to me in my hour of need and took charge of my child and household.'

'I've no doubt she was glad to do so.'

'Perhaps. She had nowhere else to go in England, that is true, but that in no way diminishes the service she did me. However –'

He broke off, and Charlotte studied his expression, sensing the complicated emotions that lay behind his hesitations.

He has no fondness for the woman, she thought thankfully. A dutiful gratitude, perhaps – but there is no real warmth in their relationship. The realisation cheered her a little, for she felt it armoured her against the blatant hostility she felt sure she would receive from Madame Colbert.

'She is far from young,' she said. 'Perhaps she would welcome a chance to give up her duties.'

'I could buy her a cottage close to the friends in Richmond she prizes so highly – see she wants for nothing –' For one moment Gabriel's voice had sounded hopeful and enthusiastic, but then he laughed ruefully and shrugged his shoulders. 'I am deluding myself if I imagine that the matter will be settled easily. She adores Elise, just as she did her mother, and she'll not want to relinquish her hold over the child. The problem, I fear, is not one that will be solved without a good deal of unpleasantness.'

'And I the cause of it all!'

Charlotte's expression was contrite, but she longed to be contradicted and was not disappointed. Gabriel turned and took both her hands in his, looking with love on the innocent face, as yet unmarked by experience, of the girl who would be his bride. He saw the clear, peaty-brown eyes with their fringe of dark lashes. He saw the vulnerable mouth, its parted lips seeming to ask a question which he would for ever be unable to answer.

'You will be the cause of much happiness,' he said. And in the saying of it, he felt his heart would break.

There were a few stormy days and people shook their heads and said that the weather had broken and that summer was surely now at an end. However, they were proved wrong, for the skies cleared again and the sun shone with undiminished warmth.

Gabriel and Charlotte walked through the woods to inspect the house at Flewett's Cross. It was known as Whiteacres and had once been a farmhouse, belonging for several generations to a family called White who, starting from humble beginnings, had prospered and added on rooms as their wealth increased. In those days its roof had been neatly thatched, the garden surrounding the house well tended, but it had now passed into the ownership of a lawyer in Canterbury who had no wish to live in such rural seclusion. He had sold the land to a nearby farmer, but for the

118

moment the house stood empty, still furnished but in a state of disrepair.

It was, in effect, little more than an oversized cottage, but both Charlotte and Gabriel were charmed by it.

'What a strange thing atmosphere is,' Gabriel said, standing in the main, central room. 'If I were a pagan, I should say there were benign spirits here.'

'It's been a happy house, I can feel it. Do take it, Gabriel!'

He wasted no time in negotiating a lease for the rest of the summer with Mr White. As his strength returned he fretted more and more about his business and his daughter, and though Dr Bonnet counselled caution, he announced that the time had come for him to go back to London to see how matters progressed in Freedom Street, and to collect his daughter and Madame Colbert from Richmond.

'But have no fear, we shall be back here as soon as possible,' he said. 'I have no wish to stay in London in this weather. Much as I hate to admit it, I know I am not fully restored to health yet.'

It was planned that once he had returned with Elise, they should stay at Whiteacres for the whole of September, at the end of which Gabriel and Charlotte would be married before the return of the entire family to London, which should by then be cooler.

Madame Bonnet had personally overseen the cleaning of the house and the engagement of two village girls to look after the Fabian household, and both she and Charlotte were present when the carriage arrived bringing Gabriel, his daughter, and a sour-looking Madame Colbert to their temporary home.

The absence, though short, had induced a shyness in Charlotte. Suppose he had experienced second thoughts while he had been away from her; suppose the reunion with his daughter had made him think that a stepmother would be not an asset but an added complication?

His smile and the expression on his face told her at once that he had done no such thing.

'Come, my darling,' he said to Elise. 'Come and meet your new maman.'

Beyond a polite and formal greeting, Charlotte did not look at Madame Colbert, but concentrated instead on the child, taking her hand and leading her inside the house. Even so, she was aware of the hostility that seemed to flow from the woman.

There was no such reaction from Elise.

'Are you really going to be my maman? I have always wanted one! I hope you will be like Madame Belamie! Oh, I was sorry when we left there to go to Richmond, for Anne-Marie was my friend and we had lovely games together, and Jean had a pet rabbit that had babies. Can I have a rabbit? Please say yes! Tantine says there is only one place for rabbits and that's the pot, but they are so soft and furry and I loved to stroke Pompom – that's what Jean called her!'

'The child is over-excited,' Madame Colbert said repressively. 'Come with me, Elise –'

'Leave her, Tantine.' Gabriel spoke kindly but with great firmness. 'She and Charlotte naturally wish to get to know each other.'

Madame Colbert, pink with fury, left the room. She returned moments later, having been shown her chamber by Madame Bonnet, to complain bitterly about its size, furnishings and lack of light.

'I can see,' Madame Bonnet said to her daughter afterwards, 'that you will have to be on your guard against that woman. Let her know from the beginning that you will be mistress of your own house.'

Charlotte sighed. 'It will not be easy,' she said. 'She hates me.'

'She must have known that Monsieur Fabian would take a wife some day,' Madame Bonnet said bracingly. 'You must simply refuse to be intimidated.'

Charlotte would have found little to comfort her had she been present at Whiteacres that evening. Madame Colbert had settled Elise for the night and come down to the parlour where she did not sit down to take her ease, but stood before Gabriel, twisting her hands together.

'You wish to say something, Tantine?' he said.

'Only, monsieur, to ask if you have taken leave of your senses.'

Gabriel marked the place in his book with a finger and looked at her, fighting down his anger.

'In that case, madame, it would be best if you kept silent,' he said evenly.

'How can I?' She swirled away from him angrily, paced up the room and back again. 'That chit, half your age – she had designs on you from the moment you arrived there. Oh, you didn't see

120

it, you were far too ill, but I could see it well enough. What kind of a stepmother will she be? I think only of your child's good, monsieur. And yours, of course.'

He smiled cynically at this afterthought. He had been aware for some time now that she disliked him thoroughly, had always disliked him, ever since he had taken her beloved Celestine away from her and allowed her to die on a crowded fishing boat.

It had taken him years to appreciate the fact that she blamed him and him alone for everything that had happened. At first she had seemed like an answer to prayer. He himself was distraught in the early days, and he had seized with gratitude her offer to take charge of his child and his household. He was lucky, everyone told him, that Madame Colbert had come to London at this time, and he himself had agreed with this view for a longer time than he now believed possible.

As well as gratitude he had felt pity for her, for her life had not been a particularly happy one. Nature had not endowed her with grace or good looks, and only a sizeable financial settlement had brought about her marriage to a man many years her senior who had treated her coldly once it became clear she would never bear children.

Only her intense love for Celestine, her sister's lovely daughter, had redeemed a bleak and cheerless life. Gabriel had not realised how obsessive that love had been until one winter's night, the anniversary of Celestine's birthday, when Elise was almost three years old.

The thought that his young wife would have been twenty-one years old on that day had she lived had filled him with the sort of pain that no amount of prayer and supplication had seemed able to ease. He had sat on into the night with the fire no more than an ember and the candles guttering, staring unseeingly at a page of his Bible, his agony of loss so great that he felt he would die from it. In that moment the door had burst open, and a wild-eyed Madame Colbert had stood in the doorway, white hair snaking about her shoulders, one hand supporting her against the jamb. Her face seemed to be contorted with a pain equal to his; but hers, he saw, was pain heavily laced with hate.

'You are suffering,' she said, her voice no more than a hiss. 'I see it, and I am glad of it, for no matter what you suffer it is not near enough for what you did to that angel, my Celestine, the sweetest and most beautiful child that ever lived. I hope you suffer for ever!' Her eyes glittered balefully. 'You risked her life. You brought her here, long after it was safe –'

Shocked into silence until then, at last he was moved to remonstrate.

'She begged me to do so – and how could I have brought her earlier when I was in prison?'

'You should have died there, so that my lamb would have lived!'

'You think I have not told myself that? You think that I've not asked why? God sustained me, for reasons of his own –'

'Hah!' There was no attempt made to hide her scorn. 'Your pride sustained you, monsieur. Pride and self-glory.'

She had left him then, the knowledge that she was not wholly wrong forcing him to his knees in an agony of guilt. The teachings and example of his saintly aunt and uncle had influenced him, without doubt, and he believed passionately in the cause of Protestantism; and yet, and yet – oh yes, pride had entered into it. He had refused to humble himself before the dragoons, and now there was pleasure to be gained in seeing the light of hero-worship in the eyes of those among the Huguenot community who knew his past history, a thrill that was like no other when he spoke to the congregation and felt them kindle with enthusiasm.

That night had left him as low in spirits as he had ever been and it marked a change in his relationship with Madame Colbert. He hoped that she was motivated by remorse and not entirely by the desire to keep a roof over her head when, later, she apologised for her immoderate words. The apology was accepted at its face value and they continued to inhabit the same house, treating each other with politeness and – at least on Gabriel's part – with consideration. He was under no illusion, however. Madame Colbert thoroughly disliked him and if it had not been for the fact that no one could have cared for his daughter with more devotion, he would have found some reason to rid himself of her long ago.

Now, surely, he had found one. He put his book aside.

'Pray sit down for a while and take a glass of wine,' he said. 'Calm yourself, do, for there is something of importance I have to say to you.'

She stopped her pacing and looked at him warily as he rose from his seat and poured wine for them both.

'Let us make one thing quite certain,' he said when they were both seated. 'I shall tolerate no criticism of Charlotte. I love her, and she is to be my wife. Is that understood?'

'You love Celestine!'

For a moment he said nothing, but looked at her with pity.

'Celestine is dead. She has been dead these six years, and there is no man could have mourned more sincerely. But life goes on.'

'And I? I who have devoted six years of my life to you and your child? Am I to be cast aside now that you have found someone else to care for you?'

'Of course not. Your friends in Richmond, Mesdemoiselles Bouverie, surely they would be pleased if you were to live closer? I would gladly buy you a house there and grant you a regular pension –'

'Never!' Her skin was pale except for two spots of colour. 'I shall never, never go so far from my darling! When would I see her?'

'I should not keep her from you. She is far too fond of you for that, but you must see that my wife would naturally wish to oversee her own house.'

'All I see is a scheming little minx who wishes to throw me out of my home and come between me and the child who has known no other mother but me.'

'Silence!' he snapped, and she subsided, glowering. When he spoke again, he had moderated his voice, but it was as firm as ever. 'I have no intention of making the break a brutal one. Elise may visit you and you may visit her just as often as you please.'

'It is I whom Elise loves.' There was a note of desperation in her voice. 'She will be upset by this. She is sensitive, highly strung. Such a shock could drive her to madness.'

'I think not.' His small stock of sympathy for the woman was ebbing fast and his voice had hardened still further. 'You must have surely realised from the beginning that a second marriage was a possibility?'

'I never believed you would put another woman in Celestine's place.'

'Celestine will have her own place, and always will. But Celestine is dead.'

'So.' Her green eyes narrowed and she pursed her lips. For a long moment she said nothing but looked away from him and sipped her wine. When finally she looked at him once more she smiled thinly, though her eyes were as cold as ever. 'It was a shock, monsieur.'

'I know. Believe me, madame, I understand something of your feelings. I can only ask for a similar understanding on your part.'

'I understand very well.' She settled back in her chair, her face shadowed. 'I shall accept your offer of a house with gratitude. You are more than generous.'

'I could do nothing less. You must know how grateful I am for all your devotion of the past.' His voice expressed relief that at last she seemed to have accepted the situation.

'When is the ceremony to take place?'

'The end of September.'

'So soon!'

'There seems little point in delay.'

'I am to be granted one more month, then – one more month with my darling.'

Gabriel made an exasperated gesture.

'Come, come, madame, no one is in a hurry for you to go. You will return to London with us, of course, and must take whatever time you need to find a suitable house. Neither I nor Charlotte wish to be unkind. No doubt she will be glad to have you to introduce her to life in London.'

There was a triumphant glint in Madame Colbert's eyes. This concession might be no more than a stay of execution, but who knew where it might lead? Time was what she needed.

'Then let us drink to your future, monsieur,' she said, as she lifted her glass towards him. 'And may Mam'selle Charlotte find in marriage the happiness she so richly deserves.'

'You will be a maman like Madame Belamie, won't you?' Elise returned to her theme of the day before. 'I hope that you will.'

'I shall certainly do my best,' Charlotte replied humbly, 'for there is no one I admire more.'

She was walking alone with Elise in the orchard at Providence House, welcoming the opportunity for the two of them to become better acquainted.

'Tantine does not admire her,' Elise went on. 'Tantine says that Minette and Louise and Anne-Marie do not behave like young ladies should and that Madame Belamie should chastise them more.'

'I have always found them perfectly charming.'

'*I* think they are charming, too. They said I was like a princess, with hair of spun gold and eyes like cornflowers.'

'They said that, did they?' Charlotte's tone was dry.

'Minette said that when she was married, she would hope for a little girl just like me.'

'I don't wonder you liked them, if they said such pretty things to you!'

'Oh, I *loved* them! I wish I had some sisters – and brothers too, of course, though boys are rough and noisy and Jean put a spider in my bed.'

'Like Paul!' Charlotte smiled, remembering the cockroach.

'No, not at all like Paul. Paul is a man, not a boy, and was always kind to me when he came to see us in London. Now he has gone away, and no one knows when he will be back. If I had brothers and sisters I should always have someone to play with.'

Charlotte, touched by the wistful tone, took the child's hand in hers.

'Well, now you have me,' she said. 'I want to be your friend, Elise.'

'And you won't stop Papa loving me? Tantine said –'

'I don't want to hear what Tantine said!' Charlotte crouched down beside the little girl so that their eyes were on the same level. 'Listen to me! I should never, never dream of doing such a thing – nor could I, for he loves you more than anything in the world.'

'If you had a baby,' Elise said with apparent inconsequence, 'would you want it to be a girl or a boy? I think girls are nicest.'

'I am happy with the little girl I have already.'

At that, Elise wrinkled her nose engagingly.

'I kept telling Papa to find me a maman,' she said.

'Does your papa always give you what you want?'

'Oh, always, mam'selle.' Elise spoke with a matter-of-fact air of satisfaction.

'Then you are a most fortunate little girl.'

'I know.' Elise smiled beatifically, and in spite of a puritanical instinct that made her feel no child should be indulged quite so much as this, Charlotte thought it was not hard to understand why Gabriel loved to please her. In another ten years, her beauty would match that of her mother.

Gabriel was delighted with the way the two of them had taken to each other. Already Elise called her 'Maman', which pleased and amused everyone, with the exception of Madame Colbert who had her own way of making her displeasure felt. Charlotte was left in no doubt of it one day in September when Gabriel was having a long-delayed meeting with Monsieur Herault. She and Elise had been walking in the lanes around Whiteacres searching for early blackberries in the hedgerows and had half filled a small basket by the time they returned, a harvest which Elise proudly lifted to show to Madame Colbert as she came to the porch to greet them.

'Look, look, see what Maman and I have picked.'

'Take them to the kitchen, *chérie*.' The tone was repressive. 'Walk – *walk*, I say, like *la petite héritière* you are. Remember *you* are no country bumpkin.'

The slight emphasis on the 'you' made the remark little more than an insult directed at Charlotte, and when Elise had gone Madame Colbert turned and surveyed her, a scornful smile on her face.

'I must discover what kind of sorcery you use, mam'selle, that all who meet you come under your spell.' The words were neither pleasantly said nor meant, and Charlotte was under no illusion to the contrary. 'However, a word of warning; I called her an heiress and I did not lie. She has money in trust from her maternal grandfather. Monsieur may seem over-indulgent, but he demands a high standard of behaviour, for such a one will make a brilliant marriage. It is her destiny! With both looks and fortune, a dukedom would not be beyond her.'

Charlotte gave an incredulous gasp of laughter.

'Madame, she is but six years old!'

'She is not too young to learn to comport herself like a lady. I have no wish to see six years' work blown to the winds.'

Later, reporting the conversation to Marianne, Charlotte was able to treat it as a joke.

'Just imagine making such plans for a mere babe,' she said. 'I cannot think it right that Madame Colbert should make Elise so aware of the fact that she will inherit a fortune – and nor does Gabriel, but she is so intimidating I could think of no apt reply.'

Marianne was brisk in her advice.

126

'Pay no heed to her. She's a jealous, foolish old crone, loath to give up her hold over Elise. To my mind it's the best day's work that Monsieur Fabian has ever done, to turn her off and hand the child to you! The woman's face would turn the milk sour, and it must have been a dismal thing for him to witness such a sight, day after day.'

'Gabriel wants me to speak English with Elise as often as possible. Since *chère* Tantine speaks nothing but French, you can well imagine this hardly endears me to her.'

'My dear Charlotte, at this moment *nothing* would endear you to her!' She repeated her advice. 'Pay no heed. She is being well treated and has no real complaint for I have been witness to the way Monsieur Fabian speaks to her, and he is kindness itself.'

'It is parting from Elise that upsets her, and though I can understand her feelings I cannot but agree with you – and with Gabriel – that the child will be better off without her. She is so possessive, so overpowering in her affection, as if she would like to smother her. Perhaps I am exaggerating the matter, but there seems something almost unhealthy in it.'

'So long as you don't allow her to spoil your happiness, Charlotte.'

'Oh, nothing could do that!'

Her cousin seemed to glow with wellbeing, Marianne thought, and could not help being amused that Charlotte, who had always professed herself totally uninterested in entering the married state, could have changed so completely.

As the wedding day drew near, so the momentum increased. Charlotte's gown, made from a length of bronze silk provided by Gabriel, was decorated with embroidery in gold thread, worked by Charlotte herself. Nan was given the task of helping with the plainer sewing, and the two girls spent hours together bent over their tasks, their conversation ranging far and wide.

'So there was Ma,' Nan said one afternoon, engaged in recounting a family disaster at her home the previous Sunday. 'Fallen right through the chair, she had, with the cane bottom gone, and Pa rushing in from outside with his foot caught in a bucket as Molly had left by the door, and the baby a-squalling fit to raise the dead, and the dog a-puking on the floor –'

'Oh, stop, stop,' Charlotte implored through her laughter. 'I can't believe such a chapter of accidents.'

'As God's my witness, miss, 'twas just as I've told you.' Nan paused, looking carefully at Charlotte as she bit off a length of thread. 'And if I may say so, it does my heart good to see you like once you was. It's a treat to see you laugh again, miss, that it is. 'Tis a wonderful thing, what the good Lord has in store, say what you will. It seems too good to be true, you marrying a fine man like Monsieur Fabian, and him a hero and all. Though there was a time,' she added, settling down once more to stitching a seam, 'when you swore his tongue was too sharp for your liking.'

'Did I?'

'Aye, that you did. *You* wouldn't have him, not if he did ask, you said.'

'Everything has changed.' Her needle busy, Charlotte smiled, not lifting her eyes from her work. 'I did not know him then.'

'We none of us know what's round the corner, and that's the truth.' Nan looked sideways at Charlotte and giggled, catching her lip between her teeth. 'Though I reckon I know what's in store for you on your wedding night.'

Charlotte stitched on serenely, not responding to Nan's mild bawdiness.

Let them speculate, she thought. Let them all guess and gloat and watch my waistline.

She felt her heart would burst with gratitude, and knew that Nan was right. Whoever could have imagined that all would work out as happily as this?

7

Gabriel was determined that Charlotte's first sight of London would be from the river. It was, he told her, the only way to see the skyline and appreciate the size of the place, and his face glowed as he spoke of the vessels she would see – ships that had come from all over the world to this, the largest and the most important commercial centre.

Accordingly, a week after the wedding, the newly married couple, together with Elise and Madame Colbert, took the coach to Rochester, staying overnight there at the inn and rising early the following morning to travel in company with several others – a lone and silent gentleman on a dappled horse, a carriage belonging to an important government officer on naval business, and a merchant who dealt in leather and could speak of nothing else.

They were to leave the main London road to go to Gravesend, Gabriel told her, and it was folly to attempt this particular stretch of the road alone since it passed over Gad's Hill, long notorious for the highwaymen it attracted.

'Would it then not have been preferable to stay on the main road?' Charlotte asked, not caring to think of losing all her new finery before she had even unpacked.

'No, no – this way is best, I promise you, and with all this company we shall surely be safe. From Gravesend we shall take to the water, and I pray that this drizzle will have stopped and the sun will be shining, for there is no finer sight than London from the river.'

'The stench of it is appalling,' Madame Colbert said, drawing her mouth down with distaste.

'Well yes, perhaps,' Gabriel allowed. 'But not near so bad now that the cooler weather has come.'

'I shall not notice it.' Charlotte spoke firmly and lifted a determined chin. Even if she did, she resolved, she would not give Madame Colbert the satisfaction of hearing her complain of it. The warfare between them was unspoken, overlaid with a cool politeness, but it existed all the same. She prayed heaven that it would not be too long before the woman found a house to her liking.

The week that had passed since the wedding had not been a comfortable one. In any number of ways Madame Colbert had underlined her position in the household, not so much by asserting her own authority but by deferring to Charlotte in an ostentatious way.

'Whatever *you* wish, madame. You are the mistress now,' she would say, when consulted on small domestic matters.

Her manner was calculated to intimidate and to an extent she succeeded, but finally Charlotte found the resolution to speak.

'I think it best if you carry on just as before,' she said. 'The servants regard you as the mistress.' She saw the light of triumph in Madame Colbert's eye and nerved herself to continue. 'However,' she went on, grasping the nettle, 'once in Freedom Street, everything will be different.'

'Different?' Madame Colbert glared at her.

'I shall, of course, be the mistress then.'

Madame Colbert pursed her lips as if in disbelief – whether at the situation itself or at Charlotte's effrontery in speaking in this way, she did not know.

To be truthful, Charlotte could hardly believe any of it herself, and from time to time felt like pinching herself to make sure she was not dreaming. The wedding ceremony, with all its sermons and exhortations, had passed her by, as irrelevant as if it had been happening to someone else.

And afterwards – afterwards when they were alone together –

She felt herself growing hot with discomfort at the memory, preferring to think of her husband as the urbane gentleman he appeared to the outside world, sure of himself, master of any situation. At the wedding there were far more eyes on him than there had been on her, new gown or no, and she had felt proud and grateful and more than a little in awe of him.

But afterwards – oh, he had been nothing like the man she had known! They had talked for a while, sitting before the fire that had been lit in their large, damp-smelling chamber at Whiteacres, sipping wine and laughing a little at Tante Hortense and the poem she had written in honour of the occasion, and at the vile, blood-red gown favoured by poor, raddled Madame de

Mailly who had been a beauty in her day and could not come to terms that her day was long past and her beauty gone.

They ate a few sweetmeats and talked some more, and as the evening wore on Charlotte was conscious of a deep contentment. It was all going to be perfect, she told herself. This was what married life would be like; an end to loneliness, a loving friendship. Then suddenly, between one breath and the next, it had all changed.

Gabriel reached out and drew her to her feet and as he stood looking down at her she saw that all the laughter had gone from his face which now looked drawn and haggard. He gazed at her hungrily, his eyes full of pain.

'Oh Charlotte,' he said softly. 'Sweet Charlotte! I so long for your happiness. May you never hate me for what I have done this day.'

'Hate you?' She looked at him in astonishment. 'How could I? You have made me happier than I have ever been, and I am grateful.'

'Grateful!' His expression darkened. 'Don't say that! No man deserves your gratitude less.' With rough, impatient hands he loosened her hair so that the curls tumbled on to her shoulders, thick and unruly, and he seized them and held them so tightly that she would have cried out but was prevented from doing so by the strangeness of his expression. The fire had died, the candles were burnt low, and in the half darkness his face was bone-white. Slowly he relaxed his hold as if it cost him a great effort to do so, and his hands became gentle as he stroked her hair and cheeks.

'You'd best go to bed,' he said softly. 'The hour is late.'

The bed with its white hangings was on the wall facing the fire, and Charlotte glanced towards it and back again to him.

'And you?' she asked.

He said nothing in reply but took her shoulders in a grip like iron and propelled her towards the bed. She had long since changed her fine gown for a loose robe, and now she saw him swallow with difficulty, saw the line of sweat on his upper lip, as he slipped the fine wool garment from her shoulders.

She could feel her heart pounding, was conscious of the rising panic that she had thought had gone for ever. She could not speak or move, but lay back against the pillows, her eyes fixed on his face.

He came no nearer, but stood and stared at her in an unnerving silence until, with a sudden movement and with an exclamation she could not hear, he turned on his heel and went swiftly from the room.

What had happened? Why had he changed so suddenly? She understood nothing and for a long time she could not sleep, dimly aware of her husband's need and frightened by it. But the day had been a long one and finally she slept. The next thing she knew it was morning and Gabriel was sitting on the bed as calm and good-humoured as ever, just as if nothing untoward had happened.

Throughout the rest of the week his control had not slipped again. They had visited friends, and been visited in their turn. They had supped together, played with Elise, walked with arms linked through the lanes and the woods, and the memory of that night's unease had faded. They had even slept in the same bed, a chaste kiss their only contact.

It was going to be all right after all, Charlotte assured herself. Gabriel was the perfect husband. Everyone told her so, and for once they were not mistaken.

And now they were on their way to their own home and she was so excited by the thought that in the wherry they took at Gravesend she sat on the edge of her seat and looked this way and that, anxious to miss nothing of this momentous journey.

There was so much of interest to see. No sooner had she exclaimed at the fishing smacks, burdened with such a weight of canvas that she thought they must surely capsize, than her attention was caught by the colliers, beating upriver with a cargo of what Gabriel assured her was coal from Newcastle.

'And look there,' he said. 'Those are hoys, from your own county of Kent. Perhaps they have Phillipe Belamie's vegetables on board.'

Her eyes sparkled and her cheeks were flushed.

'I never dreamed there would be so much to see!'

'The stench,' said Madame Colbert, like some recurring chorus, 'is terrible.'

Charlotte refused to show that the foul smell affected her in any way, though she had to admit that for once Madame Colbert's opinion had something to be said for it. It was, she told herself firmly, quite easy to ignore, and she occupied herself in looking at the merchantmen sailing for the Indies and the ceaseless, restless activity, both on the river and in the villages and shipyards alongside.

At Woolwich the sun glinted on the gold of the King's yachts, and a mile beyond was Royal Greenwich, where Sir Christopher Wren had enlarged the Queen's House to create a building of such beauty that she gaped in admiration.

'Oh Gabriel,' she breathed. 'I have never seen such a wonderful place! And look – look – can that be the King himself?'

A gilded barge sailing towards them was manned by liverymen dressed in red and gold. A solitary, richly clad gentleman was being carried in great state. He could, Charlotte thought, quite easily be the King; but Madame Colbert's sour snort of amusement told her that she had made a fool of herself and she bit her lip and kept her silence, allowing Elise to chatter without competition until a small war threatened between their waterman and the owner of a skiff laden with fruit who kept calling to attract their attention and was now dangerously close. Charlotte clutched her seat in fright.

'Gabriel, tell him to go! He will overturn us.'

Without a great deal of success, Gabriel did as she asked, wincing at the insults hurled from the skiff and echoed from the wherry.

'The language of the river is hardly fit for ladies,' he said apologetically.

'As to that, pray don't concern yourself for I understand not one word,' Charlotte said. 'How strangely they speak! I thought I understood English well.'

'The dialect of London is quite different from any other. Be thankful it's incomprehensible.'

'Oh Gabriel, it's all so wonderful! I never dreamed there would be so many boats.'

'It's London's highway.' Gabriel was smiling with a proprietorial pride at her excitement. 'But alas, it's London's midden, too. Still, on a day like this when the sun shines on it and it gleams silver, one can forget its filth. Even the wind favours us today, for all that Tantine complains. I've known the stench far worse, believe me. It's said you can smell London from miles away. Look – we're passing through the second greatest ship-building centre in the world.'

'Only the second?' Charlotte smiled at him teasingly, sensing his pride in this city he had adopted as his own. 'Where, pray, is the biggest?'

'Amsterdam.'

'Like Paul.' Elise tugged at her hand. 'Paul is in Amsterdam. I wish he still lived in London. He used to come and see us.'

'He'll come again, *chérie*, when his work in Amsterdam is done. Look, Charlotte –' On her other side, Gabriel caught her arm. 'This is Limehouse – and there's the Tower up ahead –'

'They have wild animals there, Maman.' Ignoring Madame Colbert's restraining hand, Elise was bouncing up and down in her excitement. 'You will take us, won't you, Papa? Maman has never seen a tiger, for she told me so herself.'

'They are not common in the streets of Canterbury,' Charlotte admitted, smiling at her.

She looked at the bulk of the Tower as they passed by and shivered a little at the thought of the desolation of those who, for one reason or another, had passed through Traitor's Gate. Like Gabriel, they had not always been guilty of anything more heinous than nonconformity.

'Poor things,' she whispered beneath her breath, but not too low for Gabriel to avoid hearing her.

'Aye,' he said grimly. 'Incarceration is a dreadful thing.'

'And torture worse.'

She pressed his arm and looked up at him with her eyes bright with sympathy, sick with the thought of his sufferings even as she acknowledged that had they never been, then she could never have brought herself to marry him, much as she admired him.

It was a moment that quickly passed, for now they were approaching London Bridge. Eighteen arches spanned the river and above them was a double row of shops and houses at least six storeys high that seemed to lean at a dangerous angle over the river.

This was journey's end and there was more activity than ever. More gilded barges, more liverymen; vendors and fishermen and muddy boys grubbing on the blackened strips of shingle left by the receding tide, the shouts of watermen and those selling their wares almost drowned by the roar of the cataract beneath the bridge.

Charlotte clung to Gabriel's arm, overwhelmed by it all, but at the same time exhilarated by the colour and vitality even though she was forced to follow Madame Colbert's example and hold a handkerchief to her nose.

The ladies were assisted from the wherry and left to stand in a comparatively quiet corner surrounded by their belongings while Gabriel engaged a hackney coach, but even so Charlotte drew Elise even further back to avoid the press of traffic and the mud that was sent flying by mudlarks fighting over a coin flung to them by a fine gentleman in lace and velvet.

'You'll find life here very different from Canterbury,' Madame Colbert said with a kind of anticipatory relish in her voice, as if she would enjoy the sight of Charlotte rueing the day she left rural Kent.

At last, their trunks hoisted to the top of the coach, they began their slow journey towards Spitalfields along a road congested with other similar conveyances, as well as wagons and drays.

'I could never believe,' Charlotte said faintly, peering first to one side and then to the other, 'that so many people could live in one place.'

Bells clanged, wheels rumbled; men cried chairs to mend and scissors to grind, while a crone hawked old clothes and a girl, fresh from the country, shouted that she had fine, white-hearted cabbages for sale. There were apple sellers, too, and tinkers and coalmen.

'Such a noise!' she said, laughing; and she shook her head helplessly as Gabriel leaned towards her, the better to hear her.

Their way led through Gracechurch Street, past the end of Lombard Street (where Paul Belamie had once worked, so Gabriel managed to inform her, raising his voice to combat the hurly-burly outside). Now they were coming to finer buildings. Leaden Hall was on their right, Gresham College a little further up on the other side, and scarcely had Charlotte finished marvelling at them than they were passing through Bishopsgate. She had, by this time, removed the handkerchief from her nose, albeit cautiously, for here the streets ran with less filth – a matter for which she was heartily thankful, for it was at this point that they were delayed by an altercation between the driver of their hackney coach and that of a dray laden with barrels over which of them had the right of way, a quarrel that threatened to become violent until both of the men united in common cause against a footman who preceded his noble master's carriage.

Gabriel smiled at her shocked wonder.

'Patience, my dear Charlotte,' he said. 'I regret such delays are commonplace.'

135

'They should be flogged for such language!' Madame Colbert's face had grown pink with outrage. 'Elise, cover your ears.'

The little girl did as she was told, at the same time screwing up her eyes and pulling such a comic face that Gabriel and Charlotte both laughed with amusement, looking at each other to share the moment. How wonderful, Charlotte thought, to see him so calm and sanguine, so untroubled by the demons that at times rose to torment him. She leaned closer to him and under cover of Elise's chatter murmured softly:

'All will be well, Gabriel. I know it. I shall be happy here.'

'I hope so.' He was not smiling now. 'Oh, how I hope so.'

'I am sure of it.'

The quarrel outside seemed to be reaching a crescendo and suddenly Charlotte longed for it to be over so that they could proceed on their way. It was not only fatigue that made her anxious to reach the end of their journey, but the desperate longing for a new beginning.

All her life until this point had, she felt, been lived under the shadow of a nightmare she could explain to no one. Now it seemed as if she had stepped out into the sunshine. These past few days, with Gabriel so kind and companionable and at the same time so undemanding, had shown her how blissful married life could be, and she was loath to wait another moment to see her new home.

'How did Freedom Street come by its name?' she asked, remembering a question she had long meant to ask him.

'The first Flemish refugees found freedom there. They followed the Baptists and the Quakers and all the other dissenters to Spitalfields.'

'So it has always been a place of refuge?'

'Refuge, and healing. There was a hospital there once, hence "Spital".'

'Freedom Street.' Charlotte seemed to be savouring it upon her tongue. 'It's a good name.'

'And we shall soon be there.'

Charlotte, peering from the coach window at the tall house with its wooden spool hung over the door, had trouble in seeing the topmost storey.

'I did not expect it to be so high,' she said. 'But oh, it's a fine house.'

136

Madame Colbert's voice interrupted her inspection.

'You have a visitor already, monsieur.'

There was a dark-clad man loitering near the steps that led to the house, but it had not occurred to Charlotte that he was more than a casual passer-by, one among many; now she saw that he had gone up the steps and was pounding on the door.

'Who is it, Gabriel?' She looked to her husband for enlightenment and saw to her astonishment that all the calmness, all the contentment, had left his face so that once more he looked gaunt and ill.

'Gabriel?' She put a hand on his arm, suddenly anxious. 'What is it? Are you in pain? Is something wrong?'

He did not reply and she could see that his eyes were on the man who continued to knock on the door.

'Who is that man?' she asked. And again, 'What is it, Gabriel?'

She looked at the man who appeared to have had such a profound effect on her husband and saw an ungainly, gangling figure clad in the dark clothes and white bands of a pastor, clothes that looked travel-stained and tattered. As she looked, the door was opened by a maidservant, and as she gestured towards the coach, she saw the visitor turn and look in their direction. He had a long, thin face with a nose that was too large for it and a curiously undershot jaw.

'He is a friend,' Gabriel's voice was devoid of all expression. He sighed heavily. 'Come, my love. We must go and bid him welcome.'

Charlotte heard the watch call out the hour at one o'clock, and still the voices continued from the adjoining room.

The man had been introduced to her as Etienne Boyer, a fellow prisoner who had shared Gabriel's ordeal. Though her heart had sunk at the thought of such an unprepossessing stranger joining them when they themselves were both tired after the journey, she did her best to welcome him politely and begged him to stay and share their meal.

'I had hoped for more than a meal,' he said, with what Charlotte considered unpardonable rudeness. 'I had thought, Fabian, perhaps a bed for a few nights –'

'Of course, of course.'

Newly married as she was, Charlotte knew her husband well enough to recognise that his heartiness was false – and no wonder!

The man seemed to have no social graces at all, or any knowledge of common politeness. She felt understandably piqued that he had barely acknowledged her existence, beyond a long, astonished stare as Gabriel had introduced her as his wife of a week.

It was Boyer's voice that predominated as she listened from her bed, just as it had predominated all evening, strident and insistent, lacking all refinement. She had been brought up to respect any man who followed a pastor's vocation and expected a solemnity and gravity beyond that of ordinary men. It did not, therefore, surprise her that he seemed unable to smile or to utter the empty pleasantries that constitute the small change of most conversations. She would have accepted as perfectly normal any tendency on his part to insist that they join in prayer, or even to deliver a homily on the sanctity of married life. What did surprise her was this man's obvious lack of cultivation, his utter boorishness.

It had been made clear to him from the first that his hosts had come from a distance – that indeed, this was their very first evening in Freedom Street as a married couple. It seemed to Charlotte that good manners would demand that he allowed them a little privacy. Even close and much-loved friends might think their presence out of place on such an occasion, but no consideration of this kind appeared to trouble Monsieur Boyer. Instead he gave every impression of regarding *her* as the interloper, talking volubly to Gabriel throughout the entire evening, to her complete exclusion.

Even Gabriel had little to say, though from the few questions he was allowed to interject it was learned that Monsieur Boyer had left the college in Lausanne where he had gone to train for the ministry after escaping from prison, but that for the past two years he had been back in France, in the Cévennes, ministering to those Huguenots who still worshipped in secret – the Church in the Désert, as it had come to be called.

'I am like John the Baptist and live in the wilderness,' he said. 'I move from place to place – from cave to shepherd's hut and back to cave. The faith lives on, Fabian. Never be in doubt of that.'

'Such brave souls!' Gabriel spoke the words in a low voice, full of emotion.

'Aye, brave indeed. Not for them the Church in exile, secure and comfortable and free from harassment.' These words were

138

said in a sneering way and Charlotte burned with anger on Gabriel's behalf at the expression on the man's face as he looked around the room with its panelling and good, solid furniture. 'You are not forgotten, Fabian. Memories are long in the Cévennes and you are spoken of still – with admiration, of course, though I cannot speak for what folk would say could they but see the comfort in which you live now.'

Charlotte gasped with outrage on Gabriel's behalf.

'Is there wrong in that?' she asked, and Gabriel turned to her with a tight smile.

'Etienne claims the licence of an old friend,' he said. 'We have shared much. We were captured and imprisoned together – aye, and tortured together.'

'And together we escaped.' At last Boyer deigned to address her. 'I owe your husband my life. It was he, under God, who secured my escape, for it was he who found the words to convert the guard and persuade him to let us go.'

All the more reason to treat him with courtesy, Charlotte longed to say, but did not. Instead she sat for what seemed an eternity as endlessly Boyer talked on, of this man's witness and that man's execution; of near disaster when a secret meeting was almost ambushed by dragoons, of the iniquities of King and court and of the blasphemous beliefs of Rome. Endlessly he spoke of the papists.

The unpleasant voice appeared never to weary. The words gushed from his lips like a torrent, his long and curiously mobile jaw giving a strange shape to his words. Indeed, thought Charlotte as she looked at him with distaste, torrent was an apt word, for as he grew ever more voluble and wild-eyed, the spittle gathered in the corner of his mouth and sprayed the air about him.

He is a fanatic, she thought as she watched him, and she felt a chill of fear, for fanaticism frightened her whatever form it took, papist or Protestant. Though he acknowledged that Gabriel had saved his life and Gabriel himself had described him as an old friend, there seemed no warmth in him, no affection. From beginning to end she had detected only resentment and an assumption of scornful superiority.

She had retired to bed at last, tired out by the events of the day and worried by the pale, exhausted look on Gabriel's face. She had begged him not to delay his rest, but still she could hear the voices from the next room.

139

Questions chased themselves in her mind. Why had Boyer come to England, if he despised those who had sought safety there? And how, indeed, had he managed the journey, when a state of war existed between England and France?

Whatever his mission, she hoped it would be swiftly completed so that he could take himself off. She did not like the effect he had on Gabriel, who had suddenly looked like a stranger to her. It seemed to her, as she had bidden him goodnight, that all the closeness and companionship of the past few days had gone as if they had never been and instead she could see only torment in his face, as though all the ghosts of the past had risen once more to haunt him.

She awoke with a start, shocked into wakefulness by a noise which for one moment she could not identify. Then she remembered. She now lived in a weaver's house, and the noise was that made by the looms as they sprang into action, just as Gabriel had warned her. Though silk waste and shavings were put between the floorboards, he told her, nothing could subdue the noise. She was still gathering her wits when Gabriel came into the room.

It was only then that she realised he had not shared her bed, and she looked at him in bewilderment.

'Why did you not come? Where did you sleep?'

'In my own room.' He stood looking at her from the foot of the bed, his hand on one of the bedposts, and her heart sank as she realised he was still as remote from her as he had appeared the previous night.

'Is – is something troubling you, Gabriel?' She struggled up against the pillows, pushing the tumbled hair from her eyes. 'Have I done aught to displease you?'

He laughed at that, short and mirthless, and turned from her towards the window as if he had looked at her more than long enough.

'No, no, of course not.' There seemed to her to be a trace of impatience in his voice. 'I did not imagine you would want me here now we have sufficient rooms to keep separate. It was different at Whiteacres.'

Oh, so different, she thought. Where had the companionship gone? What of the small jokes and quiet talk? Had he forgotten them?

He had walked away from the bed towards the window and

now stood with his back to her so that she could not see his expression. She looked towards him uncertainly.

'I – I did not mind it,' she said awkwardly.

'Perhaps it was harder for me than for you.'

'Then you must do as you think best.'

He swung round to look at her then, his expression determinedly cheerful.

'Well, that's decided, then! I'm sorry for the noise of the looms.'

'No doubt I shall grow accustomed to them.'

'No doubt.'

'You and Monsieur Boyer had much to say to each other last night.'

He rubbed a hand wearily across his eyes.

'Pray bear with him, Charlotte – and with me,' he said. 'Etienne is not the most comfortable of companions, I grant you, but I cannot turn my back on him. He is the voice of my conscience.'

'What does he want of you?'

'Nothing that I am prepared to give him – except monetary support, of course. That I give ungrudgingly.' He sighed, and moving to the window again, leaned his forehead momentarily against the glass pane. 'Nevertheless, he says much that makes sense to me.'

'Gabriel!' Charlotte's voice was low and pleading. 'Come and sit close to me. I had so looked forward to our first night here, and it was all different from my expectations.'

'I know. I'm sorry.'

For a moment he hesitated, but then did as she asked and came to sit on the bed. He did not touch her, however, nor even look at her, but sat staring down at the hands clasped between his knees, his head hanging despondently.

'Oh Gabriel, what is it?' she asked, putting her hand on his arm. She could feel its resistance through the stuff of his coat. 'What has that man said to make you like this? You were happy yesterday before you saw him.'

'Any fool can be happy if he closes his ears to the promptings of his conscience.'

'What can you mean?'

He stood and once more began his restless movements.

'Forgive me, Charlotte. My mind is in something of a turmoil and I must beg you to allow me to resolve matters in my own way. I have a great deal of work to do. I have lost orders during my long absence and must make calls in the city to announce my return, so I beg you, devote yourself to Elise and to the house while I go about my business.'

She felt like a small child, sent to play in another room.

'I should not dream of detaining you,' she said.

It was perfectly true that he had a great deal of work. The need to make up the time lost in sickness was pressing, but more pressing still was the need for escape.

He went, as always, to the river he loved so well. No matter how many times Tantine remarked upon its offensive smell, still the sight of it and the traffic upon it released the tension within him, as if the vessels sailing to all points of the globe demonstrated the magnitude of the universe, the unimportance of everyday concerns.

He took a ferry to the south bank, to the fields of Battersea. The trees were becoming autumnal, a sheen of gold on them a foretaste of the riot of red and russet that was to come, and the sky was blue beyond the haze of smoke that hung as a perpetual cloud over London.

He loved this city of his adoption. It was in this unlikely place, with all its squalor and its majesty, its narrow alleys and gracious crescents, and its dogged, long-suffering population who could see a city burned down yet have the will and optimism to rebuild it so that thirty years later it was more vigorous than before, that he had found peace of a kind, had made a new life for himself, had come to terms with his sins and infirmities.

Or thought he had! He sank down on a fallen tree beside the Thames, the fields around him occupied only by incurious cows, and rested his head in his hands.

He had been impervious to the invitation he had seen in the eyes of many young women, society beauties and the daughters of churchmen alike. Marriage was out of the question and he had schooled himself to accept the situation without bitterness, thankful that he had work that fascinated him, a daughter he adored, and a faith that sustained him.

Now, suddenly, all was changed. Emotions that he had thought dead for ever were stirred into life, and by whom? As unlikely a subject as one could imagine – a child, no more, with no

142

knowledge or understanding of what he suffered at the sight or nearness of her. A child so fearful of men, so unawakened, that he had seen her turn pale at the most innocent of touches, so frightened of childbearing that her senses swam at the thought. Though, inexplicably, his own blood had raced at the purity of her profile and her childlike mouth, nothing would have induced him to propose marriage had it not been for her own need for protection.

So he told himself, bolstering the arguments he had used against Boyer the previous night.

Of all men to arrive out of the blue, just when it seemed that he and Charlotte were establishing a form of marriage that, if unusual, was at least tenable! Boyer, by virtue of their close confinement, knew him more intimately than any man, and he alone saw through the façade which Gabriel presented to the rest of the world to the sin and pride that lay underneath. Like a surgeon, he cut through the skin and subcutaneous tissue to reveal the underlying rottenness.

Etienne Boyer was undoubtedly a most unlikeable man, but he had the virtue of single-mindedness. There were no halfway measures with him. He followed his own particular star, seeing his duty clearly and sacrificing everything to carry it out. Was it any wonder that he despised as selfish and lily-livered the efforts of a man such as Gabriel Fabian, whose qualities of leadership had been demonstrated over and over, when he saw that man devoting himself to laying up treasure on earth?

'All here,' he had said the previous night as he looked about him, 'is to the glory not of God but of Gabriel Fabian.'

Now, thinking of these words just as he had thought of them all through the night, Gabriel knew that there was just sufficient truth in them to make them unforgettable.

The three days that Etienne Boyer had been with them had seemed like an eternity to Charlotte. His uncomfortable presence seemed to invade every corner of the house, every corner of their lives, and still there was no word of his departure. It will all be different once he has gone, she told herself. When he goes, I shall be able to talk to Gabriel again.

She longed for that time. It seemed now as if Gabriel were a stranger, unhappy and morose. Not since some of the worst days of his convalescence had she seemed so remote from him.

143

They had expected Boyer for the main midday meal on that fourth day, but he had not come. If Charlotte had expected any *rapprochement* with Gabriel on account of his absence, she was disappointed. The main talk was of a cottage in Richmond, visited by Madame Colbert the day before.

'I could not think of taking it,' she said. 'It was dark and damp and far too near the river. My friends tell me it has been flooded many times over –'

'Then clearly it is unsuitable and you must not think of taking it.'

Gabriel spoke perfunctorily, his mind on other things, but Tantine was not content to leave the matter there and continued to enlarge upon the meanness of the accommodation offered, the lack of light, the danger of flood. Charlotte, with a sinking of the heart, saw suddenly that this litany of objections was something that was likely to be repeated many times over before Madame Colbert was suited.

'As I have said from the beginning, the decision must be yours.' Gabriel spoke tightly as if holding his irritation in check, and making his excuses he rose from the table. 'I must go. We have a complicated pattern to set up this afternoon.'

'May I see?' Charlotte had, on her first day, gone up to see the looms and had been fascinated by the complicated arrangement of treadles and heddles with their loops for lifting the warp threads. Something of an appreciation of the magic of silk had been born in her and she longed to see how, by translating a design into perforations in cards, a composition of beauty could result.

'Not this time.' He made an effort to soften his brusqueness with a smile, but it was a poor attempt and Charlotte's disappointment was in no way ameliorated by the look of triumphant amusement on Madame Colbert's face.

'Elise and I are taking the air in Hoxton Fields this afternoon – are we not, my little treasure? Unless, of course, you would prefer some other arrangement, madame? Naturally I defer to your wishes – it is only that the little one has complained that she sees so little of me these days.'

'I wish you a pleasant walk,' Charlotte said.

What should she do with her time? She could write letters, of course; but somehow the prospect did not please her and instead she sat in the parlour above the street, stitching a footstool cover,

144

telling herself that she would, undoubtedly, become accustomed to her new life before too long and that all would be different when Gabriel, she and Elise had the house to themselves. She had been there only a short time when Etienne Boyer returned.

She had angled her chair to catch the best of the light, for the panelled room was shadowed even on the brightest day. She heard the footsteps with a sinking of the heart, knowing they could belong to none other than Boyer, but she looked up with a smile as he came in.

'So you are come at last,' she said, doing her best to sound normally friendly. 'We were afraid you might have been set upon by footpads. I hear they are quite a danger in London.'

'I have nothing any footpad would wish to steal,' he said. 'My treasure is not upon earth, madame, where moth and rust doth corrupt.'

As if to underline his unconcern with mortal things, he walked past her and took the most uncomfortable seat in the room, a hard chair with a straight wooden back. Outside could be heard all the usual street noises and overhead the looms kept up their incessant vibration, but in the room there was an oppressive silence which lengthened uncomfortably. Etienne Boyer did not believe in light conversation.

'I trust your business here progresses well,' Charlotte said at last. He had come to raise money from friends and supporters for the propagation of his work in the Cévennes, she had gathered over the past few days. It had seemed not to occur to him that had other Huguenots adhered strictly to his own unworldly policy, he would have precious few sources from which to obtain such funds.

'It was not my errand that delayed me,' he said, leaning forward with his hands on his knees and shooting out his long jaw towards her. 'I was caught up in a hanging.'

Charlotte shuddered.

'How hateful,' she said. She supposed hangings were necessary; certainly many far more learned than she thought so, and still more regarded them as a side-show to be enjoyed.

'Hateful? No, madame. A salutary lesson to those watching who may thereafter turn from wickedness, seeing the fate that can befall the felon. But it is not of hangings that I wish to speak to you.'

145

'Oh?' She had returned to her stitching, but at this looked up to find him regarding her intently.

'It is of your marriage I wish to speak, madame. It is a mockery. You know it and your husband knows it. I entreat you, cut yourself loose and return to your parents.'

'*What?*' In astonishment she held her hand poised over her work and stared at him, her mouth open. 'Have you taken leave of your senses, monsieur?'

'When the good Lord saw fit to afflict your husband in the way he has done – yes, madame, I alone among men know it – it was for his own purpose, a higher purpose than marriage. I tell you that Gabriel Fabian will suffer the tortures of the damned until he admits it to himself, that it is not in the arms of a woman he will find happiness but in service to the Almighty.'

The words were emerging in their usual flood, one tripping over the other, saliva flecking his lips. She looked at him with revulsion, trembling with outrage but unable to find the words to express it.

'He seemed – not unhappy,' she whispered. 'Before you came, that is. He will be happy again when you leave.'

'Never!' He flung himself out of his chair and strode the length of the room, gangling body hunched and ungainly, arms waving wildly. 'God is not mocked, madame. There is no good can come of this marriage. Again I urge you, abandon this blasphemous liaison –'

'Blasphemous? How can it be blasphemous?'

'What else, when the sole purpose of a woman's existence as ordained by God is the procreation of the species? Abandon it, I say.'

He had walked to the end of the room and back again and now stood before her like some avenging angel, stabbing a forefinger in her direction.

'Your marriage is a sin, madame, an abomination before the Lord, a crime against God and against nature –'

'Oh, please!' Trembling, she rose, sending silks and canvas and needle cascading to the floor. She clasped her hands together as if in supplication. There was such power in him, such force, that she was almost beginning to believe that he had right on his side. 'How can I leave my husband, monsieur? How can you ask it? We exchanged vows before God –'

'He is no husband. Your marriage is an evil from which only

146

evil can spring. Gabriel Fabian is needed for God's work, even though he closes his ears to the call.'

Sudden realisation of his purpose brought her up sharply. Her arms fell to her sides and she stared at him.

'You want him to go back.' Her voice had strengthened, hardened. 'You want him to go back to France! Then monsieur, you must surely have taken leave of your senses. He would risk certain death.'

'As I do, daily.'

'That is your choice, monsieur. Do you imagine he would leave Elise, even if he would abandon all else?'

'There are those who would care for the child, as you must know. Madame Colbert would be willing.'

'Oh, indeed she would! But does the love of a father for his child mean nothing to you?'

He opened his lips to answer, but the words died stillborn for at that moment they heard the sound of Gabriel descending from the workshop and, at the same time, the arrival of Elise and Madame Colbert below.

'Papa, Papa –'

'Come, my heart's darling, tell me where you have been and what you have seen.'

Gabriel's voice sounded more carefree than it had been for some days, as if an afternoon devoted to the practise of his craft had been a soothing experience. Had Charlotte needed an illustration of his feeling for his daughter, she could hardly have arranged it more neatly.

'You have no chance of success, monsieur,' she said. 'He might part with me, but never with Elise.'

Shoulders hunched, fists clenched, Boyer stood before her, breathing hard as if he had run a race.

'The good Lord will have the last word, madame. God is not mocked.'

He went again to seat himself in the hard chair and after a moment Charlotte bent to pick up her silks and canvas so that when Gabriel came into the room with Elise in his arms there was every appearance of serenity. But although the room was quiet, the echoes of that angry voice still clamoured for attention, harsh and ugly and so insistent that it seemed they would reverberate for ever.

8

Boyer left the following day, but if Charlotte believed his depar-ture would mark a new beginning in her married life, she was to find herself mistaken. Gabriel was polite and pleasant, as if to a stranger, but the feeling of friendship she had discerned during the first days after their marriage had gone as if it had never been.

I might just as well have come as a governess after all, she thought; then tried to rally her spirits by reminding herself of all the advantages she now enjoyed. She had the status of marriage without its repugnant duties; she was free of her mother's harass-ment; Gabriel was generous, grudging her none of the inviting gewgaws offered for sale and urging lengths of silk upon her to be made into gowns. No – she had little cause for complaint, she told herself. He had married her out of pity in order to protect her from a less suitable match, and it ill became her to pine for his constant approval and attention.

Life settled into a routine; lessons with Elise in the morning, shopping or paying calls after the main meal of the day which was normally eaten at two o'clock. There was no shortage of callers during those early days, for there was a great deal of interest shown by the ladies of the church in the fortunate young woman who had at last been chosen as Gabriel Fabian's bride.

Madame Colbert continued to find fault with every dwelling offered for her consideration and stubbornly stayed on, clearly delighting in the fact that Charlotte was too timid to impress her own personality upon the household while she ruled in the kitchen.

This delight was shared by Berthe, the cook, who seemed some kind of alter ego to Madame Colbert. At first, Charlotte had been duped into believing that Berthe looked on her kindly, but it took only a short time for her to realise that, although smiling and obsequious to her face, the instant she left the kitchen – and often sometimes before she had done so – covert smiles would pass between the two of them at her naïveté.

The bond between them was understandable. They had escaped from France in the same boat, together with Berthe's sister Marthe, the sisters having the good fortune to find work as cooks within a few streets of each other. Marthe was a constant visitor. Both sisters, in Charlotte's view, were equally detestable, with their identical boot-button eyes and wiry hair and the same falsely ingratiating manner, but she hid her feelings, for Berthe was far too well entrenched for her to do anything else. Once Madame Colbert had taken herself off, things would be different, she assured herself.

However, she did venture a protest at Madame Colbert's treatment of the three young apprentices – a protest that elicited nothing but a snort of derision.

'Idle, good-for-nothing ruffians,' Tantine grumbled. 'Tracking in with their muddy boots, wolfing their food – I've not seen one yet that's been worth his keep. As for that Pierre –'

The two little maids who worked in the kitchen covered their mouths and giggled, and Joseph, who combined the job of spit-boy with that of general handyman and porter, contorted his face to hide a grin. Pierre Jourdaine, the youngest of the apprentices, was a comic, a born mimic, and though Madame Colbert's opinion of him was low, it would have been lower still had she known of his wicked parody of her manner and voice.

Even so, she detested Pierre more than the other apprentices, for all that he was the one French boy among the three. He was the only one that Gabriel had accepted without charge, for he had come across Madame Jourdaine in the course of his charity work with La Soupe and had been touched by the gallantry she had shown in her struggle to make a new life for herself and her children without the support of a husband. In his kindness, Gabriel often gave Pierre the added chance of earning a few shillings a week by carrying out tasks beyond those which would normally be expected of him. Such a contribution, in addition to the three good meals which he ate each day in Freedom Street, meant all the world to Madame Jourdaine.

Never was a boy more undeserving, in Madame Colbert's opinion. Pierre talked and laughed and pulled faces that made the servants giggle, and in short, behaved as if he had every right to be in the silk-weaver's house instead of being dependent on charity.

149

'You should send him packing, monsieur,' she said to Gabriel. 'The wretch causes nothing but trouble.'

'Is he good at his work?' Charlotte asked him when Madame Colbert had left them, and Gabriel laughed.

'He's no better and no worse than many. Oh, he's no saint, I grant you, but he's a likeable little rogue and will, perhaps, be as competent as any in the end.'

'I like him,' Elise stated firmly. 'He makes me laugh.'

'Then the matter is settled.' Gabriel smiled at her. 'There is no question of getting rid of Pierre if he makes Elise laugh! Seriously –' He turned to Charlotte. 'I could never bring myself to turn him off except for some overwhelmingly good reason, for his mother and the younger children are dependent on him. It would be tantamount to condemning them to starvation, and that I should not wish to have on my conscience.'

He was the best of men, Charlotte thought. She should be so grateful that he had married her. It was little less than sinful of her to long for more.

Among the lad Joseph's many duties was that of guide. It was he who was always assigned to accompany Charlotte and Elise when they went shopping, for he knew every inch of London's streets, having been born and bred in the liberty of Southwark. His, she often thought, was the face of a typical Londoner; thin, astute and foxy, but full of humour.

It was on a day in November that he accompanied them to a mercer's establishment on London Bridge where Charlotte was hoping to buy trimming for a new gown. She was disappointed, however, when she saw how little there was on display, and was only too ready to listen to Joseph's assurances that she would find everything she wanted, and more, if only she would go to Covent Garden.

'Ain't you never been there, madame?' he asked her incredulously. 'Why, 'tis the best place of all, is the Garden, with shops in plenty, and tumblers and jugglers besides.'

'Oh, *please* let us go!' Elise was dancing with excitement. 'I want to see the jugglers! Please, please Maman!'

'Is it far?' Charlotte asked, dependent upon him for advice for her knowledge of London was still poor.

'Bless you no, madame. A coach will get us there in no time. Oh, a grand place, is the Garden!'

Charlotte was already a little dubious about the idea before they reached the Strand for she had not previously realised how dark the afternoon was becoming. There was a heavy mist from the river drifting over the rooftops – but the look of disappointment on Elise's face when she suggested abandoning the idea persuaded her to go on.

Long before they reached Covent Garden she knew she had been guilty of gross misjudgment, for they did not, as Joseph had promised, get there in no time. As she should have foreseen, they became involved in a press of wheeled traffic in the Strand and were delayed a full thirty minutes as the wheels of their coach locked with another, and the drivers of each indulged in a brawl which in the end threatened to embroil half the street. Elise was frightened out of her life and burst into sobs, while Charlotte was herself not far from tears – though her tears were caused more by anger at her own stupidity in allowing this situation than by fear.

Meanwhile the mist had thickened and had become a regular fog. Once the wheel was successfully freed, she told the coachman to forget Covent Garden and to turn around to take them to Spitalfields.

His language, on receiving this request, even made Joseph blush, but was perhaps understandable since it proved almost impossible to turn. By the time they had managed to do so, the fog had become so dense that the congestion was even more frightening. Horses loomed up close beside them and they were dreadfully shaken by a cart running into them at the rear, and all the time there were passers-by peering in at them and banging on the side of the cab.

'Make them go away, make them go away,' Elise screamed, terrified out of her life.

'They don't mean no harm,' Joseph assured her. 'Look, they're a-smilin' at yer.'

It was true. They appeared perfectly good-humoured as if the fog created a kind of carnival spirit in them, but Charlotte was scarcely less frightened than Elise to see these strange faces leering at them, gap-toothed and straggle-haired.

The lanterns that were lit at intervals along the Strand did nothing to dispel the gloom. Their light was so diffuse that they looked pale and ghostly; nor could the link-boys who had emerged early from their doorways and holes in the ground to light

151

travellers home do more than illumine a step at a time. The cab's progress was no more than a slow walking pace, and Charlotte had ample time to imagine the anxiety that Gabriel would be feeling and to contemplate the reception that would surely be hers.

Her thoughts brought her little comfort. It was true that she depended on Joseph for advice, but the ultimate decision to make this ill-fated journey had been hers and hers alone.

By the time they turned into Freedom Street, she calculated that they had been four hours from home. The door beneath the wooden spool stood open and light from inside the house spilled out on to the cobbles. Gabriel, lantern in hand, stood at the foot of the steps. The fog was not quite so dense here and she could see that he had neither hat nor cloak, and was clearly in a state of agitation. Elise leapt from the cab almost directly into his arms, pouring out all the horrors that had beset them so that they sounded ten times more frightening than the reality had been.

Gabriel cradled her head against his shoulder and soothed her with soft words.

'Oh Gabriel,' Charlotte said as she climbed down to the road. 'I am so sorry – so very sorry.'

His face was stony as he looked at her, then at Joseph who was doing his best to slink away in the shadows.

'Go straight to the kitchen, Joseph,' Gabriel said harshly. 'There is much I have to say to you. Come, Charlotte. Let us go inside out of this accursed cold.'

'Gabriel –' she began again.

'Explanations can wait.'

He paid off the cab as she preceded him inside and up the stairs, as nervous and tongue-tied as a schoolgirl, and though he spoke to her with restraint, saving the worst of his fury for Joseph, her nervousness remained long after she and Elise had drunk the soup and the hot possets that Madame Colbert provided for them, her mouth drawn down in stern disapproval.

Elise was borne off to bed, and Charlotte looked at Gabriel fearfully, waiting for the storm to break. His anger might be controlled, but she could feel it in the atmosphere, as corrosive as the fog itself.

'Gabriel,' she said, when at last she could bear the silence no longer. 'Believe me, I had no idea how far we had to drive or how bad the fog would be. I would not have put you through such anxiety for the world.'

'Evil things happen in a fog,' he said. 'Thieves and footpads regard it as licence to do their worst, and no one is safe. Horses bolt, coaches shed their wheels and passengers and passers-by get caught up in all manner of brawls.' Swiftly he rose from his chair and went to fill his glass, and as he raised it to his lips she saw that his hand trembled. 'Anxiety is not strong enough a word,' he said harshly. 'I went through hell, not knowing where you had gone.'

'I swear I shall never put Elise at such risk again, not wittingly.'

'Nor yourself, I hope.'

'It was not pleasant,' she admitted. 'People peered in at us so inquisitively! But Joseph said they meant no ill, and I think he was right. Besides, I can take care of myself.'

He slammed his glass down and strode over to her, pulling her from her chair and holding her wrist with a grip like iron.

'You little fool,' he said, his eyes glittering. 'It was you I worried about, quite as much as Elise. More! Look at yourself.' He propelled her towards a long, gilt-framed mirror that hung on the wall, and holding her shoulders thrust her towards it. Her wavery reflection looked back at her, his face dark and taut with anger behind.

'Look hard,' he said again. 'What do you see? A young girl on the verge of life – lovely, unblemished, vulnerable, at the mercy of anyone. *Anyone!*' Loosening his grip, he turned from her. 'Except from her husband, of course,' he said bitterly. 'From him she need fear nothing.'

The hurt and bitterness in his voice shocked her into behaving in a way that was purely instinctive. In one movement she bridged the gap that had yawned between them over the past weeks and, as she might have comforted a child, she turned and put her arms around him.

'Oh Gabriel – please!' His pain seemed to be hers, even though she could only dimly understand the cause of it. 'Please don't torture yourself so.'

Not responding to her embrace, he stood with his eyes closed as if he could not bear the anguish of looking at her. His arms hung by his sides, his whole body sagged.

'I have done you so much wrong,' he said. 'I knew it from the first, of course. I said as much before, but my conscience was lulled. It took Etienne Boyer to waken it –'

Charlotte stamped her foot with a force so uncharacteristic of her that Gabriel's eyes flew open in surprise.

'Damn him!' she said. 'He knows nothing and understands nothing.'

'He knows our marriage is like no other.'

'But we could have been happy, Gabriel. We *were* happy until he came and made you see things differently, made everything look sinful and ugly. Oh, forget him and all that he said.'

'He spoke to you?' His expression tightened with anger as she nodded. 'He had no right.'

'He told me to leave you, forget my vows. He wants you to go back to France like a sacrificial lamb. I said that you would never leave Elise, but he swept that aside. There were others to care for her, he said. Why should the love of a father matter?'

'He says the Church in the Désert needs me. The people need me, he said; and I need them, for only by doing God's will can I rid myself of the sin of pride which separates me from him.'

'*He* talks of pride!' Charlotte took a step away from him and put her hands on her hips. 'Ha! What gives him the right to speak as if he and he alone is privy to God's will? You have responsibilities here – a daughter, men who depend on you for their livelihood, a wife –'

A small and almost unwilling smile appeared at the corner of Gabriel's mouth.

'Madame, you are a fearsome sight when you are angry!'

'How dare you mock me!' Tears of anger stood in her eyes. 'What should we do without you? Should I do as he said and go back to my parents?'

'Do you want to?'

The question, asked in a quiet, unemphatic voice, caught her off balance, and for a moment she stared at him, lips apart, the fight seeping out of her.

'No,' she said, and she pressed a hand to her mouth as a sob welled up in her throat. The tears spilled over and ran down her cheeks. 'I want to stay here and be a good wife to you. I want us to be friends as we were in the beginning.'

He held out his arms to her and she went to him, sobbing against his shoulder. He stroked her hair and pressed his lips to it and murmured soothing endearments, and when at last she had composed herself a little she looked up at him imploringly.

'You won't send me away, will you?'

Gabriel shook his head.

'No,' he said. 'I won't send you away.'

'No matter what Etienne Boyer says?'

'No matter what he says.'

She smiled at him then, still pink-nosed and pink-eyed.

'I knew you loved Elise far too much to think of risking your life.'

For a moment he looked at her in silence, his expression unreadable.

'Does it not occur to you, my dear Charlotte, that I love you too?' His arms tightened around her and his voice roughened. 'I love you so much that there are times –' He faltered, unable to continue. 'Never mind,' he said at last, cradling her head against his shoulder just as he had cradled Elise not so long before. 'I cannot expect that you should understand.'

'So long as we are friends,' she said. She did not see the bitter expression on his face as he repeated the word.

'Friends,' he said; then once more, with a different, more hopeful note in his voice. 'Friends.'

And as she stayed in his embrace, holding him close, she had no awareness of the fact that it was now his turn to weep.

The fog was late lifting the following morning, but when it finally disappeared it revealed a day that, though hazy, was bright and as warm as spring. Gabriel came into the parlour where Charlotte and Elise were sitting over their books and decreed that the entire day should be a holiday.

'Look, the sun is shining,' he said. 'Who would have believed it possible after the horrors of yesterday? Heaven alone knows when it will appear again, so forget your lessons and come with me on the river.'

He was at his most eager and charming, all the gloom of the past weeks apparently forgotten, and neither Elise nor Charlotte needed to be persuaded. Everything amused them, from the shouts of 'Rumbelow' of the watermen who touted for their custom, lining the slippery stairs that led to the river, to the impudent backchat of the fruit vendors, and the small black dog that raced alongside them at Barn Elms, barking furiously as if

155

they threatened his territory and he was determined to defend it.

It was there that they turned for home since the sun appeared to recollect that this was November and not April and retired accordingly behind gathering clouds. It appeared again briefly just as they approached Westminster and as Charlotte looked at the rooftops of London, speared by the spires of many churches, and saw the great houses with their gardens bordering the river, she understood Gabriel's pride in their adopted city. Seen from the river, all the eyesores for the moment hidden away, it had a proud elegance. There was energy, too – a strong and steady heartbeat, a feeling that this was the centre of the world, and she felt exhilarated at being a part of it.

Seeing that Gabriel's eyes were on her, she smiled at him.

'I am the most fortunate of women,' she said, and in response he covered her hand with his.

'May you never find cause to change that opinion.'

'I never will.'

He looked at her in silence for a moment and there was a hint of sadness in his smile.

'I have always believed,' he said, 'that there are two words that promise the impossible. One of those words is "never".'

'And the other?'

He took a moment to reply, though his eyes never left her face.

'The other is "always",' he said at last.

The barrier that Etienne Boyer had erected between them was down, and though Gabriel still occupied his own room, there was a warmth and comradeship, a coming and going between them that dispelled all the unpleasant recollections of that unhappy time.

It was during this period that Charlotte began to perceive, albeit dimly and without full understanding, the importance of the dimension that was missing from her marriage. Her longing for closeness was as yet no more than that of a child who climbs upon her father's knee seeking comfort, yet she could see now how a shared passion might diminish difficulties and misunderstandings. She wasted little time in thinking of such matters, however. There were so many other pleasurable things to occupy her; friends to be entertained, places to see. At last, and much to Elise's joy, they went to the Tower to see the wild beasts, and in Hyde Park they took their place in the parade around the balustraded ring in company with the rich and the fashionable.

Her confidence was growing, despite the continued presence of Madame Colbert, who found fault with every house that was offered to her. It had become a joke now – something to laugh at with Gabriel, who gave it as his opinion that only St James's Palace was likely to attain her standards. And what joy it was to join in this conspiracy of laughter! She blossomed in the new atmosphere of contentment, finding that where once she had been overawed in the company of Gabriel's friends, unable to take part in the conversation, now – though ever mindful of the fact that she was a woman and hardly qualified, therefore, to express opinions on business matters – she felt able to hold her own where a view was sought on art or music or the theatre. Such subjects were considered of great importance by the French émigrés who constituted their circle of friends, and there were societies in Spitalfields for enthusiasts in all the arts.

She no longer felt self-conscious and unwanted when she went upstairs to the weaving loft which drew her like a magnet, despite the fearful noise of the looms and the somewhat intimidating presence of Simon le Bec, a skilled journeyman and Gabriel's right-hand man.

He was a large man of enormous girth, loud of voice and volatile by nature, and Charlotte – just as much as the apprentices – was in awe of him at first and equally anxious not to incur his wrath. However, she soon realised the truth of Gabriel's words when he said that the man was a true artist, dedicated to his craft and highly skilled in its practice, and the two warmed towards each other for he saw that she shared his enthusiasm.

She still thought of it as some kind of magic, the way that a material of such beauty could result merely by opening the warp and wefting with the shuttles in a certain order, but that did not prevent an eagerness to know the mechanics of it. Monture, necking cords, leashes and simples – he named each part of the loom and described its function, and though she soon learned that the patterned silk that resulted was the end product of a highly ordered process, the magic remained.

'How clever the pattern-makers must be,' she said to him one day, fascinated as always by the way a drawing could be translated into the perforations which dictated the movements of the shuttles.

Le Bec shrugged.

'It is a skill that can be learned. I learned it myself and practise it still. It is designing that comes from within and cannot be taught – or at least, only in part.'

Charlotte, studying a sheet of paper on which was a lattice of leaves and flowers, frowned thoughtfully.

'The drawings in themselves are simple –'

Le Bec was polite enough not to roar at her in the way he would have done at the apprentices had they made such a remark, but she could tell by his expression that she had said something foolish.

'Further study will show, madame,' he growled, 'that the spaces are as important as the pattern. They do not occur by accident. And any designer of experience must avoid the appearance of stripes up or down or across by directing the eye elsewhere. Such things cannot be left to chance. Then there are mathematical considerations. No matter how many times the pattern is repeated, it must be wholly contained in the design, otherwise there is waste when the silk is joined.'

'I see.' Charlotte was suitably humble before the weight of his experience.

'If it appears simple it is because there is an art which conceals art.'

'I understand, monsieur. I can see now that it is not simple at all.'

The young apprentice, Pierre Jourdaine, who chanced to be sweeping nearby during this exchange, caught her eye as le Bec moved to straighten a thread, and he pulled a face that caricatured only too accurately the awe that the journeyman inspired. Charlotte bit her lip to keep from smiling. The boy was a scamp, there was no doubt about that, but even so he surely could not deserve all the abuse that Madame Colbert heaped upon him. Scarcely a day passed without complaints from her regarding his behaviour. He was presumptuous, she said. She did not trust him. He did not know his place. He distracted the maids.

Charlotte, an infrequent but observant witness, saw that it was not the maids' reaction to Pierre that caused Madame Colbert's anger but the fact that he was a favourite with Elise. The boy was full of the tricks and jokes beloved of a six-year-old child, and this was something that pleased Tantine not at all. *La petite héritière*, the little girl destined for a duke, was too far above an apprentice to be treated so.

Christmas came and went, and now spring was upon them with the trees in parks and gardens bursting into leaf and the caged birds making their appearance at the doors of houses in Spitalfields, adding their trilling to the other, less tuneful street sounds. Often, now that the better weather was upon them, they walked in the fields that lay so close to London's heart, or took a boat on the river.

Gabriel was delegating more and more of the work at Freedom Street to Simon le Bec, for there was much else to occupy his time. As more and more refugee weavers flocked to Spitalfields, outwork became more common so that while the manufacture of expensive flowered silk continued in the loft at the top of the house, he employed others in their own homes to make lustrings and alamodes, satin dimitys and tabby and the cheap half-silk that was popular with the working classes. He supplied the mercers on Ludgate Hill and was even beginning to export to America.

In the midst of all this activity he was ever mindful that summer was approaching. He now had two hostages to fortune and was determined that Charlotte and Elise would spend the warmer weather well away from London. He set in train arrangements to lease Whiteacres once more.

Accordingly, on a day which ironically was cool and wet, he accompanied them on the coach to Canterbury. Madame Colbert was left behind, much to her annoyance, clearly unimpressed by Gabriel's remark that she would now be able to devote her entire time to finding alternative accommodation. It would take more than the summer to settle the matter, Charlotte thought. The joke was wearing thin, and she was heartily glad to leave the woman in London.

She was even more glad to see her parents again after such a long absence. They, too, were overjoyed at the reunion and exclaimed at how well she was looking, how improved was Monsieur Fabian's physical state since last they had seen him, how greatly Elise had grown and how pleased they were that the family had come to Kent.

'It can do you nothing but good to avoid London's air at this time of the year,' Dr Bonnet said. 'It will set you up for the winter.'

'If we do not die of the cold first,' Charlotte said. 'Whiteacres is not at all weather-proof.'

'You should buy the house, monsieur,' Madame Bonnet stated in her usual forthright way. 'That would be my advice. Mr White would sell, I have no doubt, for he has no interest in the place, then you could refurbish it as you wish. No doubt it would be beneficial for all of you to enjoy the country air regularly.'

She spoke generally, but her eyes were on Charlotte's waistline. It was clear that she was consumed with curiosity. Surely, one could see her thinking, a child must be on the way by this time. If not, why not?

'I might well buy the place if the price is not too high,' Gabriel said.

'Capital, capital!' The doctor beamed upon his son-in-law. 'Nothing would please us more than to think of our daughter coming here regularly – not to mention our future grandchildren, of course. My wife longs for them! Is that not so, my dear?'

'Such matters are in God's hands,' Madame Bonnet said stiffly, but there was a tremulous look about her mouth that revealed her longing, and Charlotte felt unexpectedly sad that her mother's hopes were bound to come to nothing. For herself, she had no maternal longings that were not fully satisfied by Elise, for whom she had a genuine affection. Undoubtedly she was a demanding child, accustomed to getting her own way, but Charlotte did her best to temper Gabriel's more blatant acts of over-indulgence. At bottom she was a merry, good-humoured child and undoubtedly of high intelligence.

With typical perversity the weather stayed wet all the time that Gabriel was in Kent and it was not until the day he returned to London that the rain stopped. There followed a succession of sun-filled weeks during which Charlotte and Elise grew daily more indolent and undisciplined, roaming barefoot in the fields to add to the collection of wild flowers that Elise was intent on compiling, gorging themselves on the fruit that grew in the garden, forgetting lessons and resenting the times they were forced to dress up to pay or receive calls. Charlotte was aware of how greatly her mother disapproved of such behaviour, but she paid no heed. A bond was being forged between herself and Elise at this time and some innate wisdom assured her that it was something of far more value than lessons or propriety.

The garden, like everything inside the house, had been sadly neglected, and while Mr White sent a man to scythe the grass so that the air was full of the scent of new-mown hay, roses bloomed in riotous profusion and a border of lavender had grown to an excessive size, encroaching on numerous other smaller plants that struggled for life in its shadow.

Madame Bonnet, when visiting, shook her head over it and was full of instructions for cutting back this and digging out that, but Elise and Charlotte decided privately that they liked it wild; besides, time enough to begin labour, Charlotte felt, if the house ever came into their ownership. Meanwhile, many were the happy hours of idleness she spent lying in the shade lost in one or other of the books she found in the house.

One in particular interested her more than the others, for it was an account of the way silk had been made in ancient China. She was diverted to find that the draw-loom had scarcely changed at all in the intervening years, and for some reason that she could not quite fathom, she found it both exciting and satisfying that such a vast number of years should be bound together in this way despite the differences in time and cultures.

They had been there some weeks when Marianne came to stay with her young son. Already she was expecting her second child – though by the time of its birth, she told Charlotte, she would be far away from Canterbury. Her husband had inherited a farm in Devon and sooner than she cared to think, they would be taking possession of it.

'Devon!' Charlotte echoed despairingly. 'So far away! Shall we ever meet again, Marianne?'

'Of course we shall! I shall come to London and you must show me the sights.'

'I should love that above all things.'

Charlotte spoke warmly, but privately she doubted that such a visit would take place. Marianne had changed in some indefinable way. Where once they had conversed without effort, now there was need sometimes to search for a topic to bridge an awkward pause, and little was said of any real importance. To be honest, Charlotte found much of Marianne's conversation trivial and repetitive, concerned only with her home and her child. If *this* is what motherhood does to a woman, she found herself thinking, then I thank heaven it is beyond my reach. Yet little baby John was an appealing child, and she loved to feel his small hand in hers.

'I hope that you will soon have a baby of your own, Charlotte,' Marianne said as they sat together on her last night.

Charlotte smiled and said nothing.

'It is strange how easy it is for some and how difficult for others. I swear that Robert has to do no more than unbuckle his breeches! Why, you are blushing! Fie Charlotte, you are not shocked, are you? You, a married woman of close on a year!' She sighed heavily. 'I could wish it different, I can tell you. Much as I want babies, I could wish to enjoy a little bed-sport without becoming *enceinte*.'

'Just look at that sky,' Charlotte said, rising deliberately, without haste, from her chair. 'Did you ever see such a colour? It will be another fine day tomorrow, I'm sure.'

'Perhaps my Robert and your Gabriel should exchange intelligence on the matter, for both, it seems to me, could do with the skill of the other.'

Charlotte yawned, patting her mouth.

'Dear me – forgive me, Marianne. I am quite unconscionably tired this evening. The heat drains one of energy, don't you agree? If you have no great objection, I shall retire early.'

It was, she thought, typical of Marianne to be so – so *blatant*. As if she, Charlotte, cared to know of her secret life! Nothing could interest her less or be of so little concern.

Yet it had to be admitted that the conversation, if such it could be called, had unsettled her, revealing as it did that there was a world she would never know, strange urges that she would never experience.

How strong those urges must be, she thought – irresistible even to a woman who had one small child and carried another. Despite her fatigue – and she had not exaggerated it by much – she lay sleepless for many hours that night, inexplicably forlorn, dimly aware at last of Gabriel's loss.

A week after Marianne's departure the weather broke. All day it had been dull and sultry and during the afternoon the first flash of lightning split the sky, followed by a thunder clap so loud that Elise, engaged in making a representation of Freedom Street at Charlotte's suggestion, dropped her paint brush in terror, running to her and burying her head in her lap.

Charlotte, who had been in a strange mood since Marianne's departure, soothed her, feeling no fear herself but rather a wild exultation as the rain began, slashing against the windows,

162

tearing blossoms from the bushes, the thunder and lightning almost continuous. There was a strange kind of release in it, she found. Her instinct was to run outside and stand with arms outstretched in the centre of the grass, her face lifted to the sky while the tempest roared about her, purging and cleansing her.

She did not, of course. She stayed with Elise and stroked her hair – that lovely, silken, pale gold hair – looking over her head to the deluge that continued unabated outside the windows.

The following day was fresher but showery. Elise returned to her painting and Charlotte, without enthusiasm, took up some mending, but all the time she stitched she was aware that something of significance was tugging at her elbow, as if some forgotten matter was demanding her attention.

Restlessly she put aside her sewing and wandered over to the table where Elise was working, tongue held in the corner of her mouth, her face fierce with effort and concentration. She had drawn a long row of houses and before them a frieze of people, stiff and wooden with legs at odd angles.

'That one is our house,' she said, setting to work on adding the wooden spool over the door.

'Do you miss it?'

'Well –' She considered the matter, dripping brush held in the air for a moment, head on one side. 'Whiteacres is prettier, but Freedom Street is where we belong, isn't it? It isn't the same here without Papa.'

'He will be here next week.'

'I wish he would not leave us again so soon!'

'I miss him too.'

Charlotte must have spoken with more feeling than she realised, for Elise shook her head sadly.

'Poor Maman,' she said with compassion. 'You should paint, like me. You would not think of your troubles then.'

Charlotte stared at her for a moment, then laughed. Out of the mouths of babes, she thought. She had painted nothing of significance for months, putting it aside as if such occupations were no more than time-wasting, childish exercises that had no place in her life now; yet once Elise had mentioned the matter she realised that this was what had been nagging at her consciousness. She, too, wanted desperately to create something – but what? Now that she looked back at the flower paintings she had once indulged in with such enthusiasm it seemed to her that there was

163

an aridity about them. They had been too stiff and formal to be hailed as good reproductions, yet not stylised enough to be regarded as design.

She picked up a large sheet of paper from the table.

'Finish your picture, Elise,' she said. 'I shall embark on my own experiment.'

All day long she worked. She could not bear to leave it, and Elise was forced to look to Molly, Nan's younger sister who had come to help her, to entertain and keep her company when she wandered abroad looking for her flowers.

Inspired, perhaps, by the days she had spent outside, Charlotte designed a wreath of roses, within its circle a spray of leaves and pendant blossoms, but though this was the final result it was not achieved without many sketches being tried and discarded until the mass of crumpled paper was like a sea washing around her ankles and she felt guilty at the waste. Paper was expensive and not to be treated lightly, but still she persevered.

Thanks to the instruction she had received from Simon le Bec and from Gabriel – and also, in a small measure, from the book she had discovered in Mr White's collection – she understood now what woven silk demanded in a design, and what was possible. When she had at last drawn something that seemed both suitable and decorative, she took up a sheet of paper and divided it into squares then, reduced in size, she reproduced the design, repeating it five times over in the first row of squares, three in the row beneath it, then five again until the whole page was covered.

For a long time she stared at it, then began again. Repeated so frequently too much of the base material was covered, for she remembered le Bec's maxim, that the spaces were of equal importance to the design. This time the design was a little more sparse and she saw when it was finished that this was indeed an improvement. She liked the colours particularly. The base colour was cream, the design in yellow, green and gold.

She realised when it was finished that she had enjoyed nothing so much since the working of the coverlet that now adorned her bed, and she could not imagine why she had not taken seriously to trying her hand at the task long before. She did not count her first sketchy attempt, carried out at Gabriel's suggestion long before when she had no knowledge of silk manufacture. Even now she was aware how superficial her understanding of it was, but despite that she knew without doubt that her design had merit. Even if Gabriel, looking at it with his professional's eye, saw flaws in it, she had no doubt that it would be possible to adapt and alter it to meet his requirements.

The restlessness of the previous day had left her completely, she found to her relief, and she was full of excitement, longing for Gabriel's arrival so that she could show him the fruits of her labours.

He looked pale and tired when he arrived, and he assured her that she and Elise had been fortunate to have passed the previous weeks in the country since the heat of London had been unendurable.

'You must rest while you are here,' Charlotte said anxiously, as they sat together after dinner, for she was worried by his pallor and obvious exhaustion. 'Is the pain bad, Gabriel?'

He shook his head dismissively, as unwilling as ever to dwell on the fact that he still bore the legacy of his ill treatment.

'I shall be right as rain tomorrow. The journey was tiring but a night's sleep will restore me. Tell me, my love, how have you been occupying yourself? Entertaining Elise right royally, I know, for she hardly stopped talking of all your doings from the moment I arrived to the time she fell asleep, but apart from that – have you been happy?'

'I've missed you sorely,' she said, with perfect truth. 'But Gabriel, it hasn't all been play. I've not been idle. There is something I have to show you.'

She felt nervous now that the moment was upon her. Suppose, after all, her design was amateurish, falling short of the standard he demanded? Would he tell her, or would he find it embarrassing to do so? He looked at her quizzically while she hesitated.

'Well?' he prompted.

'You must promise me that if it is no good, you will say so. You must promise to tell the truth –'

'I always tell the truth! How mysterious you are. If *what* is no good?'

'Wait!'

She went quickly from the room, returning in a moment with the design she had laboured over for so long, and she saw the indulgent smile he gave her as she handed it to him.

'Ah! I guessed as much,' he said.

She watched his expression apprehensively, not knowing how she would be able to bear it if he dismissed it with some light, kind word. Her nervousness had created a strangely painful vacuum inside her, and only afterwards did she become aware of how her nails had dug half-circles in the palms of her hands.

His smile died, his eyes narrowed. She had all of his attention, she could see by the way his lip was caught between his teeth. He looked up from the paper in his hand and for a moment seemed to study her as if she were a stranger, his brows drawn together. He doesn't like it, she thought; the disappointment was almost too much to bear.

'This is quite excellent,' he said wonderingly at last.

'Oh Gabriel, do you really mean it?' She dropped on her knees beside him and clung to his arm, searching his face. 'Is it really good?'

'I would not have believed it!'

'Please, I beg you, do not be kind to me. I will not have you saying things just to be kind –'

'I am not just being kind! There is a professionalism about this that astonishes me. You must have drunk in every word le Bec has spoken to you! Yet there is a freshness and delicacy about it, an originality –'

'Oh Gabriel!' She was incapable of saying more, and felt near to tears. She had never heard words that sounded so like music.

'Is this the only one?'

'It's the only one I have finished, but I've made preliminary sketches –'

'Fetch them!'

She scrambled to her feet, picked up her skirts and ran from the room, returning seconds later with two more sheets of paper.

'I know the colour is not quite right in that second one. I meant it to be more russet and gold – autumnal, you see, with the circlet of leaves and the spray of blackberries giving a touch of purple. The scale is not perfect, either –'

'My dear, the very fact that you can see that for yourself is important. It's nothing that cannot be easily rectified.' He turned to the second sheet and smiled with pleasure. 'Now this is delightful – holly and ivy and Christmas roses, oh so cleverly intertwined! I had not realised you were quite so talented, my little one –'

166

'A long time ago, before we were married, you said I should try my hand at design.'

'Yes, but –' He did not finish, but looked at her with a smile that was positively sheepish.

'You did not really think I could do it!'

'I certainly imagined nothing quite like this. You are full of surprises, my Charlotte; a veritable box of delights.'

'I cannot translate it into a pattern.'

'Of course not – and who would expect it? Men serve apprenticeships for such a skill and it takes years to learn. I could do it, though – or better still, le Bec. How I wish I had had these to show the merchants from America I saw in London last week! Never mind, there will be other opportunities.'

'You mean – you really will use *my* designs?' Charlotte sat back on her heels and stared at him, eyes bright with excitement. 'You're quite sure they are good enough? Oh, I can't believe it!'

'They are more than good enough.' He reached towards her and she came closer to kneel beside him, his arm encircling her.

'It gave me such pleasure to do it.'

'I know. One can see it.' He looked at her with the expression of mingled love and sadness he sometimes wore. 'And God knows, I'm glad of it.'

'But that is not why you're being so kind –'

'Madame!' He was laughing at her. 'I am *not* being kind! I propose to snap up your designs before some other unscrupulous weaver exploits your talent. We'll be true partners, Charlotte.'

She could not conceive of a more delightful arrangement. This was a union both satisfying and productive, and the thought of its possibilities filled her with joyful anticipation.

'I can do more,' she said eagerly. 'Oh, so many more! I can see them in my mind's eye –'

'True partners,' Gabriel repeated; and with excitement they smiled into each other's eyes, knowing that, in spite of all, the future had much to offer.

Book Two

9

The flowers were delivered in the early morning, still wet with dew, baskets and baskets of them; daffodils and tulips, pale narcissi and anemones, and deep blue irises in a shade that lifted Charlotte's heart.

The task of arranging them she had jealously kept to herself. Let others prepare the fish and the meat with their elaborate sauces, the spiced ham, the iced desserts, the tarts and gâteaux. It was said by some that Madame Fabian kept the best table in London, and she knew that any interference on her part would not improve matters but would only serve to upset the chef, Jean Louis.

It was to be the first large assembly ever held in the new home that Gabriel had built at the far end of Freedom Street, where once dilapidated cottages stood close to the teasel ground. Now the street culminated in a small square where on three sides were the gracious homes of several wealthy merchants and master craftsmen, that occupied by the Fabians no less fine than the others. It was made of brick with a wide front door recessed between two pillars, above them a graceful arch ornamented with curlicues. Over the porch was the central window with two others on each side of it, both with their twin beneath, with two dormers projecting from the pitched roof.

No longer did the looms perform their macabre dance in the loft. Instead a two-storeyed building had been constructed at the end of the garden to accommodate them, connected to the house by a covered way. Here, too, lived the apprentices. It was all a great improvement on the old and rather cramped quarters of the previous house and Charlotte was looking forward to presenting it to their friends; however, this was not the main reason for the party. Elise's sixteenth birthday had provided the impetus for it and persuaded Gabriel to sanction it, and Charlotte, her hands occupied with the flowers, smiled as she thought of her stepdaughter's excitement. One tended to smile at the thought of Elise, though more often than not it was a smile of humorous resignation. Elise was a child still, with a child's impulsive thoughtlessness. She could be wilful – but that was not the whole of the picture. No one was a livelier or more entertaining companion, and she possessed a great generosity of spirit.

On the whole Charlotte had great hopes for her, and took great pleasure in seeing her fearless development from girl to woman, remembering how different it had been in her own case, how painful her progress towards the kind of self-confidence she now enjoyed. She had been a prey to so many anxieties. Not so Elise! She gave the impression of standing tiptoe on the threshold of life, eager to seize and hold and savour it, touchingly convinced that only good things lay ahead.

As if summoned by her thoughts, Elise danced into the outer scullery where Charlotte worked and exclaimed with delight at the sight of the flowers.

'Oh, how beautiful! May I take some to Tantine? She loves anemones.'

'Of course. I'm glad you're going to see her. It's been too long.'

'I know – but oh, I do dislike Berthe. She is quite horrid, with her fawning ways and little piggy eyes. How Tantine puts up with her I cannot imagine.'

Charlotte said nothing, but could not find it in her heart to utter any reproof despite Elise's immoderate description. Berthe was not likeable, and she had been thankful when she moved from the house in company with Madame Colbert.

'Run along with you,' she said. 'Be sure to tell Tantine we look forward to seeing her tomorrow.'

'Pray try not to excite yourself *too* much,' Elise said pertly, laughing as she gathered up a small bunch of flowers and left the room.

Little minx, Charlotte thought. She would turn heads tomorrow night at the ball, for her new gown was a confection so beautiful that even Elise had been rendered speechless for a few moments as she studied her reflection with something approaching awe.

Charlotte's own gown had been ready for some days. Though she designed some of the finest patterned silk in the country she had come to realise that ornate designs were not for her. She had developed a style of her own, plain and distinctive, but always in glowing colours that set off her pale skin and dark hair. Gabriel had chosen the silk for her on this occasion, and as always she trusted his judgment.

Life, she mused, had been unimaginably kind to her. She had been denied the experience of physical love, that was true – but oh, what joys she had been granted in its place! The friendship of a man like Gabriel, his support and companionship and the way he had educated her in the best sense of the word, drawing out of her the ability to design the silk that had made them both household names, enabling them to enjoy the new house with its fine furniture and paintings, the carriage and pair, the acquisition of Whiteacres as their country home, and a life-style of restrained elegance.

Their friends were drawn from the wealthier émigré class, for the most part; all those master craftsmen who, like Gabriel, had brought their skills and energy to England and now made such a great contribution both to its commercial and cultural life. They possessed lively minds and wide interests, patronising the arts and supporting charities. This was Charlotte's life, and it was one in which she found great contentment.

Was Gabriel equally contented? Physically he seemed stronger, suffered less pain, and she knew he was delighted that the prophecy he had made on first seeing her designs had come to pass. They had become true partners, her talent contributing in no small way to their present prosperity. Still there were times when she saw deep sadness in his eyes and he withdrew to a place where she could not reach him.

She considered him now, even as she placed her flowers carefully, one by one. It made no sense, that a man who had endured so much should be plagued by guilt because he had not endured more! Had he always been so? As a child, had he suffered black moods, shunning the company of his friends? She would like to have been able to consult the aunt who brought him up, or his mother –

His mother! She paused, the tulip in her hand momentarily forgotten. There were times when she felt uneasy about the woman he refused to mention, the woman he rejected as faithless. Was it right to be so unforgiving? She could not believe that it was. He acted as if he had forgotten her, erased her from his mind; yet how could that be so? Hers had been the hand that had held his as he took his first steps, the hand that had wiped

173

away childish tears. Others might find his attitude understandable, but to Charlotte it seemed less than worthy of him.

She shook her head helplessly, knowing that in this matter she was powerless to influence him. Any attempt to do so on her part had only resulted in anger. She turned her attention once more to the flowers. She had finished the huge bowl that would stand in the hall and now began on the twin urns that would be set on pedestals on each side of the double doors that led to the drawing room.

'Madame!'

'Yes, Nan?' She did not need to turn her head to recognise the speaker.

'The new coat for monsieur has arrived, but there is no shirt or stock with it. I thought they were to come together.'

'So they were! Oh, how tiresome.' A spray of pale green leaves in her hand, Charlotte stood frowning in thought. 'Has the mercer's man left? Then send Joseph to the shop directly.'

'Joseph is gone to collect the mail, madame.'

'Then send him the moment he returns.' She paused, her head cocked on one side. 'I can hear him now. Joseph!' She raised her voice, calling to him. 'When you have taken the mail to monsieur, I need you for an urgent errand.'

Joseph came into the cool outer kitchen where she was working, pointed nose reddened by the cold wind outside.

'Monsieur already has his letters, madame. This one is for you.'

'Oh?' She was studying her arrangement as she spoke.

'Looks like it's from Canterbury, ma'am.'

'Oh!' The exclamation was the same, but the inflexion quite different. Hastily she wiped her hands on her apron and took the letter from him, breaking open the wafer and scanning it rapidly.

Nan, watching her, saw her already pale face pale still further, saw her eyes widen, her mouth fall open.

'What is it, madame?' She took a few steps nearer. 'Is it bad news?'

'My mother,' Charlotte said faintly, then repeated it as if she could barely believe it. 'My mother, Nan! My father writes that she is ill and like to die.'

They stared at each other, seeing that strong uncompromising, seemingly indestructible figure in their minds. How she had harried them both in the past! Yet they both wept as they clung together, their involuntary movement towards each other sending a cascade of daffodils tumbling to the stone-flagged floor.

Elise clinked down Freedom Street on her pattens, avoiding the puddles left by the recent shower, the March wind whipping the corners of her cloak, the hood falling back to reveal hair like spun gold. The grimy waif on the corner who was selling lavender, dressed in rags and with hands that were chapped with the cold, gazed at her open-mouthed, dumb with admiration and envy, but the men unloading barrels from a dray were more vocal, shouting out invitations and comments that amused more than shocked, though Elise lowered her eyes modestly as she passed them.

She went by the old house where she had lived as a child without a second glance, as if it meant nothing to her. She was thinking of the apprentices, one of whom she had seen as she left home. He had wished her good morning, and she had rewarded him with a dazzling smile, laughing to herself at the way his face had blushed fiery red.

They were silly fellows, all three of them, she thought. She extracted great amusement from the way they vied with each other to speak to her or attract her notice, and sometimes played cruel games with them, seeming to favour first one and then another. Secretly she thought of all of them as exciting as three bowls of gruel, all but indistinguishable.

Apprentices had come and gone over the years, but there had not been one worth noticing – at least not since that one – what was his name? Pierre something. She remembered him because he had made her laugh when she was a child, but he had disappeared suddenly under somewhat mysterious circumstances. No one had ever explained why and she knew no details. She had hardly thought of him again until that moment.

Maman had been angry about his disappearance, she could remember that, for it was an event so unusual it had stayed in the memory. Somehow the whole matter was bound up with the suddenness with which Tantine had made up her mind to take the cottage at the other end of Freedom Street which she had previously dismissed as far too small, the cottage towards which she was making her way on that fresh spring morning.

Her mind was full of happy, inconsequential thoughts, light as thistledown. How pretty her new gown was! How the compliments would fly when she appeared in it, and how wonderful it was to be sixteen so that no one could regard her as a child any more. She hoped that Catherine Maxwell's brother would be able to come to the ball. He was an officer in the Coldstream, the Second Senior Regiment of Foot Guards, and never had she seen a man more handsome in his uniform. He had been abroad in the Netherlands but was home now and Catherine, her very best friend at Mrs Amlott's Seminary, had said he admired her greatly. So pooh to the spotty apprentices and all those moon-faced boys who gazed at her in church on Sunday!

These weighty matters occupied her pleasantly on her way down the street and as always she was greeted effusively by Tantine.

'Come in, come in my heart's darling! Oh, you have come alone! Is there no one in attendance, not even that peasant that was engaged to wait on you? No, I cannot approve of that! Is there no one now to care for *ma petite héritière*?'

'Tantine, the distance is nothing, and everyone is far too busy with preparations for the ball to come with me, heiress or not!'

'Madame should not have allowed it.'

'She sent you these flowers.' Let Maman take the credit, Elise thought, with careless generosity. 'And she bade me say how she looks forward to seeing you tomorrow.'

'Hm!' Madame Colbert looked sceptical, but she took the flowers, turning to ring a small bell that brought Berthe hurrying in from the kitchen. She was plumper now, small eyes lost in her fat cheeks, and she greeted Elise almost as effusively as Tantine had done.

'See what my darling has brought me,' Madame Colbert said, handing her the flowers. 'Pray put them in some water for me, Berthe. And bring some chocolate for our little one, and the macaroons she loves so well.'

'*Bien sûr*, madame.'

All conversation was in French here, not in the kind of hybrid language now French, now English that was heard at the other end of the street. In fact, Elise thought as she looked around her, there seemed a strange, foreign air about this room. She had never set foot in France herself but could well imagine that this was a replica of the provincial house that Tantine had inhabited during the days of her marriage in Nîmes.

Her own home was quite different. It was lighter, for one

thing, with fewer hangings. The new house had required considerably more furniture than the old, and her father had chosen a less cumbrous style. The tables had slender, cabriole legs and the chairs were actually designed to follow the shape of a human spine. In the hall stood a magnificent bench made to a design by Daniel Marot, the gifted Huguenot architect, and there was work, too, by Jean Pelletier, the carver and gilder who had been acclaimed for the picture frames and stands he had provided for Hampton Court Palace.

'Come and sit down, *chérie*,' Tantine said. 'And tell me of your gown.'

'Oh Tantine, it is the most beautiful thing you ever saw!' Elise ignored the invitation to sit, but pirouetted around the room in her excitement. 'Just wait until you see it! It has a low, scooped neck and underskirts of cream with blue flowers – oh, just the most heavenly colour, Tantine – looped up with trailing panels at the back. And Maman says that Nan will dress my hair in ringlets in the very latest style. Nan is so clever with hair –'

'Hm!' Tantine said again. The importation of Nan from Kent was something she regarded with the deepest disapproval. In her opinion, Charlotte had allowed the girl – who was, when all was said and done, no more than a country bumpkin – to take a position in the household that was quite out of proportion to her accomplishments. She had been promoted from the kitchen to the role of lady's maid, no less – and if that was not enough, her younger sister, Molly, had lately come to attend Elise. It would not be so if *she* still had the running of the silk-weaver's house. Elise, conscious of Tantine's views and of her own tactlessness in speaking so highly of Nan, hurried on.

'I shall look such a lady, Tantine, that you will not recognise me! But what of your gown? You have told me nothing of it.'

'I?' Tantine raised her shoulders and lifted her hands. 'What does it matter what I wear? I am the poor, forgotten relation, old now and in indifferent health. Who cares for me?'

'I care,' Elise assured her. 'And when Papa was making the list of guests, your name was at the very top. I saw it myself.'

'Hm!' Again the dismissive grunt. 'Well, no matter. Given that I am well enough to come, I shall wear my best black silk, of course.'

'Why always black, Tantine? Next time you choose a new gown you should have mauve or bronze. Many widows do. Bronze trimmed with black can be so chic –'

'It is not my widowhood I mourn, *chérie*, but the loss of my darling, your mother, Celestine. Sometimes I think I am the only person who remembers her.'

As she spoke she leaned forward from her chair and reached to clasp Elise's hands, holding them fast. Elise was embarrassed and wriggled a little on the stool that she had pulled up beside Tantine's chair. What was she supposed to say or do? Of course she was sorry she had never known her mother, that went without saying, but it seemed a fruitless exercise to be constantly miserable as a consequence.

'I do not believe Papa has forgotten her,' she said now. 'He keeps a miniature of her in his room, after all.'

Tantine loosed her hands and sat back in her chair. Casually, in a way that she hoped would give no offence, Elise abandoned the stool and went to sit across the room where she could not be touched.

'The house is as busy as an ants' nest, with all the preparations for tomorrow,' she said, but Tantine was not to be deflected.

'Perhaps your father thinks of her more than I give him credit for,' she said. 'After all, he must see that his second marriage was a mistake.'

Elise moved uneasily again and began to wish she had ignored the impulse to come and see Tantine. She hated it when the old woman criticised Maman so unfairly.

'Oh, come –'

'Has God seen fit to bless it and make it fruitful? Has your father a son to carry on his name?'

The question was plainly rhetorical, but in any case Elise was saved the necessity of making any response to it by the arrival of Berthe with the chocolate and the macaroons.

'Mam'selle is in good health?' Berthe asked, beaming at her over her shoulder as she put down the tray. 'Such excitement there must be at your house! Marthe tells me there is a constant stream of coaches delivering this and that.'

The lace merchant who employed Marthe as cook had moved into one of the other new houses at the end of Freedom Street – a matter of some annoyance to Charlotte since it meant that

178

little went on in the Fabian household that was not reported eventually to Madame Colbert.

'Marthe misses very little,' Elise said coolly. 'One would have thought, since she spends her time in the kitchen, she would not see so much.'

Berthe continued smiling, but her eyes were suddenly cold as if she suspected irony and she turned from Elise, busying herself with pouring the chocolate.

'Naturally, she takes an interest, mam'selle. Such a fine house-hold, that of your dear papa –'

'You are much too kind.' Elise did not add 'and much too inquisitive', but the words seemed to hang in the air as Berthe left the room.

The moment they were alone together, Tantine returned to the topic that Berthe had interrupted.

'How truly it is said,' she mused, 'that a hasty marriage gives ample time for repentance. That such as she should be put in my darling Celestine's place!'

Elise nibbled a macaroon and said nothing. Defending Charlotte to Tantine was, she had learned long since, nothing more than a waste of breath, but she still found it difficult to remain silent. Why, a blind man could see that her father regretted nothing, and that he and Charlotte were closer than many other couples she could name.

'Tantine, the ball is going to be wonderful,' she said with determination. 'Nothing is to be spared. Papa particularly wants it to be a success, and *everyone* is to be there!'

'Oh? The Queen and Prince George and my Lady Marlborough, no doubt!'

Elise trilled with laughter at this sally.

'Everyone we know, I mean. Papa said yesterday that when all our guests are gathered under one roof there would be more skill and artistic ability in one square foot of space than in the rest of London put together. And almost all of them Huguenots! He is so proud of being a Huguenot.'

'As well he might be.' Tantine was smiling again. 'And my little darling the most lovely of all the fine ladies! Your papa must watch out. You will soon be stolen away from him.'

Elise smiled and said nothing, but her blue eyes glowed. It filled her with excitement to know that somewhere in the world, he waited. He did not know her and she did not know him, but one day they would meet and at first sight she would recognise him, the man she would love for ever.

'He will have to be someone *very* handsome,' she said.

There was some competition among the serving wenches at the Bull in Rochester when the tall, fair-haired young man from the London mail took his seat at the trestle table and called for ale.

'You can leave this one to me, Meg Hawkins,' Betsy Fanshawe said. 'You tend to the clergyman.' She was smiling as she smoothed her red curls and adjusted the neckline of her laced bodice.

'Why should I?' Meg asked pugnaciously.

It was a question Betsy did not deign to answer in words, for her down-turned smile said enough. Meg was smaller, paler, more diffident. Spineless, Betsy said, but then Betsy had enough nerve for two and the kind of showy good looks that always attracted the smiling glances of the men customers.

'He wants rabbit pie,' she said to Meg as she came swaggering back. 'I told him he could have it with my love, and anything else he might want –'

'You never did, Betsy Fanshawe –'

'Oh yes, I did! Give anything to a man like that, I would.'

'You'd give anything to any man, and that's a fact. No one come in here in breeches can feel safe.'

'You'd ha' been there yourself, did you have a bit more spirit. Have you seen to the parson?'

'Him and his lady want the private room, but I tell him it's already engaged. Well then, he must have a seat by the fire, he says. There's not one vacant, say I – so *he's* not best pleased.'

'Tell them ostlers to move over. They got no right to spread themselves like that, rude monkeys, taking all the warmth.'

'I can't –'

'Oh, go *on* Meg Hawkins!' A push sent her in the ostlers' direction once more, but still the smaller girl hesitated.

'You do it, Betsy,' she said. 'They'll take more note of you.'

'Oh, give me patience!'

Betsy swept Meg aside, crossed the room with a provocative roll of her hips, and ordered the ostlers out of their warm seats. She settled the parson and his wife with their small ale, and undulated back again, taking care to pass close to the young man's table.

He smiled, more to himself than to her, and there was more than a hint of ruefulness in his expression. On any other night he might have been pleased to take up the clear invitation, but thirty-six hours of travel including a rough crossing had made him long for a night's rest.

Meg, going about her duties, yearned a little. There was something about him that appealed to her, for Meg was a romantic and had always been drawn to looks of the finely chiselled variety. She liked his profile – the straight nose, the clean lines of cheeks and chin. He was too good for Betsy Fanshawe, anyone could see that with half an eye.

'He looks sort of – sort of different,' she said when there was a lull in their tasks and they stood together again.

'He ain't English, that's why. Oh, he speaks it well enough, but funny like.'

'I knew that coat weren't made in London.'

'How would you know that? You don't know no such thing!'

'The cuffs ain't big enough. And his linen's creased, like he's been travelling.'

''Course he's been travelling! He wouldn't have got here, else.'

'You know full well what I mean.'

'I know full well you'd best go and find out what that wench wants. She's the maid from the private room.'

'Why me?' Meg asked, but there was a note of resignation in her voice, and she pushed herself away from the wall even as she asked the question, leaving Betsy to fluff her curls again and tilt her head, narrowing her green eyes to smile at the young man who had given her no definite signal yet, she was forced to admit to herself, but surely would before long.

He did not smile in return. He did not even appear to notice her, for his attention had switched to Meg and the other woman with whom she was now in conversation. He was looking at them intently, a puzzled frown drawing his brows together.

I'm not having *that*, Betsy thought, and approached him boldly.

'Did you enjoy your vittles, sir?' she asked, leaning over him to ensure that he could enjoy an excellent view of her cleavage. 'Is there aught else I can fetch you? More ale, maybe?'

'That young woman,' he said, indicating her with a nod of his head. 'The one in conversation with the other serving wench. Do you know who she is?'

Betsy tossed her head.

181

'Just somebody's maid, sir. They arrived in a carriage just before you. A miserable couple they were, her and her mistress. Not a smile for anyone between the pair of them.' She frowned as he continued to give the woman all of his attention. 'She looks a bit long in the tooth to me, sir,' she said saucily. 'She'd not be much sport.'

'She looks familiar. I know her, I feel sure.'

She stood where Meg had left her, as if waiting to be served. She was soberly clad, but not as old as the wench had implied – though she was no young girl, that was true. About his own age, he reckoned; six – or perhaps seven – and twenty. Was she a girl from Sandwich? Someone he had known in the village or at church?

Her clothes looked as if her master and mistress were people of some standing, and the appraising look which she turned on the tavern and its occupants as she waited appeared thoughtful, almost contemplative, yet the mouth was such that it seemed as if it could break into a smile at any time despite the seriousness of her expression.

Surely she would turn and face him squarely in a moment, he thought, and then he would know, but infuriatingly she seemed more interested in the antics of the group of ostlers. It was only when they became aware of her regard and responded to it by the kind of jokes that brought a blush to her cheeks that she turned her back on them and looked directly towards him. For a moment she, too, looked puzzled, then her brow cleared and she came towards him.

'It's Mr Paul, isn't it?' She caught herself up, gave a little bob, and smiled at him. 'Mr Belamie, I should say, begging your pardon, sir –'

'Nan!' Watched coldly by Betsy from the far side of the room, Paul rose from the table and seized both her hands. 'Nan! Of course! I thought from the moment you came in that you were someone known to me, yet it's been so many years since I saw you, I couldn't be sure.'

'Oh, Mr Paul, I've never been better pleased to see anyone! You were always able to cheer madame like no one else.'

'Madame Bonnet?' His question carried more than a touch of incredulity.

'No, sir. Madame Fabian – Mam'selle Charlotte, as was. I'm in her service now – have been these past five years and oh sir, if she ever needed cheering, she needs it now.'

182

'Charlotte is here?'

'In a private chamber upstairs, sir, and in as low a state as you could ever imagine. A sight of you will do her the world of good.'

Charlotte felt chilled to the bone despite the fire and the fur-trimmed mantle she had kept wrapped around her.

'Eat, ma'am,' Nan had urged her when they first arrived. 'You'll feel better with food inside you.'

The pie that Nan put before her seemed tasteless and leathery and she could get down no more than a morsel before she pushed the plate to one side.

'I cannot, Nan,' she said.

'Then take some wine, ma'am. That'll put heart in you. Mulled wine, that's the thing, then bed with a hot brick at your feet. Did you ever think the night would turn this cold? It's like the depths of winter.'

No, Charlotte thought, sitting without moving, staring at the log that glowed and spluttered on the hearth. No, I had no idea it could ever be this cold.

This morning there had been a chilly breeze but the sun had shone and she had been surrounded with flowers in all the bright colours of spring. The daffodils in the orchard at Providence House would be in bud just now. They were always later than those from the west country, but her mother would likely not live to see them, however late.

A seizure, her father had said, that had come upon her without warning. The odd-job man had found her lying in the kitchen garden. The next few hours would be crucial, it seemed, but there was little hope.

Did she live still? Charlotte wondered. Inside the helpless shell that was her body did she – the essential she – wait happily for eternity or did her restless soul chafe and rail at the thought that there was still so much for her to do, so much that others would be too incompetent to perform?

Go in peace, if go you must, Charlotte silently urged her. You always did your duty, more than your duty. Rest now, and if you are aware of my regrets, have none yourself for the barrier between us was of my making.

Perhaps that had not always been so. When she was young she would have thought differently – would have blamed her mother for lack of understanding. Now, with the benefit of maturity and hindsight, she knew that she, too, had been at fault. In her mother's presence she had always felt less than herself, conscious of her lack of worth, her silent withdrawal giving the impression of sulkiness and furtive discontent.

She should have been more her own person, then perhaps she would not have been such a disappointment. Even her marriage to Gabriel Fabian, which at first had seemed such a notable achievement, had in the end proved less than satisfactory since no children had resulted. The acclaim she had received for her designs had been no substitute; in fact her mother had, in some obscure way, blamed her preoccupation with work for her inability to conceive, as if it were all a matter of will and determination and finding the time.

I should have told her, Charlotte thought. I should have explained the reason for my childlessness. For Gabriel's sake she had not done so. She had maintained the secrecy, held herself aloof. Now it was too late and the chasm between them would remain for ever unbridged.

The grief she felt surprised her with its intensity. Sadness – yes, she would have expected that – but not this paralysing emotion, this desolation of regret. How strange the bond between parent and child, she mused, and thought again of Gabriel and the rejection of his mother. He was wrong to be so bitter, she was sure of it now. When she was beyond his reach, he would realise it and would suffer for it.

She longed for Gabriel's presence to buttress and comfort her. He had offered to come, to postpone the ball, cancel all arrangements, but she would not allow him to do so. Too many people were coming from out of town – perhaps were already on their way from their country estates to their town houses – and who, if not the invited guests, would eat the mountain of food that was already in the kitchens? Was it all to go to waste? And what of Elise's disappointment? No, cancellation was not to be thought of. Elise would step charmingly into the role of hostess and perform so well that Charlotte would scarcely be missed.

He had seen the argument and regretfully conceded. He would stay and the ball would be held while she went to Canterbury; after all, Madame Bonnet still lived as far as they knew, and could yet recover. Joseph would drive her in the carriage and Nan would accompany her, and on the day after the ball he would take the Mail and hurry to her side.

But he should be here *now*, she thought, knowing that she was being unfair and illogical. She needed him far more than hot possets or heated bricks, or whatever else that Nan had gone for.

She made no answer, did not so much as turn her head when she heard the tap on the door. She felt incapable of making the effort required to look up and smile and behave in what she would normally consider a civilised manner. Nan would understand and forgive, she knew.

'Lottie?' Only one person had ever called her that. She turned abruptly and, bewildered, peered into the shadowed area beyond the orbit of the guttering candles.

'Who's there? Who are you?'

'It's Paul.' He came in and put a tray with a bottle and glasses on the central table, turning to bend over her and take her hand, looking at her pallor and dark-fringed eyes with concern. 'I saw Nan downstairs. I couldn't believe it at first – couldn't even remember who she was, it's been so many years! She told me what has happened, about your mother. I'm so very sorry.'

'Paul! I can't believe it!' She was astonished by the sight of him. It was so totally unexpected, yet at the same time there seemed a strange inevitability about it, as if it were only right that a figure from her childhood should reappear at such a time.

He had changed, she saw; had grown taller and broader, and his face had thinned. Yet at the same time he seemed not to have changed at all.

'Paul!' she said again, and suddenly and inexplicably was overwhelmed by tears as if his sympathy and his presence, so evocative of times past, had proved her undoing.

'I have brought brandy – no, you must take a glass! It's purely medicinal. Your father would approve, I'm sure.'

Obediently she took the glass and sipped, feeling the warmth of the spirit seep through her body.

'Good girl,' he said, and smiled at her. The smile warmed her, too. No, she thought. He hasn't really changed at all.

'What on earth are you doing here, Paul? Where did you come from?'

'I arrived from Deptford an hour or so ago.' He gave no other explanation. He had taken a chair opposite her and looked at her over the rim of his glass as he raised it to his lips, studying her closely. 'Madame Fabian!' he said wonderingly after a moment. His smile was affectionate. 'Little Lottie! Whoever would have thought it?'

Such clear, steady grey eyes, Charlotte thought, suddenly shy. She bent her head and sipped again, unable to meet them.

'I am truly sorry about your mother,' he went on softly. 'You must not give up hope. She may live still, Nan tells me.'

'I know nothing since my father's letter which was written some days ago. He held out little hope then.'

'You are shivering. Here, take another drop of brandy while I mend the fire.'

'The room is warm enough. The cold is within me.'

'Tell me of your husband – and Elise and Tantine, and all your doings. You have become famous since last I saw you –'

'Oh Paul, such a long time you have been away!'

The cry was wrenched from her as if only now did she realise how much she had missed him.

'Ten years.'

'Why so long?'

'Letters have passed between me and Monsieur Fabian. You must know that the completion of my indentures coincided with a disastrous flood in Holland, and that a fund was set up to help the victims, all monies paid into Charpentier's Bank –'

'Yes, yes, that I know. And you took on the administration of the disaster fund and became Monsieur Charpentier's right-hand man. But so long without a visit home –'

'My parents came to me; and though visits were planned, somehow there was always some reason . . .' His voice trailed away uncertainly as still he looked at her. 'I should have come,' he said softly. He looked away from her for a moment and when he looked back and spoke again it was in quite a different tone, heartily impersonal.

'I was so glad to hear of your success, Lottie, and have never done boasting that I knew Charlotte Fabian before she became a famous silk designer, and that once she drew moths and birds and all manner of creatures to illustrate my learned treatise! My mother has it still, you know. She says the pictures have stood the test of time better than the text.'

'No doubt it was good training for me. Are you home for good, Paul?'

'I hope that I am. You remember that my Monsieur Charpentier had a brother in London? The goldsmith to whom I was first apprenticed?'

'He died recently.'

'Which is why I have come. I am to take over his business in Lombard Street with a view to developing it more as a bank than a goldsmith's establishment, though that side will be continued.'

'Monsieur Charpentier must indeed think highly of you.'

'No higher than I deserve!'

'Modesty was ever an attribute of yours.'

'Second only to my irresistibly agreeable nature.'

Charlotte laughed, and the sound of it took her by surprise. She sobered quickly, remembering her reason for being here, but her eyes were warm as she looked at Paul.

'It is indeed agreeable to see you again,' she said. 'It brings back more carefree days.'

He looked at her thoughtfully for a moment.

'Somehow I never thought of you as carefree,' he said at last. 'You always seemed to be in the grip of some private agitation.'

Charlotte stared at him in astonishment.

'You thought that? Then you were more percipient than I realised.'

'I worried about you – needlessly, as I see quite clearly.' Humorously he raised his eyebrows. 'I detect quite a difference in poor little Lottie.'

'You can hardly call me carefree – and I *still* hate being called Lottie!'

'My apologies!' He continued to consider her carefully. 'No, of course you are not carefree. You have more than your share of woes at the moment, but the agitation has gone. There is a maturity about you, a calmness.'

'I have marriage and Gabriel to thank for that. Why have you not married, Paul?'

He laughed and shrugged and twisted his mouth in a way that she had forgotten, a way that, inexplicably, made her feel full of happiness as if her world were a brighter place now that Paul had returned.

'I have not met the right woman,' he said. 'And it has not been the right time. I have had other dreams.'

'Banking?' She laughed at him. 'It sounds a little dull.'

'If you think that, then you are wrong. There's excitement in it, Charlotte. I said so years ago to your husband, and I have seen nothing since to make me change my mind. Using the money of others to invest, seeing it grow – that's power!'

'So money has become your god? What do your parents say to that?'

'Stop putting words into my mouth. I'm still a good Huguenot – well, a Huguenot, at least! Money is not my god – which is not to say that I am not ambitious.' A log snapped and the fire flared up suddenly, highlighting his face as he bent towards her, brandy glass held between his two hands. 'Shall I tell you my dream, Lottie? You must promise not to tell a soul –'

'I can keep a secret!'

'I remember. Well – laugh at me if you will, but one day I shall have my own bank that will stand comparison with Charpentier's or Hoare's or any of the others.'

'That sounds sensible enough.'

'There's more. Lottie, the wideness of the world fills me with excitement. I dream of taking a hand in the opening up of territories so far unknown, lands that are as yet undiscovered. I can see them – great, empty wastes, waiting.'

'But –' Charlotte began, and fell silent. She was thinking of London; of the river and the gracious buildings. Of St James's Palace and the dome of St Paul's. Once, she presumed, it had all been wasteland. Men of vision were vital to any age, or nothing would change. It did not entirely surprise her that Paul should be of their number, for he had always been anxious to see what was over the next hill; what did surprise her was the stirring of reciprocal excitement that she felt herself. More than excitement, she realised wonderingly. There was a touch of envy.

'Remember when I used to climb up behind you, and we'd ride off to look at our birds and beasts?' she asked with apparent inconsequence.

'Are you offering to climb up behind me now and gallop to the ends of the earth?'

She laughed, confused. What had possessed her to say such a thing?

'I am a staid matron! Much changed from those days.'

He did not answer her, and the expression on his face was unreadable. The feeling of comfortable familiarity had gone, its place taken by a moment of awkwardness and tension, and to relieve it she began talking rapidly of Elise and the ball, and all the preparations that had been made, and all that had been abandoned. Through it all he listened and smiled and watched and said little, but gradually the ease between them was restored and when finally the tiredness which his appearance had kept at bay suddenly threatened to overwhelm her and she struggled to overcome a yawn, he rose from his chair.

'You are almost asleep,' he said. 'And I must go.'

'It's been so good to see you, Paul. I am glad you're back.'

'We shall meet again, no doubt; if not tomorrow morning before I leave here, then very shortly.'

She gave him her hand and taking it, he pulled her gently to her feet. Clasping her shoulders he kissed her first on one cheek and then on the other – then, after a momentary hesitation, he kissed her a third time.

'My honorary sister,' he said. 'And the best of friends. It has been as though we met last week.'

He left her then, and though she had thought herself composed, she found that once he had gone, she wept again.

Grief for her mother was the cause of it, she told herself. But she knew that the sadness went deeper than that. She felt alone as she had not done for years, and she could not understand the reason for it.

10

From the moment she saw her father's face, Charlotte knew she had arrived too late and that there would be no final moment of communication with her mother.

The diminutive figure of Dr Bonnet seemed even smaller, his face bone white and pared of flesh within the flowing wig. Calm and competent with others, in the face of his own loss he gave way to helpless grief and it was Charlotte, her own crying done, who made funeral arrangements, attended to the printing of black-edged cards, arranged refreshments, ordered mourning rings and battled with Tante Hortense, who seemed determined that no flamboyant ritual of death should be ignored, however tasteless.

It was Tante Hortense who engaged the professional mute to stand outside the house miming the agonies of grief; she who sent the glover from town to provide black gloves to be worn by those who came to pay their last respects. Impatiently Charlotte dismissed them both. What, she wondered, would her mother have said regarding such a misuse of money – particularly when perpetrated by Tante Hortense? She was thankful when Gabriel arrived to take charge of everything with such authority that no one dreamed of questioning it.

Elise did not accompany Gabriel. She was staying in St James's Square with her friend Catherine Maxwell, he told her. Charlotte looked concerned at this news.

'Oh Gabriel, I wonder if that is wise? I have heard nothing of Miss Maxwell that makes me think her a good influence.'

'Mrs Maxwell pressed the matter most kindly at the ball. She was sad not to see you there, as was everyone, but I have to say that Elise played her part well. My heart wasn't in it, but I think we can count the occasion a success. Don't worry about Elise! I felt it preferable to permit the visit to the Maxwells rather than bring her with me here.'

'Or send her to Tantine.' Charlotte sighed and pressed a hand to her head which seemed to be bursting with troubled thoughts and emotions. 'No doubt you were right.'

Even after the funeral was over and the house had regained some semblance of normality, with the black hangings removed and the shutters opened once more to admit the spring sunshine, Dr Bonnet seemed unable to do other than sit in semi-darkness, crouched in his chair, not reading, not talking, merely rubbing his hands together with a dry, rasping sound as if they were cold and would never be warm. He had aged overnight and seemed to have lost interest in everything, even his appearance which had always been of the greatest concern to him. It was Charlotte now who pointed out to him that his cuff lace was soiled, his stock spotted.

For some time his work had been confined to the Infirmary which he regarded as virtually his own creation, but now he greeted news of it with little interest, ignoring all Charlotte's gentle urgings to return to his duties.

'There are many who need you there, Papa,' she told him, but apathetically he shook his head.

'Later, perhaps. I cannot go just now.'

'What can we do with him?' Charlotte appealed to Gabriel. 'I suggested that he should come to London with us for a time, but he would not hear of it. Yet I cannot leave him like this.'

'He needs time, *chérie*. I must return home, but perhaps you should stay a while.'

She had come to that conclusion herself and was glad that Gabriel accepted the inevitable so readily, and with such understanding. Not all husbands would do so, she told him, standing for a peaceful moment within the circle of his arms.

Monsieur and Madame Belamie had naturally attended the funeral, and Paul alone among their children had come with them. Minette, Louise and Anne-Marie were married and lived at a little distance, and Jean – the baby who had caused such consternation with his cries in the cellar at Nantes – was apprenticed to a bookbinder in Tunbridge Wells.

In view of their long-standing friendship, and hoping they would be of some comfort to her father, Charlotte urged them to stay for a night or two, and though her father seemed almost unaware of their presence, as always she herself found strength in Madame Belamie's company.

'Your mother was one of the most indomitable women I have

ever met,' she said to Charlotte as they sat together on the day following the funeral. 'She had her critics, I know, but there was not a soul who did not respect her – witness the great crowd that gathered yesterday! There was one man who had walked from Dover. She saved his life when he was sick and destitute, he told me, and he owed her everything. He was not alone. Many others would have had a similar tale to tell. She was a great lady, Charlotte, tireless in her work for those less fortunate.'

'I know. I cannot imagine how my father will manage without her.'

'He has his work. It will reassert its importance in time, I feel sure.'

'I hope you're right. The practice of medicine has always been his life.'

'Your husband will help him, if anyone can.'

Gabriel did indeed spend a great deal of time with Dr Bonnet, but he was also delighted to be reunited with Paul, his protégé, and to receive a face-to-face account of the years he had spent in Amsterdam.

'He has exceeded my every hope for him,' he said privately to Charlotte as they walked in the garden where a watery sun had supplanted a brief shower. 'His grasp of commerce and business is impressive. He has a great future ahead of him, of that I'm certain, yet there is nothing arrogant or cocksure about him. He is undoubtedly a fine young man.'

'With such a family behind him, it's hardly surprising. He's very conscious of all he owes to you, too.'

'He would have achieved nothing without ability.' Gabriel walked for a moment in thoughtful silence. 'I have plans for him,' he went on, 'but I will not speak of them now. They are for the future. Of more immediate interest, Phillipe has told me the family is now naturalised and they propose to anglicise their name. In future they will be Mr and Mrs Bellamy. Phillipe's brother considers it will be good for business.'

Charlotte felt little surprise, in fact she had been aware that such a distortion of their name had been in general use for some time. As for naturalisation, she and Gabriel, among countless others, had become British years before. Still more had, less expensively, taken out papers of denization.

'And Paul?' she asked. 'Will he be Bellamy too?' Bellamy's Bank, she was thinking. It had a good ring to it.

'I believe so.'

'So many of us woven in,' she said. 'All merging into the pattern so that when it comes from the loom, nowhere can the addition be seen.'

'Yet the pattern is the richer for it. As for Paul –' He paused a moment and Charlotte looked at him questioningly. 'I think, perhaps, topaz, do you agree?'

Charlotte considered the matter.

'Perhaps,' she said at last, undecided. 'Though I would have thought a deeper shade; amber, say.'

They looked at each other, sharing their amusement, for this was their own private game that few would understand, and the newly named Mrs Bellamy smiled as she saw them. She had gone to the window of the drawing room to see if the rain had stopped, and had been captivated by the sight of them.

'How happy they are in each other's company,' she said to her son who was in the room behind her. 'It must surely be a marriage made in heaven.'

'Hm?' He looked up from the book he was reading. 'I beg your pardon, mother, I did not hear –'

'Gabriel and Charlotte.' His mother sat down beside him, taking up her sewing. 'Their marriage has worked so well.'

'I'm delighted to hear it,' he said, and returned to his book.

'I'm delighted to hear it.'

He heard his own banal words echoing in his head and found the words on the page before him no more than a meaningless blur.

He *was* delighted, he told himself; surprised, but delighted. He had always looked up to Gabriel Fabian, seen him as larger than life, and was warm in appreciation of his benevolence.

He had never devoted much thought to the kind of woman Gabriel might take as his second wife, but had he done so he would undoubtedly have envisaged a lady of mature years – in her thirties, perhaps – godly, naturally, but also cultured, poised, elegant, sedate, decorous, full of grace and wisdom. In short, a woman of supreme self-confidence.

Instead he had chosen timid little Lottie – and somehow a miracle had taken place, for here was Lottie ten years on, not timid any more but as poised and elegant and self-confident as any creature he could have imagined.

193

As children they had been good friends – she admiring, he protective – and he had always been fond of her and had felt sorry for her. Madame Bonnet might have been a benefactor to all the widows and orphans of Kent, but despite the iniquity of speaking ill of the dead, she was the most terrifying woman he had ever met. In her presence, Charlotte had been too scared to open her mouth. Such a transformation he would never have believed, had he not seen it with his own eyes.

He had to agree with his mother. Somehow, surprisingly, she had become the perfect wife for Gabriel Fabian – and yes, he was delighted. It was quite nonsensical to feel even a breath of wistful regret for the artless little creature he had befriended and who had gazed at him so admiringly all those years ago.

Charlotte Fabian, well-known designer of fine silks, wife to the master-weaver, was a woman to be reckoned with now.

The Bellamys returned to Sandwich the following day, and Gabriel left the day after, taking Joseph and the carriage but leaving Nan.

Charlotte was very conscious of her own house, beloved White-acres, standing shuttered and empty only a few miles away, and the longing to go and see it grew until it was almost a physical pain. She felt alien in her old home. It was fanciful, she knew – irreligious, even – but the power of her mother's personality was so great here that she felt unable to move an article of furniture or countermand some long-standing directive without feeling the chill breath of disapproval.

Rain fell for a whole week, fine and relentless, so that the countryside was shrouded in a grey veil and the rooftops of Canterbury were all but obscured. The flood of mourners come to pay their last respects to Madame Bonnet had naturally ceased since the funeral, and now there was no one. Marianne was far away in Devon. Tante Hortense was arthritic and did not care to walk abroad, especially in the rain. Charlotte felt as if the whole of life had withdrawn from her, leaving her marooned in this cheerless, silent house.

Nan hated it as much as she did.

'Never thought I'd long for London's dirt so much,' she said to Charlotte.

'I can't leave my father yet, Nan.'

'I know that, ma'am. Poor gentleman, he's got the miseries

good and proper, and who can wonder at it? A pity 'tis he won't go back to the Infirmary. 'Twould give him other trade for his thoughts.'

Charlotte heartily agreed, but was at a loss to know how to awaken his interest. It took a visit from Tante Hortense, venturing out one morning when the rain had given way to pale sunshine to bring news that a young patient in whom he had long taken an interest was no better and now seemed near death.

'Though Dr Hoad has bled him – which I know well you do not approve of, brother, even if others think it essential. Only one thing remains. Dr Hoad is sending him to London to be touched for the Queen's Evil –'

"*What?*" The roar of rage, coming as it did from a man who had barely spoken above a whisper for the past two weeks, made both his listeners start with surprise. 'That is no more than necromancy and can do no good.'

'There have been cures –'

'Cures? By the touch of a mortal woman, herself far from healthy?'

'Queen Anne is God's anointed, Anton, when all is said and done.'

'The boy has scrofula, Hortense. He needs rest and good food and fresh air, and with God's help he may grow out of it. The Queen's Evil, indeed! And bleeding! One would have thought Dr Hoad entirely ignorant of the circulatory system. I have a mind to go tomorrow and confront him.'

Charlotte squeezed her aunt's arm as later she saw her to the door.

'I cannot thank you enough, Tante Hortense,' she whispered. 'You have made him so angry!'

'I often do, my dear, but this is the first time I've been thanked for it. Now, take care of yourself, I beg you, for you look pale and peaked. You must walk abroad a little now that the weather has changed for the better. Come to see me, I beg you.'

'If Papa picks up the threads of his old life again and I have the leisure to do so, nothing would please me more,' Charlotte assured her.

There was one visit she intended to make before any other, however, once she had the opportunity. The thought of

195

Whiteacres nagged at her like an aching tooth. There was no point in taking up residence there, she knew, but when on the day following Tante Hortense's visit her father rose early and dressed carefully, ordering the carriage to be prepared to take him to the Infirmary, she determined to walk through the woods just to feast her eyes on the house and to remind herself that it stood ready and waiting for their summer stay.

Though the clouds had rolled away and the sun now shone from a pale blue sky, strangely distant after the lowering clouds of recent days, every blade of grass in the garden still shimmered with raindrops and Nan was open in her opposition to the proposed walk.

'You'll get soaked through,' she said severely. 'The trees and bushes will be that wet, and the path will be naught but a mire. Don't I know it! I've walked many a time through the woods after rain, and cried at the ruin to my shoes. Leave it a day, ma'am. Whiteacres will be there tomorrow.'

'But who's to say the sun will shine tomorrow?'

'You could go by the road.'

'Three miles there and three miles back! Oh, it's not the distance I object to but the time it will take.' She sighed heavily. 'I suppose you're right, Nan. Perhaps Papa can be persuaded to come with me in the carriage tomorrow.'

Regretfully, for she was all prepared to leave the house, she began to untie the strings of her mantle, but was interrupted by the timid voice of one of the maids.

'If you please ma'am, there's a gentleman to see you.'

'A gentleman by what name?'

'Mr Paul Bellamy, ma'am.'

'Oh!' Her expression lightened. 'Send him in, do. Paul!' She went towards him as he entered the room, her hands outstretched. 'You are most welcome!'

'But I see you are dressed to go out.'

'Nan has dissuaded me. I had intended to go to Whiteacres, our house at Flewett's Cross, but sensible Nan rightly says that the path through the woods will be a quagmire after all this rain. What brings you here, Paul?'

'I had business in Canterbury, but naturally could not leave without making enquiries of you. We were most concerned about your father. How does he do now?'

'Very well indeed! He has gone to the Infirmary for the first time today. I'm so hopeful that this is the beginning of his recovery.'

'My parents will be pleased to hear of it – and I can report the good news to Gabriel, too, for I am off to London tomorrow and must bid you a temporary goodbye.'

'Very temporary, I hope. I am anxious to get back myself before long for I have several commissions to complete and for some reason find it difficult to work here. Paul, pray excuse me while I remove my mantle –'

'Wait!' He put out a hand to detain her. 'Your house – Whiteacres? – is it far? Could we not ride over? My horse would take us both. It wouldn't be the first time you've ridden behind me.'

'We were younger then.'

'And what has that to do with the matter? Come, Lottie! It's a beautiful morning, far too lovely to stay within doors – and I should love to see your house.'

She looked from him to the sunshine outside the window and was persuaded, though she had doubts as to the seemliness of the enterprise. She was, after all, still in deepest mourning and a staid married woman to boot – a far cry from the girl who had clung to Paul's waist as they had bounced over the fields in their search for material for their studies. All doubts were swept away, however, as she stepped outside into the full glory of the spring morning. She felt like a prisoner newly released from jail.

'I had no idea how warm it was,' she said to Paul, as he brought his bay horse round to the front of the house. 'This is the first time this year there has been any strength in the sun.'

'Do you ever think of France?' Idly he stood for a moment, slapping the reins against his hand.

'Only in dreams. I can recall very little, and most of that is confused.'

'I remember the warmth and the light. I long for it sometimes. Perhaps I shall go back to find it one day.'

'I suppose there will be peace between England and France sooner or later. At the moment it seems that no sooner does one war end than another begins.'

War seemed unreal on that April day. As Paul swung into the saddle and reached down to pull her up behind him, she felt a moment's self-consciousness at his touch, at the necessary proximity, but he seemed so natural in his manner, so much the boy she knew, that the moment swiftly passed.

They conversed very little as they rode along, but she was aware of a feeling of harmony with her surroundings and of a great calm – a calm that had eluded her of recent weeks. The bitter regret she had felt at her mother's death had by this time melted into a sad acceptance of it. Now, suddenly and for the first time, she felt a lifting of the heart, as if the loveliness of the spring morning was evidence of the earth's renewal and underlined the essential rightness of life's pattern.

She found herself smiling. There were primroses and aconites in the hedgerows, dangling lamb's-tails and furry buds of willow, and all around was the joyous chorus of birdsong. The sun was warm on her back. Paul shared her contentment and feeling of ease, she felt certain, for he was whistling softly under his breath, only interrupting himself to ask directions.

'Right at the crossroads,' she told him. 'And right once more.'

At first she had held herself stiffly, but she had relaxed now, aware not of herself nor of him but only of her delight in the moment. Paul might have been a stranger, so long had he been away; yet he was not. Honorary sister, he had called her. Gabriel appeared to regard him as an honorary son, making her mother, not sister – an amusing thought, which made him smile when she communicated it to him.

He turned to look at her over his shoulder, grey eyes creased with mirth behind thick, gold-tipped lashes.

'I doubt that I could ever see you in that light,' he said. He continued to look at her for a moment and his smile died, its place taken by an expression of faint bewilderment as he turned from her as if his perception of her was none the less changed.

Charlotte was waving to children in a cottage garden. They stared back at her impassively, showing neither interest nor surprise. Even their rustic apathy seemed amusing on this wonderful day.

'They are British to the core,' she said. 'Stolid and unemotional.'

'Do we French instantly become the same once we take out our papers of naturalisation?'

'No, no! We remain volatile and fascinating, temperamental and thoroughly unreliable.'

She laughed as she spoke, but sobered instantly as she thought of her mother who, of all people, was surely the antithesis of all those things.

'Generalisations are foolish,' she said. 'Tell me, do you approve of your sisters' husbands now that you have met them?'

'Excellent fellows, both of them. Not brilliant or wealthy, you understand, but good craftsmen of estimable character. Stolid and unemotional sums them up admirably, but they are steadfast too.'

'I'm glad. Wealth is not of prime importance.'

He looked at her over his shoulder, smiling.

'So speaks one who lives in comfort.'

She pulled a face at him, a child once more, wholly at ease in his company.

'Turn into this next track, Paul. There, that's Whiteacres. As you see, it's hardly a palace.'

They halted in the small back courtyard. Paul swung himself out of the saddle, but Charlotte sat still for a moment, looking at the house without moving as if taking stock of it, noting where the thatch had been repaired, a stone wall rebuilt. The kitchen door still bore the scars inflicted by the gardener's dog and there were crocuses blooming under the rowan tree, wilting a little now that the spring was far advanced.

'It looks so sad when it's empty,' she said, with a small, defensive smile at her own fancy.

Paul reached up to help her dismount.

'Who looks after it in your absence?'

'The herdsman and his wife from the farm up the lane. They seem to be performing their duties well.'

She led him round to the front of the house and unlocked the door with the key she had brought with her. Once inside, she opened the shutters, and instantly the dim room sprang to life. Smiling, she made a tour of it, running her hand lovingly over the carved back of a chair, lifting a chess piece from a board on the table, straightening a pair of miniatures that hung on the wall.

'No, not a palace,' she said softly. 'But a home I hold in great affection, nevertheless.'

'You have been happy here.'

'Oh, yes!'

Her smile was brilliant, holding no memory of rainy days or petty annoyances, as if time spent here was for ever bathed in light.

'How pretty you have grown, Lottie!' There was a faintly astonished note in Paul's voice, and she laughed at him as she turned to lead the way into the garden, amused by his surprise but pleased and flattered as well.

Compliments did not ordinarily evoke this response. Over the years men had looked at her with admiration and had made flowery speeches, but she had remained discomfited by them, though she had learned to conceal the fact. She was smilingly distant with them, never indulging in the kind of flirtation that was common in London society.

Opinions about her varied. She was a deep one, people said. Utterly virtuous, said others, while a few rebuffed gentlemen considered her cold and unfeeling. None guessed the truth – that she was as unsure of herself as any schoolgirl, still unawakened.

Paul, following her into the garden, sat down on the step in the sun, patting the stone beside him as an invitation to Charlotte to join him. After a moment's hesitation she did so, arranging her skirts to avoid a patch of mud.

'Will you ever live here permanently?' he asked.

'I doubt it. With all its faults we love London.'

'So do I.' At ease he leaned back, elbows on the step behind him, long legs crossed. Appreciatively he raised his face to the sun. 'I thought it the end of the world when Gabriel first suggested I went to Amsterdam, but I grew to like it. Even so, I'm glad to be back.'

'How odd it is, knowing nothing of what happened to you there – or nothing but the bare outline.' She wondered again at the unaccountable ease that existed between them, the feeling of familiarity with someone who had, after all, grown from a boy to a man in the years since they last met. 'You should seem like a stranger, yet you do not.'

'I feel the same about you. Most of the time I wonder where poor, shy little Lottie has gone – then suddenly I catch a glimpse of her and all the years since our last meeting disappear in a puff of smoke.'

'She's there, right enough.' Charlotte spoke with feeling. 'Though I hope not near so foolish as once she was.'

'Tell me.' He turned towards her with a smile, settling himself more comfortably. 'How do you care for the task of stepmother? Are you and Elise in accord?'

'Yes, indeed.' Charlotte answered quickly, then laughed.

200

'Well, most of the time. The only disagreements Gabriel and I ever have are concerning her. He can never say "No" to her, and there is no doubt she is dreadfully indulged. This is strictly between us, Paul. I speak to you as an old friend.'

'Gabriel has always seemed to me so wise in other matters, so balanced in his judgment.'

'Elise is his Achilles' heel. He can deny her nothing. Oh, I should not speak so for she is a lovely, lovable girl, with all the spirit that I never had. Life is always a little brighter, a little more amusing, when Elise is about.'

'It is a pity you have no other children.'

Charlotte looked away from him to hide the cheeks that she knew had grown hot.

'Such matters are in God's hands,' she said.

'And what of *la belle* Tantine?' he asked after a moment. 'You said she had moved to another house, but I cannot believe she doesn't plague you still. I always considered her a gorgon and a pernicious influence on Elise when she was a child. Are matters different now?'

'Tantine!' Charlotte gave a short laugh that ended on a sigh. 'She is not easy to contend with, I must confess. She is still too fond and foolish with Elise, but has less influence now she is growing up. She regards me with dislike amounting to hatred – and she dislikes Gabriel, too, I think, but is perforce polite to him for he pays her bills and even bought her the house.'

'Which must have been a relief to you!'

'Indeed it was! We began to think she would never shift.'

She became aware suddenly of the passage of time and looked at the watch that hung at her waist.

'Paul, we ought to go. I should hate my father to return to an empty house.'

'Very well.' He stood up and offered a hand to pull her up beside him. 'Thank you for bringing me here.'

'Oh, I'm the one who should be grateful. I would never have come, had you not given me a ride.'

For a moment they stood side by side, looking at the garden – at the robin who cocked a beady eye at them from the side of the urn at the bottom of the steps, at the drift of daffodils beneath the trees at the side of the garden.

'I had forgotten how lovely an English spring could be,' Paul said.

'You stayed away too long.' Charlotte lifted her arms as if she would embrace the garden and the flowers and the glories of the day. 'Oh, I feel like some dull old crow in my mourning clothes.'

'Black becomes you.'

'I have never thought so!' She turned to look at him with a smile which turned to a look of surprise as she saw the strangeness of his expression. He had been watching her again, and now his eyes seemed to have darkened and they held a look of dazed enquiry. He lifted a hand as if to touch her cheek, but stood as if turned to stone, unable to complete the gesture.

She was not conscious now of the garden or the birdsong, or of anything except his presence. For a moment they seemed to be insulated from the world, apart from it, encased in a crystal bubble.

Her eyes were fixed on that half-lifted hand, and she willed it to move onward and upward so that she would feel it against her skin. Already she could imagine it. It would be gentle, but at the same time it would burn like fire.

With disbelief she saw him lower it, and she knew by its trembling how much effort this retreat had cost him.

'You are right,' he said huskily. 'I stayed away too long.'

And with that, he turned and walked away from her.

So this was love!

Twenty-eight years old, she thought with wonder; and she had known Paul Bellamy for sixteen of those years without once ever guessing that he had the power to lift her to this state of ecstasy by the mere fact of his presence in the world. Twenty-eight, and she was as bemused as any schoolgirl, wholly possessed by the thought of him.

Odd images came to her without warning and set her heart singing. The shape of his hands as they held the reins; his grey eyes and the creases at the corners of them when he smiled. The way he whistled that little jigging tune as he rode along, and the power that she sensed in him, in those wide shoulders and long legs.

What did he think of her? He was not indifferent, she felt certain of it. She had only to think of the difficulty with which he had lowered his hand, almost as if he were fighting an adversary who was pulling it towards her. Sitting alone in her room at

Providence House, she pressed her own hand against her cheek and closed her eyes in longing.

It was a longing that would go for ever unfulfilled, but the thought did not at this moment dismay her. She asked for nothing, she told herself, except to know that Paul was in the world, and that he loved her too. And he did love her, he did, she was sure of it.

No, she asked for nothing and expected nothing. She was married to Gabriel and would never hurt him; how could she, when he had been so good to her? When he loved her so? When at times she could see such torment in his eyes?

There were days when he was brusque with her; days when he spent long hours in the loom shed or away on business concerns in the city, disappearing with no explanation at all, returning home drawn and silent. But such times had grown more and more infrequent, as if he had come to terms with his disabilities. She could do nothing to shatter this fragile peace. He was too fine a man.

At some time Paul would marry; it was inevitable. She faced the thought, there in her room at Providence House, and though it took her breath away momentarily, she told herself that when the time came she would accept it sensibly. Perhaps they could be friends, she and Paul's future, unknown wife, for her love and his would remain unspoken and unacknowledged. It was enough, she told herself again, that he should *be*!

Meantime she would pray for strength; strength to withstand this emotion and keep it secret. Nothing so wonderful could in itself be sinful, she thought; only any outward manifestation of it.

Her father noticed nothing. To her joy, he had been drawn into the Queen's Evil controversy, passionately defending his opposition to Dr Hoad's outmoded ideas. There was talk of Dr Hoad's dismissal, meetings with the Infirmary Guardians, battle lines drawn. For all of this Charlotte was profoundly thankful, for it brought him to life again, and though she found the interminable arguments rehearsed for her benefit every evening hardly the most absorbing of subjects, she was thankful that she was not required to participate – or at least, to do no more than give the occasional murmur of agreement.

Behind the mask of her polite smile and concerned expression, she thought of Paul. He was in London now. No doubt he had already called to see Gabriel – or would do so before much time had elapsed. It gave her a strangely bitter-sweet pleasure to think of him in surroundings she had made so much her own. Would he feel her presence there, she wondered? Sense her influence in the decoration and graceful furnishings? Suddenly it seemed unbearable that she should be absent any longer.

'I must go back to London,' she said one day at dinner, breaking into her father's discourse without warning. 'Now that you are back at work you will not miss me – and after all, we shall be at Whiteacres for the summer before many weeks are past.'

'Oh?' Dr Bonnet looked startled and dismayed. She had interrupted his account of the battle of words between Dr Hoad and himself, a battle in which he had been quite clearly the victor. He had been looking forward to the telling of it all day. Now she saw by the change in his expression that he had lost all heart for it. His chin trembled, and quickly he dabbed at his mouth with his napkin to hide his emotion. 'Well, if you must go, then you must, of course. No doubt you should think of your duty to your husband. Though as for not missing you –' He reached out and patted her hand. 'I assure you, my dear, I little know how I shall face each day.'

'Then I shall tarry a little longer,' she said gently.

11

'There is nothing,' breathed Elise ecstatically, 'nothing quite so stirring as the sight of soldiers in uniform.'

'And in such quantity!' Catherine murmured, lips close to her friend's ear, mouth curved in an appreciative smile of agreement.

The two girls turned their eyes from the colourful spectacle of the parading troops to look at each other and exchange conspiratorial giggles.

The vantage point afforded by Mrs Maxwell's four-in-hand was first class. They had come early to Hyde Park, knowing that there would be a great press of people, and even then the postillion had been forced to jockey for a place. Now they saw that all the waiting had been worth while. The sound of fife and drum above the shout of commands and the jingle of harness was a fitting background to the sight of the three troops of guards, clad in scarlet coats laced with gold with white feathers and great knots of ribbons on the sides of their hats. All were mounted on black horses and by any standard they were a magnificent body of men.

'Let the French match that,' Mrs Maxwell said, moved almost to tears. 'How proud the Queen must be!'

'There's Frederick,' Catherine said excitedly. 'There, on the right – no it's not.' She subsided disappointed. 'How alike they all look!'

'He said he would come and find us when the parade is over, he and Lieutenant Moore. How pleasant it will be to see the lieutenant again! It seems an age since our last meeting with him, does it not, Catherine?'

'Far too long, Mama.' Catherine's reply was demure. This time the girls did not look at each other, but pretended absorption in the parade, biting their lips to prevent the tell-tale giggles that threatened their composure. Mrs Maxwell might be among the most easy-going mothers of Elise's acquaintance, but even she would have been scandalised to know that only the previous night, the two girls – discreetly masked, of course – had walked in St James's Park with the amiable lieutenant and Captain Maxwell, long after the hour when all supposed them to be in their beds.

Not that Elise's affections were seriously engaged. It was a game, nothing more; a springtime flirtation. If it were not for the uniform, she admitted to herself, Frederick Maxwell would appear quite ordinary. It concerned her not at all that both men were on duty that night and that a meeting was out of the question.

Catherine, who was wildly in love with Lieutenant Moore, was far less happy.

'Suppose they are not on duty,' she said as they lay in bed that night, the candle snuffed. 'Suppose it was an excuse –'

'You goose, why should it be? They are soldiers, after all!'

'It would not in the least surprise me to learn he is betrothed to some landowner's daughter from the shires.'

'He is not concerned with marriage. He has a war to fight.'

'I should wait for him, if he did but ask.'

'Men!' Elise settled herself on her pillows. 'They have everything their own way, don't they? They go off to war, they choose to marry, or not to marry –'

'While we have to wait to be chosen.'

'Well, I have no wish to be chosen by anyone yet.'

'What about this man your father has in mind for you?'

'Paul Belamie – Bellamy, I should say *à l'anglaise*, for he has changed his name along with the rest of his family.'

'Well, what about him?'

'I've not seen him since I was six years old. Papa thinks him wonderful, which makes *me* think he will prove to be dull and strait-laced – though I do recall that he made me laugh. He was a great one for jokes and tricks.'

'Then perhaps you won't find him dull at all!'

'Shall I confess something to you, Catherine?' Elise raised her head and looked towards the pale blur that represented her friend's face. 'I am heartily tired of Huguenots – tired of hearing about how worthy they are and how hard they work and how much they contribute and how they suffered for their faith and how foolish the French king was to make life impossible for them and how greatly England has benefited from them.' She drew in a deep breath and let her head fall back against the pillow with a thud. 'I am tired of life being so serious and righteous. I want to kick up my heels and enjoy myself. One day I shall fall in love, no doubt, and I shall marry – but it will be with someone amusing, someone I choose myself.'

'I expect it will,' Catherine said, a note of envy in her voice. 'I cannot imagine your father saying you nay.'

Elise yawned cavernously.

'He knows better than to try.'

Paul and Elise?

Charlotte stared at the letter from Gabriel, feeling as if the breath had gone from her body. Gabriel had written:

They have not yet met, for Paul is not due to present himself here until this day week. However, I cannot avoid the hope that they will find favour in each other's eyes for Paul has ever been as a son to me and there is no man to whom I would rather entrust my beloved daughter. I ask you to join your prayers with mine, that God should grant a happy outcome to their meeting.

But she is a child, Charlotte thought, letting the sheet of paper fall on the table before her. He cannot love her!

Where now was her high-minded resolve to accept the fact of Paul's marriage when it arose with dignity and resignation? Restlessly she rose from her chair and moved about the room. She could not bear it – no, it was too much; far, far too much. How would it be possible, to see them together? God would surely not devise this torture for her.

She picked up the letter and read it again.

'They have not yet met –'

He will not love her, she assured herself. She is too immature, too young and foolish.

And since when did youth and immaturity and foolishness prevent a man from falling in love with a pretty face, she asked herself? Any man could be forgiven for doing so.

She must go home. Though her presence was unlikely to affect the outcome of events one way or the other, and though it would be agony to stand by and be witness to the so-called happy outcome that Gabriel so fervently desired, it would be still worse to be stuck at Providence House not knowing how events were shaping in London.

Her eye fell on a page of the letter that had fallen to the ground unnoticed. Now she picked it up and read on.

The best news I have kept until last. This very morning I was visited by an emissary from St James's Palace, commanding my presence with samples of silk for the Queen's use.

I am to go in two days' time and propose taking your pansy design, also the Chinese and the gold curlicue as well as plain colours and shot silk. No doubt Her Majesty will require an exclusive design but these will serve as examples of your skill.

She felt nothing. She had dreamed of this once, but now it seemed of no importance compared to the rest of his letter; but at least she saw in it the excuse she needed to leave Canterbury at last.

She need feel no guilt, she told herself. She had done her duty by her father; now she would tell him that her designs were in demand by the Queen of England herself and that she must return home at once. He would understand – would feel the pride that was so strangely lacking in herself.

Meantime she would write to Gabriel to tell him to send the carriage for her.

Yes, indeed, she said in her letter. Of course she would pray for Elise, as she never failed to do. She managed, however, to avoid being more specific.

There was a prosperous air of solidity about the house, yet the pillars on each side of the portico were graceful. It was, Paul thought, a great improvement on the old house at the other end of the street and was evidence of Gabriel's increasing wealth.

It was clear, however, by the delight with which the silk-weaver rose from his chair with hand outstretched at Paul's appearance, that he had not changed in his affections.

'Welcome, welcome my boy,' he said warmly. 'Welcome, indeed. Molly, will you please serve tea now? We shall have it by the fire, for though the almanack may tell us it is almost summer, my bones say otherwise. Now sit down and make yourself comfortable. I must hear all your news. How goes the world with you?'

His interest was so warm, so genuine, that Paul had no

hesitation in confiding everything to him; from the resentment that he had encountered from one or two of the older silversmiths employed by the late Monsieur Charpentier to the pleasure he had taken in being reunited with Harry Porter who had once been a fellow apprentice when he had previously worked in London.

'It was so good to see him again,' he said. 'And as for the others, I think they have learned now that I shall not interfere with their work but will have concerns of my own. I've spent much of this past week visiting customers who bank with us in Amsterdam despite being residents of London. We hope they will agree to transfer their accounts when the bank here begins to function.'

'The day you begin trading, I shall make a substantial deposit myself.'

'That's more than kind of you, monsieur. Your confidence in me won't be misplaced.'

'I know it will not. Even if I did not know you well enough myself, I am assured that Monsieur Charpentier's faith in you is well founded. There is a matter that has been on my mind of late –' He cut himself short and Paul looked at him questioningly. 'No matter,' he continued. 'Time enough when you are open for business.'

'Naturally, if there is any way I can be of assistance –'

'It is Elise's inheritance that perplexes me.'

'Ah – *la petite héritière*! Does Madame Colbert still refer to her so?'

'I fear that she does! It gives quite the wrong impression for it is no great fortune, merely a comfortable portion. I have contrived to scotch talk of marriage to a duke, I believe. No, it's no fortune, but it is a substantial amount, left in trust by her maternal grandfather. It will be hers when she marries or comes of age, whichever is the sooner. I am not convinced it is invested as advantageously as it might be, but as I said, all can wait. Tell me, do your premises please you?'

'They'll do well enough, once the building is done. We are enlarging at the back so that there is room for an office behind the shop.'

The maidservant who had shown him upstairs to the drawing room returned with tea at this point.

'Is Mam'selle Elise ready to join us, Molly?' Gabriel asked.

'Pray tell her that Mr Paul Bellamy is here and that tea is served.'

Molly bobbed a curtsey in response.

'Molly is Nan's younger sister,' Gabriel went on with a smile. 'She and Elise played together as children in the fields of Kent.'

The maid was clearly flustered at being the topic of conversation, and she flushed scarlet.

'A pleasant girl,' Gabriel commented as she fled from the room. 'A little feather-brained, perhaps, but devoted to Elise. She, by the way, should be with us in a moment. I have no doubt she wanted to change her gown before meeting you. She remembers you well – says she used to ride on your back when she was six years old.'

Paul laughed.

'I remember it myself! A sound beating she was wont to give me if I should be too slow. I daresay she has changed somewhat since then.'

'She's a young lady now. We shall be thinking soon of marriage.'

He said no more and the words had been uttered with studied casualness, but there was something in the look he gave Paul which seemed full of meaning – an unspoken question which lingered in the air.

Me – a possible suitor for Elise? Paul asked himself incredulously. Surely not! What had he to offer? Yet there had seemed an unmistakable intent in Gabriel's manner. Was the mention of Elise's inheritance a hint that his own lack of means would not be an insurmountable objection?

When he had last seen Elise, he had thought her delightful in many ways, but hopelessly spoiled by her doting father. Nothing he had heard since his return had persuaded him that much had changed. And even if it had, such an idea was out of the question.

Because of Charlotte? No, no, of course not! That strange moment at Whiteacres had been a wayward temptation born of springtime and youth and the unaccustomed sun. He had resolutely put it out of his mind, or at least to the back of it. It had been so unexpected, that wave of emotion that had shaken him to his foundations. He had never wanted anything more than to reach out and touch that velvety skin, nor found the denying of any impulse more difficult, but he had known then that it would have been disastrous to give way to it.

The truth was that he had no wish to marry at all just yet – and when he did, he would choose his own bride, not agree meekly for the purpose of pleasing others. No doubt he had been mistaken. Gabriel Fabian would surely look far above Paul Bellamy to find a suitable husband for his daughter.

As if on cue, she entered the room. Delicately made, golden-haired, dressed in palest pink with a stiffly boned bodice trimmed with white lace, Elise Fabian looked as if she were made from sugar icing.

She greeted him coolly, with exaggerated dignity, and as she took her place at the small table to pour the tea Paul thought she seemed like a child acting the part of a society hostess.

'I was reminding your father of the quite unmerciful way you insisted on treating me when you were little more than a babe,' he said jokingly.

She did not smile in return, but lifted elegant eyebrows.

'It was so long ago. Really, it has gone from my mind.'

'Come now, Elise! You have often spoken of Paul and how he played games with you.'

Languidly she handed him the tea.

'So much time has passed. You must forgive me if other things now occupy my mind.'

Paul hid his amusement. She was clearly striving hard to prove how far she was now from the boisterous, demanding child he remembered. But she was a child still, that much was clear – lovely beyond words, but a child.

'Has Charlotte said when she is returning?' he asked.

'I am sending the coach for her first thing tomorrow. We have had some excitement here, Paul. The Queen wants her to design some silk! I was bidden to St James's Palace a few days ago and the samples I took with me met with great favour. The Queen would like some more.'

'What great news, monsieur! I offer my congratulations.'

'It was fortunate,' Elise said knowingly, 'that the Duchess of Marlborough is away from court since the death of her son. I have it on the best authority that she is mean as dirt, and as Mistress of the Robes –'

'That will do, Elise.' For once her father looked at her with reproof. 'That is no way to speak of Her Grace.'

Elise lowered her lids and said nothing, but her expression was omniscient as if she knew much that was hidden from her father.

Paul sipped his tea to hide his amusement at her pretensions.

'I am pleased for le Bec's sake, as well as for my own,' Gabriel went on. 'And for Charlotte, of course, who works so hard at her designs. We are all in this together, with none of us able to work independently of the others.'

'I trust I am to be shown the new weaving shed,' Paul said.

'My dear boy, if you are sure you would not find it tedious –'

'I should like nothing better, I promise you.'

Elise accompanied them on the tour which took place as soon as they had finished their tea. Paul was astonished by the size and scope of the operation. In one section were the looms set up to weave the most complicated patterns; in another, those which made half-silk, alamodes and lustrings. The clatter was unceasing, the number of those employed there many times greater than when Paul had last been in Spitalfields.

Simon le Bec had changed little. He was more grizzled, his face a little more seamed, but his welcome was warm. He clasped Paul's hand in his own great paw – apparently so clumsy, yet with fingers as delicate as a woman's when it came to setting up a loom.

His greeting of Elise, however, was more restrained and it was not difficult to see the reason for this. Her presence was an obvious disruption. One young apprentice suddenly found it necessary to sweep endlessly at the same point close by the visiting party, stealing glances at her as he did so until peremptorily ordered to the other end of the shed. Even the older workers seemed tempted to slow down and gaze at her in admiration, while her effect on the younger ones was disastrous.

Having been shown the extent of the place and different looms in various stages of production, Paul stood, fascinated, watching an intricate design take shape before his eyes.

'Did Charlotte design that?' he asked Elise, who was standing close by. She made a gesture and shook her head, indicating that she could not hear him for the noise of the looms.

'Did Charlotte –' Paul began again, then shrugged his shoulders, defeated.

Elise turned to leave, and he followed her. Gabriel was at some distance, in discussion with le Bec, apparently engrossed.

'It is as well that we leave before production falls too markedly,' Paul said.

'Apprentices are so stupid!'

212

'Yet I imagine you would not like to be ignored.'

'I'm sure I do not care!'

'Elise.' Laughing, Paul reached for her arm and pulled her to a halt. 'Why so hoity-toity? We were friends once – I cannot believe you have forgotten, child though you were.'

She shrugged away from him and continued walking, her head in the air.

'What is it, Elise?' Paul remained at her shoulder, rapidly though she walked back to the house. 'Surely we can be friends still?'

She stood still, turning to face him. Her expression was stony.

'Has my father put you up to this?' she asked.

'Put me up to what? To asking if I have done aught to offend you?'

At this apparent bewilderment, something of the fierceness left her.

'Well,' she said uncertainly. 'I could not be sure.' She hesitated for a moment, biting her lip as if unsure whether to speak. Then she took a step closer to him and lowered her voice.

'He wants us to marry,' she whispered, her eyes blazing with the enormity of it. 'Just so long as you understand such a thing is *out of the question*, then we can be friends again. I will *not* have a husband chosen for me!'

'To be honest, I'm not much in favour of the idea myself.'

'It's not that I don't *like* you.' Her eyes were wide and serious. 'I should not like you to think that. I should not like you to be hurt *in any way!*'

'Believe me, I am not.' Paul was equally serious, though his eyes gleamed with amusement. 'For my part, it is not that I don't consider you pretty as a picture – simply that, like you, I intend to determine my own fate.'

'Then we'll shake on it.' Elise extended her dainty hand. 'Let us make a bargain to resist all pressure.'

'To be friends and nothing more,' Paul agreed as he took her hand in his.

'And never, never to marry – unless, of course –' she hesitated for a moment – 'unless we should chance to fall in love. Not,' she added hastily, 'that I think it in the least likely, if you will forgive me for saying so. I have lately been mixing with officers of the Coldstream Guards –'

'With whom I should never dream of attempting to compete!'

'Then that's settled.' She let out her breath in a puff of gratitude. 'Thank heaven. Now I don't have to worry about you.'

'Does that mean you can start behaving like a girl of sixteen and not a dowager of sixty?'

'There is no need,' Elise said, with a return to her former haughty manner, 'to *presume* on friendship.'

Charlotte's expression gave no hint of the relief she felt at hearing that Elise had made it quite clear to her father that she would entertain no thought of marrying Paul.

'I cannot imagine why,' Gabriel said. 'Things were a little cool at first, but after a while they seemed to be in accord. Still Elise is quite adamant.'

'She is very young, Gabriel. There is no hurry to arrange a match for her. Indeed, I should think it positively undesirable. Leave her to follow her own inclinations.'

'And allow her to choose some coxcomb with nothing but a handsome face to recommend him?'

'Her own affections must surely be regarded!'

'I should so like to have Paul as my son in fact as well as fancy.'

'I cannot believe it right for a marriage partner to be foisted on anyone.'

'Foisted?' Gabriel looked taken aback at the word. 'I have no intention of foisting anyone upon her – no one, at least, to whom she could possibly object.'

'No?' Charlotte sounded sceptical.

'No!' He looked at her angrily. 'It is not that I seek money or position. Paul is a fine, steady young man with considerable business acumen, but more importantly he has a background of love and stability. That is what I want for my daughter, and I consider it my duty to guide her in the right direction. If I had more worldly goals – money, or a title, for example – then I would deserve criticism, but that is not the case.' He had been pacing agitatedly, but now stood before her, hands extended as if in supplication. 'Tell me, is that so wrong?' he demanded in ringing tones.

Laughing, Charlotte imprisoned his hands between hers.

'You are not addressing the Consistory,' she said. 'And Paul is not the only worthy young man in the world.'

'I suppose not.' Gabriel laughed too, a little shame-facedly. 'Forgive my vehemence. I am fond of the boy, as you know, and always have been so. And there is no doubt that his affairs would benefit greatly from Elise's inheritance. I should hate it to fall into the wrong hands.'

'Surely you didn't mention it to him? Gabriel, we agreed that it would never be mentioned, lest it attract the wrong suitor –'

'But Paul is the *right* suitor! Or would be, if either of those two young people had any sense.'

'Leave it, Gabriel, I beg you. As I said before, there are other worthy young men beside Paul.'

'We must ask him to supper now that you are back. Perhaps on closer acquaintance Elise will feel differently.'

'Ask him by all means.' Charlotte hoped that her calm voice betrayed none of the inner turmoil she was experiencing at the thought of seeing him again. 'But I do implore you to put aside for the moment all thoughts of a match for Elise, with Paul or any other. She is more immature than you realise. All her apparent confidence is on the surface, with no real substance. Let her grow up a little.'

Gabriel smiled at her affectionately.

'Perhaps you are right, my dear. I only seek her happiness.'

The invitation to Paul was issued and accepted, and on the appointed day Charlotte forced herself to work at her drawing board as if nothing unusual was afoot.

There was indeed good reason for her to do so. Not only had she been commissioned to design silk for Her Majesty, Queen Anne – a task which would result in more honour and glory than hard cash – but she had also been presented with a particularly challenging request from Mrs Belle Harkness, a leading actress at the Theatre Royal, Drury Lane. She required several spectacular gowns to wear in her role of Millamant in a revival of *The Way of the World* – a play that had not been too well received when it had first been produced a couple of years earlier, but was to be staged once more with all the glitter and glamour that its sparkling dialogue demanded.

The Calvinist in Gabriel found little to approve of in this kind of production which placed so much emphasis on marital infidelity, but Charlotte paid no heed to his objections.

'I daresay her morals are no worse than some of the society ladies who patronise us,' she said. 'And she is the best advertisement we could hope for.'

For the moment she put aside the matter of the Queen's design, for it was Mrs Harkness's commission that was the most urgent. Crimson, she thought, relieved by a golden trellis design and a flower motif, more showy than for most tastes but perfect for the stage.

As so often, she found contentment in filling her mind with shapes and colours, and the day passed quickly. She had never been more thankful for the occupation that so absorbed her, for when at last she retired to change into something more suitable for entertaining than the dark gown and fichu she had worn all day, she was forced to admit to herself that she was in a quite ridiculous state of nervousness, changing her mind no less than three times about the gown she would wear until even Nan grew exasperated.

'For pity's sake, ma'am, put on the blue and have done with it,' she said at last with the familiarity of years of service. 'Now sit down, do, and I'll dress your hair in the new way, with centre parting, puffed out a little around the cap.'

Obediently Charlotte submitted herself to Nan's deft hands and at length the maid stood back, beaming with satisfaction as she contemplated the result of her labours.

'There,' she said. 'You look a real beauty, and no mistake.'

Charlotte, stroking the seed-pearl necklace that brought out the warmth and texture of her skin, laughed.

'Never that,' she said. 'Of passable looks, perhaps, when you have dealt with me and when I am happy. But beauty? No, Nan. I count such as Elise a beauty, for she dazzles even as she sleeps.'

She could see that she looked well that night and was glad of it, but now the meeting with Paul was almost upon her she felt that she had been a fool. She had allowed her imagination to run away with her. Nothing had happened; nothing had changed. She and Paul were friends, just as they always had been.

Hold on to that, she told herself. Forget that strange, inexplicable mood of exaltation that had followed the visit to Whiteacres. It had no basis in reality. It was a fantasy, nothing more, caused by some unworthy biological need which it was her duty to subdue. And subdue it she would, she resolved firmly.

Her meeting with him under Gabriel's benevolent gaze made her feel that it was a resolution she could easily keep. Paul was as friendly as ever, but no more so. They talked lightly of affairs of the day and of the Bellamy family, of Paul's new office and of Charlotte's commission from the Queen. No, she said. She had

216

decided nothing yet. Such a matter would take great thought, and she had other orders more pressing.

'I fancy,' Gabriel said, 'that it is normally the Duchess of Marlborough we have to please, since she is the Mistress of the Queen's Robes, but it was a Mistress Hill who dealt with me.'

'While the cat's away –' Elise said. 'There are those who say Mistress Hill is supplanting the Duchess in the Queen's affections. Her Grace refuses the Queen too much finery and all her gowns are refurbished a dozen times over before she is allowed to wear new.'

'My stars! I am impressed by such an intimate knowledge of the Royal Household,' Paul said teasingly. 'How do you come by it, may I ask?'

'On the very best authority,' Elise replied. She was laughing, no longer omniscient. 'From Catherine Maxwell's mother's friend's cousin, who moves in the very best of circles – or so Catherine is always telling me. In my mind's eye I can see her, moving in very stately fashion, round and round without ceasing. It is to be hoped that she doesn't grow dizzy.'

How well they get on together, Charlotte thought with a pang. It would not surprise me if one day Gabriel had his wish.

'Truly,' Elise went on more seriously. 'Mrs Maxwell says that Her Grace is most overbearing in her manner and never ceases to press her own political views on the poor Queen. She is not allowed one moment free of them, so Mrs Maxwell says.'

Gabriel smiled at her.

'But *chérie*, you do realise that Mrs Maxwell is as ardent a Tory as Her Grace is a Whig? Her views on the matter might be thought by some to be just a little biased, as well as no more than hearsay evidence. I have a great respect for the Earl of Godolphin and feel we can safely rely upon him, as the Queen's Chief Minister. Tory he may be – and as you know, I incline more to the Whig camp myself – yet I think he is a man of integrity and more than a match for the Duchess and her excesses.'

During the course of this conversation in which she took no part, Charlotte looked towards Paul, the routine glance of a hostess made to ensure that his glass was filled, the food to his liking. Instead she found his eyes upon her and saw her own bewilderment and consternation mirrored in Paul's expression; and in that moment she knew that she had not imagined that strange sensation she had experienced at Whiteacres.

And now it was happening again. She should look away from him, she knew it. Someone was bound to notice in a moment that across the width of the table she and Paul were locked together, just as surely as if their hands had been manacled.

The moment seemed to go on for a long time, as if the whole of life were suspended. Gabriel's voice, as mellifluous and persuasive as ever, continued in the background, but she heard nothing of what he said. She and Paul were alone, conscious only of each other, the two of them the only reality.

His face, she thought, seemed wiped of expression except for the look of uncertainty in his eyes as if he had been caught by surprise and could not understand what was happening to him. She felt equally frozen, equally confused, unable to drag her eyes from him. She saw him blink as if waking suddenly from sleep, and turn to Gabriel in answer to a question.

'Forgive me,' he said. 'I was dreaming. It seems so strange to be here with you again –'

'I asked if you had any interest in politics.'

'Er – no.' He made an effort to collect himself. 'That is – I suppose my natural inclination is towards the Whigs but there seems such a deal of squabbling lately that one is tempted to say "A plague on both their houses".'

His remark led naturally to more discussion of the theatre in general and Shakespeare in particular.

'I must recommend the production of *Hamlet* at the Theatre Royal,' he said. 'I saw it last night and enjoyed it greatly. It made me realise how thankful I am to be back in London.'

'You must join us for the play one evening, Paul.' Gabriel smiled at him benevolently.

'I should like nothing better, monsieur.'

Nor I, Charlotte thought, not looking at him; but it must not happen. Somehow Gabriel must be prevented from engineering such occasions, for instinct told her no good would come from it as far as his plans for Paul and Elise were concerned. Yet how she longed for it! She glanced once more towards Paul, and once more caught his eye, but it was not bewilderment she saw in his face now but unhappiness, as if the implication of this unexpected attraction between them were only now coming home to him.

Later, as she lay sleepless in bed, she thought of herself and her childlike, unrealistic happiness when she had first realised her love. How could she have been happy? she asked herself now.

218

How could she have deluded herself that merely being in the same world was enough?

It was even more unbelievable that once the thought of a man's touch had filled her with abhorrence. Now she felt weak with longing, hollow with it, her body nothing more than one vast ache so that her mouth opened in a soundless scream and tears forced themselves from under her closed eyelids.

A mile or two away in a tavern near the river, oblivious to the serving wenches and the pot boys, the seamen and hawkers, the artisans and merchants' clerks, Paul sat alone. Joylessly he drank, savagely angry at fate, determined to blot out the pain, even though he knew that the fiery bite of the geneva would solve nothing. After all was gone, he knew that the pain would be there still.

He loved Charlotte. What a bitter, evil irony that of all the women in the world, it should be this one who moved him like no other. Merely to look at her was to know how she would feel in his arms and to experience such a surge of longing that he gasped aloud with it.

Lust, he reminded himself harshly, was one of the seven deadly sins; no doubt lusting after the wife of one's benefactor carried the penalty of the worst torments hell could devise.

Yes, he lusted after her, to the point where he could scarcely pick up a glass at dinner for the way his hand trembled; but there was nothing lustful about the dear familiarity he felt in her company, the recognition, the knowledge that here, at last, was the one person with whom he could live in harmony all the days of his life.

He poured more from the jar and drank again, feeling the passage of the burning liquid down his throat and into his gut. He longed for oblivion, was determined on it, but it seemed no matter how much he drank it eluded him and when he stumbled out into the night the pain was no less. He doubted that it would ever be.

12

'There's rosemary, that's for remembrance; pray, love, remember; and there is pansies, that's for thoughts.'

Even the pit had fallen moderately quiet at the sight of poor, distracted Ophelia, but Gabriel leaned close to Charlotte.

'I cannot help but think Mrs Harkness a little mature for the role,' he whispered, with some amusement.

Charlotte smiled at him, but made no reply. It was a week now since the night that Paul had supped with them, a week during which she had felt like a puppet worked with strings, a creation of someone else's fantasy without will or power of her own. Nothing seemed real, nothing touched her. She ate because the food was placed on the table before her, not because she was hungry. She retired to bed because the appropriate hour had struck, not because she expected to sleep; nor did she, more than an hour or two.

Even her work had lost its power to absorb her. She sat at her drawing board working on the Queen's design now that she had filled the order for Mrs Harkness, but though she tried for hours on end nothing she produced satisfied her, nothing bore the touch of freshness and originality that was her hallmark.

Gabriel was worried at her pallor and listlessness and insisted that she see a physician who pronounced that she suffered an imbalance of the four humours, blood, phlegm and both black and yellow bile, for which blood-letting was the only cure. Charlotte was too much her father's daughter to submit to this and had flounced to her room, assuring her worried husband that there was nothing amiss with her. Her spirits were low. She had, after all, only recently lost her mother, and the time she had spent with her father had been a strain.

'The sooner we go to Whiteacres for the summer, the better it will be,' Gabriel said. 'Now that we are a week into May we should be making plans for it.'

'I must finish the Queen's design.'

'So soon as you have, we shall go.'

Meanwhile, to divert and amuse her, he had taken a box at the Theatre Royal to see the production of *Hamlet* so warmly recommended by Paul.

Could one go mad for love, she wondered, her gaze fixed on the stage? She had always thought the character of Ophelia overdrawn, but now she was not so sure. Was *she* going mad?

It surely made no sense to let a sinful passion ruin a life that had, until now, run along pleasant, if unexciting, ways. Had she really no more backbone than the distraught creature currently strewing her flowers on the stage – a creature rendered more distraught than even Mr Shakespeare could surely have intended by the extravagance of Mrs Harkness's gestures?

Charlotte straightened her back with a new resolve. She would be sensible, strong and resolute, she told herself. She could not have Paul; that was an incontrovertible fact. She must accept the situation.

With determination she forced herself to concentrate on the play. Edmund Brownlea, the actor taking the part of Hamlet, was far too old, she thought. Better far to have given the role to the young man playing Laertes –

A frown appeared between her brows. She leaned towards Gabriel.

'Surely we know that man?' she said.

'Laertes?' Gabriel shook his head. 'Not that I recall.'

'He seems oddly familiar.'

She continued to watch him, her appreciation of Shakespeare's words spoiled, just a little, by the irritating feeling that she had seen the actor before. Had he played, perhaps, at Dorset Gardens, the rival theatre? Or was it a chance encounter in a street, long forgotten, that now tugged at her memory?

It was not until he leapt into Ophelia's grave and was grappling with Hamlet that she remembered.

'Gabriel, it's Pierre,' she said, turning to him excitedly. 'Pierre Jourdaine! Suddenly it came to me – I have seen him scrapping like that a dozen times. How extraordinary! Pierre Jourdaine!'

'By all that's holy, I believe you're right.' Gabriel's face expressed amusement and surprise and pleasure in almost equal parts. 'Who would have thought it? He's changed a good deal.'

'Hush!' Elise said, bending to look at them severely. 'You're as bad as the ruffians in the pit.'

221

She was as excited as they were, however, when after the play was over and bodies littered the stage, they communicated their belief to her.

'Oh, I remember him,' she said. 'At least, I think I do. He was so droll, and made me laugh – but I do not recall he was near so handsome.'

'There was always a quickness about him, a liveliness,' Charlotte said. 'He was somewhat undersized, as I recall – and now I come to think of it, he was forever playing the mimic even then.'

'They disappeared into thin air, he and his family,' Gabriel said musingly. 'I should dearly love to know his story. Come! We shall go behind the scenes and pay a call on Monsieur Jourdaine. We owe him nothing less, for he left under suspicion of committing a crime which was never proved.'

Charlotte well remembered the anger she had felt at the time. It was after that first visit to Whiteacres. She had come back to Freedom Street, buoyed up with hope and excitement, longing to practise her new-found talent, ready to make a new beginning with Tantine, only to find that there was no such spirit of conciliation in her heart.

Before they had crossed the threshold, she had poured out the story to them. Pierre Jourdaine had stolen her purse and she had turned him from the house in disgrace.

'Oh, he swore his innocence right enough,' she said. 'But I knew better! What was I to do? Allow a thief and a liar to continue to have the run of the house? No, no! I threatened him with the law, said he would go to prison or even be hanged –'

The boy, not surprisingly had fled and could not be found. Charlotte had never believed in his guilt. Oh, he was a scamp and could be impudent at times, but even Simon le Bec, who was no sentimentalist, found it hard to believe that he was a thief.

As for Gabriel, he was as angry as Charlotte had ever known him. It was he and he alone who could dismiss employees, he told Tantine sternly. The boy's guilt was by no means established and he was entitled to a fair hearing. But it was the fate of the boy's mother and family that worried him most. He had taken a special interest in them from the beginning, for he had never known a more deserving case for charity than Madame Jourdaine, he told Charlotte worriedly. Pierre was the only breadwinner –

but now he and the whole family had taken fright and gone from Spitalfields, no one could tell them where.

'Well, that proves his guilt,' Madame Colbert maintained defiantly.

It proved nothing but his fear, countered Gabriel. Wouldn't *she* be afraid at the prospect of Newgate, never mind the hangman's rope?

'But he must have taken it,' she insisted. 'He was in the kitchen that day and Berthe saw him acting suspiciously, something in his hand.'

'And you could not wait to rid yourself of him because of your unreasoning dislike of the lad. Now he has gone, and his family with him – a poor, sick, hard-working woman with small children and no resources. What hope is there for them? Their fate will be on your conscience, madame.'

It was the end of Madame Colbert's sojourn in their home. He would accommodate her shilly-shallying no longer, Gabriel told her. A perfectly good house was available close by (far too close for his liking if the truth were told), and she must take it.

Gabriel had instituted exhaustive enquiries but could find no sign of Pierre or his family. Someone in the courtyard where the Jourdaine family had lived said he thought they had gone to the west country, but nobody knew for sure, and still fewer seemed to care.

Now here he was, acting upon the London stage! She could hardly wait to hear his story of the intervening years.

It was not the first time they had been backstage, for Charlotte's association with Mrs Harkness had meant that they were at times included in parties in the green room. It was therefore to her that they first made their way, through the maze of dark and draughty passages to the cramped little cupboard that did duty as a dressing room. Exhausted after her performance, the actress was reviving herself with a glass of geneva, her face still liberally daubed with greasepaint, a loose wrapper inadequately covering her bulging bosoms. Gabriel bowed politely and fixed his gaze on an elaborate wig that graced a stand, allowing Charlotte to explain their mission.

'Pierre Who?' Mrs Harkness set down the glass and frowned at them, uncomprehending. 'I don't know anyone of that name.'

'The man who played Laertes.'

Light dawned.

223

'Oh, you mean Peter Jordan! God bless my soul, you mean he's an old friend of yours? Who'd ha' thought it!'

'He was once an apprentice of ours.'

'An apprentice, eh? Well, bless my soul, I never did, not in all my born days!' Oh, there was a great deal of drama to be extracted from this! Mrs Harkness closed her eyes in ecstasy and rested the back of her hand against her forehead. 'What wonderful news for him, for he told me himself he has neither relative nor friend in London, having just come from Ireland. How joyful he will be to see you, my dear Mr and Mrs Fabian. Come, come –' She flung out her arms towards them. 'Come, my dears, I shall deliver you to him without delay.'

With the wrapper falling open still further revealing enough plump pink flesh to make two Ophelias, she swept all three of them off to an adjoining dressing room which Hamlet, despite his leading role, shared with Polonius and Laertes. An argument was in process concerning the finer points of who had, or had not, spoiled the other's entrance, but Mrs Harkness banged on the door until they fell silent.

'Visitors for Mr Jordan,' she announced, as one making a royal proclamation.

He came to the door without stock or wig, his shirt open to reveal his chest, pot of grease for removing his make-up in one hand, cloth in the other.

'If it's creditors, I've fled the country.' He spoke amiably, but his expression sharpened as Mrs Harkness stood aside and he saw who was waiting for him. 'By all that's holy,' he said softly. 'Do you seek out the malefactor as rigorously as this, monsieur?'

'Malefactor?' Gabriel frowned at him, perplexed; then his brow cleared and he laughed. 'My dear fellow, you cannot imagine we are hounding you for some misdemeanour that never happened? We were in the audience tonight and could not rest until we had renewed our acquaintance with you and shaken you by the hand. We enjoyed your performance greatly.'

'I thank you, sir, madame.' Seeing Elise in the background, Jordan bowed in her direction. 'And mam'selle?' He raised an eyebrow in comic astonishment as Elise moved a little so that a light fell upon her. 'Can this really be *la petite* Elise, grown into a lovely young woman?'

'Mr Jordan.' Elise bobbed a demure curtsey. 'I remember you made me laugh when I was a little girl.'

'I trust the experience was not repeated tonight. You were meant to weep.'

'Aye, that I did!'

'Move aside, your honours, move aside – there's work to be done here.'

An ornate throne was being carried from the direction of the stage, and Gabriel, Charlotte, Elise and Mrs Harkness flattened themselves against the wall to allow its passage, having no time to move before more scene-shifters bearing flats inched their way past.

'This is no place to talk,' Gabriel said. 'Will you do us the favour of returning home with us for some late supper, Jourdaine? – or Jordan, as we must now call you! It would give us great pleasure. We long to hear how you have occupied the years since you left us.'

'Does Madame Colbert live with you still?' His expression portrayed terror, but he laughed as Gabriel shook his head in denial. 'Then nothing would please me more, if you'll allow me a few moments to clean and dress myself.'

'My carriage will be waiting outside,' Gabriel said.

It had been his word against that of Madame Colbert, he told them, and he could see no way of proving his innocence. His mother had been even more terrified than he, for a good friend of hers had lost a husband to the hangman for a crime he had not committed, and she had therefore wasted no time in packing up their few possessions. They had left before dawn, taking the coach to Bristol where they had thought to take ship for America. His mother possessed one item of value, a ring given to her by her grandmother, which she proposed to sell in order to buy passages for them.

However, the ring, fine though it was, had not realised sufficient money, and their plans had to be altered. Nothing would induce his mother to stay on English soil, though by this time Peter was feeling safe from detection in Bristol and had even found a job of sorts in the office of a tobacco merchant close to the docks. She had not rested until she found a ship that would take them to Ireland.

'And a putrid, stinking gut-bucket it was,' Jordan told them. 'Never were reluctant mariners more thankful to reach shore than the Jourdaine tribe landing on the banks of the Liffey.'

He had a racy, amusing way of speaking and he made light of the problems that beset the family, though they must have been grievous. Charlotte's heart ached for poor Madame Jourdaine on whom had fallen the main burden of worry. They had lived in one mean room in a tenement close to the castle, he told them, and lived a hand-to-mouth existence until his mother had managed to find work making clothes at the theatre at Smock-Alley. He, too, through sheer persistence had found work at the theatre – not as an actor, but as a general odd-job boy and scene-shifter.

'It was my aim to tread the boards,' he said. 'And by God, I did it in the end, though it took time enough.'

Elise was unusually quiet as she listened to his story, her eyes fixed on his mobile face. It was not that he was particularly handsome, though he had seemed so on the stage. At closer quarters his features seemed too large, but she liked his dark eyes and his smooth, olive skin and the smile that seemed to invite his audience to join with him in amusement at the world, and the comic eyebrows that seemed to work overtime. He was so droll, so – so *different*! There was a volatility about him which made her think that, like herself, he revelled in drama and longed for adventure.

He was not a tall man. Set beside Captain Maxwell, he would have looked positively undersized, but she knew quite well which of them she would find the more entertaining. Uniforms had suddenly lost their appeal.

'How did you learn to act so well?' she asked him.

He had drunk well of Gabriel's Rhenish, and there was an expansiveness about his gestures.

'The whole world is an actor's academy,' he said. 'I observed. I watched people in the street, on the quays, in the markets. I stood by the side of the stage and watched how actors moved – how one man would make the words unconvincing, while another could speak the same words and have the audience in the hollow of his hand. I also read every play I could get my hands on, every book I could beg, borrow or steal –' He broke off, shrugged and laughed. 'A manner of speaking, I assure you. I am no thief.'

'We never thought you were,' Gabriel said.

'My ambition was to come to London,' Jordan went on, 'for any actor worth his salt must do so. The theatre in Dublin is a small, penny-pinching affair in comparison.'

'You have not mentioned your mother.'

'She died five years ago – and of my sisters, three died in infancy of the pox and another more recently in childbirth.'

'Such a hard life!' Charlotte spoke softly, thinking of the contrast between her lot and that of Madame Jourdaine.

'Yet you must be glad you did not remain apprenticed to a silk-weaver!'

'To be honest, monsieur, I was never much suited to it. I am an actor born, and can never be other.'

It was late when he left, and Charlotte found that, glad as she had been to see him again, and welcome as the diversion of his presence had been, she was in the end glad to see him go.

'I wonder if all actors are such egotists,' she remarked to Gabriel when at last they were on their own. 'Did it occur to you that he never once asked for our health, or for le Bec, nor made any of the enquiries one might have expected?'

'Perhaps it is not so strange, bearing in mind the circumstances of his departure,' Gabriel said tolerantly. 'He's an amusing little jackanapes and I'm glad to know he has done well for himself, despite the injustice he suffered at our hands. I don't suppose we shall be seeing him again, except at a distance.'

Elise said nothing to this. She patted her mouth delicately, hiding a yawn, kissed them both, and went to bed. But as she sat before her looking glass brushing her hair, her eyes had a thoughtful gleam in them. She had no intention of allowing the distance to be too great.

On Gabriel's previous visit to the palace he had been shown into a bare and poorly lit chamber clearly reserved for tradesmen where he had displayed his designs on the heavy oak table which was the room's only furnishing.

On this occasion, however, he was escorted by a page through what seemed like several miles of corridors to a far more sumptuously furnished apartment where he was greeted by Mistress Hill, the young woman who, some said, was rapidly supplanting Sarah, Duchess of Marlborough as the Queen's favourite. She seemed a demure, insignificant little creature, but she smiled at him pleasantly enough. There was, he thought, something more assured in her manner today, compared with the last occasion. He thought of Elise's words – 'While the cat's away' – and

227

wondered briefly if it was the continued absence from court of the Duchess that was encouraging this change.

'I am charged to conduct you to Her Majesty,' Mistress Hill told him. 'She feels in good health and spirits today and would welcome the diversion,' she added, seeing his look of surprise.

'I am more than honoured,' Gabriel murmured; and he said it once more as he bowed low before the Queen. He had been about to kneel, but a touch from her had prevented it.

'Monsieur, I saw from your gait that you suffer disability,' she said. 'My own infirmities are such that I have sympathy for you and no wish to cause you further discomfort. Hill, draw up a stool for monsieur.'

'Your Majesty is most thoughtful,' he said.

Her voice was musical, with a warmth in it that was pleasing, and though she was heavy-featured and her figure was gross, she was not the unattractive monstrosity that he had been led to believe. Her smile was sweet and there seemed genuine kindness, even simplicity, in her face.

She enthused over the designs, even though Gabriel was uncomfortably aware that they did not represent Charlotte's best work, lacking the quality of originality and freshness that had made her famous.

'Hill, you must help me,' she said, and quietly Mistress Hill came forward, having removed herself to a discreet distance. 'Look,' the Queen said. 'This one is charming – yet this one also is quite delightful. Her Grace would no doubt think them too youthful –'

'Your own infallible taste, Your Majesty, must assure you she would think no such thing! This colour becomes you greatly.'

'Do you think so, Hill? Well, perhaps you are right. Shall I choose this one or that? Or perhaps this third one –'

'Why not have them all, Your Majesty?'

'All?' Musically, the Queen laughed. 'Oh Hill, you wicked creature! Such a temptress! Well, why not –?'

While the cat's away, Gabriel thought once more, with some amusement.

'To be honest, monsieur,' the Queen said, as he rolled up the designs. 'It is against my inclination to wear any colours since the death of my dear boy, but at times my duties demand it.'

'I understand, madam. I cannot tell you how deeply I sympathise.'

228

'You have children, monsieur?'

'A daughter, madam. The source of great joy to me.'

'I delight to hear it. I would give much –'

He saw the tears well in her eyes, and silently Abigail Hill moved forward, handkerchief in hand, bending solicitously over her royal mistress, at the same time making it clear with a glance at Gabriel that it was time for him to leave.

He bowed again and murmured farewells, but to his surprise Queen Anne stopped him with an imperious gesture of her well-shaped hand.

'Wait, monsieur,' she said, once more in control of herself, adding a little testily in an aside: 'Thank you, Hill, it was but a momentary weakness. I am well enough now.'

'Your Majesty?' Gabriel looked at her questioningly.

'May I ask how you came by your wounds, monsieur?'

'I was tortured for my faith, madam.'

'Yet did not abjure! For that I admire you. And now you are here in England, in a society more free, more tolerant than the one you left behind. Do you find it agreeable?'

'How could I do otherwise, madam?'

'Clearly you have done well – made a success of your new life.'

'I am grateful for it; grateful to God, to my adopted country, and to you, Your Majesty, for you are England, and England is you.'

He bowed low once more and retreated from her, but not before he had bestowed on her the smile that lit his face and tended to leave all who saw it a little breathless.

'Such a charming man, Hill,' he heard the Queen say before a waiting page closed the door behind him.

Whiteacres was as welcoming as ever, and Charlotte began to feel the hope that peace might return to her. It had not done so yet, but the possibility of it was like a haven that lay just over the horizon.

The countryside was at its best. May had started cool but by the end of the month it was as warm as midsummer and the countryside was as lovely as she could ever remember, with blossom still on the apple trees and the hedgerows bright with ragged robin and vetch, herb Robert and speedwell.

She and Elise preceded Gabriel to Flewett's Cross, and it was two weeks after their arrival that he joined them. She was shocked at his appearance. Had he looked as pale and gaunt before she left, or had she been too wrapped in her own concerns to notice it? Perhaps it was the separation that was causing her to see him with new eyes.

'Are you having much pain?' she asked as they walked by the lake the evening after his arrival. Pain was something he lived with constantly, but he hated to speak of it. Dismissively he shook his head.

'Nothing I cannot bear,' he said.

'Then something is troubling you.'

'As you well know, the news from France is far from good.'

Charlotte sighed.

'Is there to be no end to it?' she asked. 'I cannot bear to think of the killing and suffering – on both sides, not only on ours.'

'One can only applaud the guerrillas' courage.'

Was he right? Were *they* right? Charlotte no longer felt completely sure.

Guerrilla warfare had broken out in the Hautes Cévennes almost a year earlier when a group of Protestants had raided the home of a priest, killing him and releasing a number of men and women who were in the cellars and had undergone fearful tortures. The house had been burned and the group responsible had retreated into the mountains, but the Commander of the Army in Languedoc had gone in search of them and many had been captured and executed.

Once the pursuit had died down, those that were left had not dispersed but had stayed together and had grown in number, contriving to supply themselves with arms and ammunition mainly by raiding the houses of priests and leading Catholic citizens. Protestants who had previously possessed arms were required by law to relinquish them, and it was in these centres that they had been stored.

Several guerrilla bands were formed. They were known as the Camisards and each was given a specific area as their particular responsibility. It was clear from the news that trickled through that the insurgents lived rough, enduring hardships beyond belief, showing unbelievable bravery and determination in the way they harried government troops.

Of course it was wrong that Protestants should be persecuted for their faith, Charlotte thought now; but the Camisards had burned churches and killed innocents. They, too, had blood on their hands, even if their original cause was righteous. She felt confused. The Protestants were Protestants, and would never change. Equally, the Catholics were convinced that theirs was the only path to heaven. Each were so entrenched that nothing would change them. How did killing help?

'I hear that Etienne Boyer is with Jean Cavalier's group,' Gabriel said.

Charlotte pulled him to a halt, turning him to face her.

'And you feel you should be there too, is that it? Gabriel, for the love of heaven, have you forgotten you are lame, past your first youth, and as if that was not enough, a wanted man?'

His eyes were cold; two dark, fathomless pits in his pale face.

'You put it very brutally.'

'Face the truth! What good will it serve if you are broken on the wheel?' He did not answer, and angrily she shook him . 'Can you not see what an empty gesture it would be? Is your life to be thrown away for no good purpose? Physically you are not strong enough to endure what these other men endure. Think of the winters in the Hautes Cévennes! They alone would kill you.' When still he did not answer, she drew back a little and looked at him measuringly. 'Has Boyer been attempting to persuade you otherwise?'

'No. I've not heard from him directly.' He walked away from her and went to the side of the lake. Picking up a handful of pebbles he threw them into the water one by one, staring as if fascinated at the widening circles of ripples. The exasperation faded from her face. She moved to his side, and when she next spoke her voice was gentle.

'Gabriel,' she said softly. 'Why be so hard on yourself? You have suffered for your faith, and still do, though God knows you make lighter of it than most men would. You are no longer young and do much good work in London –'

'So that all men call me blessed.' He spoke savagely, with a degree of self-disgust that astonished her. His eyes were shut tightly as if the weight of his suffering were too much to bear. 'You had best leave me, Charlotte. In moods like this I am no company for anyone.'

'I refuse, absolutely.' She took one of his hands between both her own. 'Gabriel, what is it that tortures you so?'

For a long moment he did not answer. He turned and looked at her, and she saw the pain in his eyes and was chilled by it.

'Guilt,' he said at last. 'Guilt at Celestine's death and my own survival. Guilt for the self-love that makes me exult in what I see in people's eyes when they look at me – still more, when they listen to me, and I see my words taking effect on them, moving them from one position to another, completely opposite. Guilt for my marriage to you, which was the gravest sin –'

'That's nonsensical! I begged you to marry me. Have you forgotten?'

'I have forgotten nothing. I wanted you so much that any reason sufficed.'

'Oh, why do you twist everything to your disadvantage?' Urgently she tugged at his hands. 'Listen to me, Gabriel. Even if your sins are as horrendous as you seem to imagine, are we not assured there are none which cannot be forgiven?'

'"Go and *sin no more*", the Lord says. It is a command I am incapable of obeying.'

'Come,' she said coaxingly, taking his arm. 'Let us walk a little more. The wood is so beautiful at this time of the year.'

He yielded to the pressure of her hand and together they walked slowly away from the lake along a wide bridle way, the beech leaves new and green all around them.

'You said,' Charlotte ventured after some moments of silence, 'that you had not heard directly from Boyer. I surmise, however, that you have heard news of the Camisards from some source.'

'From my half-brother in Nîmes.'

She stopped short in astonishment, looking at him with her mouth open. What a strange and secretive man he was! He had not, to her knowledge, heard from any of his family in France in all the years she had been married to him; one would have expected that such a letter, after so long, would have merited some mention.

'You said nothing!'

'No.' He did not elaborate and they continued walking, Charlotte's expression showing her bewilderment.

'Did he have any particular intelligence for you?'

For a moment he said nothing, and she saw that his face had grown even more sombre.

'He wrote to tell me of my mother's recent illness,' he said. 'She has recovered now, it seems, but was brought low during the winter and forced to face the fact that she is not immortal. When she thought death imminent, she was troubled by the long silence between us.'

Since the time when he had first told her of his family's history, he had never spoken again of his mother, but looking at him now Charlotte thought she had confirmation of what she had suspected before; this estrangement was part of the darkness of his soul, one more burden for his already overburdened conscience.

'What is your brother's name?' she asked.

'What?' He looked at her in astonishment at this irrelevance. 'Jules. Why do you ask? He is a papist, too.'

'Does that make him less than human? He seems a kindly man, concerned for his mother. You say he gave you news of your friend, too. Gabriel, it's natural your mother should want to be reconciled with you – especially if she feels herself near to death.'

He continued to walk in silence, his lips a thin and bitter line, and when finally he spoke it was so quietly that she could barely hear him.

'To me she died years ago,' he said. 'Let us go back to the house, Charlotte.'

'As you wish.' They turned and began to retrace their footsteps, both occupied with their own thoughts. There was, Charlotte knew from past experience, little to be gained in trying to argue him out of a mood such as this. Still she could not resist one last attempt when they reached the gate that led to the garden.

'Gabriel – forgive me – I must speak, though I daresay you will think I understand nothing –'

He looked at her bleakly.

'Do as she wants, Gabriel. Write to her – some word of comfort, of understanding. Become reconciled with her before the hour is too late. If you do not, it will be one more regret to torment you.'

When he frowned in that way, his face seemed to Charlotte to be constructed from a series of angles, harsh and humourless, as unlike his true nature as it was possible to imagine.

'She abjured,' he said. 'She was faithless.'

'So you compound the sin by being as unforgiving and as unloving as your God appears to be!' She caught him by the forearms and pulled him closer towards her. 'Gabriel, can you not see that this is the one thing you can remedy? Nothing can bring Celestine back. You and I are married until death parts us.

You, with all your great gifts and all your faults, are as God made you. This alone can be changed. You can forgive your mother. In this regard you need sin no more.'

'Is abhorrence of treachery a sin?'

'"Judge not, that ye be not judged." It is written in Holy Scripture, Gabriel.'

'Her sin was grievous.'

She relaxed her hold on him and expelled her breath sharply, suddenly exasperated.

'How grievous? As grievous as the multitude of which you claim to be guilty? No, no – it was much worse, of course, for only then can you feel entitled to preen a little, and congratulate yourself that though you have sinned, she has sinned even more.'

He stared at her coldly, blank with astonishment, and defiantly she stared back, astounded at her own temerity. She had never spoken to him in such a way.

'Leave me,' he said. 'I should prefer to walk alone.'

'Whatever you wish.'

She turned from him and began to walk towards the house. Light was draining from the day and bats beginning to swoop around the eaves. Candles were already alight, and inside the house she could see Elise standing with her back to the window, talking to Nan, laughing and gesticulating. She was not ready to join them and she slowed her steps, idly bending to pick a flower and look into its depths.

Already she was regretting her outburst. It was no way for a wife to speak to a troubled husband, yet she had been goaded into it, repelled by Gabriel's complicated introspection. Perhaps, she thought with wry humour, she was more her mother's daughter than she realised. Brisk, practical common sense had always held sway in the Bonnet household, and she could well imagine that a strong purgative would have been her mother's remedy for Gabriel's moods.

But oh, it was hard to see him so troubled! What a strange, tortured man he was when the mood was on him, and how different when it had passed. Then there was no one like him; no one kinder or warmer or more loving. How could he have cherished this hatred for so long? It was against everything she knew of his nature. No wonder he was a soul in torment.

'Let it go, Gabriel,' she whispered. 'Let it go!'

She looked back over her shoulder to where the gate barred

the way into the wood but he had moved away and there was no sign of him. She shivered a little for the warmth had gone from the sun and a breeze had sprung up. She hoped he would have the good sense not to stay outside too long.

Again she looked towards the house. Elise had disappeared from view now. Suddenly she thought of Paul, the longing for him only intensified by the fact that he had been absent from her mind for a while. She closed her eyes as the pain washed over her, her imagination conjuring a house where he would be waiting, a house where there would be children, his and hers. Children, she realised with some astonishment, that she longed to bear – and could do so without fear.

When did the fear go? She could not tell. She only knew that, little by little as she had grown in confidence, it had withered and died, replaced until now by a resigned acceptance of the fact that motherhood was a condition she would never experience. She had thanked God that her skill at the designing board was sufficient recompense. Now she knew she would hunger for Paul's children all the days of her life, and she gasped a little, pressing her hands to her stomach as if the want of them was a tangible pain.

'Maman!' Elise was at the door, calling to her, coming down the stone steps to meet her. 'What's the matter? Do you feel unwell?'

She shook her head and did her best to smile.

'No, no. It's nothing at all. It's becoming rather cool out here –'

'Then come inside, do! Where has Papa gone?'

'He wished to walk further. He has matters on his mind.'

'Come and play bezique.' Elise's interest in her father's weighty problems was minimal. 'Do come, Maman. The cards are ready.'

'I am like a lamb to the slaughter,' Charlotte said with mock resignation.

It was true that, at the best of times, she was little match for Elise who was devoted to all card games and had shown an almost alarming precocity in that direction from the time she could distinguish a knave from a king. On this night, with her thoughts in a turmoil, she lost every hand.

'A lamb to the slaughter, indeed,' she said at last. 'Forgive me, dear. I think I will retire, for I am tired and find it hard to concentrate.'

'When will Papa be home?'

'When the mood takes him, no doubt. I think you should go to bed yourself, for of one thing you may be certain, he will be in no humour to play cards.'

'Oh, why is everyone so dull down here? I wish I was back in London.'

'Go to bed, Elise.' Charlotte rose from the table and snuffed the candles, in no mood for argument. 'I shall leave a light in the window for your father.'

'He can't still be walking in the wood!'

'No doubt he has called to see a friend. You know how he enjoys a discussion with Mr Durell or Mr Mercer.'

She was worried, though, in spite of making light of his extended absence to Elise. The thought of his physical disabilities was never far from her mind. A walk of five miles which to any other man would be negligible often exhausted Gabriel.

Once in her room, she leaned from the open window, looking towards the wood, listening to the night noises and wondering if she should rouse one of the servants to go in search of him. Something should be done, she felt – yet she knew how irritated he would be if what she had said to Elise proved to be true, as it might well be. He could easily have called at the home of one of his Huguenot friends, any one of whom would have been delighted to welcome him, even without warning.

There was no moon and the garden was in deep shadow so that at first she did not see him. One moment it seemed that the whole world lay still and empty; the next that he had appeared as if from nowhere and was dragging himself towards the house, his left leg stiff and awkward. She could not see the expression on his face, but she knew that he must be exhausted for only then, thinking himself unseen, would he allow himself to walk in such a way.

Her instinct was to run to him, put his arm around her shoulders, support him into the house, but she did not. He would not want her to see him return like this, and she moved away from the window. By the time he came to her room she was half undressed and was brushing the thick mane of her hair, for here in the country she would not let Nan attend her at night, insisting that they lived with the utmost simplicity.

She turned as the door opened, laid down her brush and rose

236

to her feet. Closing the door behind him, he leaned against it, his eyes closed and his face bleached with exhaustion.

'Oh Gabriel,' she said softly. 'I have been so concerned at your absence.'

She started across the room towards him, but as she did so he made a sound that was somewhere between a groan and a cry and moved to meet her with his arms outstretched, falling to his knees and holding her tightly around the waist. For a while he wept with long, shuddering gasps, while she pressed his head to her and murmured broken sentences and endearments.

When at last his storm of emotion was over, she coaxed him to a chair and ran to fetch hot cordial and wine; then, kneeling beside him, she begged his forgiveness for the harshness of her words to him.

'Oh, my darling!' He took a handful of her hair and rubbed it against his cheek. 'It is I who am at fault. But this matter of my mother – don't you see, if I am reconciled with her, it sets as naught the sacrifice made by all the others who suffered and died for their beliefs?'

'I don't believe that. You and the others suffered for what you believed to be right – what you *know* to be right! You were strong in the faith. Your mother was not, and for that weakness should surely be pitied?'

'But to abjure, and to marry into the Catholic faith! To turn her back deliberately on God and the hope of salvation.'

Charlotte kept silent. She had been born a Huguenot and would undoubtedly die one, yet was aware of a sneaking unease at the assumption that only Calvinists were the elect of God. It painted a narrow picture of God that she found unattractive, but she knew that in argument she was no match for Gabriel.

'If she is to be denied God's blessing in the next world, should she also be denied her son's in this?'

Gabriel sighed and closed his eyes again, and was silent for some time.

'I know nothing,' he said at last, his voice ragged with weariness. 'Nothing.'

'You are such a kind man, except in this one matter.'

'I cannot break faith with those who have died.'

'Forgive her, and you may find it possible to forgive yourself for all those supposed sins that haunt you.'

'Enough!' A vestige of colour had come back to his face, and he smiled at last as he laid a finger against her lips. 'I will consider your arguments, my little advocate, and shall pray for guidance. And I will do my best to be less of a burden to you, for I know there are times when I try your patience sorely.'

She kissed his cheek.

'There are times, monsieur, when you would try the patience of a saint – and I believe we have long established that neither of us can be so described.'

'My dearest Charlotte!' He spoke her name with love and returned the kiss. 'What should I do without you? I thank God that I am like to die before you, for my world would be a dreary waste without your presence in it.'

'Don't say such things! Besides, you have Elise and silk – twin passions, I seem to remember.'

'That was many years ago. You changed everything.'

He slept in her arms that night, and she was conscious of a great tenderness for him. He had prophesied once that one day she would hate him, but she knew now that she would not – for surely if ever she were to be capable of it it would be now? She loved Paul in a way she had never imagined possible, but Gabriel was dear to her too. He was part of the very fabric of her life; her mentor, colleague, tutor, dear companion, child. She knew she could never hurt him.

13

In the week he was to remain at Whiteacres, Charlotte tried to get Gabriel to talk more about his mother's second family at Nîmes, but beyond the fact that his stepfather was a wine merchant by the name of Arnoult whose elder son, Jules, had followed him into the business, he would say nothing. His black mood had passed, however, and seeing his contentment, she did not persist with her questions. By the time he went back to London she was thankful to see that he seemed restored and refreshed by his brief sojourn in the country.

Elise announced herself envious of him. The country was dull, she said. Only in London was there to be found any life or entertainment; however, her tune changed when she was invited with Charlotte to a ball at a neighbour's house. Not only did she create her usual havoc among the young men of the county, but more importantly she struck up a close friendship with two sisters, Anne and Margaret Denning, daughters of a wealthy gentleman who had bought a large house close by. Charlotte breathed a sigh of relief to see her so well supplied with lively company.

For her own part, she was perfectly content to be alone, but she visited her father frequently and received the usual invitations from Tante Hortense to attend her cultural soirées.

It was the custom for Mrs Bellamy to come to spend a few days at Whiteacres during the summer, and Charlotte always looked forward to seeing her. This year, however, she was busy attending Minette in her confinement, and Charlotte hardly knew whether to be glad or sorry. It would have been wonderful to talk of Paul; not, naturally, of her love for him, but merely to mention his name. On the other hand, Mrs Bellamy knew her so well that she was not at all confident that she could keep her true feelings a secret. It was as well, she decided, that the matter would not be put to the test.

In her place came Madame Colbert. Gabriel's letter telling Charlotte of the forthcoming visit had been apologetic in tone.

She had been unwell, he wrote, and for family reasons the Bouveries of Richmond were unable to have her, as was their custom. The heat in town was so excessive that he could see no alternative but to invite her to Whiteacres. He could only hope and pray that she would not mar Charlotte's enjoyment.

'Heaven send that Berthe does not come with her,' Elise said when she was informed. Charlotte looked at her in dismay.

'I had not even considered it,' she said, and was so relieved when the carriage arrived and she saw that Madame Colbert was unaccompanied, her welcome was almost effusive. As for Elise, she showed her best side by spending as much time in Tantine's company as she could bear to spare from her new-found friends, and Charlotte was suitably grateful for the relief.

Even so, the month that Tantine spent at Whiteacres dragged, though mercifully the weather stayed fine and it was only in the evenings that the three of them were closeted together within doors. Even these were broken by entertainments and social occasions from time to time, and when each was over, Charlotte gave thanks that she was one day nearer the time when Gabriel would come and Tantine would go, transported in the carriage to her friends in Richmond who were now able to receive her.

It rained at the beginning of the week when Gabriel was due. There was no doubt that the farmers were grateful for it, but it was irksome to be cooped inside, for it gave Tantine numerous opportunities to make veiled criticisms of Charlotte's household management and complain at what she was convinced was lack of respect on the part of Nan and Molly, 'that pair of peasants' as she invariably called them. But the days were running out now. Gabriel was due on Friday and Tantine's visit could be counted in hours.

The thought raised Charlotte's spirits, and when Friday dawned with cloudless skies, clear and fresh after the recent rain, she took it as an omen of happy times ahead.

She was back on an even keel, she told herself. Paul was not forgotten – that would be asking the impossible – but at least he was relegated to a suitable position at the back of her mind where he could do no harm. In fact, she told herself proudly, she was almost sure she had not thought of him all day.

Elise had been out for her usual morning ride with Anne and Margaret and on her return had dressed herself in a gown of pink dimity. However, her hair was still unbound when she heard the carriage wheels, and she rushed out of the house with it in a golden shower about her shoulders. She looked, Charlotte thought, like the creation of some poet's fantasy.

She herself had been ready for some time, her delight in Gabriel's imminent arrival no less than that of Elise. However, she was more restrained and stood at the porch, smiling in welcome, allowing Elise to dance forward, calling greetings to Joseph on the box, pulling at the door handle even before the coach had come to a halt.

She could see that Gabriel was smiling, too. He looked well and in good spirits, she noted thankfully. The black mood was not on him, praise the Lord.

As the luggage was unloaded Gabriel's eyes held hers and she saw the love that was in them and his happiness that he was back with her again, in this simple country house he liked so much.

He stepped down from the coach and she moved towards him, lifting her face to his.

'I have a surprise for you, my love,' he said when he had embraced her. 'A visitor you will welcome, I know.'

He turned with a smile to the coach and for the first time she saw he had not travelled alone. She felt as if a giant hand were squeezing her heart, as if all the breath had been knocked from her body, for it was Paul who had been his companion from town, and Paul who was now dismounting, a tentative smile on his face as he extended his hand to her.

'I *hope* I am welcome,' he said, as if he rather doubted the truth of Gabriel's words.

A thrush was singing from the topmost branch of an apple tree and the air was sweet with the scent of roses. Gabriel walked ahead, Elise hanging on his arm chattering of Anne and Margaret and the horses they owned and the parties they gave. In silence Charlotte and Paul walked several yards behind.

How often I have walked here and longed for him, she thought. How often have I dreamed that he was here beside me; and now that he is here in reality, it doesn't seem real at all.

There was no doubt about the reality of the pain, though. Would it stay just as sharp as this for ever, or would the time come when it would fade? Perhaps when she was old, with eyes dimmed and skin withered, she would be able to look back without anguish. Perhaps she would have to search her memory to recall the shape of Paul's mouth or the colour of his eyes.

She knew it would never happen. No matter if they never touched, never acknowledged this emotion that had flared between them, she would remember it for ever. The space between them seemed to quiver with tension; the silence was a vacuum she was impelled to fill.

'I never walk here without thinking of my mother,' she said in a bright, social voice. 'It was she who planted these roses. This pink one has a particularly delightful scent.'

'Charlotte –' Paul's voice was low and urgent. 'Charlotte, we must speak. I know I should not have come.'

'You know you are always welcome, Paul.'

'"You know you are always welcome, Paul!"' There was a note of savagery in his voice as he mimicked her words, as if he were angry with her. He shook his head and apologised. 'I'm sorry. There is so much between us – so much we should say –'

Charlotte paused as if inspecting a rose.

'You are right,' she said in a low voice, quite different from the one she had used before. 'You should not have come. I don't understand what has happened exactly – why, suddenly, it is impossible for us to be natural with each other. I only know that it is wrong.'

'I have told myself that. The last time, when I saw you in Freedom Street, I told myself that there was no alternative, in future we should keep away from each other –'

'Yet still you came!'

'It was hard to refuse Gabriel. You, of all people, must know how persuasive he is! He knew I was due at Sandwich next week, and it seemed inexplicable – churlish, even – to turn down his offer of a ride.'

'Hurry up, you two,' Elise called.

'We're coming.' Slowly they continued their walk.

'One thing I insist on saying while I have the chance,' Paul said. 'I love you, Charlotte. I think I always have done, since I was a child, even though I didn't realise it.'

She glanced at him quickly, almost reached to touch him, but with an effort restrained herself.

'May God forgive me, but I love you too,' she admitted. 'There, now it's said and can never be spoken again. The matter must be laid to rest, once and for all.'

242

'What kind of woman are you?' He seemed quietly, desperately angry again. 'Are you human, or some kind of spirit that you can dismiss the call of the flesh so lightly? If only you knew how I hungered for you, Charlotte.'

'I do know,' she said softly. 'I know full well. Do you think it is different for me?'

They had reached the gate that separated the garden from the wood and together they leaned upon it. She looked down to the topmost bar where both their hands rested, his right not more than an inch from her left. Had she never seen a hand before? She stared at it as if to learn it by heart – the size and the shape and the strength of it – then slowly, as if some hidden force compelled her, she raised her eyes to meet his, so conscious of his presence that she could feel herself trembling. One flesh, she thought. No matter that we have scarcely touched each other. We are one flesh.

'We are neither of us capable of hurting Gabriel,' she said. 'How could we, when we owe him so much?'

Paul said nothing for a moment but he reached to touch her hand briefly.

'I have asked myself the same question a thousand times,' he said. 'I could wish you had married a villain, not a saint.'

Charlotte smiled ruefully.

'He is no saint,' she said. 'Just a good and highly vulnerable man, whom I love.'

'As I do.' Paul expelled his breath in a long, despairing sigh. 'What a coil! You know he wants me to marry Elise? I can't do it, of course.'

'You will marry someone, some day.' How could she have thought she would ever accept it without pain?

'Perhaps. But not Elise.'

'Well, here you are!' An intrusive voice made them both start. It was Madame Colbert who had appeared without warning, not from the direction of the house behind them but from a small side path that was concealed at this time of the year by thick, leafy bushes.

How much had she heard? Nothing, probably, for they had been talking in low voices, but it was clear from her bright, darting eyes that her curiosity was aroused. A handful of ferns provided some kind of explanation for the fact that she had come from such an unexpected quarter.

243

'I believe these to be quite rare,' she said, at Charlotte's enquiry. 'I wished to take them to Mam'selle Claudine Bouverie for she is much interested in such things. Is Elise not with you?'

'She is with her father a little further on. I expect they are at the lake by now. Come along, Paul – they will think we have fallen by the wayside.'

'Will you join us, madame?' Politely Paul proffered his arm, but Tantine shook her head.

'I shall go to pack my trunk,' she said.

She did not move, however, and when Charlotte looked back over her shoulder, she still stood by the gate, watching them.

On Monday she left, and so did Paul.

'Now the summer will begin in earnest,' Charlotte said to Gabriel when they were alone in their room that night. 'I am thankful they have gone.'

'Even Paul?' Gabriel sounded surprised.

'Does it not occur to you, husband, that I like to have you to myself?'

'It never occurred to me that you would not welcome Paul! He's such an old friend. Besides –' He hesitated a moment. 'I thought it politic to allow him a little more time with Elise. I don't intend to give up my hope of a match between them so easily. You disapprove so strongly?' he added, as Charlotte gave him a speaking look.

'Elise is not ready. And she is certainly not in love with Paul, nor he with her.'

'They need time,' Gabriel said. 'Time to get to know each other. Time works magic, *chérie* – have you not seen it a hundred times?'

Charlotte said nothing. Pray God it works magic for me, she thought.

The month of August passed as pleasantly as it always did, without too many social engagements. Gabriel preferred, as he frequently said, to pull up the drawbridge when he came to Whiteacres, and if it was not possible to seal themselves off completely from the outside world, then they did the best they could, restricting themselves to family parties and visits from old friends. Dr Bonnet came for several days, and Charlotte was pleased with the way he had clearly taken hold of life again.

Tante Hortense, it was plain, kept a sisterly eye on him and invited him constantly to this occasion or that.

'You know, she would have me marry again,' he said, 'but my work is sufficient company for me. I'd not want to take a young wife and strive to please her.'

Charlotte had noticed from the first, however, that he was once more fastidious about his person and wore the latest fashion in cravats. She even saw him dance a quadrille on one occasion, which was something he would never have done in his wife's lifetime.

By mid-month, Charlotte was wishing they could always live in this quiet, rural fashion, far away from the noise and smell of the city. She had lost the ability to create designs, she confessed to Gabriel, and astonishingly did not care. She would be perfectly content to live the life of a countrywoman, concerned only with kitchen, still-room and garden for the rest of her days. In reply he raised a sardonic eyebrow, smiled, and said nothing.

However, he, too, was clearly content and at peace, and she was sorely tempted to raise the question of a reconciliation with his mother once more. He had made no reference to the matter since the last traumatic occasion and she had no notion what, if anything, he had done about it. Had he written, or had he dismissed her plea? She longed to know, but prudence kept her silent.

By the end of the month she found her thoughts straying more and more towards the city. Paul was never far from her mind, but she assured herself that his presence did more to deter than attract; she must not, she told herself, even *think* of engineering a meeting with him. Life, after all, held much of interest for her – the new theatrical season, to name only one.

'I wonder what demands Mrs Harkness will make of me,' she mused, and Gabriel smiled to himself.

When he found her at her drawing board one morning in early September, he laughed outright.

'I thought you had forsworn this occupation,' he said.

'An idea came to me in the night. No, don't laugh at me, Gabriel! It's a woman's privilege to change her mind.'

'I think it's time we went home.'

In her heart she agreed, and she had few regrets when finally the time came to set their faces towards London again. That she was not alone in this was obvious by Elise's excitement.

'Oh, I can't *wait!*' she said, clasping her hands in sheer delight.

'Yet you have enjoyed the summer, surely?'

'Oh yes. I shall miss Anne and Margaret, but they tell me they will be spending time at their father's town house, so we shall meet again. But I long to see Catherine, and – and all my other friends.' She glanced sideways at Charlotte to see if she had noticed the slight hesitation, and was relieved to see that she seemed engrossed in folding a pair of stockings, her mind on other things. She had no wish to elaborate on this theme. She had done nothing particularly heinous in her young life, but as a matter of principle she felt that the less her parents knew of her associates, the easier life would be. Evening strolls in the park, however innocent, would undoubtedly be frowned upon.

And then there was Peter Jordan. It was strange how the thought of him had returned to her unbidden at intervals throughout the summer. She hoped it would be possible to see him again before long.

'I think you should go to help Molly with your packing, Elise,' Charlotte said. 'She has much to do.'

Elise pulled a face.

'I hate packing as if it were poison,' she said. 'When I marry, I shall have *swarms* of servants, just like Anne and Margaret's mama –'

'Then you'd best go in search of the duke Tantine has picked out for you.'

'Why not? I should make an excellent duchess!'

And putting her nose in the air and holding her skirt with comic daintiness, she swept from the room.

Youth, beauty, vivacity – and a comfortable portion besides! Could Paul really hold out against such a range of attractions, particularly when they were presented to him by Gabriel with his persuasive tongue? Yes, he could, she told herself forcefully. She felt quite certain of it. She had never been more sure of anything.

Yet somewhere, on the very edge of her mind, a small, wriggling worm of doubt refused to be smothered. People often weakened, when faced with Gabriel.

Resolutely she pushed the thought away. She would think instead of the work that was waiting for her in London and all she had to do before leaving Whiteacres.

By the time they had been back in Freedom Street for a week

246

it seemed as if they had never been away. The looms were all working every hour of the day, and Gabriel was much engrossed in plans to purchase a new and complicated piece of machinery which manufactured ribbons far cheaper and more quickly than they had been made before. He was enthusiastic, too, about a new dye house which a fellow Huguenot was hoping to set up down by the river.

'De Vaux is a veritable master of his craft,' he told Charlotte. 'Do you remember how I told you once that I longed to be able to use more subtle colours? Well, de Vaux is the man to produce them for me. He needs more capital, he tells me, and I am resolved to speak to Paul on the matter. If he has clients with money to invest, they could do no better than back de Vaux.'

Charlotte smiled noncommittally and returned to the all-absorbing occupation of creating designs for which a certain facility had returned, though she was not satisfied they had achieved the same level of creativity that had made her name. However, for what they were worth, they allowed no time for unproductive thoughts of Paul, and provided some kind of balm for her soul.

Elise's days at Mrs Amlott's seminary had come to an end, for she had learned all she was likely to, Gabriel decided. Charlotte had agreed, at least in part. Elise could write a good hand and was capable of reading works of literature, even if she did not often choose to do so, and as for the more practical part of the curriculum, she would not learn to ply her needle with any great skill if she stayed at school for the next twenty years.

Instead she enrolled with a music master, an elderly émigré, who lived close by Covent Garden where she was transported daily by sedan chair to pursue her studies at the harpsichord, for which she had shown considerable talent since she was a child.

Sometimes she did not come home immediately the lesson was over, but met Catherine Maxwell for a turn about the shops, escorted by Molly. It was an arrangement that made Charlotte a little uneasy, even though she told herself that she had no reason for it. Elise was neither a child nor a prisoner; yet instinctively Charlotte worried about her and began to have some sympathy for Gabriel's desire to see her happily settled with a good husband.

Elise and Catherine loved Covent Garden. They liked the shops and the wide piazza where there were always musicians or tumblers or other street entertainers to be seen; and even if she had not been so entranced by them, Elise would still have persuaded her friend to walk there, for she lived in hopes of seeing Peter Jordan, the Theatre Royal being close by.

But the weeks passed and she did not see him. Once or twice she suggested that it was time they went to the theatre again, but the comedies that were being played were those that her father particularly disliked, and her hints fell on deaf ears. Then, just as she was giving up hope of seeing the actor again, an unexpected letter arrived for Gabriel from Jordan himself. The tragical history of Othello, the Moor of Venice, was to be presented at Drury Lane, in which production Mr Jordan was to take the part of Iago.

'Since you, dear Mr Fabian, were kind enough to invite me to your home after the production of *Hamlet*, I should be honoured if you and your family would do me the favour of attending the theatre as my guests on the night of 10 November, afterwards supping at my rooms close by Drury Lane. Upon receipt of your favourable reply I will straightway reserve a box for you and your ladies.'

'This is most kind of him,' Gabriel said once he had read the letter through. 'We must accept, of course. It would appear as a slight were we to refuse.'

'I thought you said he was a little jackanapes we should not be seeing more,' Charlotte said, with some amusement. 'How quickly your heart is touched!'

'It does him credit, that he wishes to return our hospitality – and you always enjoy the play, do you not? No doubt we can look forward to seeing Mrs Harkness as a somewhat mature Desdemona.'

A polite acceptance was sent, and less than a week later the performance took place. From the outset the Fabian family were treated as honoured guests. The moment that Gabriel mentioned his name at the door they were escorted to their box and plied with refreshment. There were whistles and shouted invitations from the pit as Elise took her seat, but she paid no heed to them, for all her attention was on the empty stage.

It's another world, she thought; another magic world, full of colour and excitement, and Peter Jordan is part of it. She leaned forward eagerly as if willing the play to begin.

Iago opened it, she knew. Oh, she could not *wait*, she told herself, hands tightly clasped together. The callow youths she had flirted with during the summer had gone from her mind as if they had never been.

There was a roar of mirth from the pit, and her mother and father were smiling too at the antics of a dwarf who was acting out some pantomime with one of the orange girls. Elise barely turned her head to look at it. The lights were being dowsed now and the noise and laughter died away, their place taken by a low murmur of expectation.

Breathless with anticipation she leaned forward, waiting for his entrance.

He had performed well and been much applauded. His obvious talent and the evil he had portrayed so skilfully made Elise feel shy of him, as if he were a creature set apart from ordinary mortals. She was glad that she and her parents were to go to his rooms as soon as the performance was over; Jordan would join them, it had been arranged, as soon as he had divested himself of his make-up. She felt it would give her a breathing space – time to pinch her cheeks and straighten her hair; time, too, to remind herself that she was not a child, but was a young lady – and a pretty one, too, if Frederick Maxwell and the youths of Kent were to be believed. There was no reason at all for her to feel so unsure of herself.

They were welcomed to his rooms by his gap-toothed, straggle-haired landlady, who curtseyed low and ushered them upstairs to the room where the table already bore the meal that was to be offered to them. It was a bare and comfortless chamber, cold in spite of the fire that smouldered in the grate, giving out more smoke than warmth.

'Kindly sit, your worships,' the landlady said. 'Mistress Cutting is my name, and right glad I am to welcome you to my humble home. Poor of worldly goods I may be, but there is none that is friend to Mr Jordan who don't receive a hearty welcome from me.' This speech was accompanied by a great deal of nodding and smiling. 'You'll take a glass of Rhenish in the meantime, I hope,' she went on. 'Mr Jordan will be here shortly, but he told me to offer you whatsoever you would like to drink.'

'Thank you, but we shall wait for our host, I think.'

Gabriel spoke firmly as he took the seat she indicated, but not, apparently, firmly enough, for she was already pouring from a flagon.

'He'd think me at fault did you not drink, sir, and you need it, I'm sure, you and the fine ladies, for there's naught makes for a thirst like the play, do you ask me, and I'm the one that should know, for didn't I work at Drury Lane twenty years and more?'

'You were an actress?' Charlotte asked, hoping that the note of surprise in her voice would not be construed as an insult. It was hard indeed to see what role this crone could have taken, unless, perhaps, it should be one of the three witches in Macbeth.

'Bless you no, madam, though there are those who say I would have made a good one. No, I was a dresser. I saw them come and I saw them go, and there wasn't one of my ladies who wouldn't say they owed their fame to me and my needle.'

'I understand Mr Jordan's mother followed the same occupation,' Charlotte said politely, making conversation. Mistress Cutting clasped her hands as if in ecstasy.

'Which is why I am like a mother to that boy, madam. Like one of my own, he is, and there's none that can say different, for where else would he have the use of such fine rooms and all the comfort of home for what he pays me? Or I *should* say, what he promised to pay me, for like as not he'll come home of a Saturday and say "Ma Cutting," he'll say, "it's the slate again, bless your heart." "You young rascal," I'll say to him' – and she shook a finger at an imaginary Mr Jordan – '"there's naught but a marrowbone and a cabbage leaf in the house!" But what can you do, madam, when he takes a body by the hands and dances around the room and kisses her soundly and promises the moon and all tomorrow? And like as not, he'll be there the next day with not one but two guineas, and for a week we'll all live like kings, him and me and Mr Cutting, the poor old slob – begging your pardon, madam, I'm sure, but Mr Cutting has never been the same since he was felled by a brewer's dray.'

Further revelations were cut short by the arrival of Peter Jordan himself, who showed no sign of the extravagant behaviour described by his landlady, but greeted them with subdued politeness, clearly determined to prove that he could entertain in as gentlemanly a way as Mr Fabian when he put his mind to it.

The fire smoked badly and the meats had long since seen better days, but the oysters were fresh (Mistress Cutting had gone to

250

Billingsgate for them that very day, as she told them several times) and for the first hour it was as correct a gathering as one could imagine.

Then the rest of the Company arrived – or at least the more junior members of it. It was clear that they had been refreshing themselves at some nearby tavern and were now looking for some further outlet for their high spirits. Jordan pointed out to them that he was already engaged in entertaining other friends, but they refused to be discouraged.

''Tis why we've come,' said the erstwhile Duke of Venice. 'We knew there'd be wine for the drinking –'

'Be off with you, there's good fellows –'

'Nay, some of us have brought our own bottles, have no fear! We seek good company, no more, and perhaps a game –'

'There'll be no gaming here!'

Jordan spoke sharply, and looked uneasily towards Charlotte and Gabriel who were attempting to look as if they had not noticed the intrusion. Brabantio, a rotund gentleman with a wide smile, had no intention, however, of being ignored and pushed his way into the room smiling broadly.

'Now, what friends are these that we should be kept from? Are you ashamed of us? No, no, I can't believe it!' He appealed to Charlotte. 'You've no wish to see us thrown into the street, have you, madam?'

Charlotte shook her head, amused in spite of herself. These raffish new arrivals were a novelty and seemed harmless enough, but in time the copious draughts of wine with which they were all regaling themselves had their inevitable effect.

Brabantio started to sing a catch and the others joined in. Jordan refilled his glass, shrugged resignedly, and bowed to the inevitable. He caught Elise's eye and gave her a look which seemed to say: This is my life and these are my associates. Make what you will of it.

She smiled at him and he grinned back widely. She felt suddenly excited. This was as far from Freedom Street and her sober upbringing as could be imagined, and she found the experience exhilarating. She would have joined in the song had she known the words, but instead she contented herself with beating her hand on her knee in time to the music.

The songs grew more bawdy. The room was now so smoky it was almost impossible to see across it. More uninvited guests

251

arrived, both men and women, and a few couples began to jig in time to a flute produced by one of their number.

Charlotte saw Gabriel's expression and knew it was time to leave. She peered across the room and saw in the haze of smoke that Elise was engaged in conversation with Peter Jordan, but as if conscious of her eye upon him he broke off and shouldered his way across the room to her.

'My dear Mrs Fabian,' he said, a look of exaggerated penitence on his face. 'I had not meant this gathering to degenerate so. I would not have subjected you –'

'Pray think nothing of it.' Charlotte smiled at him, anxious to put him at his ease even though she hated the smoke and the cackling laughter and the noise and the bawdiness. 'However, perhaps you would be so good as to tell Elise that her father and I must leave now.'

Elise was summoned and politenesses were exchanged, and it was a relief to Charlotte when at last they stood in the street and breathed the night air. Malodorous as it was, it seemed pure after the atmosphere of the room upstairs.

'And that, I trust, is the end of it,' Gabriel said as the carriage bore them away towards Freedom Street. 'Honour is satisfied on all counts. I have no wish to see or communicate with any of those people again.'

Elise, her face pressed to the window as if anxious to miss nothing of the night life of the streets, said nothing, but Charlotte was moved to utter a small protest.

'Mr Jordan meant well, Gabriel.'

'A more dissolute, disreputable, Godless set of ne'er-do-wells it has seldom been my lot to encounter.'

'They are actors, after all,' Charlotte said, as if that explained everything.

How little they understood, Elise thought. How could they judge? Their life and their associates were so correct, so humdrum, so God-fearing. Voices in their world were well modulated, never raised in anger or joy. They only half lived, that was the truth of it.

Three o'clock in the piazza, outside the fan-makers, Peter Jordan had said, catching hold of her wrist and smiling into her eyes as he spoke the words, confident that they were out of sight of her parents. She had struggled to appear mistress of the

252

situation though her heart was pounding with excitement.

'What makes you think I shall be at liberty?'

'I shall wait anyway. Tomorrow.'

There had been no time for more. She had been summoned to her parents; Maman with a polite smile on her face which said more clearly than any words that she wished herself gone; Papa not even bothering to smile, but with his face set in disapproving lines. She loved him dearly, but no one could deny that his Calvinist outlook could sometimes be a trial.

The watch was crying midnight as they pulled up outside the porch and entered the house. Fifteen whole hours must pass until three o'clock tomorrow. How could she bear it? She would never sleep, she knew it – not one wink.

But if it chanced that she did, then she hoped – oh, how she hoped – that she would dream of Peter Jordan.

She wrote a note to Monsieur Grimaud, her music tutor, that she was indisposed and bade Molly take it to him – dear, good Molly, who was not near so bright as her sister Nan, but was as devoted as a maidservant could be.

She left it until a few minutes after three before entering the piazza; it wouldn't do to appear too eager – but she looked about anxiously when at first she saw no sign of him. Perhaps it had been a joke to test her gullibility. Perhaps he had not meant it at all – or had been too far gone in his cups to remember! Perhaps she should promenade a little, look in some of the shops –

'Mam'selle!' His voice behind her made her spin round, an unguarded look of relief and pleasure on her face. 'How kind of you to come.'

'I – I –' She felt ridiculously tongue-tied, not at all her usual self. 'I had little else to do.'

'Then let us walk since the day is so fine. One would hardly believe it to be November.'

He proffered his arm and laying her hand upon it she fell into step beside him, just one among many of the couples taking the air in the piazza.

He looked very fine, she thought, stealing a sideways glance at him. His coat was of bottle green, braided in gold, and it hung open to reveal a waistcoat of green and gold brocade. His cravat had tassel ends and his hat was wide-brimmed, swept up at front and back.

'I could have done murder last night,' he said, with a rueful grin. 'I was determined to show your father that in spite of all I had turned out to be a gentleman.'

'Your friends were very merry. I was sorry to leave.'

'It must be hard to have a saint for a father!'

'Sometimes,' Elise admitted. 'Not that he would agree with that description –'

'Saint or not, I doubt he would approve of your actions today.'

'Poor man, I should not dream of burdening him by confessing it!' She smiled her little, three-cornered smile. 'It is necessary, sometimes, to exercise discretion, Mr Jordan, and in that I excel.'

'I can imagine it!'

She began to feel more sure of herself, for though she had never walked with such a man before, the look in his eyes was one with which she was entirely familiar.

'I think my father would keep me in the schoolroom for ever,' she said, preening a little in the warmth of his admiration. 'Or at least until some suitable man can be found to marry me. And by suitable, I mean Huguenot.' She pulled a face as if the word were synonymous with dreariness. 'Such a dreadful fate, Mr Jordan, when all I desire is to enjoy myself.'

'And so you shall, my sweeting.' He took her hand and kissed it, patting it as he replaced it on his arm. She widened her eyes at him in simulated horror, melting into a smile as he grinned down at her. 'Though I have to remind you,' he said, 'that I myself am a Huguenot.'

He arranged his features in an expression both pious and haughty, and she laughed outright. Oh, he was so amusing – she had never known anyone more droll! They looked at a shop window full of cravats, and at once he was the fop, lisping and mincing as he pretended to choose between them. Outside a goldsmith's, he out-Shylocked Shylock.

Suddenly he seemed to weary of these games.

'For how long can I enjoy your company?' he asked. 'I have a fancy to go to the park.'

She looked at the watch that hung at her waist.

'I must be back here to meet Molly, my maid, at half past four.'

'That's time enough.' Already he was hailing a hackney. 'The Mall will be lively today, since the sun is shining.'

'I am not sure that I should –'

254

'Mam'selle, you will be as safe with me as in your mother's arms! I guarantee to have you back here in an hour.'

He helped her into the cab and they drove to St James's Park. For the first hundred yards she sat on the edge of her seat, her back ramrod straight, her fingers twisting together anxiously. It was one thing to walk in a crowded piazza, and quite another to be in such close proximity. Then she heard him laugh, and gently he pulled her back so that her head rested beside his.

His laughter died as he touched her cheek with the back of his hand. Her mouth was dry and she could not breathe. His eyes – those brown, eloquent eyes – looked into hers, only inches away.

'"O, she doth teach the torches to burn bright,"' he quoted softly. '"It seems she hangs upon the cheek of night, Like the rich jewel in an Ethiop's ear."'

All her fragile sophistication gone, she licked her lips and swallowed painfully.

'That's from a play,' she said.

'*Romeo and Juliet*. The greatest love story ever told. It ended sadly, though. I do not care for love stories that end sadly, do you?'

Slowly, mesmerised by his eyes and his voice that had picked up a trace of Irish lilt, she shook her head.

'Ours will not end sadly, will it?' he asked her.

'I – I did not know that it had begun,' she said, and smiled with pleasure when he laughed as if she had said something amusing.

'Oh, it's begun,' he said. 'Make no mistake about that. You are the loveliest creature I ever saw, Elise. I may call you that, may I not? Elise, Elise, Elise.'

Her name had never sounded so sweet. She was unaware of the street outside the cab window – all the usual noise and traffic. It was like their own little world inside.

Their arrival at the park took her by surprise, so quickly had the journey passed. And now they were walking again, and the Mall was every bit as lively as he had promised, with all manner of fashionable ladies and their escorts promenading in the late sunshine, where a few ragged remnants of leaves still hung from the trees.

She had walked here with Captain Maxwell. How could she ever have thought him in the least attractive? To think she had allowed him to kiss her! She had been a foolish child, she told herself. Now it was different. She was almost seventeen and had more discrimination.

'Who would have thought we would ever walk together like this,' Jordan said, 'bearing in mind the manner of my departure from your house?'

'I never understood why you left until Maman explained it recently. It must have been hard for you.'

'It was.' His expression was one of grim amusement. 'Yes, it was indeed hard. One day my future seemed assured and I was a reasonably carefree apprentice – the next I was fleeing from the hangman's rope.'

Elise shivered.

'It would not have come to that! You were innocent. Papa would never have allowed it.'

'Could I have relied on that? I thought no one would believe me.'

'Were you very poor, you and your family?'

'Very,' he answered shortly.

'I suppose,' she said, her brow furrowed as she did her best to picture the circumstances of his life, 'that there were times when you had no meat to eat?'

'No meat?' He laughed at that. 'My dear Elise, there were times when we had nothing, and I would cheerfully have eaten the hide off a donkey. I remember once,' he went on, 'one cold, wet night in Dublin. I had broken my fast that morning with a bowl of thin gruel and had eaten nothing since. I had been told of work in a brewery and had walked from one side of the city to the other with boots that let water and clothes that were no more than rags. Suddenly, just as I crossed the bridge over the Liffey the rain stopped and the clouds parted, and the moon shone through. Then and there I stopped on that bridge and I swore that one day I would show the world I was not to be trifled with. "By yonder moon I swear," I said, for I was inclined to the dramatical even then.'

Elise clasped his arm with both hands.

'And you have done,' she said admiringly. 'Everyone in London knows of you!'

'Nay, I'd not go so far as that – but they will, they will. One day I shall be rich and famous.' His mouth had a hard line to it and his voice was gritty with purpose. 'You'll see. I'll show them all.' He grinned down at her, resuming his bantering tone. 'And talking of riches – keep your eyes skinned for a short fat man with a crimson waistcoat, for I am hoping to see him today. I have business with him.'

'You have arranged to meet him?' She did not care for that at all. She wanted to keep him to herself.

'No, no, nothing planned,' he assured her. 'He is just a fellow who hangs about the park and does business here.'

'What sort of business?' Elise asked, but he laughed again and made no direct answer. It was nothing, he said, that she should worry her pretty head about – and perhaps they should turn around and begin to walk back slowly or they would never be back to Covent Garden in time.

'Have you ever played Romeo?' she asked him as slowly they retraced their steps.

'Not yet.' He spoke softly. 'But I will. Next time I see a moon, I shall swear that too.'

'You want to do it so much? Then I am sure you will!'

'I wonder! Remember I am a comparative newcomer to Drury Lane.' Gracefully he danced away from her, miming sword play. Savagely he made a downward thrust into the body of an imaginary victim. 'There are those who would run me through were I to be given such a role before them. Don't be misled by all the bonhomie last night. Passions run high in the dressing room!'

'But you are so worthy!'

Laughing, he caught her wrists and pulled her towards him.

'We are of one mind, sweeting. Two hearts that beat as one! When are we to meet again? Is three a good hour for you?'

'Morning would be better. I cannot always miss my music lesson!'

'Eleven, then? This day week?'

A whole week! How would she bear it? Seven days and seven nights seemed to stretch endlessly in front of her – but at least, she consoled herself, it would give her a chance to see Catherine and concoct some sort of alibi.

'Eleven o'clock,' she said. 'This day week.'

'How can I bear to wait so long?' He looked deep into her eyes, gathering both her hands in his. His voice was low, a little husky, with that caressing lilt that sent a shiver down her spine. 'You will be my last thought every night and my first on waking. And throughout the day, I shall –' He paused, looking at a point somewhere to the left of her. 'I see a crimson waistcoat,' he said in quite a different voice. She looked over her shoulder, following the direction of his eyes. 'There he is, over by that tree, talking to those army officers. Wait for me here, dearest heart. I shall be no more than a moment. Pray forgive me.'

He hurried off, leaving Elise feeling conspicuously alone – but 'dearest heart' he had called her, and it was something of a consolation.

She would not have tolerated such behaviour from anyone else and was mildly astonished at herself. He must have bewitched her!

Her gaze followed him as he went towards the small group by the tree. The army officers moved off as he reached it, and now that she had a clear view of the man she saw that he was indeed short and fat – so fat that one might think him as wide as he was high. He was wearing not only a crimson waistcoat but a crimson topcoat as well, and the type of full-bottomed wig that had been out of fashion these five years.

What could Mr Jordan's business be with him? She chewed her lip thoughtfully; then her brow cleared, remembering something that Captain Maxwell had told her. There were those who placed bets for others on horses. There was a certain disreputable air about this man that made her think he could be one of their number, and indeed, he seemed to be reaching into his pocket and paying out money. That must be it! She felt quite pleased with herself for working it out so quickly. Mr Jordan had been gambling, that was it (oh, what *would* Papa say?) and had clearly backed a winning horse. Clever, clever Mr Jordan!

She asked him when he came back to her, but he only grinned and slapped his pocket in reply.

'Come on,' he said. 'We must get back. I can't allow you to get into trouble with your sainted parents. Nothing must prevent us meeting next week.'

He imprisoned her hands again and kissed them both, first the left and then the right.

'Nothing shall,' she whispered. 'Nothing could.'

She remembered suddenly a dell in the wood at Whiteacres where she had loved to play as a child. Joyfully, but with an edge of fear, she would stand poised on its lip, arms flung wide, before running to the bottom.

'I'm flying, I'm flying,' she would cry, as the slope added impetus to her passage from top to bottom.

258

Here with Peter Jordan she felt the same joy, the same fear, the same soaring excitement. At last, she thought ecstatically, at last my life is beginning.

14

The city coffee house to which Gabriel had invited Paul to discuss possible investment in the dye house was crowded, but they had succeeded in finding seats at the end of a long table. Here they sat in comparative isolation, engrossed in conversation, oblivious to the voices raised in argument and the deals being struck all around them.

'Why have you made yourself such a stranger in Freedom Street?' Gabriel demanded when the business talk was over. 'You have not set foot in the house since the Lord knows when, and we have all missed you.'

'The days are full and time flies.'

'Your business goes from strength to strength, I know that. I hear it on all sides – which is why I was anxious to put to you the matter of Monsieur de Vaux; but still you could surely find time for old friends?'

The warmth of his smile took the reproach from his words. I am damned if I go and I am damned if I do not, Paul thought guiltily. What's a man to do?

'I've missed you too,' he said truthfully. 'And have not yet enquired for Charlotte and Elise. How do they do?'

'Very well. Charlotte has as many orders as she can comfortably deal with – including a further commission from the Queen. I am bidden to the palace in three days' time to learn of her wishes –'

'And you say I have done well! I congratulate both of you. And what is Elise's news? She is well?'

'In health, excellent.' Gabriel hesitated a moment, a look of uncertainty on his face. 'In spirits I am not so sure. She is up and down, one moment the happy girl we have always known, the next so low it is hard to know how to distract her. Between us, Paul, she is at the age when a woman needs a husband.'

'There can be no shortage of suitors, surely?'

'There are none that she favours, it seems – and to be honest, none that find favour in my eyes either. The one that I would choose is clearly unmoved by her.'

His eyes held Paul's, and there was no doubting his meaning. Paul's gaze shifted away awkwardly.

'She seems little more than a child to me.'

'Scarcely younger than Charlotte at the time of her marriage.'

'Perhaps not. I feel sure the right man will present himself before too long.'

'I pray that you are right. All I want is her happiness. I have, perhaps, indulged her too much. She can be wilful and headstrong, I am the first to admit it, but there is a gaiety –' He caught himself up short and smiled ruefully. 'Forgive a doting father,' he said.

'You have every right to dote. Elise is a charming girl.'

Gabriel hesitated for a moment and scratched idly at a stain on the table.

'I wish,' he said at last with an upward glance at Paul, 'that you would think seriously about marriage with her. You think of her as a child, you say; well, that's a condition which, alas, changes all too quickly. The years fly faster than anyone cares to think. It is time you took a wife.'

'I have no plans for marriage to anyone at this moment. I am fully occupied with my work.'

Gabriel shrugged his shoulders.

'I can do no more than beg you to consider it. Well, thank you for your time, my boy. Whatever the outcome of our discussions, be they concerning business matters or family affairs, it is always a delight to see you.'

Paul stood and shook his hand, but sat again once he had gone and called for more coffee.

He is as tenacious as a dog with a bone, he thought. He sighed, slumped despondently in his seat.

A wife with a sizeable portion would mean a great deal to him, no one could doubt that. He had ambitions beyond managing a bank for Charpentier. One day he would set up on his own; Bellamy's Bank. It sounded good – but such a dream needed capital, and capital was something he did not possess.

There never had been such a time for amassing it, though. In previous generations, money was no more than a reflection of the power of land and status. Now money was a powerful thing in itself, and though his bread and butter business consisted of discounting bills of exchange and operating current accounts for wealthy customers, it was the wider implications that interested him – stocks and shares, and dealing in foreign currency.

Could he not, if he tried, fall in love with Elise? He had, after all, squired other women since he had last seen Charlotte. He had been mildly attracted; had even made passionate love once or twice, but always with bitter feelings of dissatisfaction and betrayal once the passion was done. It was one thing to admire the curve of a cheek, the sweep of an eyelash, but such momentary pleasures were meaningless when compared with the helpless affinity he felt for Charlotte, beside which all other attractions lost their meaning.

One day, perhaps, it would wither and die. One day, if he stayed away from her long enough, they would be able to meet again as friends. One day his admiration and gratitude for Gabriel could again be unclouded by guilt; but for the moment he would continue to stay away from Freedom Street no matter how many invitations were to be extended.

Immediately after Christmas the weather turned bitterly cold. The Thames froze hard, and though the cold was not so sustained that a Frost Fair could be held on the river as had happened in the past and would no doubt happen again, still there was skating and sliding and all manner of games for a week or two, with a brisk trade carried on in roasted chestnuts, mulled frumenty and hot pies.

'What say we take a turn about the town tonight, Paul?' Harry Porter said one day, coming into the room behind the goldsmith's shop which was already darkened by the gloom of a grey January afternoon. 'You're growing old before your time, my friend. I can't remember the last time you came tavern-crawling with me.'

Paul looked up from his books, his smile a little apologetic.

'I seem to have lost the taste for that kind of merriment,' he said.

'Then find it again, for pity's sake! Every man needs some pleasure in his life to counterbalance the dull business of making a living.'

'I don't find it dull – though I confess if I'd stuck to your trade, I'd say the same as you.' Nevertheless he laid down his quill and arched his back as if to ease it. 'We're not the two heedless apprentices we once were, Harry, and that's a fact! I suppose age has sobered me.'

Harry rolled his eyes towards heaven.

'May the saints preserve us! You've not more than half a toe in the grave yet, my friend. I suspect that good red blood still flows in your veins. Tell me.' He perched himself on a corner of Paul's desk and peered at him frowningly. 'When did you last have a woman?'

Paul made as if to pick up the inkwell and hurl it at Harry's head.

'That's no concern of yours!'

'It is when I see your face droop and your mouth turn down like a poor parson. For the love of heaven come out and enjoy yourself for once! How else can we get through this dreary winter weather?'

'I'll give the matter my earnest consideration,' Paul said, picking up his quill again. 'Now give me some peace, I beg you, for there are figures I must cast before the day is out.'

Harry pulled a face but eased himself off the desk.

'Mark me,' he said severely, 'I'll not accept refusal –'

'Get back to work!' Paul, grinning, reached for the inkwell again. 'If you chased your gold as well as you chased the bawds, you'd have been a master craftsman years ago.'

'Left to you, every one of them would be chaste!'

Paul laughed and went back to his figures, but for some reason they made less sense than they had done before. He sighed and rubbed his forehead.

Harry was right. It was weeks since he had kicked up his heels. He did not count the assemblies and receptions and parties he attended at the homes of the merchants and professional men who were beginning to be aware of his existence. Now he thought of it, he had enjoyed few social contacts where he was not regarded solely as the London representative of Monsieur Charpentier.

It had not meant, necessarily, that the receptions were dull; merely that he had felt a responsibility to behave with circumspection and the kind of gravity of which Monsieur Charpentier would approve. And always, always, he attended such occasions fearing and hoping that he would see Charlotte; and if she chanced to be present as sometimes was the case, the entire evening would be little short of torture.

When he had first come back to London, in the flush of

reunion with his old friend, he and Harry had visited taverns and coffee houses, and in the society of the men who frequented such places he had been among the liveliest. Now he was inclined to seek his own company more and more, retiring to his rooms over the premises in Lombard Street – and it would not do, he told himself now. He could not turn into a recluse simply because he loved a woman who was out of his reach.

He would do as Harry said, he decided. Tonight they would go out, just as they used to, and he would make a determined effort to join in whatever amusement was afoot, be it singing or dicing or bussing the serving maid.

When the time came to put away his ledgers until the following day he almost thought better of it, however, for the cold was enough to freeze the breath.

'There's a warm fire upstairs,' he said to Harry. 'Come and share a few bottles –'

'Never!' Harry threw his coat at him and pushed him out into the street. 'One would think you two and eighty, not eight and twenty,' he said. 'We'll be inside the tavern with plenty to warm us in a trice.'

He was right. A wave of warmth and light and noise reached out to welcome them and draw them in as they pushed open the door of the Goat and Compasses. It was a tavern close to the river and full of a mixture of men, some well clad and foppish as if recently come from Lloyd's Coffee House, others young and crop-headed, apprentices escaping from their labours. There were watermen and fishermen, a quack who was taking the opportunity to sell a sure and certain cure for the stone, sore eyes and the green sickness, several drunken sailors and an Irish fiddler.

Harry, in the lead, pushed through the crowd to the room beyond where five or six men sat round a table, sober in comparison with the raucous assembly outside, but not as sober as all that. They greeted the two new arrivals warmly and made room for them round the table.

The conversation was animated and ranged wide. One of the men was a writer of pamphlets; another a lawyer. Yet another was, like himself, a banker, and on his right hand was another writer, a satirist with a biting wit.

I have been a fool to cut myself off from such people, Paul thought as he listened to the cut and thrust of their discussion; and he had no answer when the lawyer asked him where he had been keeping himself. I have been a fool, he thought again.

The talk was of the war that still raged with France, of Marlborough's handling of it, and the Tories' distaste for it. They talked of the Occasional Conformity Bill, introduced by the Tories and hotly contested by the Whigs, that would put a stop to dissenters qualifying for public office by taking communion in the Anglican Church merely once during the year.

They talked of fashion, of court scandals, and the merits of snuff as opposed to tobacco. They talked of the latest plays at Drury Lane and Dorset Gardens, and the recent occasion when an actor at the Theatre Royal had kept the audience waiting for his entrance a full ten minutes while search was made for him, the other actors frozen in attitudes of expectation.

'Was he found?' asked the lawyer.

'Aye, in the end.' The writer of pamphlets grinned wolfishly. 'He had been locked in the passionate arms of Madam Hazard – 'tis said the fellow can't leave cards or dice or horses alone, which is much to be deplored since he is a talented actor, and I've said as much in my writings. Peter Jordan has it in him to set the stage alight, but I doubt he has the discipline.'

A serving maid brought pies and eels and oysters and the conversation moved on, Paul by this time glowing with good fellowship. These men have brought me back to life, he thought; but when at last it was suggested that the party should move on in search of a cockfight, he demurred, finding small pleasure in such things.

'Then let's go and have some sport on the river,' Harry said. 'There will be skates for the hiring, I'm certain.'

Not all were in favour of the idea and finally only Harry and Paul went to the river while the others chose the cockfight. It was even colder now but they were beyond caring for such things. The whole of London seemed to be on the ice, indulging in horseplay and laughter, as the two of them handed over their money and donned their skates, tottering to join the throng with a great deal of hilarity and little apparent skill.

'Those wenches need a helping hand if my opinion is asked,' Harry said, clinging to Paul and indicating with his head the direction taken by two girls in a similar state.

'From you?' Paul slapped his thigh and roared with laughter as Harry tumbled to the ice. 'You'd best ask for help from them.'

'I see no great talent for this pastime from you, my friend,' Harry said, picking himself up. But thank God, I see a little light-heartedness, he added silently to himself. This was more like the friend he had known.

The scene was lit by flares, the fitful, flickering lights illuminating faces that were for the most part young and eager for this novel experience. There were a few fine ladies in velvet and furs, their identity hidden by masks. There were braided uniforms and lined cloaks, but for the most part the river had been turned into a temporary playground for those who lived in crowded courts and alleyways and tenements; that faceless workforce that was making London the thriving centre of world trade. Poor they might be, but they still knew how to enjoy themselves.

'Hold on me, sir, and I'll show you how,' called a girl, cheeks glowing with the cold, red hair confined in a crimson shawl.

Paul knew very well how to skate, for he had learned the skill in Amsterdam. His clumsiness had been caused by an excess of wine rather than lack of expertise; however he was happy enough to clasp the girl's hand and listen solemnly to her instructions, and soon they were flying over the ice together. He was conscious of a feeling of sheer exhilaration, and he laughed aloud as they skated, more light-hearted than he had been for months.

They swooped back towards the crowd, and with a wave of the hand the girl left him. He had lost sight of Harry, and for a moment he stood looking around in search of him; and as he did so, he heard a woman laugh.

He turned so sharply that he almost fell, but he regained his balance quickly and looked this way and that in search of the source of that laugh. He would have missed her even then, had she not laughed again and half turned towards him. Swiftly he skated over to her.

'Elise!'

The smile froze upon her face as she turned and saw him, and he, too, looked astonished as he took in the plain dress, the homespun quality of the hood and cloak that she wore. She pressed her lips together in annoyance.

'I knew I should have come masked.' She looked up at the dark-haired young man on whose arm she was hanging. 'Did I not say, Peter, that I should have come masked?'

'I suspect I should have recognised your laugh,' Paul said. He looked at her companion closely and with some suspicion, knowing at once that whoever he was, he was no gentleman. 'Will you not introduce me, Elise?'

'Of course. Peter, may I present Paul Bellamy, a friend of my family? Paul, this is Peter Jordan –'

I have heard that name only recently, Paul thought, but for the life of him he could not remember in what connection. The men touched hands, no more, and murmured polite phrases, their eyes wary.

'Paul, you'll keep our little secret, won't you?' Wheedlingly, certain of her ability to get her own way, Elise smiled up at him. 'You'll not tattle to my father? We are friends, are we not? Did we agree? You'd not see a friend in trouble, would you, Paul?'

'It's not my habit to divulge secrets.'

Paul was aware of his voice, stiff and disapproving, and could almost see himself standing before them like some censorious parson. He made a conscious effort to relax.

'Satisfy my curiosity,' he said. 'Where does your father imagine you are spending this evening?'

'I am with Catherine.' Elise looked about her. 'She is here somewhere, I assure you, and shortly she and I will go virtuously back to St James's Square, none the worse for enjoying our fun.'

Paul looked directly at Peter Jordan, the tight smile he wore not reaching his eyes.

'I should not care to be in Mr Jordan's boots if you do not,' he said.

'I don't care for your inference, sir.' Jordan glared at him, bristling with anger. Elise patted his shoulder comfortingly.

'Pay no heed, Peter. Dear Paul thinks he has the right to guard my virtue. He stands in place of a brother to me. Come, we'll leave him to enjoy himself in whatsoever way he pleases – which is no more than the right I demand for myself!'

These last words were tossed defiantly over her shoulder in Paul's direction as she and her escort left him, and he watched them go, conscious of a feeling of deep unease. Elise was a wilful little minx; yet he knew instinctively that she was an innocent minx, if such was not a contradiction in terms, and he could not deny an affection for her. She had spoken truly when she had said he was like a brother, and at this moment he felt an elder brother's irritation with her.

Where had he heard Peter Jordan's name before? It was infuriating, not being able to remember. He was bent over his ledgers

267

the following day when suddenly the answer came to him. Peter Jordan was the actor who, it was said, could not leave cards or dice or horses alone. Or women, Paul wondered?

The thought was one which he could not easily dismiss from his mind and during the next day or two it kept recurring, insinuating itself between him and his work. On the third day when a damp grey mist had settled upon the city, lifting the temperature a little and ensuring that there would be no more skating until the next cold snap, Harry put his head around the door which led from the shop to the office.

'Are you at liberty to see Mistress Fabian?' he asked with a wink. 'If not, I am perfectly prepared to show her my wares –'

'Please to ask her to come in.' Paul rose to his feet, not acknowledging Harry's attempt at humour – though he had to admit, as Elise entered the room, that he had every reason to feel admiration. She was dressed in a mantle of dark green that threw into relief the gold of her hair, and there was a grace and lightness about her that seemed to illumine the sober surroundings of his panelled room. She glowed like some exotic flower, he thought.

'Elise!' He stepped round the desk to greet her. 'Well, I can't say I find this a totally unexpected pleasure. I thought, somehow, that you might find it necessary to call. Pray sit down –'

She ignored the invitation, but went to him and clasped his hands in hers, looking up at him with wide, appealing eyes.

'Paul!' Her voice was low and throbbed with emotion. 'I have sought the chance to see you ever since we met on the ice. I must know if you mean to tell my father of the meeting. I cannot sleep for the worry – oh, not on my behalf, but on his. He is far from strong, you know, and the distress it would cause him could only add to his sufferings. I – I cannot bear to think of it.' Her voice faltered on the last words, and she loosed her hands to delve into her muff for a scrap of lace and linen with which she dabbed the corner of her eye.

Paul grinned wickedly and clapped his hands.

'Bravo!' he said. 'Such an affecting performance could scarcely be bettered on any stage. It must be the company you keep.'

Her expression changed and she pressed her lips together with annoyance.

'You are a beast, Paul Bellamy. You like nothing better than to mock me – but you won't tell, will you?'

'Sit down, Elise.' Gently he propelled her to a chair, and leaning against his desk, he faced her with folded arms, his lips pursed in a silent, pensive whistle.

'What a goose you are,' he said at last. 'I have no wish to cause trouble and dissension in your home, and hope I shall never have the need to. But if you continue to behave like a common little hussy –'

'How *dare* you!' She half rose from her chair in her anger, but lazily he reached out and pushed her down again.

'I did not say you *were* a hussy,' he said. 'Merely that you behaved like one.'

'You understand nothing!'

'I understand that you are associating with a man of whom your father would heartily disapprove. I understand that you disguise yourself as a serving maid in order to meet him. It's not worthy of you, Elise. You're lovely to look upon, lively and spirited and full of intelligence. Don't waste it all on a man like Peter Jordan.'

'I'll hear no more of this.' She stood up angrily. 'I thought better of you, Paul Bellamy, but you are as bad as my father – just as narrow and intolerant. Peter is a man of great talent and sensibility and I love him. Do you hear that? I love him! I suppose that means nothing to you, for what do you know of love? Here you are, eight and twenty, and still not wed! Ha! You think you are qualified to give me advice?'

Paul's air of good humour fell from him and his eyes hardened. He stared at her for a second before turning away and moving papers on his desk, as if other matters engaged his attention. When he spoke, his voice was weary.

'Perhaps you're right,' he said. 'But then again – think what you're doing, Elise. You tend to be over-impetuous, you must admit, and a woman's reputation is precious. You can call it unfair, inequitable, a gross travesty of justice, and it may be all of those things. The fact remains, however. Unwise behaviour now could ruin your life, and you know it.'

As if encouraged by his change of tone, Elise came closer to him again.

'You could help me, Paul. That's what I came to ask.'

'Help you? How, pray?'

'Befriend Peter! Believe me, you would like him, did you but give him half a chance. He is a charming, talented man – an

269

actor, yes, but why should the talent of an actor be less regarded than that of an artist or a – a goldsmith, or silk-weaver.

'The life they lead –'

'Oh, pooh! He has raffish friends, I'll not deny it, and when Papa met them they showed their worst side, but that doesn't mean that Peter is worthless. Once he had the entrée to our circle, people would see for themselves, and before long they will be boasting of his friendship for he will be famous, you know, one of these days.'

'And you think I could give him the entrée?'

'Of course you could.' Her anger was forgotten, and she was all sweetness, all cajolery again. 'Do I not hear on all sides what a thoroughly worthy, wonderful man is Mr Paul Bellamy – so upright, so charming, so admirable in every way –'

'Stop it, Elise!'

'But it's all true! It would be the easiest thing in the world for you to procure invitations for Peter, and once he had become part of our circle, then Papa would look on him quite differently.'

Should he mention the rumour of gambling? Thoughtfully Paul took a few turns about the room, watched appealingly by Elise. At last she gave a little jump of impatience.

'Well?' she said. 'I'm not asking you to sponsor some highwayman.'

He returned to her and took both her hands in his.

'Listen to me,' he said earnestly. 'I am newly in business, trying to make my way in London, and for that reason it is necessary for me to make contacts through social means. I make no promises regarding Mr Jordan. It would be detrimental to me were I to introduce him only to find that his character falls short of what you suggest –'

'It doesn't, it doesn't!'

'Hear me out, do. I will attempt to befriend him, that I promise. It may be that all you say is true – certainly I have heard other than you say that he is talented – and that only prejudice keeps him out of society. Truly, I have no time for such an attitude and I'll fight it where I can. Give me a little time – and Elise, trust me to be fair to him, and to you. And one more thing. Promise me that you will be prudent and behave with circumspection. You spoke of the worry your father would suffer were he to hear of your escapades. You exaggerated nothing. He

270

adores you, you must know that. Have a little thought for him, if not for yourself.'

'Do your part, and I shall be the very model of discretion, virtuous as an angel from on high –'

'I don't ask the impossible!'

'Beast!' she said, but she smiled as she said it and wrinkled her nose in the enchanting way that reduced strong men to shivers of delight.

Paul smiled too.

'I shall see you again before long, one way or another,' he said. 'Don't come here –'

'Why shouldn't I visit a bank? I have money of my own, you know.'

'Not lodged with me.' A thought struck him. 'Does Mr Jordan know of it?'

'Why should he not?' She looked at him challengingly. 'Am I not worth loving on my own account?'

'Of course you are.' He spoke gently, but her response had done nothing to dismiss his fears. She had not denied that Jordan knew of her inheritance. If he were indeed a gambler, as he had been represented, then the news was disquieting to say the least.

'What trickery did you resort to, to account for your presence here this morning?' he asked.

'I am on my way to buy ribbons – which is no word of a lie,' she added hastily, seeing his expression. 'Molly awaits me outside.'

'Molly must be the most discreet servant alive.'

'Oh, she adores me too!'

'How comfortable it must be, to be so universally adored.'

'It is rather agreeable.' Elise smiled at him. 'It would be a deal more comfortable if *you* adored me, Paul, and I were in love with you instead of Peter, for then the whole world would smile upon me, my father included.'

'Life,' said Paul, 'seldom arranges itself so satisfactorily.'

'We shall simply have to put up with it as best we can.'

She smiled brilliantly as she waggled her fingers at him in farewell. Paul, watching her go, smiled and shook his head in bafflement – at her? At himself? He was none too sure. Some instinct, however, told him that a time would come when he would bitterly regret his involvement in Elise's affairs.

*   *   *

271

Charlotte always considered the church in Threadneedle Street an oasis of quiet in the hurly-burly that was London, but on this Sunday in February that silence was intensified as Gabriel walked painfully slowly towards the three-tiered pulpit, the men in the body of the church as rapt as the women who watched from the gallery.

He has aged, she thought with a pang, but she saw with pride that age had in no way diminished his magnetism. He could command this group of people no less surely than he had dominated that frightened band of refugees in Nantes – perhaps more, for if anything he had grown in power and assurance. His face was drawn, his expression grave, but his eyes smouldered with all their old fire as he turned to face the congregation.

'In the darkness,' he began quietly, 'even the flame of a small candle burns bright. In the darkness that is France, in this year of our Lord seventeen hundred and four, Protestantism is officially dead and buried, smothered by the evil of intolerance and bigotry.' His voice rose, soaring majestically. 'Yet beneath this foul blanket a small flame flickers still, and the flame will burn on and leap high until it can no longer be extinguished by those who would deny it life.

'There is a part of our beloved, oppressed country,' he went on, his voice low again but every word was as clear as a note plucked on a harp, 'where the flame has flared into open rebellion. Our hearts have lifted at the reports that have filtered through to us, inspiring us with their stories of bravery. In the Cévennes, men risk their lives daily to fight for the freedom to worship God in the way they believe right, and in heaven they will reap their reward.'

No one moved or coughed or took their eyes from him. What is his secret? Charlotte asked herself, no less spellbound than the rest of the congregation. How is it that he can hold us in thrall like this, even though he tells us nothing that we do not know already? She had even forgotten that by the merest turn of her head she could look down and see Paul.

He did not often come to Threadneedle Street. Sometimes he attended the Savoy congregation; sometimes, she suspected, he went to no church at all. This week Gabriel had received a note from him proposing himself for dinner following the service, and she had spent the intervening days with her emotions in turmoil, longing to see him yet at the same time dreading it.

Whenever they met at social functions, they treated each other with distant politeness. For some reason she invariably found this more difficult when they met within the walls of her own house, and she had been aware from the erratic way her heart behaved when she had seen him taking his place among the other men in the pews below that this occasion would be no different.

Gabriel, however, absorbed her now. Elise, who habitually showed a marked lack of enthusiasm for attending church and being forced to sit through hour-long sermons, was motionless, and even Madame Colbert, who sat on Elise's further side, had stopped her incessant fidgeting. Stillness and silence were almost tangible. It appeared that even breathing was momentarily suspended as Gabriel went on to give a factual account of the latest news from the Cévennes.

He spared them nothing of the horrors, and just as Charlotte felt she could bear no more his eyes fell to a list he held in his hand and with a voice scraped raw with emotion he read the names upon it.

'Pierre Briot, broken upon the wheel. Jean and Jacques Barreau, condemned to the galleys. Joseph Chamier, imprisoned in Fort Real. Henri de Chesne, broken upon the wheel. Paul de la Haye, burned at the stake. Claude Grissot, broken upon the wheel.'

Strophe and antistrophe, the litany continued. He could recite the days of the week, Charlotte remembered, and still enthral; and he could recite a list of names so that men wept.

When the names were finished he stood for a moment with his head bowed; then he lifted it high and began to speak not of vengeance or retribution, but of forgiveness and reconciliation.

There was a collective, indrawn breath of astonishment, even outrage. Had he inflamed emotions only to preach a pacifism that none could accept? Charlotte saw heads move down below – saw eyes kindle with anger and jaws snap shut, but in her heart she felt a wild joy for he was saying words that she had long since believed; that Protestants should ask for freedom of worship, not that the rest of the world should worship as they did. That those whose only sin had been to follow their own consciences should be released from prison, but in return that there should be an end to bigotry and intolerance wherever it might be found.

'For punishment is God's work,' he said, 'and should be left to him. Our work is to pray for his will to be done on earth.'

She heard his voice, but she watched the congregation too,

and not for the first time she saw the magic taking place; saw anger turn to exultation and high resolve.

What did this mean? When he spoke of reconciliation, did it refer to himself and his mother? Surely it did! He was too honest a man to propose that others should do what he could not.

And now he had lifted them to such a pinnacle of emotion that some were wiping tears away again. What was his secret? she wondered again. Oh, there was never a man like him.

For the love of heaven, Elise thought, enough is enough. Part of her was unbearably moved, the other half sat back watchfully, cynically amused. She did not normally pay much attention to what was said in church. She went there because it was too much trouble to rebel and would in any case have been useless – besides, despite the endless sermons and the sombre faces it was pleasant to see, if only at a distance, the other young people she had come to know over many years. It was pleasant, too, to be pointed out as the daughter of Gabriel Fabian whom everyone admired – though there had been a moment or two during this particular homily when she feared that his halo had slipped! However, it seemed that he now had it comfortably in place once more.

She had given little serious contemplation to beliefs that underlay the faith that sustained the Huguenots, and to be honest, found herself in something of a trance during the long prayers and harangues. Guiltily she resolved, every now and again, that she would try very hard to think nothing but holy thoughts during the course of the service, and sometimes she succeeded for all of half an hour. There was always something more important to occupy her mind; a new gown, or plans for a party. Largely, of course, it was Peter who filled her thoughts – and that was little short of sheer misery!

For all she had said to Paul regarding his charm and talent, there were times when she felt that loving an actor was akin to building a house on shifting sands. She never knew from one day to the next in what role she would find him. She only knew that she loved him – though as often as she admitted it, she vowed that she hated him, that she would never demean herself by waiting for him another minute, that she would never give him money again or tell her parents another lie to account for the lack of it.

Her father had been concerned for her, she knew. She had

seen him watching her sometimes with a bewildered expression on his face, as if he could not imagine what had happened to his sweet little girl of yesterday.

Listening to him now, seeing the effect he had on others, she felt guilty at the way she had answered his enquiries as to her welfare with such ill humour. He was undoubtedly a great man, a father to be proud of; yet even as she thought this, the other half of her that looked on cynically remembered Peter's words. 'Your father,' he had said once, 'would be a better actor than any of us were he to appear at Drury Lane.'

He was right, she thought now; and because she had been to several rehearsals and had been party to numerous conversations between the actors, she recognised that it was not only his voice or the words he spoke but also his timing that wove the spell enmeshing those who listened to him.

It made him more lovable, not less, she thought. He *was* a great man, albeit with faults and more than a touch of vanity. She had no wish to hurt him.

She looked down to where Paul was sitting in the body of the church. She had kept her promise and had barely seen Peter since her visit to Paul's place of business, but she knew that Paul had been to see him. She would soon know the outcome. Had they become friends? How she hoped so! She had warned Peter to be on his best behaviour, and he had laughed and made a joke of it, but beneath all had recognised the importance of it. He wanted, above all things, to be accepted as a member of the Huguenot circle wherein the Fabians entertained and were entertained in their turn.

Acceptance meant a lot to him. Not so much, perhaps, as the fame and wealth that he craved, but much more than his flippant air would make one think.

How complicated people were, she thought. And how complicated life was. And how hungry she was getting, and how she wished her father would stop talking. And how much – oh, how very much – she hoped that Paul and Peter were now fast friends. It was no exaggeration, she told herself, to say that her whole future depended on it.

Nothing was calculated to please Gabriel more than Paul's presence on this day of all days. There was no one alive he would rather see in church to hear both the account of heroism and his own statement of faith than the young man he had come to love like a son, the young man whose good opinion he valued so highly. Indeed, he had toyed with the idea of inviting him.

Paul's letter had removed the necessity to do so, for which he was thankful. An invitation would have smacked of self-glorification – a sin of which he was only too much aware, for his conscience continued to bother him when he thought of the sea of upturned faces and the thrill he experienced when he saw how he had moved them.

So many sins, so many sins. He was glad that he had not added this one to them.

Yet surely it was no sin to feel joy at Paul's presence when it was at his own suggestion? He should know of the extent of his countrymen's bravery, but should be aware, too, that there was need for reconciliation. Then, hard on this thought: God help me, I am glad he will hear it from me, at the height of my powers, manipulating this congregation like a conductor with an orchestra. Oh God, what manner of man am I, that I can speak of heroes and at the same time be guilty of such pride in my petty gift?

At last it was over. Slowly, deliberately, he made his way down from the pulpit amid a charged silence. Prayers were said and at last, a full hour after the usual time, the devotions were over and the congregation began to filter out into the greyness of the February day.

One lady sitting in the pew behind Charlotte leaned forward and touched her shoulder.

'Such a fine speaker,' she said. 'I have never heard anything more affecting.'

'A wonderful man – oh, a wonderful man,' said the woman beside her, and Charlotte nodded and smiled, her heart still singing at the implications of what Gabriel had said.

Madame Colbert seemed to think this a poor acknowledgment.

'Monsieur Fabian is, of course, a hero himself,' she said importantly, as if deciding that today she would forget his shortcomings. 'Which makes his talk of forgiveness so telling. He was married to my niece, you know. He suffered for his faith quite dreadfully – you will have noticed the way he walks. He was affected by the torture, was he not, madame?' She appealed to Charlotte, and receiving no reply, repeated the question a little louder. 'Was not your husband affected by torture, madame, and does he not suffer pain even today?'

Charlotte nodded again, already making her way towards the wooden stairs that led down from the gallery. Elise was hanging back to speak to a dark-haired girl she had known since childhood, but Madame Colbert seemed determined to stay close as if underlining her attachment to the Fabian family, and she scurried hastily after Charlotte.

Paul stood with Gabriel outside the church, waiting for them. Charlotte had known that he would be there. It was the moment she had longed for and dreaded; the moment she had rehearsed a dozen times, yet when it came it was the moment for which she was totally unprepared. Her eyes held his and her face blazed with unguarded pleasure for one second before her habitual caution asserted itself, and she was able to move towards him, her hand outstretched, her smile cool.

'Paul,' she said, surprised at the calmness of her voice when her heart was pounding in her breast. 'How glad we both are to see you. Are we not, Gabriel?'

'I have just been telling him so. Come, where are Elise and Tantine? The coach is waiting and the wind blows cold.'

'Elise is close behind – and Tantine, too, I think.'

'I am here,' Madame Colbert said, a look on her face that Charlotte could not interpret. 'I must have passed you on the steps, madame, but you had no eyes for me.'

15

How to find an opportunity to speak to Elise alone had been exercising Paul ever since he had joined the family outside the church. All through the meal where, painfully conscious of Charlotte, he had nevertheless ignored her and conversed almost exclusively with Gabriel, part of his mind had been engaged with the problem. One way or another he must create the occasion for a private conversation, though the moment was not one he looked forward to with any enthusiasm.

In the end it was Elise's suggestion that they should make music together, he on the flute and she on the harpsichord, that provided the excuse.

'I have a flute you may borrow,' she said.

'I am not in practice –'

'Then we shall take a little time to find a tune to suit us. There are some that are quite simple.'

'The more simple, the better it will be, I assure you!'

'Maman has a favourite I feel certain you can play – the simplest of gavottes. Isn't that so, Maman? Truly, there is nothing easier – why, Maman can even play it herself, though she is the first to admit that her ear for music is the equivalent of my hand for drawing.'

Paul and Gabriel had laughed at this and looked towards Charlotte, but she had made no response, had not appeared even to hear them.

She is thinking of me, Paul thought. She is committed as I am, and what in God's name we are to do about it, I do not know. I only know that this misery is killing me by inches.

'Charlotte is clearly preoccupied by weightier thoughts than simple gavottes,' he said lightly.

Charlotte had smiled at that and got up to precede Gabriel from the room, not seeing the momentary narrowing of her husband's eyes, the sudden penetrating look he gave her. He, too, can feel the tension in the atmosphere, Paul thought – and who, indeed, could wonder at it?

In the music room Elise closed the door behind them and whirled to face him.

'What do you think of Peter?' she asked eagerly. 'Isn't he every bit as charming as I told you?' A puzzled look came into her eyes as she saw his guarded expression. 'You did like him, didn't you? You have said nothing to Papa?'

'No, no, I've said nothing.' Paul sat down on the stool beside the harpsichord and patted the space beside him. 'Sit down, Elise. We need to talk seriously.'

She obeyed him impatiently.

'Tell me what happened, Paul. I know that you have seen him and talked with him.'

'Then you must know I called to see him at the theatre on the very day you came to see me. I saw him at rehearsal. I am sure you are right about his talent. He is a very good actor.'

'I told you!'

'I made myself known to him afterwards. He seemed to expect a call from me and was charm itself, in spite of our less than friendly exchange on the ice.'

'I told you,' she said again. 'Did I not tell you, Paul? So is it all arranged? You know we are all invited to Madame Loubigniac's ball, and I feel sure you must be too. I'm sure she would be agreeable if you brought Peter –'

'Wait, wait, Elise. Look, this is far from easy for me. The truth is –' He hesitated, and Elise pummelled his arm in her impatience. 'Ouch! Stop it, you little vixen! The truth is – oh come, Elise, you *must* know what the truth is?'

'I have no idea what you mean!'

Paul took a breath.

'He is a gambler.'

Elise stared at him for a moment, then burst out laughing.

'Who is not?' she asked. 'Why, I have known cards played for money in this very house – and I dare swear you're not beyond a little dicing yourself. And what, pray, of the Queen? She loves the horses!'

'It's something more than that. Elise, I can't be party to introducing him into our circle. For all his charm, I cannot like him.'

Elise stood up angrily.

'I don't believe this! What makes you so high and mighty, may I ask?'

'Nothing, nothing.' Despairingly Paul shook his head. 'I wish I had never agreed to your preposterous scheme, but having done so, I can only be honest.' He hesitated for a moment. He was not, if the truth were known, being entirely honest. Perhaps he should say more. Perhaps he should mention the distinct impression he had gained, that for all his surface charm, Jordan was a self-centred man of chilling immaturity, unlikely – though he could speak a playwright's words of love as if they came from the heart – to allow his own emotions to become involved.

Jordan had discovered no depth of feeling for Elise. If he wooed her, then it was not for love, of that Paul was certain, but he could not bring himself to say so. It was, in any case, unlikely that she would have believed him.

'Mr Jordan is an inveterate gambler,' he said, sticking to the trait that he felt would hurt Elise least. 'And I have no intention of being his sponsor.'

'Most men are gamblers of one sort or another.'

'Not like Jordan. Gaming is an obsession with him – almost a sickness, and for that, perhaps, he should be pitied rather than blamed.'

'Pity?' Elise laughed derisively. 'Peter needs no one's pity, of that I can assure you.'

'Perhaps not. Perhaps I should save my pity for those from whom he borrows money and neglects to pay back. The man is in debt all over London, Elise –'

'You found that, from one brief meeting?'

'It was not one, and it was not brief.' He holds his liquor badly, Paul thought in passing. Put that down to his account too. He had learned more of the man after a few bottles of wine than Elise could ever imagine. 'By all accounts, he would sell the coat off his back for a stake at hazard. Surely you deserve better than that!'

'I don't believe you.' She pushed away the thought of the fine green coat and the brocade waistcoat that she had seen once and never again. 'You are every bit as bad as my father, prejudiced against Peter because of his profession.'

'And you are blinded by infatuation, unable to see him for what he is –'

'I know him a great deal better than you do! Paul, I was depending on your help.'

Paul sighed heavily.

'I'm sorry, Elise. I'd help you if I could, but I have no intention of introducing such a man to people I respect –'

'And people you *need* for your precious business!'

'It's a consideration I cannot ignore. But since you press me so far, I'll tell you I would not introduce him to my worst enemy.'

'You're a Calvinist through and through.' Elise spat the word as if it were an insult.

'There are worse things.'

Abruptly she turned from him without a word, took a sheet from the pile of music that lay on a table beside her and threw it towards him.

'There, that one will do,' she said. 'I shall go and tell Maman and Papa that we are ready.'

Paul expelled his breath in a puff of exasperation as she left the room. He had not recounted the half of what he had discovered regarding Peter Jordan; the dismal tale of promises made and broken, debts dishonoured, friends betrayed. It was so sordid, so unrelieved by any gleam of honour that he had felt it must surely appear exaggerated to her, too heavily weighted against the man she said she loved, too much of a contrast to the picture of easy charm he presented to the world. Now he wished he had told her everything – or kept silent altogether, for certainly he seemed to have done little good.

Alone with Gabriel, waiting for the summons to the music room, Charlotte knew she should speak of the morning's service. She had been glad, she remembered; but somehow Paul's presence had overlaid the gladness. Now when Gabriel spoke of the way he had been influenced by the words she had uttered at Whiteacres, she found it difficult to give the matter the attention it deserved.

'Did you approve of my sentiments?' Gabriel asked her.

'Yes – yes, of course.' Abstractedly she picked up a piece of embroidery, looked at it as if she had never seen it before and put it down again. She gathered her fluttering wits, forced herself to concentrate. 'I was surprised,' she said. 'Pleasantly surprised. You know I have long held such views. Bitterness breeds only more bitterness.'

'The battle is hardly over. I meant merely to say that if an olive branch is extended, it should be grasped. There are those who appear to think that the guerrilla war can go on for ever, until the whole of France is Protestant, which is plainly ridiculous. We must settle for tolerance.'

'And your mother?'

He was silent for a long while. He rose to his feet and went to the window and for some time looked out at the length of Freedom Street that he could see before him and the other prosperous houses which made up the left and right sides of the small square. A thin veil of rain was falling now, trickling soundlessly down the window panes, as cheerless as the weight of depression that had fallen on Charlotte's spirits.

'Forgiveness in general is easier than forgiveness in particular,' he said. 'I shall continue to pray for grace.'

Elise came into the room then and told them that a piece of music had been selected, if they would like to present themselves in the music room . . . ?

She managed to smile, to present a composed face to her parents, but inside she seethed with fury.

It was all lies, she fumed. All lies! How could Paul say such things? Peter was not like that, not the wicked monster Paul made him out to be.

He loved to gamble – she knew that by now, but so did a million others. She knew, too, that he was often short of money. He had borrowed from her on more occasions than she could remember, but she had forgotten now the disquiet this sometimes caused her and remembered only the smile with which he promised to pay her back. He was paid so meanly, yet expected to keep up some style. It was all so unfair! People were jealous, she told herself; jealous of the attention and the applause, and the way he was sometimes recognised in the street. Certainly he was resented by others in the company. It was proof of his talent, she assured him. Proof that he was sure to be given roles that others coveted. Jealousy accounted for everything.

Well, if the virtuous Mr Paul Bellamy refused his help, then she and Peter would have to manage without it. They didn't need him. It had been a foolish idea, anyway, when in only a short time the whole of London would be acclaiming him as the greatest actor of the century. Paul would no doubt sing a different tune then! He would be begging the favour of introducing his fine friends to the shining star of the Theatre Royal.

Meantime she contented herself by ensuring that Paul made an utter fool of himself, for the music she had chosen for him was well beyond his capabilities.

'My dear Elise,' he said helplessly at last. 'This can be little entertainment for your poor parents! The best I can do is to apologise and keep quiet. You are far better off without me."

'Surely not!' she said; and only he could see the mockery in her eyes.

Plump ankles crossed on the embroidered footstool before the fire, hands folded over her stomach, Madame Colbert felt full of good food and contentment.

'Is there aught else I can do for madame?'

Berthe beamed fatly from the doorway, hands clasped over her apron. She had attended her own church in Spitalfields, for there were now several new Huguenot congregations, and had hurried home to cook dinner. Now she was due some time to herself.

And about time too, she thought, for heaven alone knew she worked hard enough during the week with only one stupid girl to help her, and if madame had the gall to think up some other task at this hour on a Sunday afternoon when she was all ready to have a cosy chat with Marthe, then she would be hard put to it to keep her temper.

'Mend the fire a little,' Madame Colbert said.

'Of course, madame.' For all the ferocity of her inward thoughts, Berthe bobbed a curtsey and continued to smile, reaping her reward when, as she straightened up from the fire, her mistress put out a hand and caught hold of her arm.

'What should I do without you, Berthe?' she asked. It was a question she posed quite often and one to which there was never any reply. If Berthe had been able to think of one, she was certainly not likely to make it.

'It's my pleasure to serve you, madame,' she said unctuously. 'You need someone like me – a friend, if you'll forgive the familiarity, for when I think of the way your family has treated you, my blood fairly boils. How long is it since you were invited up the road? How long since little Elise came here? Answer me that!'

Forgotten was the momentary pride at being connected with

the Fabians that Madame Colbert had experienced in church. Forgotten, too, the many kindnesses she had received from Gabriel's hands; the house in which she lived rent-free (it was still *his*, when all was said and done! He might have given the deeds to her, a man so wealthy – what difference would it have made to him?). She dismissed the frequent gifts of food and silk, the allowance he made her. She thought only of the way her place – Celestine's place – had been usurped by the little upstart whom Elise called 'Maman' with such disregard for accuracy.

She leaned forward, eyes bright with malicious pleasure.

'All my suspicions have been confirmed, Berthe,' she said, brushing aside the question. 'I saw her face –'

'Whose face?' Berthe frowned, for one moment uncomprehending. 'You mean *her*?' She jerked her head in the general direction of the Fabians' house.

'Madame Fabian.' Madame Colbert gave every syllable a great emphasis. 'That young fellow – Belamie or Bellamy, whatever he chooses to call himself. He was there outside the church, and I'm telling you, the look on her face when she saw him gave all her guilt away. She thought I was behind her. She thought I could see nothing; but I could see, all right, and I know what that look meant. Tantine was not born yesterday.'

Berthe clicked her teeth disapprovingly.

'It's a shame,' she said. 'A shame and a sin – and on the Lord's day, too.'

'Never mind the day.' Madame Colbert's grip on Berthe's arm tightened. 'It's my innocent little Elise that worries me. What kind of example is that for the child? Immorality and fornication all about her! One would think we lived in a sink of iniquity, no better than Versailles!' She pursed her lips and shook her head. 'Oh, I have long suspected! I caught them conversing privately – I told you, did I not, how they were skulking in the wood at Whiteacres?'

Many times, Berthe thought, but contented herself by nodding solemnly.

'Do you think monsieur knows?'

'Who can tell?' She released Berthe and lay back in her chair, gazing pensively into the fire once more. 'Who can tell?' She smiled a little as if her thoughts entertained her. 'It would serve him right if he did – putting a creature like that into my Celestine's place.'

'There, madame.' Berthe straightened the shawl that lay around Madame Colbert's shoulders. 'There, now you should keep warm. You are right, madame. It would show him the error of his ways – and not before time, too! Why, my blood boils when I think how you have been slighted! Still, I won't have you worrying your head about it. If dear little Elise is corrupted, it will be the fault of others, not yours.'

Madame Colbert gave a piteous little moan at this thought and put a trembling hand to her lips.

'Corrupted!' she repeated in horror.

'Now, you're not to take on.' Berthe, despite her boiling blood, spoke soothingly. 'How about a little port wine to calm you?'

'How well you look after me, Berthe!'

Berthe smiled as she poured the wine.

'Some would say it's in my own interests to do so, madame, for what would happen to me if aught happened to you? I've no chick or child to care for me, as I was only saying to my dear sister not two days since, and though it says in the Good Book "take no thought for tomorrow", so happy am I in your service that I cannot avoid feeling fearful of what would befall me were you to be struck down.'

'Mercy me, Berthe!' Madame Colbert looked aghast. 'I've no intention of being struck down.'

'We are all mortal, madame. There are times when I think I should take another husband to care for me in my old age.'

'No, no!' Madame Colbert's face paled visibly.

'My sister had it from the fishmonger that he would not be averse –'

'Oh pray, Berthe, dismiss such a course from your mind!'

'But dear madame, what is a poor woman to do?'

'Not that – not marry!' One hand fluttering at her throat, Madame Colbert sat forward in her chair, placing her glass tremulously on a small table and reaching for Berthe once more. 'You will be taken care of, you may depend upon it. I have not much to leave, but rest assured, except for a memento for my dear little Elise, all will be yours. The matter is already seen to, the will signed and witnessed.'

'Oh, may the Lord bless you, dearest madame!'

'There, there, no need to weep. Take yourself off, dear Berthe, and enjoy your time of rest.'

Berthe continued to dab at her eyes with a corner of her apron as once more she curtseyed and left the room, but once outside the door she let it fall and smoothed it absently, her face transformed by a smile of intense gratification.

The matter was already seen to, madame had said; the will signed and witnessed. She could hardly wait to tell Marthe.

It was ten days after his visit to Freedom Street that Paul went to the gaming house. From the moment the project was suggested, he had felt no enthusiasm for it. He enjoyed a flutter on the turf now and again and a friendly game of cards for moderate stakes, but he had little stomach for the serious gambling that went on in such establishments all over London – houses that ranged from exclusive and elegant gaming clubs to sordid dens filled with the riff-raff of society.

They had supped at the tavern, he and Harry and Ned Jolly, the writer of pamphlets, and when Ned had suggested going on to a house he knew in an alley close by Covent Garden, Paul's first reaction had been to decline. It was the thought of suffering his own, cheerless company in his cheerless rooms that stifled his objections and ensured he went along with the others. Ever since his last sight of Charlotte, depression had sat like a stone in his heart despite the fact that he had recently enjoyed a profitable meeting with some American traders and had spent a cheerful evening in their company, impressed by their spirited optimism and self-assurance. For a brief while he had managed to forget his troubles, but they soon returned.

From the moment he entered the gaming room by way of the steep and narrow stairs off the street he knew he had made a mistake. If he was ever to loose himself from the hold Charlotte had on him, it was not this way; not by frequenting crowded, smoke-filled rooms where wine-sodden clerks and footmen and low-class tradesmen wrangled and cursed and fondled the bedizened harlots they had brought off the streets.

'Come on!' Harry, it seemed, was enlivened by the atmosphere that only served to deepen Paul's depression, and he pushed his friend away from the entrance into the heart of the crowd. 'Let's find a place. I feel luck will smile on me tonight.'

'Then play,' Paul said. 'But play alone, for I'm not in the mood for this.'

'Well, take some wine, for the Lord's sake! Here, girl, bring a flagon of Rhenish. Look, there's a place. Take it, Ned, before some other beats you.'

Stumbling towards them was an ashen-faced man who had vacated his seat. He swayed a little as he cannoned into Paul, and grasped at his arm to steady himself.

'Everything,' he said hoarsely. 'All gone!'

He shambled away, helped by those who stood around laughing raucously, pushing him from one group to another until he reached the door and disappeared, one more desperate and destitute creature in a city where the courts and alleyways seethed with others of his kind.

Paul felt a tug at his arm and looked down to see a girl of no more than fourteen or fifteen, her face still smooth and rounded, her lips as delicate as those of a child. Her dress was of purple velvet, low cut and flounced with dingy lace, clearly made for a larger woman.

'Coom with me, sir,' she said. 'I'll find thee a place, does thee wish to play. There's another table in t'other room, beyond curtain.'

'I'm about to leave, I thank you.'

'Don't go, sir. 'Tis better beyond t'curtain – much finer, with nowt so many folk to press upon thee. Coom on! I'll bring thee luck, I swear it.'

Paul looked at her curiously.

'What are you doing here?' he asked. 'You're a country girl, I can tell by your voice.'

'Aye, from Yorkshire.'

'A great distance.'

'Oh aye, it is that.' She tossed her head and smiled at him provocatively. She looked, he thought, like a child dressed in her mother's clothes, acting the part of a coquette.

'Where are your parents? You're over-young to be in a midden like this.'

She frowned at him, uncomprehending.

'Don't you fret about me, sir. Coom on – coom to t'other room.' She wrinkled her nose engagingly. 'You'll not find such riff-raff there.'

Peering through the pall of smoke and the press of bodies he saw Ned and Harry both bent over the table, glasses of wine at their sides, and after a moment of hesitation he yielded to the pressure of her hand and followed her, a movement he regretted almost at the same moment as he embarked on it. Neither this child nor the surroundings had the slightest attraction for him; in fact he found the atmosphere positively repellent with its mixture of despair and raucous jubilation.

'Coom on,' the girl coaxed again, seeing him falter on the threshold of the further room. She was smiling up at him, chiding him playfully. 'You'll like it, sir, you see. It's faro they're playing here. Some say 'tis more sport than hazard.'

The second room was screened from the first by a curtain stiff with grease. The girl had, Paul saw with one glance, exaggerated its charms, for it was every bit as crowded as the outer one and no less smoke-filled. It was, however, considerably less noisy. A large table occupied the central space, lit by flickering candles each with its small plume of smoke, and round it sat men and a few women. Their features were hidden for the candles shed a fitful light. It was the hands that fascinated Paul; hands that shuffled and cut and dealt. Hands that laid down cards, picked up others, hovered as if in doubt, swooped decisively. Hands that won or lost – scooped up or threw down. And all the time there were watchers in the shadows, gaping and whispering.

One man appeared to be winning, far ahead of the others. He wore a dark wig and a flamboyant blue coat. He was half turned from Paul and other watchers stood between them, but although his view was obscured Paul could not avoid being caught up in the tension of the moment. Cards were flung down and collectively the watchers drew in their breaths as once more the hands of the dark man scooped the money towards him. There was drama here, Paul thought. One had to admit it.

A woman stood behind his chair. The man looked round and spoke to her, and Paul saw with a shock of recognition that it was Peter Jordan. In spite of his winning streak he appeared to be scowling. His mouth seemed thin with ill humour, and though it was impossible to distinguish the words he had spoken it was clear from his expression that they had not been pleasant.

With difficulty, Paul edged closer, ignoring the mutters of annoyance of those he displaced. He moved towards the left-hand side of the room where the woman was standing and saw without surprise, once he was close, that though she was on this occasion masked, the woman was easily recognised as Elise. The brightness of her hair alone was more than sufficient.

She looked round with startled astonishment when he hissed her name in her ear.

'Paul!' she said faintly.

'Yes. Paul! What are you doing here. Are you completely crazed?'

'I am more than willing to go home.' There was a note of outraged virtue in her voice as if her readiness to leave made up for her presence in such a place. 'Peter says he cannot leave while he is winning.'

Her voice trembled a little. She was nowhere near so defiant as she appeared, Paul saw, and the recriminations died on his lips. He made an angry move towards Jordan, now once more engrossed in the game, but Elise grabbed his arm.

'Oh pray, don't make a scene, Paul. Just take me home, I beg.'

Slow to anger, Paul was nevertheless capable of a violent temper when he was finally roused, and now his outrage at a man who could have brought a girl such as Elise into a place like this made his head throb and his fists burn with the desire to smash and flail and punish; but looking at Elise, he knew she was right. Retribution could come later. First he must take her home.

'I cannot imagine what madness must have possessed you.' His jaw was tight with fury as he bit back further words, and with an arm around her shoulders shepherded her through the crowd of onlookers, leading her through the outer room, down the stairs and into the darkness of the street. Once there he took her by the shoulders and pulled her close to him so that their faces were only inches apart.

'This has got to stop.' His voice shook with the anger that gripped him. 'I cannot *conceive* how any decent man could have taken you to such a place, or how you could have agreed to it. Are you lost to all decency? Don't you realise that every other woman there was a whore?' He flung her from him. 'Take that ridiculous mask off! You're a disgrace to your family. I refuse to be a party to this – this liaison of yours another moment. Believe me, when I get you home I shall tell your father all.'

'You can't! He's in Essex, gone to recruit throwsters.' Her anger flared to match his.

'And where are you supposed to be? With Catherine again?'

'No.' Elise's voice was more subdued. 'Maman thinks I am in bed. I crept down when she was asleep and came out through a window downstairs. I shall go back the same way.'

'Unless someone has closed and bolted it in your absence.'

'Molly will see to it.'

'Molly should be hung, drawn and quartered, and so should you! And as for Mr Peter Jordan –'

'I am finished with him.'

She turned away from him and began to walk towards the distant lights of the piazza. With a few strides he had caught up with her and taken her arm, forcing her to a standstill.

'Is that true, Elise?' he asked, more gentle now.

'I have never been more humiliated than I was tonight. It was just as you said. Gaming is all-important to him. He forgot my existence, once he started winning.'

'He is worthless, Elise.'

The moon was bright in the night sky and it glinted on the tears that spilled from her eyes and coursed slowly down her cheeks.

'I know. I have said it is finished. Now please take me home.'

He took her arm and they walked towards the piazza where there were plenty of cabs for the hiring. Sympathy for her grief had dissipated the anger he had felt for her. Worthless or not, she had loved Peter Jordan.

They barely spoke until they were in the cab, rattling over the cobblestones in an easterly direction towards Spitalfields.

'I'll not mention this to your father,' he said, after a long silence. 'There is no point in it, if truly it is over.'

'Thank you.' Her voice trembled, and he looked at her, uncertain of what he could say that would comfort her. He reached for her hand and held it between both of his.

'I know there is something better for you in store,' he said.

'Is there?' She gave a brief, mirthless laugh. 'A conventional marriage, that's what is in store for me. A worthy Huguenot husband, you can depend upon it, that's what the years hold for me.'

'One can depend on nothing. One thing I know is certain – they hold something better than Peter Jordan.'

She said nothing for a moment, but Paul saw that the tears were flowing again.

'Life was never dull with Peter,' she said at last. 'He made me laugh so – and cry, too, but I loved the excitement of it all. The theatre, the dressing up in Molly's clothes to meet him. It was such fun, Paul.'

'There will be fun and excitement of a different kind when you have a family of your own.'

'Do you think so?' Her voice implied total disagreement. 'Ends of things are so sad.'

'Perhaps it's the beginning of growing up.'

She said nothing. I am being pompous and sententious, Paul thought, and said no more, hoping only that the genuine sympathy he felt for her was apparent.

They had arrived in Freedom Street now, and both were silent as they approached the house. Some yards before they reached it, Paul rapped on the side to halt the coachman, and paid him off.

'We shall walk from here, I think,' he said. 'It will make less disturbance.'

'Do you not want the cab to take you home?'

'It's a fine night and I'll welcome the exercise.'

'Oh, a fine night indeed.' The words were echoed ironically, but as she looked up at the starry sky and apparently noticed for the first time the moon that bathed the street in a silvery light, her voice changed. 'It's beautiful,' she said, and she spoke with such sadness that Paul could feel only pity for her.

He walked with her to the end of the street where the house stood, a solid monument to Gabriel's wealth and endeavour. The window at the back was unlatched and he helped her to climb through it, feeling in some way disloyal to Gabriel.

'Never again – do you hear me, miss? Never again! You're to be virtuous as a nun from this time forward.'

She was recovering her spirits a little now that she had almost reached the safe haven of her room and impudently she reached up to kiss him on the nose.

'Papa don't approve of nuns,' she said.

It was indeed a fine, fine night and Paul extracted some measure of peace from its beauty and the clarity of the frosty air. Elise was soon dismissed from his mind. She would forget Jordan, he thought. Had Gabriel any inkling of how his darling had been occupying her time, heaven alone knew what the consequences would have been, but thank God the episode was over, with neither Gabriel nor Charlotte any the wiser.

His thoughts turned to his own problems. How easy it had been to assure Elise that she would soon forget! He, of all people, should know that emotions could not always be so easily regulated.

One thing was certain. Life was untenable like this. Perhaps he should seriously consider the offer made to him by Edgar Dawe, one of the Americans he had dealt with only this week.

Dawe was an importer of textiles of all kinds. Previously he had dealt with a rival's bank in Amsterdam, but now he wished to switch to a London bank since most of the goods he purchased originated in England. The discounting of inland bills, whereby the goldsmith purchased the outstanding bill from the supplier a few weeks before the amount from the purchaser became due, had been common practice for many years. Now more and more foreign traders were adopting this method of doing business, and it was for this reason that Dawe had contacted Paul.

The rapport between them had been instantaneous. They had enjoyed each other's company and parted regretfully.

'If you ever want to strike out in new territory,' Dawe had said. 'I beg you to let me know. America needs young men like you.'

Paul had grinned.

'Well, if I'm ever wanted by the constables –'

'I'm serious, Bellamy. We need young men with energy and ambition, for the opportunities are endless. We need skills. We need entrepreneurs of all kinds. We need banks, Bellamy – and I'll tell you now, any time you want to come I guarantee to raise you the necessary capital.'

He considered the matter seriously as he walked through the darkened streets. Had he yet reached the point when he needed to get away at all costs? He found that he could come to no conclusion as the arguments for and against raged in his head so that he barely noticed the heaps of huddled rags in alleyways and doorways where beggars slept, or the harlots who sidled up to him and offered their wares. He heard the watch call out 'one o'clock and a fine, frosty night' as he crossed Threadneedle Street, passing the Royal Exchange and swinging into Poultry, but he waved away the linkboys intent on lighting him home.

America. The New World. The thought had always intrigued him, excited him, as he clearly remembered telling Charlotte; but that was before he was in love with her. Even as he welcomed the thought of a fresh start in a new country, a wave of desolation seemed to wash over him. Without the hope of seeing her even at a distance, could he ever summon the strength to leave?

*   *   *

'Your sister saw him? Are you quite certain of this, Berthe?'

'No word of a lie, madame. Up past midnight, Marthe was, with the whole house in a turmoil on account of the mistress's toothache. In agony she was, poor lady, and nothing would please her but that Marthe should attend her – and attend her she did, and dosed her with her own special remedy.'

Madame Colbert nodded, her eyes avid at the revelation that Berthe had brought her. She had been the recipient of Marthe's remedies herself more than once – had, in fact, pronounced her better than any apothecary, and she showed no surprise that Marthe's mistress had demanded her services at such a late hour.

'He was walking from the house, you say?'

'No doubt of it, madame. Marthe chanced to look out, for madame swore there was a draught from the window that needed stopping up. Tight as a drum it was when my sister looked, but as you know, anyone can see the Fabian house from that window and what did Marthe see but young Mr Bellamy walking bold as brass round the side and out through the front gate. Stealthy, she said he was. Walking quiet, like, so as not to disturb.'

Slowly, savouring every implication, Madame Colbert expelled her breath.

'They've been keeping Elise from me, you know,' she said in an apparent non sequitur. 'Three weeks and more it's been since she's set foot in this house, and never would the little angel have kept away so long if left to her own devices. I know my Elise. It's madame's doing, you can be sure of it. Monsieur is away from home, of course.'

'Of course.' Boot-button eyes gleaming, Berthe nodded. 'Well, it stands to reason, does it not? She would hardly entertain her lover, were her husband at home.'

Lips pursed in disapproval, Madame Colbert nodded sagely.

'No doubt he is the last to know. It would not surprise me if the whole of London is not buzzing with the scandal. I see it as nothing less than my duty to acquaint him of it.' Her gaze wandered away from Berthe towards the fire. 'Three weeks,' she said again. 'Three weeks since Elise has been here. I have cause for complaint, don't you agree?'

Berthe, who had been shaking her head as if in despair at man's evil ways, nodded vigorously at this.

'Oh, indeed I do, madame. Ample cause.'

'Alone in the world! Cast off by my only relations!'

'Now don't upset yourself, I implore you. She will get her come-uppance, I don't doubt. Why, you could even be back in that house yourself in no time at all!'

'You think so?' Madame Colbert looked taken aback at this and raised a tremulous hand to her brow. She had not, somehow, thought of going back. It was really a great deal more comfortable to sit complaining in her own little house by her own fireside, with Berthe to attend to every want, rather than to take up once more the responsibility for the administration of a large household. Still, such selfish considerations should not deter her from doing her duty.

'The news has upset me,' she said petulantly. 'I feel quite undone.'

'I'll bring you a little something, madame.' There was tender solicitude in Berthe's voice. 'A thimbleful of brandy, perhaps? I'll add a few herbs with lemon and hot water. It will settle your nerves in no time, you can count upon it.'

'Oh Berthe!' The familiar cry. 'What should I do without you?'

The period of Gabriel's absence had been an unhappy, confused time for Charlotte. There were times when only a supreme effort of will prevented her from running to Paul. She burned with the desire to feel his hands on her skin, his arms around her body, his lips on hers. At night she lay, unsleeping, straining in the darkness to conjure his face or the sound of his voice, but during the day she felt ashamed of her folly, guilty as if she had committed all the acts she had dreamed of.

She was a woman grown, she told herself, not a romantic, addle-pated girl. Life was more than physical love; a busy, contented existence more the key to happiness than scaling the heights of passion. But how do you know that? a small, insidious voice insisted on asking. How can you tell, when you have never experienced it?

Work was the answer, she told herself briskly. She had the Queen's design to compose, and must concentrate on producing something memorable.

Shapes and patterns came to her readily enough when her mind was at peace, but with a troubled heart she could work all day yet find that the perfect design lay just outside her reach. So it was at this time.

It was not only her own guilty desire that troubled her. She was worried too about Elise, who seemed to have lost all her spirits, drooping silently about the house in a most uncharacteristic fashion. Was some man at the root of her malaise? But if so, which one? Charlotte ran through a list of possibles in her mind. There was no shortage of admirers, but so far she had seen no evidence to say that any of them had captured Elise's heart. She ventured a question or two, but learned nothing. Whatever was troubling Elise, it was clear that she had no wish to confide in her stepmother.

Charlotte was immersed in work at her drawing board one morning, sighing with frustration over her lack of inspiration, when Elise's voice behind her made her jump with surprise.

'How I envy you,' she said.

'You need not!' Charlotte put down her pen and rubbed the back of her neck, sighing dispiritedly. 'Designing is a miserable business when nothing falls into place.'

'Ha!' Elise gave a short laugh. 'Even when it makes you miserable, still you are happy.'

Charlotte smiled at the contradiction.

'I suppose you are right. Elise –' She hesitated, then hastened on. 'Elise, something is very wrong, isn't it? Can you not tell me?' She saw indecision in Elise's eyes; saw her lips part as if she were about to speak. 'I want to help,' she said.

The unspoken words that trembled on Elise's lips seemed to hang in the air between them, but then she swung away, walked over to the window and looked down into the street below.

'It's of no consequence,' she said distantly. 'You wouldn't understand.'

'I would do my best.'

'How could you understand? You have everything! A good husband, a comfortable home, and in addition a talent which others value.'

Charlotte left her desk and went over to the girl, taking hold of her arm and pulling her round gently so that she could see her face.

'There are those who would say that *you* have everything; good looks, money, health; and much love, *chérie*. Never forget that.'

Elise's face stayed closed and unresponsive. Charlotte studied her for a moment, a small frown drawing her brows together.

'What do you want, Elise?' she asked.

'Want?' Elise was still for a second, then she broke away and swirled agitatedly around the room, fists tightly clenched. When she stood still and turned to face her, Charlotte saw that her face had lost the dull, dispirited look she had worn for days now and blazed once more with life. 'Want?' she asked again. 'I want *everything*! Love, riches, excitement, acclaim. I want *drama*, Maman! I cannot bear the thought of the life most women lead, the thought of being a man's chattel, producing a baby each year, my main excitement an outing to church on Sunday. I dread it – do you hear me! I dread it!'

'I understand. I dreaded it, too. I was mortally afraid –'

'I'm not afraid!' Elise lifted her chin and her eyes blazed. 'I'm not afraid of *anything*! I want to take life and drink it to the dregs, not be cowed into doing what others think a woman should.'

'No one wishes you to be cowed. What a preposterous thought! Am I cowed? There is no place for that in a happy marriage.'

'A marriage to some virtuous, dull clod of my father's choosing!'

'You do him an injustice, Elise.' Charlotte was beginning to lose patience. 'One day you will meet someone you can love –'

'And will he wait till then? He would throw me at Paul Bellamy if Paul were willing, never mind my feelings.'

Charlotte clutched the back of a chair to steady herself.

'He is fond of Paul.'

'I am fond of Paul. You are fond of Paul. The whole world is fond of Paul, but I have no wish to be married to him. He treats me like a two-year-old idiot!' Suddenly the fighting spirit seemed to drop out of her and her shoulders drooped. 'Forgive me, Maman. I am restless and at odds with myself. I have no right to speak so immoderately to you. How little you deserve me!'

Charlotte laughed and embraced her, kissing her on both cheeks.

'Be patient, *chérie*,' she said. 'All will be well. You must know how much you are loved and how your wellbeing is our only concern. Now – may I beg for a few minutes' peace? I *must* work!'

'And what am I to do?'

'Oh, a thousand things! I know – go to see Tantine. You have neglected her shockingly of late, and she always blames me for it.'

Elise made a small grimace.

'I cannot abide Berthe. She grows more and more oily and familiar.'

296

'But Tantine loves to see you so much.'

'Oh, very well.' Elise sighed heavily and left the room, leaving Charlotte to sigh too and to wish that Gabriel would come home quickly.

Seventeen, as she could well remember, was the age for deep depressions and swings of mood, and she could hardly be surprised that Elise was proving to be no exception to the rule. She realised, however, that she was no nearer finding out the cause of this particular outburst, and she felt uneasy.

When finally Gabriel came home, it was two days before she had expected him and they greeted each other with undisguised pleasure and relief. He was tired, she saw, but in excellent spirits, having been impressed with the competence of the Essex throwsters he had seen and only too happy to accept their work.

'They are a devout band,' he said, 'and an inspiration to converse with. I felt I learned much from them. I wish you had been with me, my love.'

'I wish I had, too. For all I have achieved here I might just as well have come with you, though I could not have left Elise and she would scarcely have been the best of company. She is in a strange mood, Gabriel. Something is troubling her. Which reminds me – she called on Tantine the day before yesterday and came back with an urgent request that you should go to see Tantine the moment you return.'

'Indeed?' Gabriel raised his eyebrows. 'Trouble with the roof, no doubt – or the pump out of action or a dispute with a neighbour. Probably all three. Troubles never seem to come singly with Tantine. Well, tomorrow will be soon enough. Tonight I have no intention of moving from your side.'

Charlotte smiled and took the hand he stretched out to her.

'And I have no intention of allowing it,' she said.

16

Madame Colbert's room was, as always, overheated, but that was not the reason for the beads of sweat that stood out on Gabriel's lip and brow.

'You are a slanderous, evil woman,' he whispered, rage a red mist before his eyes. 'There is no word of truth in it.' He pointed a shaking hand towards her. 'Speak one word of this outside these four walls and you will be in the street.' His voice rose in its fury. 'Remember you owe this to me.' He reached to bang his clenched fist on the nearer wall. 'And this, and this.' A table and chair were equally assaulted.

Madame Colbert, too, was trembling. Her pale dewlaps quivered and her little mouth opened and shut.

'I tell you for your own good –'

'You tell me because you have always hated and resented Charlotte – aye, and me, too. Well, watch your words in future, you and that lying creature who serves you.'

He slammed from the house and stood for a moment on the street outside, jostled by passers-by, unable to see or to think clearly because of the anger that flamed inside him.

He began walking without thought – anywhere to put a distance between him and the house where Charlotte had been so vilely abused. Charlotte! He remembered her as she had looked the evening before when she had welcomed him home, smiling with a pleasure that surely was genuine. Would he not have discerned it, if it was not so? He knew her so well. Dishonesty was alien to her. She was pure and lovely, through and through – he would stake his life on it.

And Paul! That fine, upright young man he thought of as a son – as honourable, he could swear, as the day was long. Of course the woman lied! She was crazed by bitterness and jealousy, and always had been.

He was unaware of the curious glances he provoked as he lurched along, his lean figure bowed a little now but still head and shoulders taller than the crowd. As always he was clad in black and there was a vaguely clerical look about him, yet there was an unmistakable richness of quality in the clothes he wore; a distinction, a difference, that ensured he was noticed.

He could walk quickly when he chose despite his infirmities, though normally he did not choose to do so for the swifter his stride, the more ungainly it became. Now he did not care, gave it no thought, did not see those who blocked his way or turned to stare at him. Had he but known it, he followed the exact path that Paul had trod, the night he had brought Elise home.

He crossed Poultry and narrowly avoided being run down by a four-in-hand. He did not hear the shouts of abuse, not then nor later when he brushed against a box of oranges in the market and sent them flying; nor did he hear the bells and the costers crying their wares or the shouts of derision directed at the poor wretch in the stocks. He did not even notice that the stocks were in use.

It was not until he stood beside the river that he stopped, conscious suddenly that his back ached unmercifully. Wearily he leaned against a wall. Where now? Where but on the river?

It was a cold, murky day with an oily look to the water. A pall of smoke hung over the city. All was grey; grey water, grey sky, grey buildings save for the magnificent dome of Wren's new cathedral.

'Row,' he said to a persistent boatman. 'Take me where you fancy.'

He did not care that the man thought him mad and did not hesitate to say so to the other boatmen who stood around. As if carved from stone, he sat in the wherry, lulled a little by the rhythmic splash of the oars, staring unseeingly at the barques and colliers and barges that surrounded them until they had cleared this most populated part of the river and were beyond Chelsea.

'You may leave me here,' he ordered suddenly.

'Here?' The boatmen gawped at him. In summer, perhaps, these fields would be an attractive destination, but on this day they were desolate.

'Here.'

The boatman shrugged and did as he was told, looking with astonishment at the coins that Gabriel flung at him. The man *was* mad! This was enough for more than double the journey.

Gabriel stood on the bank and watched the boat pull away

from him, conscious for the first time that he felt cold down to the very marrow of his bones. He turned and lurched away from the river to a lane he could see beyond the fields, and here he found a tavern and a fire where he rested and refreshed himself with ale and meats served by a girl. She had dark hair and a creamy skin – like Charlotte, but not like Charlotte, for there was no one like her. This girl had a bold, flirtatious air. Charlotte was cool and restrained, and still had that touch of childish diffidence that had so moved him when he had first known her; and beneath all, she was loving. Surely, loving?

'It is not true,' he said angrily, out loud, and the sound of his voice brought the girl back to ask if there was more he wanted.

'No, no – I spoke my thoughts.'

She left him again and he sat alone beside the fire, the solitary customer in this remote inn.

It is not true. The words echoed in his head, but beneath them there was a deep sadness, an ache of loss. Staring at the smouldering log in the hearth and the sparks that flew up the chimney, he remembered and wondered how he could have been so blind.

There had always been a strangeness about her relationship with Paul; a dimension he had not understood. She had spoken warmly of the friendship they had enjoyed as children, yet always now seemed reluctant to invite him to the house. But when forced for one reason or another to do so, the reluctance was inevitably followed by a febrile gaiety.

Then there had been the meeting outside the church when she had blazed into glorious life for one brief moment. He had noticed it but had been elated himself by his own eloquence and had believed it to be directed towards him. Now he relived the moment and knew that he had been mistaken. It was Paul who had kindled that expression of joy. Yet later, at the meal, she had been tense and withdrawn.

He knew her so well. He understood the workings of her mind, could foretell her reactions; hadn't he made it his life's work to do so?

It *was* true. Anger dulled into reluctant acceptance and an agony of self-reproach. The sin was his, not hers. How could it be other, when he – so many years older than she and surely wiser in the ways of the world and human nature, had taken advantage of her childish fears? He deluded himself if he said he had married her out of concern for her. It was not true. He had seen her and he had wanted her, and even if he could never bed her, he was damned if any other should.

Had Paul?

The blame might be his, but this thought still had the power to make him gasp with pain and he groaned as he lowered his face into his hands.

'Are you ill, sir?' The serving maid was at his side again. 'You look that pale.'

His spine felt as if it were made from a series of red-hot splinters that seared his flesh, but he shook his head.

'No, I am not ill. A little tired perhaps. Is there a coach I can hire?'

'Why, to be sure, sir. We can soon get one from the village.'

'Then do so, if you please. I wish to go to the east side of London – to Freedom Street in the liberty of Spitalfields.'

The irony of the name was not lost on him. There was no freedom anywhere. Guilt and suspicion and misery were the chains that bound him now, and for the life of him he could not conceive how he would ever be free of them.

'I cannot imagine where your father can be,' Charlotte said to Elise. 'I think, perhaps, we should eat our dinner without him for it has been held back more than an hour and still there's no sign of him.'

'Did he not say something about going to Lloyd's after he had seen Tantine? He might have eaten at the chop house.'

'I suppose he might.' Still Charlotte frowned, for such behaviour was not characteristic. The main meal of the day was invariably served at two o'clock and wherever Gabriel partook of his supper, this was an hour he liked to spend with his wife and daughter.

She grew worried as the short winter's afternoon began to darken. It was true that he had mentioned something about arranging the shipping of a cargo of half-silk to New York and might well have gone to the city on this business – or even, perhaps, to the docks, for he loved the air of bustle and excitement to be found there. It was a rough, lawless part of London, however, and he would not be the first wealthy man to be found in the river with a knife wound in his back. Knaves and vagrants abounded there.

301

'I wonder if he said anything to Tantine about his intentions when he left her?' she wondered aloud.

Elise had gone to her music lesson. It would be possible to send a servant bearing a note, of course, but impulsively, seeing it was not yet quite dark, Charlotte put on her mantle and went herself. She hurried down the street with a basket over her arm in which, equally impulsively, she had put some gingerbread, knowing of Tantine's fondness for it.

Berthe's manner seemed strange as she admitted her. It was true that Charlotte had not visited Madame Colbert for some time – it was one of the reasons she had decided to do so that afternoon – but that seemed little reason for Berthe's eyes to bulge out of her head with astonishment, or her thick lips to gape so rudely.

To her surprise, Charlotte was not ushered into the parlour immediately but was bidden to wait, and she listened in bewilderment to the voices from the inner room. To allow an audience or not to allow it seemed a question that was debated for some time, but at length Berthe returned and said, without warmth or grace, that Madame Fabian could enter.

Charlotte, who had been on the point of slamming out of the house, thanked her icily and swept past her to find Madame Colbert sitting in her usual chair, tightly clutching both its wooden arms, and looking both frightened and determined.

'You may say what you have come to say and go,' she announced sharply. 'I have told your husband nothing but the truth, deny it as you may.'

Taken aback, Charlotte stared at her in astonishment.

'What can you mean?' she asked at last.

Madame Colbert laughed unpleasantly.

'Playing the innocent, eh! Well, look into your heart, madame. There you will find all the answers.'

'Have you gone mad? I came to ask you if my husband said aught of his destination when he left you.'

'He said nothing.' Uncomfortably, remembering what Gabriel had said, her eyes shifted away from Charlotte. 'I know nothing of his whereabouts. I only know he was here this morning.'

'What truth is this that you say you told him?'

'The truth concerning you and young Belamie – Bellamy, whatever you call him. He knows the whole story now, madame, though no doubt you will deny it.'

302

'What story? What truth? I demand an answer!'

'Adultery, madame.' Madame Colbert was leaning forward, spitting venom. 'Adultery. No more nor less.'

'You – said – that –' Charlotte's reply came haltingly, as if she could scarcely find the breath to utter the words. 'You said that to my husband?' Her voice strengthened. 'How dare you spread such lies! Has he not suffered enough? You are wicked, wicked –' With shaking hands she reached into the basket she still carried. 'I brought you a gift,' she said. 'Here, take it!'

Furiously she flung the gingerbread towards Madame Colbert, and though she heard an outraged squawk she did not wait to see if she had hit her target but was out of the room and out of the house in a whirl of anger.

Her passage back to her own home was as unseeing as Gabriel's route to the river, her thoughts a confused jumble of anger, guilt and fear. Surely, surely Gabriel would not have done anything desperately foolish? He would not – *could* not have believed the old harridan! Anything Madame Colbert had told him must have been pure conjecture. She and Paul had done nothing. She was innocent, innocent – yet if desires and dreams had anything to do with the matter, then surely she was as guilty as any harlot?

There was still no sign of Gabriel, but Elise had returned – or so she assumed, since she saw the coach being driven into the yard. Nan met her in the hall and exclaimed at her distraught air.

'It's not bad news about monsieur, is it, madame?'

'No, no.' Charlotte put a hand to her head. 'At least – I don't know. I was hoping he would have returned.'

'There, there madame.' Nan spoke with determined cheerfulness. 'He is a man grown, when all is said and done, and the hour isn't late. Calm yourself, do. There's a warm fire in the parlour and I shall bring tea to you, do you go and warm yourself.'

She took her mistress's mantle from her as tenderly as if she had been a child, and disappeared to get the tea. Charlotte was glad of the fire. She felt cold as stone, and she stood before it, holding out her hands to the blaze.

'So you are back! Is there news of Papa?' Elise came in and stood beside her.

Dumbly Charlotte shook her head, aware that there was a touch of exasperation in the look that Elise gave her.

'I cannot imagine why you are so worried,' she said. 'He has many business affairs to occupy him, after all.'

Charlotte opened her mouth to explain, then closed it again. It was not possible to speak of Madame Colbert's lies – not to anyone and certainly not to Elise. No one must ever know.

'I trust you enjoyed your music lesson,' she said stiffly, sitting down in the armchair beside the fire. 'How is Monsieur Grimod?'

Elise turned from her as if refusing to meet her eye. She picked up the silver candlesnuffer that lay on the mantel and examined it as if she had never seen it before.

'I am not in a position to say. I did not go to my music lesson.'

'I'm glad to hear it.' Charlotte's voice was faint, abstracted. Elise's lips tightened.

'You are not paying attention,' she said. 'I told you I did not go to my lesson.'

'Did you not?' Charlotte frowned in bewilderment as if she were trying to make sense of some incomprehensible puzzle. 'Well, I suppose it is of little moment.' She winced as Elise crashed the candlesnuffer down on the stone mantel and whirled to face her.

'I must talk to you, Maman,' she said.

Unconsciously Charlotte sighed, wearied at the thought of more self-examination from Elise when she had so much on her mind. She could not deal with it.

'Pray leave your discourse until tomorrow, dearest,' she said. 'Today I am distracted with worry –'

'Aye, about a man who is well able to take care of himself. Who cares for my troubles?'

'I do, and you know it! Stay – here is Nan with the tea which will cheer us both, perhaps.'

'I have no wish for tea.' Elise stormed towards the door, but stopped short as a thunderous knocking made itself heard from downstairs.

It could not surely be Gabriel – unless he was mad with rage? But it could, perhaps, be news of him. All three women – Charlotte, Elise and Nan – hastened down to the entrance hall where Molly was already opening the door. In the darkness outside, illumined by the lights which spilled from the house, a figure could clearly be seen.

It was not Gabriel. This man was unkempt, untidy in his dress, pale and unprepossessing of features. He looked with some surprise at the reception committee that stood before him.

'I am seeking Monsieur Gabriel Fabian,' he said. 'Is this his residence?'

It was nine years since Charlotte had heard that voice, but it was not one she would ever forget. Reluctantly she stepped forward.

'Pray come in, Monsieur Boyer,' she said. 'I regret that my husband is from home.'

'I have never *seen* such a hateful man – or been forced to listen to one,' Elise raged to Molly. 'I cannot understand my father agreeing to entertain him.'

'They were old friends, mistress. It does your father credit. He's so good and kind.'

'So good and kind that he makes me sit silent while the hateful Monsieur Boyer gobbles and gabbles –'

''Tis only good manners, mistress.'

'Ha! What of Monsieur Boyer's manners? They leave much to be desired. I uttered one word regarding Catherine's new gown yesterday at dinner and was treated to a full hour of sermonising about the sin of frivolity and vanity with no voice uplifted in my defence. It's monstrous unfair!'

Molly, busy folding the clothes that were strewn about the chamber, grinned at her slyly.

'Better say naught of the theatre, then. I'll wager there'd be a mort of sermonising about that.'

Elise knew that she was right; and knew, too, that the disapproval would not be confined to Monsieur Boyer. She could imagine only too well all that her father would find to say on the subject, and as for Paul – uncomfortably her thoughts swerved away from him and from the memory of that terrible night when he had rescued her from the gaming room, for she had broken her promise not to see Peter again.

He had explained everything. He had not been himself, he told her. He had drunk too much, cast into despair by the jealous plotting of the rest of the company, and the tyrannical, penny-pinching practices of Mr Rich, the owner and manager of the Theatre Royal. How could she possibly have refused to see him again? He had been so penitent – had even broken down and wept, and had vowed a thousand times that nothing like it would ever happen again.

She had been only too ready to believe him for she had felt miserably bereft during their estrangement. She loved him; that was the beginning and the end of it, and the rest of the world would simply have to accept the fact.

She loved the theatre too, and had become a constant visitor to rehearsals, fascinated by the magical world they seemed to reveal to her, a world where the sun always shone; where characters spoke only in witticisms and the strains of music wafted in bearing dreams.

It came as something of a shock to her to realise that despite the extravagant terms of affection which the actors employed towards each other, Peter had in no way exaggerated the jealousy and backbiting. As the despised Mr Rich's protégé he unfairly attracted more than most, he grumbled – neglecting to tell her of occasions such as the time he had been too engrossed in gambling to make his entrance.

She burned with indignation on his behalf. Of course Edmund Brownlea, nearer fifty than forty and of considerable girth, was too old to play the handsome hero – though he continued to do so, as of divine right. And of course Rupert Onslow was not to be compared with Peter when it came to looks or talent.

'Yet both have complained that I have been given roles above my station,' he told Elise indignantly. 'Let them wait! I'll show them all – I'll show the world –'

'Oh, you will, you will,' she assured him earnestly.

On the day her father had disappeared so mysteriously for so many hours, she had been to see him rehearsing the part of an over-foppish young coxcomb and acting it to perfection. Alone in her box, she was forced to cover her mouth with her hand to stifle her laughter. The comedy was by Wycherley, and of the type based on cuckoldry and marital mistrust that her father disliked so heartily. A year ago – six months, even – she would not have understood the half of it, but association with Peter Jordan had added considerably to her education and now there were few *doubles entendres* that she did not appreciate.

On the stage Peter had appeared smiling and suave, but he was much changed when he joined her afterwards in the box.

'You'll not believe it,' he burst out angrily. 'After this trifle we

306

are to do *Romeo and Juliet* – Brownlea to play Romeo, Harkness, Juliet! Is it conceivable?'

'You have a complaint, Mr Jordan?' The voice from the shadows behind them made them both turn in surprise. It was the despised Mr Rich himself who stood there.

Elise had heard no good of the man, from Peter or from anyone. He had pared salaries to the point where everyone complained. He cheated and twisted anyone foolish enough to trust him and was engaged in constant lawsuits. If Peter gambled more than he should have done, then this man was to blame, in her opinion. The wretch had no right to keep his actors so short of money. Rich was an overbearing man and few were strong enough to stand up to him, but Peter was too angry to back down.

'I suggest that Mr Shakespeare might have one,' he said forcefully. 'I submit that Romeo was conceived as several decades younger than Mr Brownlea.'

'Mr Brownlea draws crowds, Mr Jordan.'

'That is understood. Nevertheless –'

'Nevertheless, you are by nature more qualified for the role. Is that what you are attempting to say?'

'By nature, and by my talent, sir. You yourself brought me from Smock-Alley for that reason. I am a good actor, and I come cheaper than Mr Brownlea.'

A long pause followed this statement, as if Peter's final point was one that deserved careful consideration.

'Hm,' Rich said reflectively at last. 'Cheaper, eh?'

'Much cheaper, sir. All I ask is a chance to show what I can do.'

'Hm.' There was silence again from the theatre manager. 'Hm,' he said once more. 'The matter needs thought. You have not, in the past, been entirely reliable –'

'Those days are over, I swear!' Peter's voice rang with eagerness and sincerity. Elise clasped her hands as she listened to him. Oh, how could anyone doubt him?

'Say nothing,' Rich cautioned him. 'I shall reflect upon the matter.' He turned to leave the box, but paused at the door to turn and look at Peter once more. He was in the shadows, his expression hidden, but the rumble of his voice came to them clearly enough.

'Cheaper, eh?' he repeated thoughtfully as he left them.

The moment he had gone, Peter whirled round to face Elise.

307

'The role's as good as mine,' he said joyously, gloatingly. 'I know it, I know it! He can't resist the thought of saving money! Oh, I'll give them a Romeo to remember. I shall play it lithe and quick –'

'Oh, pray don't get your hopes up –'

'I'll not rant or screech, but speak the lines low and thoughtful –'

'He made no promises!'

'I shall be Romeo.' He seized her shoulders and held her tightly. 'Did I not tell you, that first time, that one day I should have the part? The whole of London will speak of it – then Rich will have to pay me what I deserve! My name will be on everyone's lips –'

'Oh yes, yes!' She had caught his excitement.

'Even your father. Even he!'

'Yes, even he!'

'He'll say "I knew Peter Jordan as a boy!"' Somehow Peter had transformed himself into the very image of Gabriel Fabian, and Elise laughed delightedly. 'He'll say "Be so good as to marry my daughter, sir." And I shall thank him kindly and do exactly as he asks!'

There was a sudden charged silence as Elise took in the significance of his words.

'Marry?' she repeated softly. The matter was not one that had ever been mentioned between them. 'You would wish to marry me?'

'Why not? Today I can believe anything possible!'

'But –' She hesitated, biting her lip. 'Oh Peter, don't you understand? I fear that in reality, no matter how talented or successful you may be, my father would never agree to it.'

She saw the joyous excitement die from his eyes, saw his lips draw back in a thin and bitter line.

'Then perhaps we shall have to dispense with his gracious approval,' he said tautly. 'Others do it every day.'

It was suddenly difficult to swallow and Elise was conscious of the accelerated beat of her heart. There was noise coming from the stage, rough voices cursing, carpenters hammering, the trilling of laughter from Belle Harkness, yet the two of them seemed isolated in their box, alone in their private world.

Marriage! Was it really possible?

'I don't know, Peter. I am frightened.'

'Of your father?'

Dumbly she shook her head.

'Not precisely. Of hurting him, I suppose. He loves me very much – I have never doubted that, not for one instant.'

Peter let go her shoulders and turned away from her.

He had gone from her, she could tell – back to the magical, make-believe world of the theatre. He looked towards the stage and a smile of gratification came to his lips.

'Romeo!' He seemed to roll the name around his tongue, savouring the taste of it as well as the sound. It was as if he had forgotten the casually uttered proposal almost before the echoes of it had died away. 'This is my chance, Elise. No matter that the skinflint pays me less than Brownlea – what do I care for that? It's the opportunity that matters. I shall make the whole of London ring with my name.'

The excitement, the confidence, were contagious. Elise found herself responding, on the edge of the dell and ready to fly again.

'Peter, did you mean it? Were you in earnest?'

'About marriage?' He took her hands again and the smile that he turned upon her was full of tenderness, just as it would be when, as Romeo, he smiled at Juliet.

'My dearest love, I was never more in earnest.'

'Then I will marry you.'

'Without your father's approval?'

'If necessary. We belong together, I am sure of it.'

What a day, Peter thought exultantly as he kissed her. First Romeo, now this. He had never thought – never *really* thought – that he could pull it off, though right from the time of their meeting he had made a small wager with himself as to the outcome. He had not doubted her love; she had been eating out of his hand for months. But he had seriously doubted his ability to get her to agree to marriage without her sainted papa's agreement. His timing had, as always, been superb.

La petite héritière! Who could have dreamed it possible? How the gods had smiled on him.

It must surely be an omen. The dice would fall his way that night.

Charlotte would approve of marriage to Peter no more than her father, Elise knew that, however she resolved to confide in her in an attempt to enlist her support. After all, she had always been more of a friend than a mother, and had never failed to listen to her with sympathy and understanding.

It was incomprehensible that now, just when Elise needed a confidante so desperately, Charlotte seemed for the first time to be unwilling to give of her time. It was all Monsieur Boyer's fault, Elise thought rebelliously. Ever since that evening when he had arrived smelling like a midden and looking like a scarecrow, everything had been at sixes and sevens. She had never been more astonished than when Charlotte invited him in, just as if he were an honoured guest.

Papa, when finally he had arrived home on the day Monsieur Boyer appeared, had looked gaunt and ghost-like and had given no explanation of his long absence. He had greeted the unexpected visitor with wary politeness rather than warmth, but still, inexplicably, had urged him to stay for however long his business in London took him. And now here he was, dominating the conversation, clearly disapproving of both her and Maman.

One would have thought that in the face of this joint disapproval the two women might have closed ranks, but though Papa had returned safe (Maman's anxiety, Elise thought with a touch of amused condescension, had been sweet and rather touching. As if there had been any real risk!). Charlotte remained withdrawn and silent, inattentive when Elise tried to speak to her on any serious subject.

'Forgive me, I have a frightful headache,' she had said when Elise came to her room several nights after Monsieur Boyer's arrival. She had retired early to escape his incessant harangue and Elise had thought it the perfect opportunity for a confidential chat. 'I have taken a draught for I have not slept for nights. Tomorrow we must have a talk.'

Elise had flounced angrily from the room. It was *now* she needed to talk to Charlotte, not at some future time which, like as not, would prove equally inconvenient when the moment came. With the self-absorption of the young she could see no misery but her own. Nobody had time for her, she thought, in spite of all their talk of love. Nothing had been right since Monsieur Boyer's arrival.

Worst of all, no one seemed to know how long he was likely to stay. He was raising money and promises of support for the Camisards and was loud in his condemnation of those in favour of responding to the French government's moves towards peace.

310

The campaign against the guerrillas was costing them dear when they needed all their resources to fight Marlborough and his troops. The new government commander, Marshal de Villars, had even gone so far as to make a public proclamation stating that all insurgents would be pardoned if they would lay down their arms, but contemptuously Boyer swept aside such overtures.

In view of her father's rousing sermon regarding reconciliation and forgiveness, Elise would have expected a more spirited argument from him, but he said little, apparently unable to bestir himself to do more than allow Boyer's rantings to wash over him as if they were a force too mighty to withstand. He, like Charlotte, seemed only half-present, sapped of energy.

Elise stared at herself in the mirror after her abortive attempt to speak to Charlotte. Life, she decided, was totally insupportable.

At Drury Lane, *The Country Wife* was being performed and *Romeo and Juliet* was about to go into rehearsal, with Peter in the main role. Mr Rich had exercised his dubious diplomatic skills, but in spite of them, Peter had reported to her, the atmosphere in the company could be cut with a knife.

'I swear Brownlea has made a representation of me and is even now sticking pins in it,' he said to Elise; but gaily, unworried. 'What should I care? The part is mine and we'll let the audience decide who has the better claim to it.'

It was all right for Peter, Elise thought. He was doing exactly what he wanted. What had she to look forward to? Not even a celebration for her seventeenth birthday, now just over two weeks away. Nothing had been planned, nothing mentioned. How unlike the excitement of her sixteenth birthday when she had been the hostess for her father in Maman's absence and had felt as if she were stepping through a door into a wonderful, grown-up world of pleasure!

Nobody cared, that was the truth of it. The years were passing, she would soon be old, all her youth gone. For all her father's love for her, he would dispose of her as he thought fit – not, necessarily to the highest bidder as many would do, but to the worthiest, the most upright.

In other words, Elise thought, to the dullest. It was not to be borne, and she would not bear it. Could not, and would not. Peter was the only one who cared. She was only alive when she was with him.

Really, she said to her reflection, there could be no alternative.

Charlotte bit her lip guiltily as Elise left her. She should have listened to what the child had to say – would certainly have listened but for the draught she had taken which was already blurring her senses, wrapping everything in a covering of thistle-down.

Child? Elise was no child! She had been born as self-confident as if she had been here before, and at almost seventeen was a beautiful, assured young woman, as different as she herself had been at the same age as it was possible to imagine.

Yet seventeen was a strange age, full of doubts and fears. She should have listened to Elise. Tomorrow, she thought, drifting in and out of the sleep she so desired. Tomorrow I shall make a point of it.

Of all times for Boyer to come!

Unwelcome at the best of times, he had picked the most difficult moment of her marriage. Gabriel had arrived only shortly afterwards, but though she longed to run to him she had been constrained by Boyer's presence and throughout that long evening had been forced to listen with overtly polite attentiveness to his monologue while secretly her thoughts were in turmoil.

Had Gabriel believed Madame Colbert? Did the very sight of her now fill him with hate and revulsion? And Paul – what could he be thinking of Paul? Not for one moment did Charlotte underestimate the hurt that Gabriel would suffer if he truly thought he had been betrayed by the man for whom he cherished such genuine affection.

That first night she had at length given up the attempt to out-sit Monsieur Boyer and had bidden the men goodnight, searching Gabriel's face for some hint of his feelings.

She had found none. He had smiled at her and in turn had wished her goodnight, only his extreme pallor and air of exhaustion making him appear different from normal. She had touched his face lightly.

'You look so tired, my dear. Pray rest soon. There is all tomorrow for talking.'

She hoped that Monsieur Boyer would take the hint, and indeed it was not long before she heard them both ascend the stairs. Gabriel's steps passed her door, but he did not enter. His room adjoined hers and for some time she contemplated going to him; she remembered his exhaustion, however, and resisted the impulse. Wrongly, she thought afterwards – but she reminded

312

herself that he had no knowledge of Madame Colbert's revelations to her and thought her ignorant of the charges. Let him rest tonight, she counselled herself. Tomorrow, as she had said to him in the drawing room, would do for talking.

The following day, however, Gabriel and Boyer left immediately after breakfast to visit members of the Threadneedle Street Consistory. She worked at her drawing board all day and astonishingly, considering her state of mind, had achieved a pattern she had at last considered satisfactory. In Gabriel's absence she took it to Simon le Bec.

'Do you think the Queen will approve?' she asked anxiously.

'Will the Duchess approve? That's what matters, for it's said she rules the poor lady with a rod of iron.'

He spread out the paper and looked at it closely, a slow beam appearing on his face as he nodded his head.

'This is good, madame. Very good. Complicated – yes, I give you that – but I can work it well enough.'

'It is your work that is the hardest, monsieur. I have never understood it.'

'Neither of us can work without the other, madame.'

It was good to be back in the weaving shed for it seemed some time since she had put in an appearance there. Though conversation was all but impossible above the noise of the looms she nodded and smiled at the journeymen and looked with interest at the work they were producing, at the glowing colours and rich patterns. Silk was a wonderful business, whatever the future held, and she was thankful to be a part of it – and a successful, essential part too. The thought of just how successful she had been filled her with sudden confidence so that when she encountered Gabriel and Boyer as she left the shed she was able to assert herself.

'Could you allow Monsieur le Bec to show Monsieur Boyer the work in progress?' she asked Gabriel. 'It is vital that I speak with you.'

Boyer looked down his nose at her effrontery, but Gabriel assented at once though he looked surprised when, even once they were alone, she dismissed the yard as a suitable venue for discussion and insisted on leading the way to her chamber. There, heart beating rapidly, she turned to face him.

'Is something troubling you?' he asked, as if puzzled by her manner.

'Gabriel, for the love of heaven stop pretending! I chanced to call on our dear Tantine yesterday and learned what she had told you.'

His eyes widened and his face became very still.

'Yes?'

'Gabriel, I beg you!' She came close to him, grasped his arms. 'I cannot bear this! I must know that you disbelieve her.'

'Of course I do.'

'I have never been unfaithful to you.'

'I know it! Come, Charlotte – I have no need of these assurances.'

'Then why –' Charlotte broke off in mid-sentence. Why do you look as if you had been mortally wounded? she longed to ask. Why so remote?

'Forget her.' He held her too, and forced a note of jollity into his voice. 'I have never been able to make up my mind on a colour of *chère* Tantine, have you, *chérie*? Yesterday I decided that she is undoubtedly the pink of an earthworm, while that noisome Berthe is that strange yellow one sees on the underside of a slug – though I have no wish to insult the most humble of God's creatures. At least a slug cannot spread slander.'

Charlotte stared up at him in bewilderment.

'What can Berthe have found to say of me? I am at a loss!'

'Her sister maintains she saw Paul leaving here after midnight last week while I was in Essex.'

'Then she lies.' There was undoubted relief in Charlotte's voice for this was something she could confidently deny. 'I have not seen Paul since that Sunday he came to dinner. I swear it, Gabriel.'

'*Chérie*, I have never doubted it! I said forget the woman – forget both of them. They are evil, motivated by spite and ill will towards us.'

She gave a sob of relief and laid her head against his shoulder.

'Foolish one!' He stroked her hair for a moment, then put a hand beneath her chin so that she was forced to look into his eyes. 'Is it forgotten?' he asked.

'It is forgotten,' she said.

That was three days ago. The relief had been immense, but once the euphoria had died she was left uneasy. If he believed her so implicitly, why had he disappeared that day for so many hours – why did he continue to seem so strangely remote? Was

314

it Boyer's presence alone that caused it, or did he harbour doubts despite his confident denials?

Or was it merely her own guilty conscience that caused her to imagine the strangeness where none existed? For she felt guilt, she could not deny it; guilt and shame – but above all, she felt desire.

She thanked God that Gabriel had not seen fit to ask the question to which an honest answer would have given the lie to all her denials.

Did she love Paul? Yes, yes and yes again, now and for ever.

17

Though a pale sun had encouraged a fashionable crowd to walk in St James's Park where the leaves of the lime trees were just beginning to unfurl, within the palace itself it was as cold as midwinter. No warmth penetrated the thick walls. No wonder the court ladies were eager to take their evening stroll in the Mall, Gabriel thought. They must feel as remote from the world here as if they were incarcerated in some fortress miles from the city's heart; yet the crowded streets were only yards away.

He had expected to deal with the Duchess of Marlborough – she of the fine eyes and the decisive manner – but instead found himself once more conducted to Her Majesty. The Duchess, it appeared, was not at court.

The Queen's apartments were warm, the room where he was received overheated and smelling of medicaments. Her feet were bandaged, he noticed, and she rested them on a footstool, but she smiled at him graciously as he bowed, and bade him be seated.

'Dear Hill will bring us a dish of bohea,' she said. 'You will consent to join me, Monsieur Fabian?'

'I should be honoured, madam.'

Mistress Hill was dismissed with a wave of the hand, though the Queen smiled at her in a kindly fashion.

'Dear creature,' she murmured, as her attendant left the room. 'She is so calm and quick. It is always so *peaceful* without . . .'

Her voice trailed away and she neglected to finish the sentence. She did not need to. Without Her Grace was what she meant, without doubt. Was the Duchess slipping from favour? It was hardly any concern of his.

The pattern was admired, the order placed.

'You must congratulate your wife on my behalf,' the Queen said.

'I will do so, madam. Nothing will please her more than to know Your Majesty approves the design.'

Mistress Hill, who had joined them for tea and sat with eyes demurely downcast as the business was concluded, rose to her feet at a signal from the Queen, and thinking this a clear indication that the audience was over, Gabriel did likewise. The Queen, however, raised a hand.

'There are other matters I wish to discuss with you, monsieur,' she said. 'Er – Hill –' She made a little shoo-ing gesture with her fingers, as one disposing of a pet kitten, and like a kitten Hill scampered away. 'Now, monsieur, pray seat yourself again. I shall not detain you long.'

'I am at Your Majesty's disposal for so long as you need me.'

He sat down once more and for a moment they surveyed each other in silence. Her face, highly coloured beneath light brown hair, seemed to peer at him questioningly, as if she were striving to see beneath his polite exterior to the man beneath.

'I have heard,' she said at last, 'that you preached a sermon, monsieur. A few weeks ago, in Threadneedle Street.'

'It was not a sermon, madam – or at least, not intended to be. The pastor relinquished his pulpit for me to give a statement of events in the Hautes Cévennes, and a summing up of my views concerning a resolution.'

'I heard about it. One of my women chanced to be present and she told me of it.'

'I see.'

He waited, not understanding quite where this was leading – unless she too required information about the Camisards. I should have brought Boyer, he thought, gloomily amused at the thought of the man in these surroundings.

'Monsieur Fabian, you probably know that Jean Cavalier, one of the leaders of the insurgents, requested arms from Britain to allow him to continue the struggle?'

'Indeed I do, madam. I also know that the attempt to land arms came to grief owing to a combination of circumstances and that they never arrived. May I ask if you intend to send more?' He thought of Boyer again. He would consider this a God-given chance to plead for aid; would think Gabriel mad if he neglected the opportunity.

The Queen hesitated, picked up an ivory fan and toyed with it, not looking at him.

'The Duchess of Marlborough is anxious that I do so. She feels that by prolonging the guerrilla war, troops that would have been

317

deployed against her husband's army would be dispersed. For myself . . .'

She hesitated again, and fanned herself slowly and thought-fully. 'For myself,' she continued, 'I cannot be so sure. I am naturally in sympathy with the Protestants – yet on the other hand –' She peered at him with her myopic gaze. 'On the other hand, monsieur, it is hard for me to sympathise with what is, after all, a guerrilla war, an insurrection against the King. It is one thing for us to be at war with him; quite another to encourage his subjects . . .' Her voice trailed away again, then picked up strength. 'Besides,' she went on, 'I understand that the French government is anxious to hold talks, that there has been the offer of a pardon. I was interested to learn that in your sermon you advocated such talks.'

'If they lead to freedom and tolerance, yes, madam. I cannot do other than agree with them.'

'But do Jean Cavalier and the other man – what is his name? Roland? Do they agree?'

'I believe Cavalier to be in favour of discussion, madam. He is more farseeing than Roland and the other leaders and understands that only in co-operation with Catholics can religious tolerance be achieved. The others regard such co-operation as dishonourable.'

'Foolish, foolish,' the Queen murmured, fanning herself ab-sently. 'I am saddened to hear of it. To continue the insurrection, burning churches and monasteries, will only result in more Protestants being tortured and imprisoned – so barbaric, so useless, a never-ending spiral of woe. What we need, Monsieur Fabian –' Her voice strengthened and she leaned forward a little to gaze at him earnestly. 'What we need is for some persuasive advocate to go there and convince them that there is no dishonour in compromise. Someone such as yourself –'

It was like a physical jolt to his system, the realisation that she was right. He licked lips suddenly dry, remembering the rack, the pain, the pitiless faces. Did she know what she asked of him?

Yet she was right to ask, he thought again, feeling the inevit-ability of it. They would listen to him. And Boyer had also said that they should never surrender, they should fight to the last Protestant. Foolish, foolish, he thought, echoing the Queen. Such slaughter could not go on. Both sides were being brutalised by the continuing barbarism.

'Do I ask too much of you?' The Queen's voice was gentle, musical to the ear. 'Please understand, monsieur, I give no orders in this matter but must leave it to you and the inner voice that prompts your actions. It is a suggestion only – a matter for you alone to decide. You must take time to think it over.'

'Your Majesty –' His voice emerged roughly and he cleared his throat. 'Your Majesty, this is a matter about which I have already thought deeply. I shall go to France as you suggest.'

'Good. That is settled then.'

She smiled at him amiably and shifted her feet on the stool as if they had become uncomfortable. She blinked sleepily.

She doesn't know, Gabriel thought, seeing again the walls that dripped blood and hearing the screams. She has no idea what she has asked of me. To her I am a persuasive Frenchman who happens to hold views of which she approves. How could she know?

'Agents come and go all the time,' she said vaguely. 'I am persuaded there is no risk to you.' She extended her hand to him. 'I shall look forward to hearing your report on your return, Monsieur Fabian. In the meantime I shall speak to Mr Harley regarding the arrangement of passage to France and all that is necessary.'

There was no doubt now that the interview was over, no risk of misinterpreting the signals this time. Gabriel bowed over her hand and left.

Outside in the park he ignored the coach that waited for him and walked some distance from it, down to the edge of the canal where he stared unseeingly at the ducks, causing a lady taking the air to look at him with some alarm as he uttered a short bark of laughter.

Who could now say that God had no sense of humour? Weeks ago in Threadneedle Street, Gabriel Fabian had indulged himself by doing what he did best. With pride and more than a touch of vanity he had used his powers of oratory; and on the word of an unknown woman in the congregation who had been impressed by it, the Queen was sending him back to the country that was the breeding ground of his worst nightmares.

And was right to do so. Yes – he was proud of his ability to sway an audience. It was his gift, his talent; and now he would be using it, not to the glory of Gabriel Fabian, but solely in a cause that was righteous. There was an inevitability about it, he thought again. A completion of the circle.

And Charlotte?

The pain which had become a constant companion over the past days clutched at his heart once more and his whole body felt weighted with sadness. He closed his eyes.

'Thy will,' he prayed in anguish. 'Thy will be done, O Lord.'

Charlotte would have given much to flee the house until such time as Monsieur Boyer had gone from it, and she felt a pang of envy when Elise was invited to stay in Villiers Street with Anne and Margaret Denning, her friends of last summer, now come at last to their father's town house as promised.

She felt oppressed by the atmosphere in Freedom Street, which was one of unrelieved gloom. Gabriel was in a strange mood, busy with affairs of which he confided nothing, apparently immersed in that dark and private world which, for as long as she had known him, waited threateningly just outside the field of vision, like a footpad skulking in the shadows.

Nothing more had been said about Madame Colbert's accusations. Charlotte, feeling they still clouded her relationship with Gabriel, attempted to raise the matter one evening, visiting his chamber for the sole purpose of doing so, but lightly he dismissed her anxiety.

'It is forgotten,' he said. 'Did we not agree?'

'Yes, but Gabriel –'

'There is no more to be said.'

He came close to her and put his hands on her shoulders, and for a moment as she looked into his eyes he seemed suddenly within reach again, as if one word – so long as it were the right word – would release him from that dark world that held him prisoner.

'I have something to tell you,' he said before she could speak. 'Something that will please you.'

'Yes?'

'I am going to France in person to make peace with my mother.'

Her eyes widened in astonishment and fear.

'You are going to France? Gabriel, that is sheer folly!'

'I thought you were in favour of reconciliation.'

'Yes, yes – of course! I meant by letter! Surely that would

suffice? I cannot believe you would put yourself in such jeopardy. Your mother would never expect it.'

'I am assured there is no danger.'

'By whom? By Boyer? He is at the bottom of this, isn't he? He has persuaded you to join him at last – to become one of the Camisards –'

'Of course not! My views are opposed to his, as you well know.'

'Then why go –'

'Listen to me, Charlotte. Yes, in one way I have been influenced by Boyer, but not in the way you think. I look at him and see a man so eaten up by bigotry and hate that I can only feel revulsion. Oh, he is undoubtedly sincere, but I see now that he is totally mistaken. I am going at the Queen's request to urge Cavalier and Roland to hold talks, to come to some honourable compromise.'

'But the risk to yourself, Gabriel! Even for the Queen's sake it is too much.'

'I think not, *chérie*. It is seventeen years since I was there last. The horrors persist in my mind, I grant you – how could I ever forget them? – but common sense tells me that I cannot still be a wanted man. As the Queen assured me, agents come and go every day. I shall carry no arms, will not proselytise. I shall merely be the long-absent son, come to see his sick mother – and not before time, for I hear from Jules that she is truly close to death. You must have no fear for me, for believe me, I have none for myself.'

'There must be some other who could go.'

'Have you not heard me? I shall be in no danger. Besides –' He smiled at her, the old, brilliant, magnetic smile. 'I can do it best. There speaks my sinful pride again.'

'When do you go?'

'Soon. Very soon. I await orders. Meantime, say nothing yet; there will be time enough to tell Boyer and Elise when plans are made.'

'I say as little as possible to Boyer, and Elise is with her friends in Villiers Street for the next few days. Gabriel, how long does that man propose to stay with us?'

'He will move on, I think, in a few days. From what he tells me I gather his work is almost done.'

'May it be soon!'

'Be prepared for much argument when he hears of my mission.'

'I expect nothing else from him.'

She longed for his departure even more now, for openness had been restored and she and Gabriel seemed closer than at any time since Madame Colbert's allegations.

He took to coming to her chamber at night and lying with her on the bed with his arms about her, talking seriously of future business plans; of pending orders that must be filled, of a journeyman who seemed shiftless and unreliable and would bear watching, or another that seemed gifted beyond the ordinary.

At first she was glad. It seemed to imply a commitment to a future that was secure, that would be waiting for him when once he returned from France; but eventually realisation dawned. He was supplying her with a plan of campaign in the event of his death.

'Don't talk like this,' she said in sudden panic. 'I don't wish to know. You are coming back to attend to it all, Gabriel.'

'Of course.' He smiled at her. 'But any journey is hazardous. One can be set upon by footpads in Hyde Park. Is death more likely because a man makes a will?'

'No,' she admitted cautiously. 'I suppose that it is not.'

'I am being prudent, no more.'

Perhaps he was right. It was the uncertainty that she hated; not knowing when the call would come for him, not knowing how long he would be away, not knowing how much longer Etienne Boyer would be beneath their roof.

She did not dare to think of Paul, but withdrew to her room and immersed herself in work. Belle Harkness presented herself (to Charlotte's relief choosing a time when Boyer was out on his own concerns) to select something spectacular to wear in her new role of Juliet.

'She is first seen by Romeo at a ball, you know,' she said. 'I thought, perhaps, crimson –'

'Something paler would give the illusion of youth,' Charlotte suggested, and hastened on feeling that she had not been as tactful as politeness demanded. 'We have some bolts of exquisite blue with a pattern of oak leaves – less costly, of course, than if the silk were bespoke, but equally good.'

The silk was displayed and approved.

'Charming, charming!' Mrs Harkness threw out her hands and closed her eyes in an excess of admiration. 'And Mr Rich can have no complaints as to the price. You must see the piece in

322

production, dear Madame Fabian – you and your husband. The scenery is to be quite spectacular, complete with musicians, Chinese jugglers and a dancing bear. And do not fear that the ending will be too tragical to be borne, for the final scene is to be rewritten and all ends in a burst of song. Neither Dorset Gardens nor Lincoln's Inn Fields,' she added, a note of great satisfaction in her voice, 'can produce anything to touch it.'

'So I imagine.' Charlotte's voice was professionally restrained, but she longed to share the joke with Gabriel – though perhaps Elise might appreciate it more.

'My stepdaughter loves the play,' she said.

'Really?' Mrs Harkness, on a plane of her own far above the other players, made no connection between the purveyor of silks and the young girl who occasionally watched rehearsals even though she had seen her on the occasion of the Fabians' visit backstage in search of Peter Jordan. Her shortsightedness was yet one more evidence of the onset of middle age which she refused to acknowledge. 'Then she must accompany you, of course.' She patted her abundant, highly coloured red-gold hair. 'I play Juliet to a Romeo who is surely nearer to Mr Shakespeare's ideal than Mr Brownlea. None but Mr Jordan, who was once in your employ, as I recall.'

'I am delighted by his success.'

'Oh, he's a charming young man! Quite the flatterer! He assures me he would liefer play opposite me than any other actress in London, for there is none from whom he can learn so much. I do like modesty in a man, Madame Fabian.'

'It is indeed a worthy attribute, Mrs Harkness.'

'Of course, there are those in the company who resent him.' Belle Harkness gave every appearance of settling in for a long chat. 'Mr Brownlea, to name but one, has had his nose put well and truly out of joint, which I suppose is only to be expected, though I trust that when the time comes for *me* to be supplanted by someone younger – thankfully distant yet, but inevitable, my dear Madame Fabian – I shall retire more gracefully. Mr Onslow, too – he is incensed that he was passed over in favour of a man who has been in the company but a short time. Still, as I pointed out to him, he has not the looks of Mr Jordan.'

'That can hardly have pleased him.'

'Oh, imagine Onslow as Romeo, if you will! He with his pudgy features and spindle shanks! No, no – Mr Jordan was the obvious choice, but I have warned him to watch his back. They'll discredit him if they can.'

'Dear me.' Charlotte's smile was as polite as ever, but she longed for Mrs Harkness to leave now, quickly. If she did so, it might give her time to share half an hour and a dish of tea with Gabriel before Boyer's return from one of his mysterious excursions. However, the actress refused to be hurried.

'He is a scamp, of course. Mr Jordan, I mean. I am thankful I am not open to his wiles, being wise in the ways of the world.'

'A scamp?' Oh, please go, Charlotte begged silently, attempting to edge her unobtrusively towards the door.

'Feckless, Madame Fabian. Well, many actors are, but I am distressed that gaming has such a hold on him, for that and drink have been the ruin of many, as I know you will agree. He has undoubted talent but is in perpetual difficulty; still, youth will have its day! There is a hardness – a kind of ruthlessness about him which makes me think he will always survive. Dearie me, how I do run on!'

She trilled with laughter, straightened her mantle, adjusted her muff, and Charlotte allowed herself to hope that she was about to make her exit. However, it seemed that the subject of Mr Jordan had not yet been wrung dry.

'Oh yes,' she went on, halfway to the door. 'That young man will survive, there is no doubt whatsoever about that! He assures me that his financial difficulties are likely to be solved quite soon.' She winked knowingly. 'An advantageous liaison, he tells me.'

'I'm so glad for him.'

'But still I tell him, "Watch your back, young man!"' She wagged a finger roguishly as if Peter Jordan were there in the flesh before her.

'How fortunate that he has a friend in you, Mrs Harkness.'

'It is to be hoped he recognises the fact. He is a charmer, no doubt about it, but there is a *coldness* about him, Madame Fabian. He is a calculating young man, in my opinion. I'm not sure that I envy the young lady.'

'Young lady?' Charlotte had all but lost track of Mrs Harkness's discourse and was intent only on getting her through the door and into the sedan chair that awaited her outside. When this was at last accomplished she breathed a sigh of relief – relief that was only short lived as she had barely waved the chair away when she saw the greeny-black, flapping figure of Boyer approaching down the street with his usual shambling stride.

'I have made my plans,' he said abruptly as he came close to her, dispensing with any greeting or preamble. 'I leave tomorrow on the mail for Colchester. I have raised as much as I can from the congregations here.'

Even formal expressions of regret were totally beyond her and she merely nodded in silent acknowledgment.

'I am to go to the Three Cups Inn at Whitechapel at six of the clock.'

'You shall be conveyed there.'

'I am perfectly accustomed to walking. There is no need to put yourself about.'

'It will not be the slightest trouble, monsieur.'

Never, Charlotte thought as she turned back into the house, had she spoken a truer word, and her spirits rose accordingly. Gabriel seemed positively light-hearted when he visited her in her chamber that night. It was almost like the old times, though the knowledge of his imminent departure was there between them, casting its shadow. He had been advised that it would take place in four days.

'I suppose,' Charlotte said to him, 'that it would be useless for me to implore you not to go, even at this late stage?'

'Useless,' he confirmed.

'I am so fearful of the danger.'

'I am assured that there is none. I questioned Etienne closely, and though he is implacably opposed to my mission, he bore out the view that I run no risk so long as I draw no attention to myself. Besides – I have to report to Her Majesty on my return. Who would dare use me ill?'

'It is I they will have to reckon with, never mind the Queen!'

'Oh, Charlotte.' When his smile died, his face had never looked more sad. 'Such a good wife as you have been.'

'And will continue to be, please God.' She took his hand in both of hers and held it to her breast. 'My dearest husband, I love and admire you more than I can say.'

'And have done nothing to deserve the misery of my black moods. Forgive me for them, *chérie*.'

'I wish I knew what caused them.'

'You say that? You say that of a husband who is no husband

at all? Believe me, there are times when my grief is insupportable, the weight of my guilt more than I can bear. Look down there!' They were standing close to the window and at this he turned and with one movement swept aside the draperies at the window. The street below them was empty of movement, full of shadows, lit by a half moon.

'Freedom Street,' he said, and laughed shortly. 'So it seemed to those who came here first. But we make our own prisons of fear and guilt and self-love and intolerance; those are the bonds that bind us wherever we live, and those are the bonds I am determined to break. Only then shall I find freedom.'

He let the curtain fall and held her close to him, and for a while they were silent.

'One thing I am determined on before I leave,' he said at last. 'I want an evening with those I hold most dear. You, Elise and Paul. I shall ask him to sup with us.'

Charlotte said nothing, her head still on his shoulder. She forced herself to breathe evenly; in, out, in, out. She was thankful he could not see the panic which she knew must show in her eyes.

'When do you have in mind?' she asked.

'When else but on Elise's birthday in three days' time, the eve of my departure?'

He was showing his trust, she told herself; demonstrating his total disbelief of Madame Colbert. She looked up and smiled at him.

'Such a good idea,' she said. 'I felt guilty that we had arranged nothing to mark the event.'

He kissed her and left her then, saying that she looked tired and clearly needed to sleep. Sleep, however, eluded her.

She thought of Paul. It was as if their relationship had changed, moved to a different plane, even though they had not met since Madame Colbert's outburst. It had become more complex – but in her mind only, she reminded herself, not in his. He still knew nothing of the accusations, and she hoped profoundly that he never would.

Meantime, in only three days' time she would have to meet him – be the cordial hostess, friendly but not too friendly. She must indulge in no private glances; yet on the other hand she must not be unnaturally cool for that in itself would seem strange to Gabriel. Was he as artlessly trustful as she had first assumed, or was this some devious plan to watch them together, observe their behaviour?

No, she did not believe so. It would be out of character for him to act in such a way – which did not mean that the occasion would not be fraught with danger.

Gabriel was preoccupied in the intervening days. Only because there was so much to arrange before he went away, Charlotte assured herself. There were orders of raw silk to be put in hand, the finished product to ship, payment to be arranged for the throwsters and outworkers.

Calmer than when Elise went away, Charlotte was assailed afresh by pangs of conscience. The talk that Elise had so ardently desired had never taken place. Somehow the right opportunity must be made, Charlotte resolved. She would make it clear to Elise that her concerns and her emotions were of prime concern, and always would be; it had been the greatest of pities that at a time of Elise's need, she herself had been in such torment.

When Elise returned, however, it seemed that the need had passed. She seemed fully restored to her usual good spirits and more lovely than ever, but though she gossiped breathlessly of promenading in the Mall and of the ball she had attended with the Dennings, and of the *thousands* of new gowns that were being made for the two girls, Charlotte felt that she learned few details of how her days had been passed. Her gaiety was so febrile, her air of suppressed excitement so apparent, that Charlotte felt quite certain that she must have fallen in love. She showed no desire to confide, however.

A summer wedding would be delightful, Charlotte thought. Gabriel would undoubtedly be home by then. And she laughed at herself for the flight of fancy even as she mentally planned the silk she would design for the occasion. Probably Elise's high spirits were no more than understandable joy at finding the looming presence of Etienne Boyer gone from her home.

Gabriel gave Elise an emerald necklace and ear-bobs for her birthday, as well as a length of silk. Charlotte's present was a fan of exquisite workmanship, and Paul brought a gold brooch fashioned by Harry, set with an amethyst surrounded by seed pearls.

The opening of these presents, the exclamations and Elise's clear delight helped to gloss over what might have been an awkward moment. Charlotte half expected Elise to mention the

327

absence of Tantine from the party, for in past years her presence had seemed obligatory; however, nothing was said.

Not for the first time in her life, she found that an occasion she had approached with dread passed more happily than many others which seemed to hold the promise of great enjoyment. Everyone seemed to take his cue from Elise. Gabriel was at his most charming and there seemed no sign of the animosity between Paul and Elise that Charlotte thought she had detected at the end of his previous visit. Paul (though she scarcely dared look at him for fear her feelings would be obvious) was as handsome and entertaining as ever, and had them all laughing at his account of the strange clients he encountered in the course of a day. Slowly she relaxed. The evening was proving as pleasant and light-hearted as any she could remember. She congratulated herself on her own control, as laughingly she reproved Paul for the jokes he was making at Elise's expense, teasing her about her recent taste of high society.

After supper they sat by the fire and Elise sang to them in her sweet, clear young voice, Paul joining her from time to time. Charlotte's face was turned towards the fire. She was as conscious of him as ever, but for once her body seemed quiescent as if, this evening, the knowledge of his nearness brought comfort, not pain. It must be relief that induced this contentment, she told herself. Relief that despite evil, lying gossip nothing had been spoiled. She and Paul were still among those Gabriel loved the best.

'I wish you were not going, monsieur,' Paul said to Gabriel when the time came to say goodbye. 'I cannot believe there is no risk.'

'I am assured there is none, if I am prudent.'

'Then I pray you remember it.'

'Thank you, my boy.' For a moment Gabriel's hand rested on his shoulder, but his eyes sought Charlotte. She smiled uncertainly, not understanding the look in them.

He came to her in her chamber that night and for some time held her close without speaking.

'I could not have wished for a better farewell,' he said at last. 'I shall remember it.'

'There will be other such occasions.'

'God willing. Keep me in your prayers, chérie.'

'Can you truly believe there is need to ask?'

328

There was little to say when the time came to part the next day. He kissed her and rode away as calm and composed as she had ever known him, but she was conscious of a deep feeling of unease, and linked her arm through that of Elise as if for comfort.

'How glad I am that you are returned home,' she said. 'I've been a poor companion to you of late. We must bear each other company now that we are deprived not only of your father but of the delightful Monsieur Boyer.'

'Pray don't mention his name,' Elise begged. 'I should not put it past him to materialise out of thin air, like some spirit come to haunt us.'

She laughed as she spoke, but was conscious of a twinge of disquiet. Was Charlotte about to become a constant companion? This would not suit at all! She had hoped that her father's absence would make life easier for her, not more difficult.

She need not have worried. Though they rode abroad together on shopping trips to London Bridge and to the Exchange, and further afield to the booksellers of St Paul's, Charlotte had plenty of work on hand to keep her occupied. Though Mrs Harkness had been satisfied with silk off the shelf for the first scene she had ordered a special design for the last, and Elise smiled inwardly as she was invited to admire it.

'For it is all to end in wedding bells and jubilation,' Charlotte told her. 'Did you ever hear of such a thing?'

Frequently, would have been the honest answer; and at great length, for Peter had been incensed by the change in the play and had talked of little else the last time she saw him. However, to Charlotte, she expressed the required amount of surprise and amusement.

'I suppose Mr Brownlea is to be Romeo,' she said mendaciously.

'No, no. You'll be surprised to hear it's none other than Peter Jordan! A good choice, I would say.'

'I agree.' Oh, there was nothing sweeter than hearing him praised!

'Though I understand that the choice has caused much heart-burning in the company. He is a comparative newcomer, after all.'

'But a *wonderful* actor!' Charlotte's eyebrows went up at Elise's vehemence.

'It is to be hoped,' she said, 'that he is actor enough to forget that Mrs Harkness will never see forty again.'

'Such monstrous casting! They should have chosen a young girl.'

'Well, what does it matter?' Charlotte, sorting through her drawing materials, was unconcerned. 'It's all play-acting anyway and hardly important. I wish Mr Jordan nothing but well, but Mrs Harkness says that the rest of the company will discredit him if they can.'

'They are all jealous.'

Elise sounded so personally involved that Charlotte paused and looked at her in surprise and some amusement.

'Well, well,' she said. 'I had not realised that Mr Jordan was such a favourite of yours.'

'I admire his talent,' Elise said stiffly, and changed the subject with all speed.

Later, when she went to Covent Garden with the invaluable Molly for company, ostensibly to choose a muff, she met Peter and told him of Mrs Harkness's warnings as they strolled among the crowd in the piazza. He dismissed this with an airy laugh.

'The old harridan cautions me constantly,' he said. '"Watch your back, my boy!"' Cruelly he mimicked Belle Harkness. 'I'm a match for them, my sweeting, don't fret.'

A match for any of them, he added silently, Gabriel Fabian included. He felt confident, invincible, as he promenaded with Elise on his arm. Charlatan, mountebank – he knew exactly how Fabian thought of all actors. Well, he would show him; he would show the whole world. Born in poverty, unjustly accused, possessed of no material advantage but dependent entirely on facile charm to bring him to this point – soon the whole of London would appreciate that his talent put him far above others of his calling. Marriage to Elise meant respectability and acceptance and – oh, bliss to think of it! – freedom from financial worries. And almost best of all, it was tantamount to thumbing his nose at the man he still saw as the epitome of authority.

Oh yes, he would show them all – all the clods in the company, all those strait-laced Huguenots who considered themselves too good for him. He would have them begging him to grace their social events –

'Maman was amused at the new ending that Mr Rich has provided for the play,' Elise said, breaking in on his pleasant reverie.

330

'Amused!' He looked outraged. 'I have never seen or heard such a travesty. Poor Will must be spinning in his grave. No matter! I shall be a Romeo that will live in every play-goer's memory. One thing is certain, once I am established as a leading player I'm damned if I intend to continue on the pittance Rich is paying me. Once the play's afoot I shall demand my rights, for I'm devilishly short of cash.'

'I have money.' Elise produced her purse and looked inside it. 'I am able to give you a guinea.'

'By God, you have a hoard of guineas in there!'

'But I must pay for my muff. You do understand, Peter, do you not? I have to account to Maman, and while a guinea might pass unnoticed, more would cause comment.'

'I shall take nothing, dearest.' Honesty and sincerity were written clear in every line of his face. 'You have given me too much already, though you know full well I am taking note of all and shall pay you back.'

'Then take this, I pray you.' She thrust the coin towards him. 'To please me, Peter. Truly, I want you to have it.'

'Well.' He turned the coin over and over in his hands as if reluctant to accept it. 'I'll not deny Ma Cutting will be glad to see it, poor soul.'

'It's shameful that you should be paid so little.'

'Shameful!' Peter agreed earnestly.

He was still holding the guinea as he drew her behind a pillar to kiss her goodbye. He waited until she had joined up with Molly once more and had left the square before walking jauntily in the opposite direction, whistling cheerfully and spinning the coin and catching it as he went.

How blind love could be – and thank God for it!

Rupert Onslow – pudgy of features and spindly of shanks, as Belle Harkness had described – was nevertheless a competent actor and had seen himself as the natural successor to Edmund Brownlea. Until, that is, Peter Jordan had joined the company. From that moment he had felt insecure and distrustful, despite the fact that Brownlea had assured him of his own personal backing.

From the first he had recognised Jordan's ambition, the hardness that Belle Harkness had mentioned to Charlotte, and he had seen, too, the elusive, indescribable quality that made him appear quite different when on stage. He seemed taller, better-looking. The eye was drawn to him. It did not surprise Onslow that such a lovely girl should be attracted to him.

From his vantage point beside a pillar close by a mercer's shop he watched them together, chewing a fingernail thoughtfully. He saw them stop; saw the girl look in her purse – saw her look up, saw Jordan shake his head and hold up his hands as if in repudiation. And saw, without surprise, that at last he relented and took the coin.

Watch for the moment when he has money, Brownlea had said.

Onslow saw the coin spin into the air, saw the smile on Jordan's face. He would need to be quick, for a guinea could be spent in no time and it would not be long before Jordan was back to his usual state of penury. Hastily he set off in the same direction that Jordan had taken and soon saw him in the street ahead, apparently making his way back to the theatre.

He quickened his step and hailed him, so that Jordan turned round, his questioning look deepening to astonishment tinged with mistrust as he saw the friendly smile with which Onslow approached him. Friendliness towards him on the part of other members of the company had been in short supply of late.

'Halloa! Well met!' Onslow clapped him on the back. 'We follow the same direction. Do you go to the theatre?'

'Where else, at this hour? It's almost time for rehearsal.'

'No, no – you mistake it.' Onslow looked at his watch. 'We've time for the tavern first. Come – I'll stand you an ale in the name of friendship.'

'Friendship?' Peter echoed cautiously, still mistrustful.

'There's been too little between us of late – whoa up, look there –' Onslow pointed at the ground as if in great delight, then squatted down. 'Move your boot, you dolt – there, see where you had placed it.'

He stood up, smiling broadly, holding a second guinea.

'You must be deep in love to have missed this one, friend. Here – take it. 'Twas your boot that covered it.'

'But your eyes that saw it.' Peter was still wary.

'Then we shall toss for it, the winner to buy the ale.'

'That seems an equitable arrangement.'

They moved off together, Onslow's undistinguished features set in a broad smile.

'I'll tell you something, friend,' he said. 'Luck must be smiling upon us today. What say we go to Woodnut's tables? Now, don't prate of rehearsals, for I know as well as you that we must be at the theatre by two of the clock, but we still have time to improve our fortunes.'

Peter wavered.

'The coin – was it an omen, d'you think?'

Laughing, Onslow shook his head.

'I know naught about omens, but I know good luck when I see it staring me in the face. Come, we can have our ale and a hand of cards at the same time.'

'Well –' Still Peter hesitated. He had been uncommonly virtuous since the beginning of rehearsals for he was aware of how much hung on the chance that had been offered him and was determined to make the most of it. The thought of a game, however, be it hazard, basset or ace of hearts, was like an uncontrollable itch he was unable to scratch. 'Well,' he said again.

'One more well and I shall proclaim the spa open!'

'It was lucky, was it not, to find the coin?'

'Well, my friend, it might happen to you every day, but certainly not to me.'

'Then let's chance a little.' Peter smiled happily now the decision had been made and playfully punched his companion's shoulder. 'You are the last man I should have expected to bring me luck, for you've not overwhelmed me with your friendship lately.'

'I was wrong.' Onslow spoke earnestly, serious now. 'Rivals can be friends. There is no place for bad feeling in a company.'

'I'm more than happy that you should say so.'

The plan was half-baked. Onslow was fully aware of that, but he had seen his chance and thought it worth acting on. At least he had achieved the first step. He had enticed Jordan over the threshold of Woodnut's. The next would be to get him too drunk to notice the time or to be capable of seeing beyond the cards in his hand. On past form, he considered it should not be too difficult. In fact – and he grinned privately at the aptness of the thought – he would not at all mind making a wager on his success.

She had never looked lovelier than she had the night of Elise's birthday party, Paul thought. Seeing her with the firelight on her face, he had felt as if his heart would break with longing. It was strange how Charlotte's dark, understated beauty was so much more appealing to him than Elise's bright prettiness.

Most would say there was no comparison. Elise's looks were those which would make any artist reach for palette and brushes. Never was skin more fine or eyes more blue; never a nose more perfectly shaped or a smile more beguiling. Yet though he could appreciate her beauty as he would appreciate beauty in any other form, it did not touch his heart. Charlotte's very imperfections moved him unbearably; the dark, sweeping brows, the childish lips, the smile that revealed a crooked tooth.

He would go to America. He had decided finally, after the supper in Freedom Street, for he had realised then that Charlotte was not for him, could never be for him, and that to spend so much time in longing for her was not only immoral but plainly foolish. He had always known it, of course, but at some unexplored level there had remained a vague hope that somehow, somewhere, they would be together. He knew that she felt the attraction as strongly as he did and experienced as much difficulty in resisting it. On the night of the party, however, she had seemed different, remote from him, as if she had finally relinquished her hold on the dream that could never be made reality.

From the dim room behind the shop he could hear the muted sounds of the street and with a pang realised how much he would miss London now that he had renewed his acquaintance with it. He would miss the noise and the excitement and the bustling vitality; the tavern by the river and the group of friends who argued every subject so fiercely and laughed so uproariously. He would miss the huddled houses and the fine, tall residences in the new squares, and the parks and countryside that circled this biggest, most exciting city in the world.

Resolutely he picked up a pen and continued with the letter he had begun before the remembrance of Charlotte's downbent profile had come between him and the sheet of paper on his desk, but before he could add more a knock sounded at the door.

'Enter,' he called, expecting a member of his staff to answer the summons. Instead it was the foxy-faced Joseph who obeyed the call.

He had grown from the lanky, whippet-like youth who had accompanied Charlotte around London in the early days to a cheerful, if emaciated man who was normally seen with a smile on his face. However, on this occasion the smile was nowhere to be seen and it was clear that something was badly amiss.

'Mr Bellamy, madam says would you come, sir. In a right state, she is – a-cryin' and a-'ollerin'.'

Paul was on his feet immediately.

'What is it, Joseph? It's not monsieur, is it? Not bad news?'

Joseph wiped a horny finger across his nose.

'Nah,' he said. 'Not monsoo. Nine lives 'e's got, do you ask me. We'll see 'im back 'ere, safe and sahnd, you mark my words. Nah, it's the mam'selle. She's gorn, sir. E-loped, as the sayin' is.'

'God in heaven!' Paul stared at him, aghast, paralysed for one moment as he took in the news. Then quickly he started for the door. 'Lead on, man – let us waste no more time. I'm going out,' he called to Harry as he passed rapidly through the shop.

Oh, the little fool! How long ago had it happened? Was it too late to find her? He fired these questions and others at Joseph who raised his shoulders helplessly and sucked his teeth.

'I don't know nothin' sir, and that's a fact. You'd best wait and ask madam. It was 'er what found the note.'

How *could* she – now, while Gabriel was away, while Charlotte had to cope with the situation on her own? How could she do such a thing? He swore savagely, cursing the selfishness that would make her act in this way, but beneath his anger he could not avoid a feeling of responsibility. He should, after all, have told Gabriel of Elise's escapades with the wretched Jordan – for surely it was he who had enticed her away? But she had sworn to him it was over, and foolishly he had believed her.

Charlotte was more composed than Joseph's graphic description had led him to expect, but she was clearly shaken and he could tell that she had been weeping. She came running down the stairs to him as soon as he entered the house.

'Oh Paul – thank God you have come! Did Joseph tell you? Elise has gone – and with Peter Jordan, of all people! I had no idea there was anything between them.'

'What did her message say?'

'Read it!' She thrust a sheet of paper towards him. Elise had written:

Forgive me, *chère* Maman. I have no wish to hurt you or Papa but I love Peter and cannot live without him. He has been cruelly treated, has been cast from Drury Lane and is returning to Dublin where he knows he has friends and will be welcomed.

335

By the time you read this we shall be married. Once in Ireland I shall write to you again. Pray do not be angry for I am very happy.

'For how long?' Paul asked cynically, handing back the note.

'Paul, for the love of heaven, what am I to do? She was in my charge! Gabriel would be distraught if he did but know of it.'

'When did you find the note?'

'Not until this morning. She must have left last night.'

He looked with compassion at her, and saw her pallor and the tears that welled once more in her eyes.

'Come into the drawing room,' he said. 'We are surrounded by prying onlookers here.'

It was true. Two saucer-eyed maids stood beside the steps that led down to the kitchen. Above them, another peered over the banisters. Charlotte went with him unresistingly, though once inside the room she broke away from him and buried her face in her hands.

'I cannot think what to do,' she said. 'I cannot think at all!'

'What has Molly to say about it?'

'Molly?' Charlotte lowered her hands and looked at him. 'You think she was privy to this?'

'Why not? She was privy to most other things.'

'She appeared to be as astonished and upset as I. It was she, in fact, who brought the note to me – she found it on Elise's pillow when she went to call her this morning. I have no reason to think her distress was anything but genuine.'

'Perhaps!' He was silent for a moment, his thoughts darting this way and that. 'I will go to the theatre,' he said at last. 'There must be something I can find out there. Perhaps he has a friend there to whom he confided his plans. At least I might find out whether they intend sailing from Bristol or Liverpool.'

'But if it is true, that they are married already, what is to be done? Gabriel will never forgive me. I shall never forgive myself!'

'Hush, Charlotte.' He captured her as she swirled agitatedly past him and held her tightly. How ironic, he thought, that the first time I have her in my arms, I am the last thing on her mind. 'You are not to blame. Elise is not a child and she knows right from wrong. Try to be calm, at least until I return with more news.'

'I'm so grateful to you for coming, Paul. I could not think who

336

else to ask. Go now – and come back quickly – no, stop, stop!'
She halted him as he reached the door. 'I have just remembered.
We know where Jordan had his rooms. They were above the
hatter's in Cross Keys Alley. Perhaps his landlady would know
something – I disremember her name, but she appeared to be on
friendly terms with him.'

'I shall go there before the theatre,' Paul assured her.

He found the place without difficulty, but Mistress Cutting
was in a state of outrage and could be of no help to him.

'I never would have thought it,' she said, quivering with
indignation. 'Like a mother I was to that boy, and what does he
do to repay me? Flits at dead of night, owing two weeks' rent,
never mind the mussels I fetched him the night before last! Run
and get a coupla dozen, Ma, he says to me, and I'll give you
the cash come next pay-day on account of being temporarily
embarrassed. Oh, it's shameful, sir, shameful!'

'He said naught to you of marriage, or of going to Ireland?'

'Not a word. Oh, he'd spoke of marriage, of course – said he
would soon be tying the knot and all his troubles would be over,
but he led me to believe he had nothing hasty in mind. It was
them at the theatre done it, of course, throwing him out when
he was so pleased about the part he had.'

'What caused that? Did he tell you?'

She pursed her lips and lowered her eyes, as if even the
contemplation of his downfall shocked her sensibilities.

'Drink,' she said. 'And gaming. That's what done it. He was
always a one for the tables, but I thought he'd turned over a new
leaf. That's what he told me, anyway. "Ma," he says, "I'm a new
man. Virtue is my middle name."' She sniffed disgustedly. 'If
that's virtue, I'll take a good honest crook any day.'

'How much does he owe you?'

'Three guineas. Four,' she amended, seeing Paul's hand go to
his pocket. 'Yes, I misremembered. It's four, not three. Has he
taken the young lady with him, then?'

'I'm afraid so.' Paul spoke heavily, more depressed by the
minute.

'She'll rue it.' Mistress Cutting shook her head with a kind
of macabre pleasure. 'She'll rue it, sir, and on that you may
depend.'

Enquiries at the Theatre Royal were no more enlightening,
and it was with a heavy heart that Paul returned to Freedom

Street. He was ushered directly into the drawing room where Charlotte came swiftly towards him, her face anxious.

'Is there news?'

'Nothing. He seems not to have had a friend at the theatre. He left under a cloud: some story about having gambled heavily and missed an important rehearsal. And at his lodgings it was the same story. He left without notice, owing money.'

'What are we to do?'

'Charlotte, are you quite certain Molly knows nothing? After all, she was an accomplice from the start.'

'I don't think –' Charlotte began, then broke off and stared at him, puzzled. 'What do you mean, Paul? How do you know that she was an accomplice?'

He shrugged and lifted his hands.

'It stands to reason.'

'You know something.' She took a step closer and looked into his face, forcing him to meet her eyes. '*Did* you know, Paul? Did you know they were meeting?'

He sighed.

'Yes, I did – but she swore it was over, that she was finished with him.'

'How did they meet?'

'How? My dear Charlotte, you sadly underestimate Elise's ingenuity if you think she found it at all difficult. There were her music lessons, her visits to Catherine, her shopping excursions alone with only her maid for company.'

'And you *knew*?' Charlotte's face blazed with anger and her fists rose as if she would strike him. 'All the time you knew, and you said nothing? How could you, Paul? Was this how you repaid Gabriel's kindnesses? Oh!' She swung away from his despairingly. 'I would not have believed it possible, not from you.'

'Charlotte, calm yourself and listen to me.' He grasped her shoulder and swung her round to face him once more. 'Are you fool enough to think I smiled upon her deception and allowed her to think I approved of it? Do you think I said "Well done, Elise; lie and cheat and dupe your parents and I will aid and abet you"? Of course I did not! I told her she was a fool and that Jordan was a gambler and a debtor and I made it clear I would tell her father everything if she did not mend her ways. She promised me that it was all over and I saw no need to worry Gabriel unnecessarily.' He sighed heavily, the momentary spurt

338

of anger dying. 'Which is not to say that I am not weighed down with guilt. In retrospect I see I was wrong.'

Charlotte's anger died too.

'I am the one who must be blamed,' she said. 'Elise was in my charge.'

'But Gabriel indulged her always. Perhaps we all share the blame.'

'Which helps Elise not one jot. I am grieved for her, for I cannot believe she will be happy with a man like that, but oh, I am so angry with her, Paul.' She came close to him again. 'She has no wish to hurt us, she says, yet she can do something like this that must surely break her father's heart.'

'Hearts don't break, Charlotte.' He was looking at her steadily. 'We should know that.'

Her eyes held his for a moment and she swallowed painfully.

'Paul, I am so grateful to you for coming. I have taken up far too much of your time.'

He made no move to leave but rested his hands on her shoulders.

'When did you last eat?'

The unexpectedness of the question took her by surprise and she gave a small laugh, shaking her head.

'I really cannot remember. Last evening, I suppose. I shall have some little repast now, perhaps.'

'Which I am not invited to share?'

'I think not, Paul.' It was one of the hardest things she had ever been called upon to say. He continued to look into her eyes and she found it impossible to turn away.

'You will not weep or give way to pointless self-recrimination when I have gone?' There was a note of intimate concern in his voice, and she was acutely conscious of his touch and the beating of her heart.

'You must go, Paul,' she whispered, but she could not break the link between them. Still he held her, still their eyes were locked together.

The thought of Elise receded, lost its power to hurt. It would return, she knew, but for this moment Paul was the only reality; Paul and the strength of the feeling between them which she had for so long tried to deny and which denial had served only to make stronger.

'Charlotte –' He spoke her name on an upward inflection as if there were more to follow, but nothing came. Instead, almost as one in a dream, she saw his head bend towards her and felt the warmth of his breath as his lips sought hers. His touch was gentle, tentative, and she submitted to it rather than returned it with any passion. Nevertheless it was hard to breathe with the excitement that filled her, and when he drew away she saw that he trembled, and with a sound that was almost a groan his arms went round her once more and he kissed her again, not tentatively this time but fiercely and longingly; and fiercely and longingly she returned his kiss, her whole body melting with the heat of her desire for him.

The clock chimed, bringing her back to the everyday world. She pulled herself away from him.

'Paul, we must not. You know we must not.'

'I love you, Charlotte.'

She closed her eyes against the pain of the longing that swept through her; yet there was joy there, too. In her heart she had heard those words so often, spoken by him, in just those tones. Still she walked away from him, the width of the room.

'There is nothing to be done,' she said.

She had her back to him, but she knew that he had followed her.

'There is this to be done,' he said. He turned her to face him and once more took her in his arms. This time, when the kiss was done, he did not relinquish her but held her within the circle of his arms.

'If only you were not the wife of Gabriel Fabian,' he said bitterly.

'But I am.' She laid her hand against his face, willing her fingers to remember the feel of his skin. 'I am, Paul.'

Her expression was one of infinite sadness, and she repeated the words of a few moments before.

'There is nothing to be done.'

18

The pastor of the church in Threadneedle Street – good Monsieur Bayard, whose opinions were respected by all – was quite certain that it would serve no purpose to attempt to get word to Gabriel.

'What good would it do?' he asked her, when she solicited his advice. 'He can do nothing. The girl is married, and that's an end of it. The news would only serve to trouble his mind when he needs all his wits about him.'

'I feel so helpless, so alone.'

'My dear, you are not alone. You have the prayers of many friends, and above all, the love of God.'

It was the answer she had expected and she felt guilty that she found it of so little comfort. She had never felt so greatly distanced from God, so resentful of the constraints that a strict moral code placed upon her.

She hungered for Paul. To say that she loved him was part of the sum that made up her feelings for him, but only part. For the rest, she was riven by a longing that demanded physical expression, and the strength of it astounded her, as if she had turned into a woman quite different from the one she had always believed herself to be.

He called on her as often as she would allow it, and they kissed and sat with clasped hands as if neither could ever bear to let go, but though the clamour of their bodies was almost unendurable, she would not yield to him.

'Not here,' she said. 'Not here. This is Gabriel's place.'

'Then come to my rooms. Please, Charlotte.'

Still she hesitated; and the reason she did so was not solely because she disliked the thought of breaking her marriage vows. There was also the shame of her virginity to consider – and yes, it *was* shame; not to her, but to Gabriel. To divulge this secret to anyone, and most of all to Paul, would be the ultimate betrayal. And yet she longed for him so.

At last a letter arrived, short and uninformative but cheerful.

Gabriel had seen his mother, he wrote. His half-brother, Jules, was a fine fellow and much in favour of reconciliation. At the time of writing, Gabriel was about to leave Nîmes to venture into the mountains where he hoped to meet both with Cavalier and with Roland. He had no doubt that God would sustain and protect him for he felt certain that his task was righteous.

He said no more, except to assure Charlotte of his devotion and to advise her to take Elise to Whiteacres without him if the warmer weather should arrive before he could return to London.

The cold winds of March had given way to a fitfully sunny April, and the newly green trees in the parks ensured that Charlotte's mind turned more and more frequently to the country-side, though no one yet could call the weather hot. A fresh breeze tugged at her skirt as she threaded her way through the crowds to Lombard Street to let Paul know of this latest news of Gabriel, but the sky was blue beyond the haze of smoke that always hung over the city and the flower-sellers' baskets were full of daffodils and tulips, primroses and violets.

Paul read the letter that she handed him.

'It sounds as if he expects to be away for some time yet,' he said.

The dimness of his office was relieved by light from the high window. Motes danced in the solitary beam of sunlight that found its way into the room.

'There will be primroses in the orchard at Whiteacres,' Charlotte said. 'We were there last April. Do you remember?'

'Of course! It was then that I –' He stopped and looked at her in astonishment, as if he had only just taken in the meaning of her words. 'Was it only a year ago? I seem to have loved you for ever. Listen, Charlotte –' He took both her hands in his. 'We could go there again.'

'No!' She spoke sharply, then took a step closer to him, moderating her tone. 'I couldn't, Paul. Whiteacres is Gabriel's place.'

'Whiteacres is his place – Freedom Street is his place. Where is *our* place? You love him still, don't you?'

'Of course!'

He looked at her without speaking for a moment, then shrugged and laughed shortly.

'Of course,' he echoed flatly. 'And the damnable thing is that I do, too. So there is no hope for us, Charlotte, no hope at all, and since meeting as we have done these past weeks is little short of torture, we had better part and meet no more.'

She felt physically sick, as if her blood had turned to ice. Her mouth was dry and no words would come. She looked at him in silence, searching his face to see if he was in earnest, her heart sinking as she saw his face, sharp with misery but set and implacable. He has had enough, she thought; and I am not so much changed, after all. I long for him, yet find a hundred reasons for holding back.

'Paul?' She managed to speak at last and there was a note of entreaty in her voice.

'Please go, Charlotte.' His voice was brusque and he did not look at her. 'You must! I cannot bear it.'

For a moment longer she stood without moving, then swiftly, without another word, she left the room.

For the first time she found the house in Freedom Street inimical and cheerless. Restlessly she wandered from room to room, unable to settle to any of the occupations that normally kept her happily busy. Even the servants added to the gloom, for Nan blamed Molly for her complicity in Elise's affairs, and the two sisters had quarrelled bitterly.

It was not Molly's behaviour, however, that caused Nan's expression of horror when she came to the drawing room one afternoon to announce that Charlotte had a visitor.

''Tis Monsieur Boyer, madam,' she said agitatedly. 'He's come back.'

Mistress and maid stared at each other with almost equal dismay. Charlotte collected herself quickly.

'Pray ask him to come up, Nan.'

She stood to receive him, full of anxiety. Had he heard news of Gabriel? Undoubtedly he was in touch with events in France.

He denied this when she put the question to him. He had heard nothing, he said. He had been on his travels around England to the different Huguenot communities.

'But be assured he is in no danger, madame,' he said. 'I could almost wish that he were, so misbegotten is this scheme of his. It is no less than an insult to those who have died. It is treachery, madame, sheer treachery.'

Her expression showed no sign of the revulsion she felt for his insensitivity, but her fingers tightened on the back of the chair where her hand rested.

343

'And are you now on your way back to France, Monsieur Boyer?'

'After a few more days in London, that is my intention.'

Charlotte smiled at him.

'And where do you intend spending those days, monsieur?' she asked silkily.

'Where?' His loose mouth hung open in astonishment. 'Where, madame? Where but here, beneath the roof of my friend, Gabriel Fabian?'

'The man you could wish in danger? The man whose honest intentions you despise so much? Come, Monsieur Boyer!'

'We are not always in agreement, that is true, but our association has deep roots. I still regard him as my friend.'

'Alas, Monsieur Boyer, your friend is from home and I am alone. You must surely see that to entertain a gentleman such as yourself –' She gave a regretful smile, and shrugged her shoulders. Boyer, for once at a loss for words, gave the impression of trying to swallow a hen's egg, shell and all.

'You cannot imagine, madame, that I am any threat to your virtue?' he said at last.

Or I to yours, Charlotte thought, but merely shrugged again.

'It is out of the question, monsieur.'

'Then where shall I stay?' He thrust forward his ungainly head, his jaw shooting out towards her. 'Your husband, madame, would not like to know of this. He has ever offered hospitality –'

'Offered, monsieur? It occurs to me that on occasions it has been not so much offered as –' she paused for a fraction of a second, raised her hand and snapped it shut – 'snatched.' She smiled at him again. 'I am too mindful of my reputation either to offer it or to have it taken from me summarily, monsieur. I feel sure you must understand. There are taverns in plenty where your custom will be welcome. Allow me to offer my coachman to take you to one.'

'I am astonished, madame. Astonished!'

'How truly it is said, monsieur, that life is full of surprises. Will you take tea, or shall I ring for the coach now?'

He made no response to this but took an agitated turn or two about the room before coming to rest only inches from her, forefinger upraised.

'I was a stranger and ye took me in,' he hissed at her, face contorted with fury. 'Are we not exhorted in the Gospels to do

344

likewise? Should not the naked be clothed, the sick and the prisoner visited?' He swung away from her in disgust. 'Oh, that your husband were here to see this day. How he would burn at this affront to his friend!'

'But, monsieur –' Charlotte's smile remained as ingenuous as ever. 'Are we not also exhorted to avoid not only evil, but the *appearance* of evil? You, I feel sure, would be among the first to rebuke me were I to fill this house with itinerant gentlemen while my husband was away.'

'I shall not argue further. Keep your tea and your coach, madame. I have no wish to be a burden upon you or your servants.'

'Then I shall wish you good day and a pleasant journey.'

Charlotte was conscious of a heady feeling of power as she stood at the window and watched him stalk angrily down the street. How she would have loved to share this moment with Elise!

She remembered the girl she had once been, cowering voiceless in her chair as he had thundered his rebukes. I *have* changed, she thought, and knew a moment of great satisfaction. She did not even ask herself if Gabriel would have approved her action. She merely knew that another visit from Etienne Boyer, its length unspecified, was more than flesh and blood could bear.

I have grown up, she thought with delight. I am a woman now.

Except in one particular. Was that country, so familiar to others, to remain unexplored by her? Standing at the window, looking down on the street, she remembered Gabriel's words; that it was fear, guilt, intolerance and self-love that created the prisons people built for themselves – that prevented them living in Freedom Street.

My bonds were forged in the foolishness of youth, she thought, when I was full of fear and understood nothing. In ignorance I built my own fortress, and now I am to be incarcerated for ever.

She closed her eyes as the oppressive weight of her separation from the world seemed to bear down on her. For a few moments she stood unmoving, then swiftly she went to the escritoire and took a sheet of paper.

Her breath was coming quickly, her colour had risen. She dipped the quill in the ink, held it suspended a moment as she collected her thoughts, pondered her words. Then, rapidly with no more hesitation, she began to write.

Life went on and work went on, but in nothing was there any pleasure.

'Just leave me, Harry,' Paul said shortly when his friend urged him to go to the tavern and meet with the others. 'I am in no mood for it.'

'Come – some entertainment will lighten your mood –'

'*Leave me!*'

And seeing the face which Paul had turned upon him, Harry had left him, anxious and bewildered, but silenced by the depth of misery he could see.

'Best leave him,' he advised the clerks and the silversmiths and the other employees in Lombard Street, and they were glad to do so, for this silent, withdrawn, scowling man had little in common with the Paul Bellamy they knew.

For his part, Paul could only feel thankful for the work that absorbed him. Figures, he thought, were logical and reliable, and in future they would provide all the excitement he required. He gritted his teeth and forced himself to concentrate on matters of business, rising early and staying late at his desk, hoping that by these means he would soon become unaware of the gnawing loss where once had been his love for Charlotte.

Not that he did not love her still. Of course he did – and always would, he knew that. No amount of work could change that. It might, however, render the situation less painful.

He was casting a long column of figures when the tap came at the door and a clerk brought in a letter.

'Put it down,' Paul said, not taking his eyes from the ledger. Whatever it was, it could wait. A bill of exchange – a request for withdrawal? It was of little consequence and could wait its turn.

There was silence in the room, a silence that was unbroken until he threw down his pen with an oath. The total was different from the time before and the time before that. Were even figures becoming unreliable now? Was he to find no solace anywhere?

His eye fell upon the letter, and his heart leapt with disbelief. There was no mistaking that delicate, pointed, artistic hand. Charlotte had written to him.

To say – what? He snatched up the letter but hardly dared to open it, holding it in his hands for a moment and staring at it hungrily.

'Let us still be friends' – depend upon it, that was what she had written. 'Surely we may still meet from time to time?' It could be no more, he would stake his life upon it. And he would be so tempted – but he was *damned* if he would agree to it, to put himself through that torture again, seeing her and loving her, knowing that he would never possess her. No – they had parted and they must not go back on it. Somehow he would have to find the strength to write and tell her so.

Such thoughts raced through his mind as he broke the seal, but as he scanned the words she had written he found himself numb with disbelief. He read the letter again. A pulse thudded deafeningly in his ears; he felt on fire with joy.

She had changed her mind. She was bidding him come to her. She hungered for him – would do anything he wanted. Exultantly, magnificently, she was admitting her need – and the thrice-damned figures could wait!

His passage through the shop was such that those within it stared after him, feeling as if they had been caught up in a whirlwind.

'Is aught amiss?' Harry called, but received no reply. Only a grin and a wave of the hand and a look of such blazing happiness that, in view of the recent gloom, he shook his head in disbelief.

Deception, Charlotte found, was quite ridiculously easy once one gave one's attention to it. No wonder Elise had found it so simple. It only became detectable when others were on the look-out for it; and in her case, though Nan seemed a little mystified that she should suddenly take it into her head to go to see her father on her own with no servant to attend her, asking only that Joseph should take her as far as the Bull Hotel in Rochester from where she would complete her journey by Mail coach, she felt certain there were no suspicions of wrongdoing.

'Are you sure you'll not be needing me, madam?' Nan asked.

'Quite sure.' Charlotte smiled at her. 'In fact I have another plan for you. I am distressed at the bad feeling between you and Molly. Truly, you should not blame her so. She acted foolishly, I know, but Elise can be persuasive and Molly is devoted to her. I think it would be an excellent plan for both of you to have a change of scene. Take advantage of my absence and pay a visit to your brother in Colchester, as you have longed to do. Put this household out of your thoughts for a while, and patch up your difficulties.'

'You are very good to us, madam.'

Charlotte felt humbled by this undeserved praise. She was not good, but bad; sinful, faithless, adulterous – well, not quite the latter yet, but undoubtedly she would be before too long. So radical had been her change of mood that she cared little. She still would not be unfaithful to Gabriel beneath his own roof, but had become firmly of the opinion that what he didn't know, wouldn't hurt him.

'Why do you not allow Joseph to take you all the way to Canterbury, madam?'

'And what if monsieur should return? No – Joseph should be here in case he is needed. He can collect me at the Bull in ten days' time.'

Nan appeared to accept this strange plan without question, and if there remained any trace of bewilderment in her mind, it was effectively forgotten when, to the relief of everyone, over a month after her elopement, word from Elise arrived at last.

Her letter was full of endearments and apologies and entreaties for forgiveness, in spite of which there sounded throughout an unmistakable note of happiness which somewhat allayed Charlotte's disquiet. If it had not been for the post-script scrawled beneath the signature, she might have felt that, after all, good might come of Elise's rash step. The addendum, however, gave her pause for thought:

'Please send the monies due to me under my inheritance without delay,' Elise had written. 'We are in dire need of them.'

Dire need? Was that nothing more than Elise's customary extravagant way of expressing herself, or did it mean that the couple were truly in desperate financial straits?

'I imagine that they are,' Paul said, when Charlotte went to him for advice. 'Jordan was in debt when he left London.'

'But Elise writes happily of taking rooms near the castle and of meeting Jordan's friends and entertaining them. It hardly sounds like a state of penury. Still, I must send her something, Paul. Can you arrange the transfer of money on my behalf? This inheritance of hers is invested, and I cannot deal with it. It must wait until Gabriel returns. The best I can do is to send her an advance on what is legally hers.'

'Considering how she behaved, you're being more than generous,' Paul told her, but Charlotte shook her head.

'I am merely tying up loose ends,' she said. 'While I am with you, I intend to think of no other.'

In the same spirit she wrote to Madame Colbert, making a transcript of Elise's letter, with the exception of its worrying afterthought.

News of the elopement had been a shattering blow to poor Tantine. That Elise could go without a word of farewell – could run off with a worthless actor, could deny all the maidenly virtues instilled into her from childhood by Madame Colbert herself, could cast aside the chance of a good marriage – all these had brought Tantine close to collapse.

She blamed Charlotte, naturally. Had she not said her beloved Elise would be corrupted? She made her views quite clear in the emotional, tear-stained letter she had dashed off when she had first heard the news.

The letter had angered Charlotte who was no less worried and upset by Elise's flight than Madame Colbert, but when the anger had died a little she could not help feeling a pang of pity for the poor woman in spite of all the mischief she had caused. Elise had been her life, and now she was gone.

And so, as if scoring off one more matter that might weigh on her conscience to spoil the days that were to come, Charlotte sent news of Elise to the woman who adored her, and having done so, felt able to concentrate at last on her own affairs.

Nothing more remained to be done. She was ready in every way for her time with Paul, and the prospect of it was so sweet, so full of promise, that she trembled, conscious as never before of her own body. Suddenly it seemed to her that it was transformed, changed from a mere collection of bones and veins and arteries into a finely tuned instrument, awaiting the hand of the musician to conjure from it some haunting melody. There was no fear in her now, and no remembrance of fear. Only a longing.

At the Bull she was given the best chamber, as on so many other occasions, and if there was any surprise that she had come unattended, no one was impolite enough to show it.

She slept little but rose feeling more alive than ever before, knowing that Paul would be with her very soon. It seemed right, that he would come to her in this room where they had first met as adults after their long separation. She remembered how sad she had been then, and what a joy it had been when Paul had appeared so unexpectedly.

Now he was coming again, but nothing else was the same. She looked into the mirror and could see the excitement in her eyes, the unaccustomed flush on her cheeks. She looked almost beautiful; for once she could see it.

She could only pick at the food that was served to break her fast; then, suddenly, he was there, and they were looking at each other smilingly like two children sharing a daring escapade, laughing at nothing with a catch of nervousness in their voices.

'You are lovely,' he said, his eyes devouring her. 'So lovely!'

'Did you bring the horses? Is everything ready?'

'Everything.' He held out his hand to her. 'Come, my dearest.'

It was still early when they trotted out of the inn yard between the pillars that flanked the entrance. Charlotte had hoped for fine weather, and she was not disappointed. The River Medway glinted on their right hand as they rode along beside it, and the square-built castle reared solidly against the sky on their left. There was not a cloud to be seen, though there was a chill in the air. It was not the chill that made her shiver, however, as she looked at Paul and smiled at him.

'You have no belated regrets?' he asked.

'No regrets at all.'

Soon the track began to lead upwards, traversing farmland; bare, windy country, with rolling fields and few trees. But still the river gleamed in the sun below them, and beyond the river the hills were hidden in the haze.

They left the main path and took a smaller track which led more steeply to the North Downs. It seemed as if they had the world to themselves. In the folds of the downs they saw hamlets, cottage roofs, church spires pointing to the sky, but they went near none of them, keeping to the pathways that wound around fields and the woods that clothed the higher hills.

At midday they stopped in a clearing to eat the food they had brought with them from the inn. The sun was stronger now and out of the wind the air was warm. Birds darted all around, engaged in frenzied activity, seeking for food for themselves and their nestlings.

'That nuthatch must have a nest in the tree,' Paul said. 'Yes, there's a hollow below the second branch; do you see it? See how she makes her way there with her haul. There'll be a horde of open beaks to greet her.'

'While her mate perches on a bough and sings merrily, no doubt!'

'You do him an injustice. He takes his share of the feeding and what appears to be singing is the marking of his territory. To be honest –' He looked at her with a grin. 'I cannot tell if that busy bird is a mama or a papa. I recognise a threat when I see one, though. Look at that sparrowhawk hovering over yonder.'

'You still have your fondness for wild creatures?'

'Of course.'

He had spread his cloak on a grassy bank and now lay on his side, propped on one elbow and looking at her as if he could never look his fill.

'You could say,' Charlotte said, 'that we were introduced by a cockroach.'

'We have shared so much.'

Charlotte knew his eyes were on her. Suddenly she felt nervous. She rose from the bank and wandered off as if something had caught her attention in the bushes.

'Hey,' Paul called after a moment. 'Do you tire of me so quickly?'

'No.' She stood still, abandoning the aimless search. She had picked a bluebell and stood for a moment twisting it in her fingers. 'Paul,' she said at last, her voice betraying her uncertainty. 'Paul, there is something I have to tell you.'

The frivolous answer he would have given died on his lips. There was something in the set of her shoulders and the way she hung her head that showed she was deeply troubled. He rose and went to her, turning her to face him.

'My dearest heart, what is it?'

'There is no easy way to say it.' She would not meet his eyes. 'The secret is not mine alone to tell, yet tell it I must. I – I have never lain with a man, Paul.' The words came in a rush and she looked at him directly at last. 'I am a virgin still.'

'What?' His thick, fair brows drew together and bewilderment clouded his eyes. 'But you have been wed these many years!'

'I am a virgin still.' She repeated her words. 'Gabriel was tortured horribly. He calls himself half a man and feels shame because of it, though why he should do so I cannot fathom. Men

351

seem to feel strongly about such things. One would think the blame his, though of course it is no fault.'

'The fault was to marry.' He shook his head as if the matter was beyond belief. 'I cannot comprehend this, Charlotte. How could he do such a thing?'

'There was no fault,' Charlotte insisted. 'He hid nothing from me. Please, Paul – I have no wish to speak of it.' Indeed, even the mention of Gabriel's name had opened the door to feelings of guilt. Helplessly her hands fluttered and the blue flower fell limply to the ground. 'I felt the need to explain why I, though wife in name, am as untouched and ignorant as any maid. Otherwise I would have kept silent. I *should* have kept silent!'

He captured her hands and drew her close, kissing her lightly, restraining his passion.

'You will find there is nothing to fear,' he said gently.

He took her to a place not far from the Pilgrims' Way, a huddled collection of buildings that was part farm, part inn. They arrived in the late afternoon when the sun was beginning to stain the sky with pink and gold.

'Are you sure this is a place for travellers?' Charlotte asked.

'I stayed here once with my father, long ago. Look, there's the sign – The Travellers' Rest. Nothing could be more appropriate.'

There was little sign of life, but a plume of smoke rose vertically from the chimney and as they clattered into the small yard the landlord came out to meet them. He was a morose man and showed no curiosity, but took the horses and called for his daughter to show them to their chamber.

Charlotte's heart had sunk a little at the initial appearance of the place, for it seemed dark and gloomy. The public room was sparsely furnished and so full of smoke that her eyes smarted. However, she gasped with pleasure when she saw their private room, for here the small windows that were all that could be seen from the front had been enlarged to give a wide view of the valley that was now spread before them, calm and lovely in the light of the dying sun.

''Twas done for my mother,' the innkeeper's daughter told them. 'She was bed-rid many months and liked to lie and look at the sun as it set. Father – he seems harsh sometimes and if he spoke so to you, then I'm sorry for it – he'd have done anything for her. He's grieving still. She died last autumn.'

'The poor man! I'm so sorry. He has my sympathy – you both do.'

Charlotte spoke genuinely enough, but nevertheless when the girl had gone she turned to Paul, smiling with delight.

'We all die, but few can have done so in a more beautiful place. What an end the poor woman must have had!'

'Is it trite to say it makes a wonderful beginning for us?'

'Trite or not, I give you leave to say it. Oh Paul, how clever of you to arrange it so! Did you ever see such a sight?'

'It was chance, I confess, not cleverness.' He was gladdened by her change of mood. He could feel that she was smiling as he kissed her. 'It is but the first of many pleasures, I promise.'

The room was simply furnished, the bedhangings threadbare, but all was spotlessly clean, and when a fire was kindled in the hearth and a table laid before it, no palace would have seemed more charming.

They kept the shutters open until the last light had gone from the sky. Together they watched it die, his arms encircling her from behind, her head against his shoulder, counting the stars that appeared one by one. Charlotte's nervousness had returned and she was conscious of the pulse that beat in her throat.

'We should make a wish,' she said, her voice light and breathless. 'A wish that time could stand still for a while, that the hands of the clock should not race around so fast.'

'We can only make the most of each moment.'

There was a catch in his voice, too. Still within the circle of his arms, she turned to face him.

'Why do you not close the shutters?' she asked softly.

With his left arm he held her close; with his right, he did as she suggested, fastening the shutters against the night.

'There is no cause to fear.' His lips caressed her cheek as he spoke.

'But you are trembling too.'

He laughed breathlessly and with sudden urgency reached for the fastenings of her dress, kissing her bared shoulders and breast until her fever mounted and she twisted from him, impatient with the masculine fingers that were so awkwardly slow with tapes and buttons.

Desire was a tide that swept aside all doubts and fears, all thoughts of modesty or guilt. She had longed for the feel of his lips and his body, but there was a sweetness here that was beyond

353

dreams, a hunger that he delayed fulfilling until she was on fire with it.

'I didn't know,' she whispered when finally they lay together, spent and exhausted. 'I didn't know.'

She thought of all the staid married couples of her acquaintance; women who had sat at her dining table and spoken of their servants and their children, their lace-making and the orchestra they had heard at Dorset Gardens; men who seemed interested only in the purchase of a carriage horse or the conduct of the war. To think they went home to this!

It is not always so, Paul thought; but he said nothing. Other times, other women meant nothing to him and were certainly not matters to be brought to Charlotte's attention at such a moment.

She was made for love, he thought. What could Gabriel Fabian have been thinking of? He had always believed him to be both sensitive and unselfish – yet surely to marry a girl of seventeen and condemn her to a lifetime's celibacy showed a want of both attributes?

I could hate him for it, he thought, breathing the scent of her hair. What was to become of them?

'At least we have the present,' Charlotte said, just as if he had spoken.

They stayed eight days at the inn, and every day the sun shone.

'More like June-month than April,' the innkeeper said. 'We'll pay for it later. We're not done with winter yet.'

He paid no more regard to them than if they had been a pair of drovers, and his daughter was scarcely more communicative. To Charlotte it was a magical, enchanted time during which she was barely conscious of the rest of the world.

They walked the Pilgrims' Way and explored the wooded hillsides. There were dark thickets of yew trees where the spreading branches shut out the sky and where, on the hard-packed, needle-strewn earth, they made love. The trunks of the trees were a shade of olive green. Will olive green mean ecstasy to me for the rest of my days, Charlotte wondered?

Sometimes they found a sheltered spot and drowsed in the sun. Sometimes they talked of time past. They shared memories, but they never spoke of the future. Of each other, they could never have their fill.

It was towards the end of the sixth day that they came upon the dead robin, half eaten by some predator.

'Cruel nature,' Charlotte mourned.

'His mate will find another to replace him. Sometimes it takes them less than an hour, faithless creatures.'

He could have bitten his tongue out as he saw the light die from her face.

'Faithless!' she repeated the word bitterly. 'Infidelity is not a pretty attribute, is it?'

'You are not faithless, Charlotte.'

'No?' She looked at him sadly. 'Then what am I, taking such pleasure in a man not my husband?'

For a moment Paul was silent. He dared not think of Gabriel, for such thoughts were dangerous. He could so easily hate him for what he had done to Charlotte; yet how could he hate such a man – a man he had looked up to all his life? A man he knew to be generous and kind? He wished he were cuckolding almost any other man, yet the affection was gone and there was resentment in its place, he could not deny it.

He took her hand and traced the lines on it with his finger.

'Your marriage could be annulled,' he said. 'It is no marriage at all.'

She snatched her hand away.

'That's unthinkable! Gabriel has suffered enough.'

'Is that reason for you and me to suffer? Look at me, Lottie –' The childish name took her by surprise. She obeyed him and he saw the desolation in her eyes as if she realised that although this was not quite the end of their time together, the hours were numbered. He reached for her hand again and held it tightly. 'I love you, Lottie.' He caught his lip between his teeth and shook his head as if in frustration at having to use the same, tired old words that had been used for centuries. 'We are two parts of a whole – you know it, you feel it, just as I do.'

She nodded.

'I feel it,' she said heavily.

'Then how can you go back to life as it was before? Listen, my dearest love.' He pulled her closer to him. 'I have decided to go to America.' She gasped soundlessly, eyes widening in pain. 'Yes, it hurts, doesn't it? I cannot bear the thought of parting from you, but neither can I bear living in the same city, seeing you at regular intervals, exchanging meaningless pleasantries under the eyes of a thousand others – not to mention those of your husband. So I have decided to put an end to it. But it need not be the end, Lottie. You could come with me.'

He saw her eyes kindle with hope, her lips part. Then she sighed and the light died.

'I cannot hurt him, Paul. He has done nothing wrong. How many blows can any man endure?'

He expelled his breath slowly, relaxing his hold.

'Consider it carefully, I beg. Will you promise me that, at least? There is not a court in the land would not grant you an annulment.'

'And the scandal would be the talk of London! Imagine it, Paul. Think how Gabriel would suffer – a man as proud as he is, to be mocked and ridiculed.'

'Think carefully, Lottie. I want no answer now.'

She said nothing. She did not even protest at his use of the name she hated, but there was an added frenzy about her response to him that night and afterwards she wept and could not be comforted.

The magic time was over. The gates to the outside world had been flung open and it was impossible now to close them again.

'When do you think of leaving for America?' Charlotte asked as they looked at the sunset on their last night.

'In a month or so.'

'So soon! Does Monsieur Charpentier know of your intentions?'

'He is sympathetic, yes –'

'What do you mean?' She twisted round to look into his face. 'He surely knows nothing of us?'

'I mean he understands my wanderlust, my fascination with the New World – which, I might say, would seem ten times more fascinating were the woman I love to agree to share my bed and board!'

'Please, Paul! Don't!' Her voice was tight with pain.

'Have you thought that a child might result from this?'

She was silent for a moment, examining her feelings. That such an outcome would complicate matters no one could deny, but she felt no panic. She was not a frightened girl any more, but was strong, assured. Made so by Gabriel, her conscience insisted.

'I suppose that it might,' she said.

'And what then?'

'Then –' Her voice died and she sighed, as if in defeat. 'I don't know, Paul. I cannot tell. We must wait on events. Do you think such a decision easy?'

'I think it is not.'

'Imagine his feelings. Elise has gone from him and when he discovers that, it will hurt unbearably. How can I possibly hurt him more?'

'Elise!' Paul gave a short laugh. 'Would that she shared your care for him. I wonder,' he added after a pause, 'how that marriage goes?'

She had disliked the parson Peter had found to marry them. He had a bulbous nose and suffered from boils and his cassock was dirty, spotted with the remains of many meals. She disliked, too, the squalid hovel where the ceremony was performed in a back alley of the district known as the Mint in Southwark, long infamous as the haunt of debtors and felons of all kinds; but when once they had been proclaimed man and wife and the ring had been put on her finger, Peter had turned her towards him and kissed her and suddenly a wild elation had taken hold of her and the sleazy surroundings and leering parson were forgotten.

It was exciting, romantic. The nosegay of flowers that Peter had bought from a girl at the corner of the street was celebration enough. Love for him swept aside all other feelings, so that even her genuine regret that it had been necessary to hurt her family melted away. It was a great pity, she felt, but what was her alternative? Her parents would undoubtedly forgive her once they realised how blissfully happy the marriage had made her. After all, when had her father desired anything other than her happiness?

They had taken the Mail to Liverpool and the packet to Dublin, and if a narrow bunk in a cramped and stinking cabin provided an uncomfortable marriage bed, she remained optimistic, her spirits buoyed by Peter's assurances that at the theatre in Smock-Alley he would be welcomed with open arms by Joseph Ashbury, the long-time manager.

''Twill be like going home, dearest,' he told her. 'I've so many friends there you'll not believe – and they're warm and loving, not cold like that London crowd who could not bear a newcomer to have any share in the applause. Ashbury will be delighted to see me back, you mark my words.'

Ashbury, however, had managed to contain his delight very

well; in fact his welcome was grudging, and if it had not been for the sudden illness of one of the players, he would not have allowed Peter back in the company – a matter which, for the first few weeks of their stay in Dublin, Peter was able to conceal from Elise.

Once the invalid was restored to health, it was a different matter. Ashbury made it clear that Peter had left him in the lurch when he went to London and that he did not trust him to refrain from doing so again in the future, if the fancy so took him.

'I've no place for you here,' he said brutally. 'I like those about me I can rely on.'

'Then devil take you, and your company,' Peter shouted angrily. 'I can act any of them off the stage, and well you know it.'

He had stormed back to the chamber at the tavern where he and Elise temporarily dwelt pending the acquisition of funds by one means or another, revealing to his bride of six weeks a side of his character she had not suspected. Though the charm and the humour that had so appealed to her were not so often in evidence these days and she knew now that he could be morose, she had not seen any trace of the furious temper he now displayed.

It frightened her – not so much because of the violent anger, which was something she had never been exposed to throughout the whole of her young life and was frightening enough, but because of the change in him. He turned into a man she could not recognise. His face altered, took on a pinched, vicious expression with staring eyes that seemed the eyes of a stranger. He flung himself about the small room picking up any object that came to hand, hurling it to the floor with curses and obscenities that were new to her.

Fortunately it was mainly the contents of her wardrobe that were so mistreated and therefore nothing was broken, but the sight of her garments being thrown about in such disarray moved her as perhaps nothing else would have done. She ran to him, seizing his arm and shaking it like a terrier.

'Stop it, Peter – stop it this minute!'

'It's your fault.'

'What?'

'These clothes.' He gestured wildly at the petticoats and gowns that now littered the room. 'They should not have been about.

358

Do you expect a servant to wait on you? You're not in Freedom Street now, you know.'

The monstrous injustice of the remark made her gasp. It was true that her clothes had been in view, but only because there was no cupboard or press in which to keep them. They had been neatly enough arranged until he had vented his fury on them.

'Where are they to be kept, then? There is no place –'

'So you dislike the home I can provide, do you? Well, you know the remedy! Should I like it any better? I thought I could expect some help from you. 'Twas said often enough.'

'Not by me.' The thought that he did not truly love her, had married her entirely for money, made her feel strangely hollow inside, as if she might faint.

'*La petite héritière?* How many times when I was an apprentice in your father's house did I hear your precious Tantine say those words?'

'She was foolish –'

'Oh, so far above us poor creatures were you that we felt we should genuflect each time the little princess passed by. Destined for an earl, you were – even a duke! And here you are, married to me.' He laughed harshly. 'And I yet to see a brass farthing.'

'There will be money! It's mine and they must send it – but is that all you care for?' Sobbing, she ran to him and threw herself into his arms. 'Don't you love me at all? You swore that you did!'

He calmed down and kissed her. Yes, of course he loved her, he said in an exasperated way. But she must surely see that the lack of money was a sad disappointment, particularly now that Ashbury had refused him work?

When the next day they received a bank draft for one hundred pounds from Charlotte to 'tide them over until business matters can be straightened out', life took on a brighter aspect and he was all smiles again, so that she forgot that sickening moment when he was so angry.

'Now Mistress Flynn can be paid her reckoning,' he said.

Mistress Flynn was their landlady at the damp, dark hostelry known somewhat incongruously as the Angel Inn where they lodged – the 'rooms close to the castle' as Elise had described it to Charlotte, as if its nearness to the castle somehow invested the dwelling with a vicarious grandeur instead of merely over-shadowing it. As for describing their one small chamber as 'rooms' – well, that could be passed off as a slip of the pen, Elise assured herself. Anyway, it was only temporary. Ashbury would surely see the error of his ways soon, and would employ Peter once more – and before long the rest of her money would arrive so that they could find accommodation more to their liking.

Meantime they bought food and a new coat for Peter since it was important that he keep up appearances, a few flagons of wine because it was equally important that he entertain his friends. He had not entirely given up hope of his old associates being able to persuade Ashbury to change his mind regarding employing him, he told Elise. But since he had not yet done so, and he needed to make money, he would borrow some of Charlotte's gift for the gaming tables.

Her feeling of unease was quieted when he won and came home in high spirits, kissing her soundly and presenting her with a bunch of daffodils.

'Now can we find somewhere else to live?' Elise asked.

'This isn't such a bad place.'

'I cannot like Mistress Flynn!'

The woman was fat, with a large, slab-like pink face and a frizz of yellow hair. At first Elise had thought her kind and motherly. All too soon she realised that Mistress Flynn was a prying, meddlesome busybody who took a prurient interest in 'my two young lovers' as she insisted on calling Peter and Elise.

'Sure, there's no harm in the old sow.'

He was a chameleon, she thought. They had been back in Ireland only a short time and already he had picked up the speech patterns of his associates, the way of speaking that must have been his before he came to London.

'She questions me.' About what, Elise refused to say. It embarrassed her, to remember Mistress Flynn's nudges and winks and innuendoes. The quality and extent of Peter's prowess in bed seemed to obsess the woman.

'Then write home again, for the love of heaven. Tell them to send the money that is yours. God knows we have need of it.'

'I have explained the situation,' Elise said wearily. 'Maman has done what she can. Until my father returns home her hands are tied.'

'Or so she says!'

'She would not lie.'

'Not even to get you away from me?'

'She knows we are married, Peter. And she *did* send us money!

It will last us for a while – and you have added to it today.'

'Sure, it goes nowhere,' Peter said sullenly, all his elation gone.

He had been right in one respect. He did have many friends in Dublin, and they all appeared as warm and open-hearted as he had described them. It was through their representations that, just as he had hoped, Ashbury relented and gave him a small part in the next production.

'Though I'll not tolerate any nonsense,' he said. 'I'll give you one chance and one chance only.' This warning, needless to say, was not communicated to Elise, who received the news that he was once more employed at the theatre with jubilation.

Everything would be different now, she thought. This separation from the stage – from the profession he loved so much and excelled at so greatly – had been a kind of death for him. All his bad temper, all his moodiness could be accounted for by his frustration. Now he would return to the charming, loving man she had known in London.

While Peter rehearsed she explored Dublin. The castle dominated the city with its round towers and thick walls, but the poverty in the surrounding streets appalled her. Peter had lived here when he was young, she reminded herself. How could she, who had wanted for nothing all her life, begin to enter into his feelings regarding money?

She had seen nothing like it, not even in London – not even in Spitalfields and Whitechapel which had more than its share of privation. However, she liked to watch the barges unload at the quay in the centre of town and to walk beside the Liffey where there were meadows overlooked by mountains. And in the better part of town there were grand buildings which would have done credit to London itself.

Rain drove her indoors, but to avoid Mistress Flynn she went to the theatre. It was a shabby place with shabby actors who played each night to houses where only the upper gallery was filled and the rest of the theatre almost deserted. No wonder Peter had left to try his luck in London – and no wonder Mr Ashbury had no wish to re-employ him since money was so short.

But if money was scarce, there was no shortage of rumbustious company. Peter's cronies among the players were a raffish, tatterdemalion crowd, the women no better than they should be, the men hard-drinking and hard-gambling, boisterous in their enjoyment of life, full of noise and argument. Sudden fights were common, but the next moment they could be full of uproarious bonhomie, swearing undying friendship.

There was Jonathan O'Hare who could sing like an angel, and often did so when in his cups; there was Finbar Dooley, who never stopped talking, and Seamus McNicholas who was thin and lugubrious but possessed a dry wit. There was Patrick Casey who was quick to take offence and equally quick to throw a punch, and Christopher Connor, who tended towards the maudlin when there was liquor inside him.

Elise thought them wonderfully entertaining – delightfully and amusingly different from her father's associates. She blushed prettily at their extravagant compliments and welcomed them to the Angel and their humble room with all the grace of a society hostess. They were so entranced with her that they came again – and again, and again, and again. It became too much for her to stomach, no matter how fulsome the compliments. The drinking bouts were long and noisy, and since she had no other room to retire to it was impossible for her to ignore them or to sleep, however tired she might become.

'We are never alone any more,' she complained to Peter.

'I thought you liked my friends!'

'I do, I do! It's just that we have no time to call our own, no privacy.'

'Well dearest, you shall have all the privacy you need tonight. I propose to increase our fortunes –'

'You're going to the gaming house? Oh, don't – please Peter, don't go! I don't want to be alone tonight.'

He turned up his eyes in mock resignation.

'Complaints one moment because we are never alone, and the next because tonight you may have a quiet evening –'

'I want a quiet evening with you, Peter. With my husband. Is that so much to ask?'

'On this occasion, sweeting,' he said as he kissed her, 'I much regret that it is. Use the time to write home again.'

Charlotte's money had gone, and the daffodils had long wilted. He was paid a pittance, and she knew that his friends openhandedly staked him at the gaming house while debts piled up.

She wept a little when he left her, but after only a few moments she resolutely dried her eyes and looked about the room. There were empty bottles on a table, together with the remains of a meal and some sewing materials, for she had mended Peter's cuff just before he left. Clothes were littered everywhere; not only hers but his as well, for he was far from neat in his ways.

It was a far cry from Freedom Street and she could not suppress a sharp pang of homesickness, but though she had her share of faults, Elise was not one to sit and weep. She would transform this wretched room, she resolved. She had chosen this life, she had chosen Peter, and in spite of all she loved him. She was not defeated yet. This was as good a way as any of demonstrating the fact.

She picked up the strewn clothes, folding and stacking them as neatly as she could. She tore a strip from an old petticoat and dusted and polished the few sticks of furniture, tipping plates and bottles into the portion that was left and dumping the bundle unceremoniously in the dim cavern that served as kitchen to the inn. She had no compunction in doing so for the rent was supposed to include service. That Mistress Flynn had no guarantee of receiving next week's reckoning had nothing to do with the case, in her opinion.

'What's this, what's this?' The lady in question was toasting her toes by the peat fire and leapt up at the sight of Elise and her bundle, but with no more than a hasty word Elise fled, unwilling to enter into any conversation.

Back in her own room she looked around once again, this time with more satisfaction. It needs something more, she thought – and with a sudden inspiration delved into the trunk where she had packed away her clothes and from its depths brought out a crimson velvet cloak which she spread on the bed.

If only the daffodils had not died! Tomorrow she would ask Peter for a few farthings to buy more, and they would light up the room and make everything seem brighter, more hopeful. Even now the improvement was startling. She could hardly wait for him to come home and admire her efforts.

She remembered then his instructions to write home. Had her father returned yet? There had been no word of him. She hoped he was safe. She hoped he would forgive her. Surely he would have written to her, if he were back in London?

Perhaps she should write again, asking once more about the money. Pride had kept her from making too much of an issue of it in previous letters, but maybe the time had come to sound a more urgent note. She gathered pen and ink and paper and sat herself at the table, now free of clutter. It was hard to know how to begin; hard to think of a way to express her urgent need despite Charlotte's gift, yet at the same time ensuring that she sounded blissfully content. She sighed heavily and drew the paper towards her.

My dearest Maman,
At last I have a quiet evening in the round of pleasure that has engaged us since Peter's triumphal return to the Dublin theatre, and I take my pen to acquaint you of my health and perfect happiness.

She stopped, stared dismally at the page, and try as she might she could not find the words to continue. Indeed, she could not see what she had already written, for through her tears the lines shimmered and blurred.

Daffodils, she thought, as the tears spilled over. What possible difference would daffodils make?

19

Gabriel had forgotten how fierce the sun could be; how even here where the path wound between pine and chestnut trees it would sift through the leaves and fall on the ground like burning coins so that one went from sun to shade with profound gratitude. It was hard to remember the softness of an English spring; hard, too, to remember the patois which had once been so familiar to his ears that he could slip into it without thought.

They had left the gorge an hour earlier, he and the man who had come to lead him to Jean Cavalier. Beyrac was a huge, silent man, his shaggy head set on wide shoulders, his thighs solid as English oaks. Gabriel envied him his strength as he strode ahead, making light work of the uphill path. He himself rode on a mule, his long legs dangling almost to the ground. He was thankful for the ride, knowing full well that he could never emulate Beyrac, that he was unequal to this climb. Already he was having to make the familiar effort to ignore the searing pain in his back.

Beyrac spoke seldom, indicating the direction by thrusting out a massive arm this way or that. Always the path led upwards, sometimes dwindling almost to nothing between bushes and outcrops of rock. The scents of the forest brought back to Gabriel as nothing else the childhood he had spent in this beloved and beautiful country.

Beloved, yet now so alien that he felt himself a foreigner, struggling to understand the tongue, struggling to come to terms with the noonday sun. And it was not yet high summer! How the years had changed him.

Beyrac paused in a pool of shade and looked back.

'Is all well?' he asked.

'All well. How long more?'

'We shall be there before nightfall.'

As Gabriel approached he offered a goatskin flask and watched with a look of amused superiority on his face as he saw the relief with which Gabriel drank. He took a brief sip himself, wiped his mouth with his sleeve, and set off once more with no attempt at conversation.

Gabriel was glad of the silence, for he had much to think of. Relief and sorrow were equally mixed in his thoughts; relief that he had reached his mother while there was time; sorrow that he had thought of her harshly for so long.

She had been desperately ill but quite lucid when he had first arrived, and had wept with joy at the sight of him, tears in which he had shared.

'My son, my son –' For some time she could say little more, and Gabriel, seeing the joy his presence had bestowed and that death was indeed close, had not reproached her or pressed for reasons for what he had regarded as her faithlessness. He had sat beside her with her hand in his and they had talked of days gone by before the persecutions, when he had been a child, the family together, with no thought of the divisions that the future would bring.

'Tell me of your wife,' she demanded one day. Gabriel was silent for a moment as he thought of Charlotte.

'She is dark,' he said at last. 'Thick, dark hair, dark eyes, and skin like the petal of a camellia. She is a gentle person and moves with such grace and lightness you would think her a dancer, but though she loves music, it is design that is her gift.'

'Your voice changes when you speak of her,' his mother said. 'You love her very much.'

'Yes.' His throat seemed to close on the word, and he coughed.

'And she loves you?'

He paused again and his mouth twisted a little as if at the bitterness of his thoughts.

'More than she should, perhaps.'

His mother laughed, almost without sound as if she were conserving her strength.

'How can a wife love a husband over much?'

'By thinking of his good, perhaps, when she should think of her own.'

'What else is loving?' She was silent for a moment. 'I loved your father,' she went on softly. 'When he died, I felt as if part of me had gone, too. My marriage to Monsieur Arnoult was another matter, yet we have not been unhappy. He is a good husband, a good man.'

'So is Jules a good man. I am glad to have him as a brother. They are both good men.'

And both Catholics, he thought wryly. Both sure that their path to heaven is the right one, even as I am sure that we Huguenots have the answer.

He did not much consider what he would say to Jean Cavalier, though he prayed for guidance as the mule picked its way over the rough path. When the moment came, he felt sure that the words would be put into his mouth, and he asked that they would be powerful ones that would convince the guerrilla leader that somehow the killing and the carnage must stop, that the Camisards had demonstrated their strength and determination and now must show a softer side, a willingness to compromise.

All his information led him to believe that Cavalier would agree. It was the other, Roland, who had to be convinced – but Roland was at some distance, not easy to reach, his group of insurgents more deeply hidden in the mountains. Meeting with one would pave the way to meeting the other. Surely even Roland would recognise that now, with king and country so occupied with the foreign enemy, this was the time to make demands for freedom and tolerance within France's borders? Gabriel was relying on Cavalier's backing in his effort to put the argument to Roland so that at least an effort to make peace could be initiated.

He did not delude himself that it would be easy, even with Cavalier's agreement. These people of the Languedoc were a dogged, intractable race. They were tough, accustomed to privations, firm in their faith – a faith only strengthened by the persecutions they had endured. He himself had, after all, been as inflexible as any. What had changed him? He pondered the question as he rode.

Life had changed him. Charlotte had changed him. And at the thought of Charlotte, never far distant, a deep sadness engulfed him and he bowed his head as if this pain, unlike the physical one, was more than he could bear.

'My thoughts,' Jean Cavalier said, 'have been travelling this path or one very like it for some little while. Have you heard of de la Bourlie? He was in touch with us some months ago,' he went on as Gabriel shook his head, 'urging us to stop the warfare against Catholics and to join with him in a rising of both Catholics and

367

Protestants, united in common cause against the tyranny of the court, the aim to restore liberty of conscience.'

'You agreed to this?'

'I did, yes; the others?' He tipped his hand first one way and then the other, indicating irresolution. 'Nevertheless, it was finally agreed we should provide a force for a combined rising.'

'What happened?'

'Carnage, monsieur. It might have been a different story had a leader been chosen for this force who had a grain or two of tact or common sense – but the others chose a man called Catinat who failed to see that the whole success of the operation depended on co-operation between Catholics and Protestants. He laid waste every church, every monastery. He spread devastation and terror among the Catholics. Those, monsieur, are the type of men you must convince.'

The two men sat in the dimness of a cave lit by guttering candles. They had shared a rabbit stewed with herbs, and black bread with cheese, but though the meal had been sparse Gabriel gained the impression that it had been an unusually magnificent banquet provided in his honour and he had been suitably grateful.

With the meal over, the serious talking began, and for this, the other men – Cavalier's lieutenants, who had shared their meal – had withdrawn, leaving them alone.

'What is to be done, then?' Gabriel asked. 'It has to be understood that there will be no material help from England. I had it from the Queen herself.'

'I grieve still about the consignment of arms that never reached us. Bad weather, garbled messages, the capture of an agent – everything conspired against us. It was the worst possible luck –'

'Or God's will, perhaps? You and the Camisards have nothing left to prove, Cavalier. No one can doubt your bravery, your commitment. You have taken everything they have done to you. I have heard it all from Etienne Boyer – the scorched-earth policy, the devastation of villages and farms in the region, innocent people put to the sword. When one group falls, another rises to take its place.'

'We are at least three thousand strong.'

'But you have suffered bad reverses recently – is it not so?'

Cavalier nodded and sighed.

'Yes, it is so. It was the last gesture of Marshal de Montreval. Despite the scorched-earth policy you mentioned he failed to wipe us out, and the King decided to replace him with de Villars. De Montreval's pride was stung and he mounted a powerful offensive against us from three points of the compass. We lost stores and equipment as well as men.' He shrugged, palms outwards. 'Yet here we are – my group here, others elsewhere in the mountains.'

'You have nothing left to prove,' Gabriel said again.

'It is the new Marshal, de Villars, who has made the public proclamation that all Camisards who lay down their arms will be pardoned. Good, as far as it goes, but we want more.'

'Then ask for more! You are bargaining from a position of strength. After two years you are undefeated. Can you seriously believe that Louis has any wish to fight his own countrymen when he has a major war on his hands? Ask for the release of prisoners. Ask for liberty of conscience. This man de Villars has opened the door a crack; use your strength to kick it down, man, not kill innocent civilians.'

'You are preaching to the converted, my friend. It is the others you have to convince.'

It was, Gabriel thought with inward amusement, like the prospect of a bullfight to a champion matador.

'Take me to them,' he demanded. 'All I ask is a chance to talk to them.'

'Roland is several days' march away, further up in the mountains.'

'No matter.' Lightly Gabriel dismissed the heat and weariness and pain. 'I shall doubtless survive.'

'You are in no hurry to return to England?'

'I shall stay until the matter is resolved.'

'Then let us drink to our success.'

Cavalier poured wine into cups, handed one to Gabriel and raised his own.

'To freedom,' he said, and Gabriel echoed the toast.

'To freedom.'

The day that Ashbury angrily dismissed Peter Jordan, shouting that he would never act upon the stage at Smock-Alley again while he had the management of it, he came home to the Angel Inn with a bunch of gillyflowers – gold and russet, with a scent so sweet it seemed as if summer had entered the room in their company.

Elise was surprised to see him, for it was an hour when she would expect him to be at rehearsal.

'Oh, 'twould be a crime to stay indoors on such a day,' he said. 'Even that old fool Ashbury has the sense to see it. Put on your bonnet and come to the park.'

She had not known him so lively, so ready with his smiles and charm, for a long time. It was like a return to the days of their courtship, to the time when he had set himself out to please, and she responded at once to his gaiety, kissing him in return for the flowers and happily agreeing to abandon the gloom of the Angel Inn for a walk with him.

'Now, aren't you the loveliest thing?' he asked her with a smile when she was ready to go out. 'I'll be the envy of the entire city, with a girl like you on my arm.'

Compliments had become a rarity and she glowed with pleasure to receive this one. Everything was going to be all right, she told herself. He had been difficult and thoughtless recently, but only because he was worried now that he was responsible for her as well as himself. A good wife must make allowances.

But it seemed there would be no need for forbearance that day, for his only concern was to entertain and amuse her. He made her laugh with his stories and mimicry; and when they came to a fallen tree trunk, he leapt upon it and struck an heroic pose, declaiming Henry V's Eve of Agincourt speech dramatically but in comic Irish until she wept tears of mirth and implored him to stop. Oh, Elise thought, how grand it was to see him restored to his old ways like this. How wonderful to laugh and be carefree!

And when he drew her towards a seat in the shelter of a wall, pulling her close and kissing her with the kind of tenderness that had been missing for some time, she relaxed against his shoulder and smiled with contentment.

'I was beginning to think you did not love me after all,' she said, and he turned to kiss her again.

'Sweet Elise,' he whispered, running his finger down her cheek. 'Lovely Elise.' Gently he kissed her again. 'You must never doubt me.'

He continued to caress her, his hand with a touch as light as thistledown moving to stroke her forehead, her ears.

'So pretty,' he murmured. 'Always so pretty.' Gently he was toying with her ear-bobs now. 'As these are. Rubies, are they not?'

370

'Garnets.'

'But gold. The gold must be worth a pretty penny, *ma petite héritère.*'

'Don't call me that – I hate it!' She pulled herself away from him. Now he was spoiling things, and she bit her lip in disappointment. When after a moment's silence she looked up at him determined to say some loving word that would restore the atmosphere of accord that had previously been between them, the pretty speech died on her lips. His face had changed. He was still looking at her closely but there was a look of calculation in his eyes and his mouth was twisted, as if he wanted to speak but could not find the words.

'What is it?' she asked him. For a moment he said nothing. Then he smiled and reached out to touch the ear-bobs again.

'Let me have them, sweeting. They'd keep me going a week at the tables, and at the end I would buy you a dozen more –'

She stared at him, the happiness drained from her face.

'At the end you would have nothing,' she said stonily. 'And I would have lost my ear-bobs that were given to me by my father. I won't do it, Peter.'

'You may have to. Gaming is the only occupation left to me now.'

'I don't understand.'

'Then allow me to explain.' He sighed heavily and paused for a moment before going on. His voice when he spoke sounded weary and sullen, with no trace of his earlier gaiety. 'You had to know some time. That whoreson Ashbury has turned me off.'

'But *why?* I don't understand.'

'He's been turned against me.'

'By whom?'

'It's of no consequence by whom.' He hunched his shoulders, angling himself away from her. 'I knew I had enemies in the theatre. I did not expect my wife to be against me too.'

'How can you say that?' She was hurt and angry.

'Then stake me.' He turned and looked at her full in the face. 'What other choice is there? If Ashbury won't employ me then I am finished in the theatre – at least in Dublin. But who cares for that? Sure, it's a worthless place, only good for getting out of. We'll go to America, you and me, and make a fresh start. For that we need money.' He gripped her hands tightly. 'Listen to me, Elise. I am capable of living on my wits. Yes, yes – I know,

I need no telling, I have lost at dice these past days, but if you will only stake me, I shall win tonight. The tide has turned! It always does, in the end. The trick is to keep your nerve, keep going. I lost last night. Tonight will be different.'

'Last night?' Elise seized on these words, disregarding the rest. 'You were at the theatre last night!'

'Sure, it's a piddling, useless role the man gave me in this play. Finbar spoke my lines as well as his own and no one would have missed me had not Ashbury been at the front of the house instead of at home with a rheum as we thought –'

'So *that's* why –'

'Sweeting, forget Ashbury and the theatre. I'll make far more at the tables, then we'll go to America and I'll try my luck on the stage there. With your money and my winnings –'

'Neither of which we have at this moment. In the meantime we have to eat and pay the rent.'

'And so we shall, do you but stake me. Just one pair of ear-bobs! It's not much to ask, is it? You have others.'

'Aye, and how long before they are gone too? I'll not sell my jewels.' Elise got to her feet, all her enjoyment of the day gone. 'I'll not see them thrown away.'

She began to walk back towards the town and Peter hurried after her.

'Sweeting, you misunderstand!' He had adopted a reasonable, mildly humorous tone. Which of his many voices would he choose next? Elise wondered. 'There is a science in these matters, a rule of averages. A man can lose so much, but eventually he must win. Tonight is my turn to win. I feel it! I'm certain of it!'

'And last night? What did you feel then?'

'My heart's darling, will you listen to me?' Coaxing, smiling, he turned her to face him. 'Sure now, be kind to this rogue who is full of sin but loves you dearly.' It was to be cajolery then, Elise thought cynically. 'Try to understand. There are nights when one loses. Equally there are others when one wins. If I kept a ledger you would see it clearly over the course of a year – income would exceed outgoings.'

'There's been precious little sign of it so far.'

'How long have we been wed? Six weeks? It's not long enough, sweeting. If in another six weeks I have not recouped all and made enough to take us to America, then I'll pack you in a trunk

372

and tie you with ribbons and send you back to your father. How's that for an offer?'

'It would be humiliating beyond words.'

The afternoon lay in ruins about her. She wrenched herself free of him and walked home, his persuasive voice in her ears at each step, still attempting to cajole and charm.

Fear and misery sat like a stone in her stomach. Had he ever loved Elise Fabian? she asked herself; or was it only *la petite héritière* he had wanted to possess? Soon the cajolery would turn to anger, she knew him well enough to be sure of that now, and he would show her that thin, cold face that was the face of a stranger.

In the end she gave him the brooch that Paul had given her for her seventeenth birthday, and Peter kissed her and told her he adored her, there was no one like her and no man possessed a sweeter, more understanding wife.

Possessed was the word, she reflected as he took the brooch and left her, making no promises regarding the time of his return. She was his possession. In law he could take anything of hers he wished. The pleading was merely a concession to the niceties.

As doomladen as a funeral bell, the thought occurred to her that the day would come when the pleading would cease and the plunder begin. Would love die then, she asked herself miserably? Would she be indifferent? Would she hate?

One thing she did not want to do was to skulk back to London, tail between her legs like an ill-used bitch. She clenched her teeth and her fists determinedly. She would not. *She would not!* Somehow, somehow, she would create order out of this chaos.

Her optimistic nature resurrected itself a little. Perhaps Peter spoke truly. Perhaps he would win, make a fortune, start a new life in America. There must surely be theatre of some kind over there. It was possible, after all. If only he could get the recognition he deserved he would be different, she felt sure of it. His was a talent worth saving, worth fighting for. Meantime, there were gowns she could sell, he was right about that.

She shook herself out of her lassitude and began to go through them, making a pile for disposal. It was to be hoped, she thought grimly, that Peter was equally profitably engaged.

Casey's was a small tavern with a room behind where there was always a game in progress – cards or dicing, whatever was demanded. It was popular with the acting fraternity for no particular reason except that once one had started frequenting the place, others followed; consequently Peter could depend upon finding someone among the tatterdemalion clientele who welcomed him extravagantly, asked what he was drinking and how was his lovely wife and what was the latest scandal from Smock-Alley. The place was smoke-filled and none too clean, but it was friendly and he had the feeling of homecoming as he ducked under the lintel and heard voices raised in greeting.

Where Mr Goodbody came from nobody knew. Afterwards some said he was a distant relative of Casey's wife; others that he had come from Casey's home town of Clones. All Peter knew was that suddenly Goodbody was there most nights, as unlikely an habitué of Casey's as it was possible to imagine, being thin and clerkly and respectable-looking, with a little pursed mouth that seldom smiled, still less shouted with laughter or roared obscenities as did the rest of the company.

He liked a game, though, even if he showed no emotion, neither pleasure nor dismay when he won or lost. It was Goodbody who had cleaned Peter out the previous night when he should have been at the theatre, scooping up his winnings with a joyless, matter-of-fact air which had only added to Peter's annoyance. Now, armed with the proceeds from the sale of Elise's brooch, he was out to get his revenge.

Casey was a genial man with a wide grin and a turned-up nose like a blob of putty. The grin died as he saw Peter that evening, despite the greeting he had received from cronies around the fire.

'Now look,' he said without preamble, going over to him before he had advanced more than a few feet into the room. He took his arm and spoke softly. ''Twould be a lot easier if you'd play elsewhere tonight.'

'What?' Peter stared at him blankly and laughed in disbelief. 'What are you talking of, man? I'm playing here.'

'Look – Goodbody has some bee in his bonnet –'

'What should I care? Is my money less acceptable than his?'

'So you've money in your pocket tonight, eh?' Goodbody challenged him across the width of the room. 'Where did you come by it?'

'What's it to you?' Mystified, Peter looked about him, conscious of an atmosphere he did not understand. Even men he had thought of as friends seemed ill at ease, avoiding his eye. He looked at the landlord who seemed as embarrassed as any. 'What's afoot here, Casey? Answer me, is my money not good enough?'

'So long as it is your money.' Goodbody sneered.

Peter became very still. Only his eyes moved as he looked towards the unimpressive little man in the black coat.

'Would you please be good enough to enlarge on that remark?' His voice was silkily polite, but chilling as splinters of ice.

Casey tugged at his arm.

'Sure now,' he said pleadingly. 'We don't want any trouble.'

'Quiet, Casey.' Peter pushed the landlord from his path and walked over to where Goodbody sat in a corner of a settle, tankard in hand. 'Now, sir, if you have something to say, may I ask that you say it boldly? Pretend that you're a man, not a mealy-mouthed pervert.'

'I'll not play with thieves.' Goodbody spat the words venomously, holding his tankard before him like a shield.

Its contents rocked dangerously as Peter reached out and hauled Goodbody to his feet. The little man's mud-coloured eyes widened with terror and his nose twitched. However he defiantly stuck to his guns.

'I'm right and you know it! You took my purse last night. 'Twas after you left I discovered the loss of it. Who could it have been but you? "If he comes in here with money in his pocket, we'll know for sure," I said, "for he'd not a penny last night by the time I'd finished with him."'

Peter's face had thinned and whitened. Elise would have recognised the signs at once.

'Say it straight,' he said, bending to whisper the words menacingly into Goodbody's face. 'Say "Peter Jordan, you are a thief!"'

'Now, see here Jordan –' Casey tried once more to take hold of him but was shaken off. 'See here, I want no trouble.'

'Then allow me to play this whoreson liar.' Peter whirled round, dropping Goodbody so suddenly that he rocked back on his heels and the ale in the tankard almost spilled again. As if emboldened by this increased distance between them, Goodbody spoke out.

'You are a thief, Peter Jordan – a common thief, and here's the proof, that you've money in your pocket –'

Thief, thief, thief – he had run from the accusation before and it had taken years to break free from the memory of Madame

Colbert's shrill voice. Now the cry had come again, setting the echoes ringing, and blindly he struck out, sending Goodbody reeling and the tankard flying from his hand.

Casey tried once more to restrain him but it took only a moment for the entire room to explode into violence, sides taken, battle lines drawn. Fists smacked into faces, blood spurted, men grunted and groaned and laughed wildly with the sport of it. The settle crashed over and bottles smashed to the floor.

To most it was all a game, a chance to let off steam and enjoy a scrap as if they were boys again. They were Irish, after all, and what better sport could there be than this, even if it meant bloodied noses and broken heads?

Only Casey pleaded for calm. To him it was no sport, for the damage it was causing made him wild with despair; neither was it sport to Peter, who continued to punish Goodbody viciously for his groundless accusation, standing white-faced, blind-eyed, throwing punch after punch, left and right, left and right, until the little man fell senseless. He kicked him then as hard as he knew how, heard the crunch of bone and kicked again unheeding, until others stopped and looked and became aware that it was a game no longer and that to Peter it had never been so.

The men round him seized him and held him, and still he struggled in his determination to punish the man who now lay senseless on the floor.

All around the room, the combatants shook their ringing heads to clear them, mopped the blood and grinned ruefully at each other. Some limped into the night towards the comfort of their beds; others found their pots where they had fallen to the floor and looked to refill them.

The knot of men around Peter was silent, suddenly sober. Casey, crouched on the floor beside Goodbody, stood up slowly. His mouth was stretched in a kind of rictus and his face was ashen as nervously he wiped his hands down the sides of his breeches.

'He's dead,' he said hoarsely. 'Goodbody's dead.'

In the stunned silence that followed these words, the eyes of all the men turned to focus on Peter. The only sound that could be heard was the rasping of Casey's breath.

'And you killed him,' he whispered. 'You murderin' bastard – you killed him.'

* * *

From the moment she had returned to London, the time spent in the Kentish hills took on the quality of a dream, yet Charlotte knew it had changed her for ever.

They had not been back a week when business took Paul out of town, much against his will. He had no wish to leave her, but had been summoned to Bristol to deal with the financial affairs of two wealthy but elderly sisters who were not fit to come to London, and he felt it his duty to go.

'If I do not we may lose their business,' he said. 'Which seems hardly fair to Charpentier.'

Charlotte moved to hold him closer, but did not argue. She had stuck to her resolve not to allow Paul into her chamber at Freedom Street but had agreed to go to his rooms – though even that was not without difficulties. She understood all too easily why Elise had found it necessary to employ Molly as an accomplice. Keeping Nan and Joseph ignorant of events was a major problem, but for Gabriel's sake she was determined to do so.

'Of course you must go,' she said now. 'In some ways it will be easier.'

He asked for no explanation of this statement, understanding it all too well. Living apart, yet so close in terms of distance, had been difficult for many months. Now it had become a refined form of torture for both of them.

'It is like a bereavement,' she said to him dismally before he left. 'Like consciously mourning for one's own death.'

She wondered at times if life would ever hold pleasure for her again, and in tune with her mood, the innkeeper was proved right and winter returned. Rain fell incessantly, droplets trickling down the window panes like tears, rank upon rank of them as if they would never end.

She was not carrying Paul's child, she found – a circumstance which caused her a certain amount of bitter amusement. Perhaps she was barren – and if so, what a waste of emotion had been all her childish fears!

A letter from Gabriel arrived after she had been back in London some ten days.

All was going well, he wrote, with Cavalier proving of the same mind as himself. He was in no danger, was among friends, and she was not to worry about him. He had stayed with his mother, he told her, until she gently and peacefully relinquished her hold on life, and her final words had been of her joy at seeing him once more.

And my thankfulness that I was with her is so great that I find it almost impossible to express. For this as well as for so many countless other things, I must thank you, my dearest wife, whom I hold constantly in my thoughts and my prayers.

A further blessing has been the meeting with my brother Jules Arnoult, and the friendship and respect that have grown between us. Though in matters of religion we do not agree, we are as one in our determination to see liberty of conscience restored in our land. I hope that in happier times you, too, will meet with him and will rejoice with me in the brother I have discovered so late in life.

May God keep you and my dearest Elise. I hope to be home in less than a month, my mission safely accomplished.

Charlotte gave Paul the letter to read when he called to see her on his return from Bristol, and he read it in silence.

'He sounds well,' he said as he handed it back to her. 'Confident and in the best of spirits. Charlotte –' He hesitated and she looked at him questioningly. 'By the time he returns, I shall be gone.'

She had moved to place the letter in the escritoire but at this she whirled round, slamming the lid, staring at him with panic-stricken eyes.

'Paul, no! It is too soon.'

'I cannot bear to see him, Charlotte.'

Painfully she swallowed.

'Perhaps you are right.'

'I feel I am deserting you – yet if you *will* stay, my presence will accomplish nothing but to make matters more difficult for you.'

Slowly she nodded and gave a small, unhappy laugh.

'I suspect I am able to dissemble better than you,' she said. 'If he saw us together, he would have no doubts, I feel certain.'

'Come with me, Charlotte.' He had said the words so often – sometimes pleadingly, sometimes angrily. Now he spoke dejectedly, head drooping as if all spirit had gone from him, not looking at her. 'He has had you for so many years. Is it not our turn now?'

378

She was silent for such a long time that he began to hope. He raised his head to look at her, but when their eyes met he saw that hers were full of tears.

'I cannot, Paul,' she said.

Slowly, painfully, as if he had suddenly grown old, he rose to his feet.

'Then the sooner I go, the better,' he said. 'While in Bristol I made provisional arrangements to sail on a barque in early May. The tenth.'

'The tenth of May.' She repeated the words tonelessly.

'I must go to Sandwich before then to take leave of my parents.'

'Of course.'

The tears spilled over and ran down her cheeks, silent as the rain, and he moved to take her in his arms, holding her as if he could never bear to let her go. Finally, though, he gently dried her eyes.

'What news have you of Elise?' he asked unexpectedly.

'Elise?' Charlotte struggled for composure. 'Nothing! I am very worried about her, Paul. There has been no further word from her, though I have written begging for intelligence.'

'I ask because the barque on which I sail puts in at Dublin with cargo of some kind and may anchor there for some days. If you tell me where I may find her, I shall make enquiries.'

'Oh Paul, would you? I should be so grateful. It will be good reason for you to write.'

'I will not dare to commit to paper the words I shall be longing to say, but you will know them anyway. I love you, Charlotte. Always.'

Reluctantly he left her and it was some time later that Nan found her sitting in half darkness, alone and still.

'I cannot prevent myself worrying about Elise,' Charlotte said, as if in explanation. 'Though Mr Bellamy is to go to Dublin en route for New York and has said he will call on her. That is good news, is it not?'

'That young miss will be well enough,' Nan replied briskly. 'She's one to land on her feet, is Mam'selle Elise. You mustn't fret so, madam. If you'll forgive me, you're looking real peaky — now what will the master say when he comes back to find you've took ill?'

'I cannot imagine what he will say when he finds Elise gone –'

'Oh, it's a crying shame! No wonder you look like a ghost! Your little holiday did you no good at all, if you ask me. But try not to fret, madam, for it won't mend matters.'

And it won't stop the days trickling away like grains of sand in an hourglass, Charlotte thought.

Paul went to Sandwich and stayed there several days, coming back laden with kind and loving messages from his mother to Charlotte and the earnest hope that they would be meeting at Whiteacres before too long.

'She must have been saddened by the thought of your going,' Charlotte said. 'How long will the voyage take?'

'Much depends on the weather and the time lost in Dublin.' They were lying in each other's arms on a night when her servants thought her to be attending a ball in Soho, and Paul's words were punctuated by kisses. 'It will be a few weeks, I reckon.'

'I am so glad you are going to Ireland, Paul. There is still no word from Elise.'

'I'm not sure her husband will welcome me.'

'Never mind him! I must know if she is well and happy. Tell her I have word that her father is in good health and hopes to be home in a few weeks.'

'You have heard from him again?'

'Only a brief word, scribbled from some remote place in the mountains. He was delighted with Cavalier, and most optimistic about his chances of success.'

'Who can resist him?' There was a bitter note in Paul's voice; then he sighed and repeated the words, but ruefully this time, almost with affection and amusement. 'Aye, who can resist him! Would that I had his gift of persuasion.'

'Dearest Paul.' Her lips moved over his cheek, his throat, and he closed his eyes with the sweet pain of his longing. 'You have other gifts.'

That night was one on which they were able to block out the thought of their imminent separation and could talk of other concerns. It was not always so. Particularly it was not so on the last night they spent together when the fact of their parting was suddenly so real and immediate that they were shocked into silence, with no words that could give comfort one to the other. There was no comfort to be found.

And then he was gone and there was nothing – nothing at all except an aching emptiness.

20

The Camisards: named, it was said, for the ragged cotton garments they wore.

Ragged they were without doubt. Gabriel stood on a crumbling wall, braced against the trunk of a chestnut tree, and surveyed them. They had come in their hundreds – how many? Seven hundred, eight hundred? He could not guess. He only knew that they filled the natural amphitheatre hidden away in the heart of the Hautes Cévennes. It was a strange, secret rock declivity, ringed by the forest, impossible to find without a detailed knowledge of the area.

The Camisards had that knowledge, for it was here that they lived, among the trees and the ravines and the fast-rushing streams. They were hard men, uncouth, battle-scarred, burnt nut-brown by sun and wind, a strange similarity between them, with their watchful, obstinate faces scored prematurely by lines that hardship and determination had etched deep.

They are the greatest challenge I shall ever meet, Gabriel thought as he looked at them. How best can I move them?

He reached into his memory and found that the patois of his childhood had returned to him, and in simple words he sketched a picture of a land where religious freedom was denied, where a minority was persecuted. The listening men nodded and murmured their recognition.

'I speak not of France,' he said to their astonishment. 'But of Palestine at the time of Christ's birth. He came to a country as troubled and oppressed as this – and what, I demand of you, was his message? Was it to hate? Was it to burn? Was it to kill?'

He hammered home the questions in ringing tones, then paused for just the right fraction of time before answering them himself.

'Love your enemies,' he said, in the voice that could surely charm a raging beast. 'Blessed are the peacemakers, for they shall be called the children of God. Blessed are the merciful, for they shall obtain mercy. That was his message.'

He compelled their attention, and when he had them firmly in his hands, he dropped his voice a tone or two so that they were forced to concentrate on each word that he spoke.

He spoke of matters close to them: the country their children would inherit if the present state of affairs was allowed to continue, the legacy of bitterness, the killing that would go on from one generation to another.

'You are Huguenots,' he cried, raising his voice to a thrilling pitch once more, 'and rightly proud of it. No one has the right to deny you this privilege, but while you live as exiles within your own country you have no influence, and denial will be the result. Your voice is unheard in the councils of the land. You may say that without the gun and the sword you have no voice in any circumstances. I say you are wrong –'

'You preach capitulation?' It was a young man in the front who spoke, dark, with flashing eyes and a nose that curved like the beak of an eagle.

'I preach reconciliation, a joining together with like-minded Catholics who believe in freedom of conscience.'

'Treachery!' the young man shouted.

'Faith!' Gabriel's reply was swift as a ricochet. 'Faith in Christ's words, that the Kingdom of Heaven is like unto a grain of mustard seed – the least of the seeds that grows to a tree so great that the birds of the air can lodge in its branches. Thus we will bear witness to our faith – not hidden in the forest, but like a beacon set on a hill. Let your light so shine before men –'

Were they with him? They were so still and watchful, showed so little emotion, it was hard to tell.

'Let no man call me a traitor,' Gabriel continued quietly, every word clear as a droplet of crystal. 'I, Gabriel Fabian, was tortured and did not abjure. I lost my youth, my strength, my health – aye, and I lost my manhood at the hands of my torturers, but I kept the faith.'

What had made him say that? He had guarded the secret jealously until that moment, but now the words were said before this great multitude he felt a sense of liberation, a heady mixture of elation and pride.

'Yes, I kept the faith and shall do so until death, but I say to you now, reconcile or perish. Accept the olive branch that has been held out to you. Insist on your demands being met, but accept it, for surely God must weep to see the slaughter and bitterness between Protestant and Catholic when the highest aim of each should be to glorify him. Accept it, for if you do not, babes now in their cradles will die for your intransigence.'

He stood for a moment without moving, a moment that lengthened unbearably as he allowed his gaze to travel from one side of the amphitheatre to the other and back again, assessing their reaction.

Are they with me? he thought again. I think that they are. But even as his optimism rose he caught the eye of their leader, Roland, who sat beside the dark young man at the front and he knew without doubt that here was a man who remained hostile, unswayed either by reason or eloquence.

Roland stood up and faced the crowd.

'No one doubts Monsieur Fabian's sincerity,' he shouted in a high, angry voice that echoed and re-echoed. 'But he is wrong. We have not fought so long and so bravely to give up now.'

'We shall put it to the test.' As before, Gabriel's words were both low and clear. 'Those who wish to accept the offer of an end to hostilities on terms to be negotiated, form in this part –' He flung out his right hand. 'Those in favour of continued fighting, to the left. Make no instant decision, I beg you. Pray to your God, consult your hearts, and in one hour, make your choice.'

He stepped down from the wall, suddenly exhausted.

'You have them,' Cavalier said, taking hold of his arm, his fair-skinned face bright with enthusiasm. 'I swear you have them.'

'Perhaps.' Gabriel sank down and leaned against the wall, his eyes closed. 'I am not sure that your own convictions do not blind you –'

'Say what you will, you're a traitor, Fabian.' At this harsh, intrusive voice Gabriel's eyes opened. The dark young man stood before him, mouth drawn back in a snarl. 'We'll never give in! Shall I tell you what they did to my entire family – to my young sisters –?'

'No one denies the suffering.'

'You'll have support from the likes of Cavalier, but we'll not turn our coats here.'

'Then God have mercy on you.'

The young man swung away towards a knot of men who were engaged in earnest talk.

'Who is that?' Gabriel asked Cavalier.

'Durel, a henchman of Roland and even more of a fanatic.' Leaning together against the wall they conversed in low voices, as they watched the scene before them where many groups talked heatedly together while others appeared to be taking seriously Gabriel's exhortation to pray. 'One thing strikes me, Fabian,' Cavalier went on after a moment. 'Whatever the outcome of this, you must not delay your departure.'

Gabriel turned his head to look at him, frowning.

'That sounds like a warning.'

'I intended it to be so. There are too many hot-heads here who will be against you, even though I believe you have carried the majority.'

Gabriel said nothing, but turned to look back at the amphitheatre, at the men far and near, the comings and goings. He was silent for a long time.

'Am I now to fear fellow Huguenots?' he asked. 'I think not, Cavalier. I must see matters through to their conclusion.'

The sun sank lower and a strong breeze sprang up, lifting the hair on their heads and swaying the branches of the trees in the surrounding forest. Gabriel bowed his head, praying silently that men's hearts would be moved, and as the time for choosing approached he found himself unable to look up, suddenly fearful that the wrong decision would be made. Was Cavalier right? Was his own life in danger? Would this horde of hardened killers, no less deadly because they were strong in the faith, turn their wrath against him? He could not know the workings of their minds for there were many among them who had been driven by cruel persecutions towards strange, mystic practices. Some who claimed to speak in tongues; others who vowed they could stand in the midst of a fire and not be consumed; still other fanatics who pursued the rite of physically breathing the Holy Spirit into the mouth of another. How could he have expected to reach out to such men? Surely it had been a supreme example of the arrogance and pride that bedevilled him?

Lord, if I am to die, so be it, he thought. Slowly he raised his head.

There was a general movement in progress, a heaving of the

crowd. Some went one way, some another. For a time it was impossible to see where the majority had taken up a stance, but then suddenly all was still.

Slowly Gabriel and Cavalier got to their feet and Roland, closely followed by Durel, swaggered over to join them.

'Well?' Roland asked unpleasantly. 'What now, monsieur?'

'What, indeed?'

To any observer the crowd appeared equally divided. Perhaps there were a few more in the right-hand section of the amphitheatre – fifty men, or perhaps a hundred, but it was far from the overwhelming endorsement that Gabriel had hoped for.

'We have a majority,' Cavalier said stubbornly. 'I am empowered to negotiate.'

'We need a further test,' Roland said. 'We should meet again in Nîmes where others can join us.'

Gabriel was conscious of a feeling of impending calamity which only deepened when he chanced to look up and find Durel's eyes on him, piercing in their intensity, burning with malice. Nevertheless he calmly spoke in agreement with Roland.

'Spread the word, then,' he said. 'Let us all meet in one week's time in Nîmes. If Huguenots sweep in from all points of the compass, coming not in supplication but in strength, then de Villars will accede to our demands.'

It was Cavalier who addressed the crowd, Gabriel who listened on this occasion, though in truth he barely heard what was said. If I am to die, he was thinking, let it not be a shabby, pointless death, with nothing achieved. Let it not be a knife in the back on a darkened street.

When Cavalier had finished speaking, those who filled the amphitheatre prepared to move away, back to their home villages or to the forests where they were in hiding. Some were deputed to ride towards Nîmes and beyond, spreading the word in all directions, that there would be a tremendous gathering of Protestants, one that would shape their entire future.

Exhaustion threatened Gabriel like a gaping pit and he sank down again with his head resting against the wall, summoning the strength he would need to begin his own journey, content to let others make arrangements, to speak of times and places. But even though his eyes were closed he became aware of scrutiny and opened them to see Durel standing a few yards away from him. For a moment they looked at each other, saying nothing, then Durel spoke.

'We shall meet at Nîmes,' he said.

There were elderflowers growing thick where they camped that night, close to a stream, and high white asphodels on stony ground beyond. The scent reminded Gabriel of his childhood. His old grandmother always said the elderflowers would keep better when picked on a waning moon, and he remembered her filling her apron with the blossom, using it to make a lotion for sore eyes and for boils. Would it cure a sore heart? he wondered.

He lay and listened to the nightingale and could not sleep for thoughts of Charlotte and the wrong he had done her, though there was not one bone in his body that did not scream out for rest. Sometimes he could think of her without pain; sometimes he was aware of the tiny flicker of hope at the back of his mind, the hope that he was mistaken and that he would return safely and that all would be as it had been before. Sometimes it burned brightly, but never in the cold, grey hours of night when he could not sleep. At such moments all hope seemed dead – yet often, almost to his annoyance, a new day would see the flame rekindled. He loved her so. How could he relinquish hope?

At daybreak he rose wearily and the long journey down from the hills continued, through the twisting streets of Mende with its high-spired cathedral; down and down until they crossed the River Pecher at Florac. More elderflowers here, and yellow gorse, and butterflies brightly trembling everywhere like living flowers – swallow-tails, orange tips, fritillaries; Paul would know them, Gabriel thought, and felt the knife twist inside him.

They passed through the bustling town of Alès, the sky darkening above them, and they were given shelter that night by a sympathetic farmer and his wife. The rain fell, hard and unwavering, for several hours, but in the morning the sky was clear again. The trees hung heavily, but the air was sweet with all the scents of summer, intensified by the rain.

Gabriel lost count of the exact number of days taken up by this journey, for the time seemed endless, his body on fire with pain. He felt no fear but only exhaustion and as he rode pictures came and went in his mind as if he slipped in and out of a dream-filled sleep.

One moment he thought he was at Whiteacres; the next, he

could hear the noise of the looms and he looked up, expecting to see le Bec. Always there was Charlotte. It is inconceivable, he thought, that I shall not see her again. I *must* see her again! Soon this will be over and I shall be home, and this is the part of my life that will seem a dream.

At one point Cavalier rode alongside him when the path grew wider.

'Have you thought more about leaving for England before this gathering in Nîmes?' he asked. 'I think it would be prudent.'

Gabriel blinked and cleared his vision, and saw that they were about to enter the streets of Nîmes.

'It is the culmination of my mission,' he said. 'I must be there to speak to them.'

'But do we not tempt the fates too greatly? Your presence has passed unremarked so far, but we must not forget that no treaty has been signed yet. We cannot be sure that you are no longer a wanted man.'

Gabriel rode for a while without speaking, then he smiled at Cavalier.

'Pray don't be fearful,' he said. 'We are all in God's hands. Tell me,' he went on, injecting a lighter note into his voice. 'Shall you lodge with me at my stepfather's house?'

'I think not, I thank you. I have some good friends here who will expect – what's this?' He reined in his mule as ahead of them three troopers appeared on horseback from a track to the side of the main road and ranged themselves across it, barring their way. There was no avoiding them, no way of escape. After a moment's hesitation, the two men continued slowly towards them.

'Is either of you men Gabriel Fabian?' called out one of the troopers who appeared to be their leader.

'What of it?' Jean Cavalier spoke defiantly. 'We are unarmed travellers, come to see Marshal de Villars.'

'That one's Cavalier,' said another of the horsemen. 'I've seen him before.'

'We've orders to let him through. It's the other – are you Gabriel Fabian? Answer me,' he snapped, as Gabriel remained silent. He was a young man, Gabriel saw, with a bad skin and close-set, pebble-hard eyes.

'Yes,' he said quietly. 'I am Fabian.' His voice gave no indication of the accelerated pounding of his heart.

'You will come with us. Not you –' the trooper shouted at

Cavalier who had moved closer to Gabriel. 'Get on your way and keep out of trouble. It's this one we want.'

'May I ask why?' Still Gabriel sounded calm.

'You know why.'

'I am an unarmed traveller, as Monsieur Cavalier said –'

'You are an escaped prisoner, a wanted man, and by God, you've kept us waiting long enough. You are to come with me. Be off with you, Cavalier.'

'Where are you taking him? He's done no wrong.'

'My orders are to arrest him. Now get out of my way – move, move –'

He hit about him with the flat of his sword and Cavalier was forced to retreat.

'Go, Jean,' Gabriel said. 'All will be well.'

'Such a proud steed,' said one of the troopers mockingly, taking the mule's reins in his hands. 'A fine mount indeed.'

'A donkey was good enough for Christ.'

'Blasphemy!' roared the trooper. 'This is our man, right enough. This is Fabian.'

People going about their business in the town stopped and stared, to look with curiosity at the small procession as they rode along; first the officer, then Gabriel flanked on either side by the troopers. Poor devil, they thought, and wondered briefly what crime this man had committed, before turning back to their marketing.

'He don't look like a criminal,' an old man said, sitting idly in the sun and relishing the feel of its warmth seeping into his bones. 'Does he look like a criminal to you, Henri?'

His companion hawked and spat thoughtfully into the dust at his feet.

'Who can tell?' he said indifferently. 'Who can tell?'

Charlotte looked daily for a letter from Paul, but she heard nothing. Her loneliness and sense of isolation induced a kind of paralysis, and she found it impossible to work. She slept poorly and even resorted to the apothecary for a draught which did little to help her.

'That Marthe would give you something,' Nan said.

'Marthe? Berthe's sister?' Charlotte shuddered. 'I would not touch any brew of hers. I mistrust the pair of them.'

'She's quite the herbalist, madam. She treats all about here.'

'Well, she's not treating me.'

She tried the apothecary's draught again, and this time she slept heavily. It was not a refreshing sleep, however, but a sleep plagued with dreams. One confused image followed another until suddenly everything was very still and she seemed to be in a huge, empty space – a dark room with a high ceiling, only the far end of it lit by a small, barred window, such as one might find in a dungeon.

There was a man at the end of it, standing with his back to her. He was dressed in a long, black cloak, and though she could not see his face, she knew that it was Gabriel and that he was in danger. She tried to reach him to warn him of it, but could not move and could only watch from a distance when, as if from nowhere, men came and tried to drag him away towards a trap door that had suddenly appeared in the floor. She opened her mouth to shout, but no sound came. He turned just the same and she saw that his face was a skull's face, but still he spoke to her.

'Tantine killed me, Charlotte. But it was with your help.'

She woke at that, trembling and crying. Her skin was clammy and she felt physically ill, so sick that she scrambled from her bed and vomited helplessly in the china basin that held water for washing.

She had helped to kill him, Gabriel had said in the dream. Back in bed she pulled the covers up to her chin and lay rigid, her teeth chattering.

It was not true! There had been no truth in Tantine's story – not then, not when she told it. Surely he had believed her denials? She had begged him not to go to France, but he had made light of her fears, deriding them so successfully that she had dismissed them. He was visiting Nîmes as the long-lost son of Madame Arnoult, he had said. No one would be interested in him or his past.

But he was in mortal danger, she was sure of it now; and it was her fault, for though Tantine's tales had been slanderous lies, she and Paul had made them true. But why should that put him in danger? Was she being punished through him? No, no – God was not a fiendish, merciless judge. She had dreamed dreams before and they had been proved unfounded. She was no prophet; merely a worried, guilty woman who had mislaid her peace of mind.

So she attempted to convince herself and gradually the shivering ceased. However, she could not entirely dismiss the feeling of terror, the sense of looming disaster. Dawn was only just breaking, but she could not sleep again. She lay awake listening to the birds' chorus and watching the sky grow lighter. It would be fine once more, yet she felt as oppressed and threatened as if the air were heavy with thunderclouds, and as she lay there conscious of fear like a weight in her stomach, the trembling began again and she shook as if she had an ague.

When at last Nan came with chocolate for her to drink, she felt her mistress's forehead with concern.

'You did never ought to have taken that draught,' she said severely. 'It's upset you proper, no doubt about it.'

The draught! Of course, that was it. That was what had caused the nightmare, not any kind of foreknowledge or prophecy. There was relief in the thought, but she still felt uneasy, for all the world as if a sword were suspended over her head.

'You should stay a-bed, do you ask me,' Nan said. 'You've taken some kind of chill.'

'I've work to finish,' Charlotte insisted.

She did her best to dismiss her fears and to concentrate on her design, but she could not keep her mind on decorative flower patterns and scrolls and curlicues, and finally she flung down her pen in disgust and left her work table, drifting aimlessly towards the window where she stood looking down into Freedom Street.

Here where the street widened into the little square there was never so much traffic or so many pedestrians as further up, closer to the main road and the market. Still tradesmen came and went to the big houses, and there were always servants coming and going. There was no reason for her to take an interest in the man who stood on the corner, except that he seemed irresolute, as if unsure where to go. He has come too far, she thought, and now finds that there is no way out of the square except the route he took into it.

He looked like a seafaring man, and none too respectable. She toyed with the idea of calling Joseph to send him on his way but before she could move from her vantage point she saw him hail a footman from one of the neighbouring houses who happened to be passing by. For a moment they stood and exchanged a few words, then she saw the footman turn and indicate her own house. The stranger raised his hand as if in thanks and began to make his way towards the gate.

It was a message from Gabriel, she thought at once – a letter he had entrusted to a sailor instead of to the regular mail, for it was through all manner of hands that his previous letters had reached her.

The fears that she had tried to dismiss returned, redoubled, and she ran downstairs, opening the front door before the sailor had even knocked so that she caught him with his hand raised, a surprised look on his face.

'Is it a letter?' she asked breathlessly.

'Aye, and one I am to deliver to Mistress Fabian and none other, for so the writer told me –'

'I am Mistress Fabian. I beg you, give it to me.'

He fumbled at the pouch that hung at his waist while in an agony of impatience Charlotte waited. Were ever fingers so thick and awkward? It was all she could do not to snatch the folded sheets from his hand, but at last she had them in her grasp. Still the man waited – he wanted paying, of course. A coin – where was a coin? She had no purse about her, but Nan would see to it. She called her frantically and was thankful to see that she came at once.

'Nan, give this man a penny or two,' she said as she ran up the stairs towards her own chamber, not able to wait another second to discover what Gabriel had to say to her.

In the privacy of her room she broke the seal with fingers that trembled; only then did she realise that the writing was not Gabriel's, and she stared at it blankly. Thoughts of her husband had so dominated that day from the moment of her waking that it had not occurred to her that another hand could have written the letter. Then suddenly she gasped, shocked. Paul! Of course, of course, this was the letter she had longed for, the letter she had looked for every day – how could she not have thought of it?

She sank down in a chair close to the bed to read it.

My dearest Charlotte, I scarcely know how to begin this letter or how to acquaint you with all that has happened since I arrived here. You cannot conceive of the horrors I found waiting for me in Dublin and I shrink from the need to tell you of them, however there is naught else I can do.

I found Elise in circumstances so squalid that they defy description, and in considerable distress. Peter Jordan had, that day of my arrival, been found guilty of the crime of murder and was sentenced to hang two days later. The crime occurred in a tavern brawl after Jordan had been unjustifiably accused of stealing a purse which later was found in the possession of a noted thief.

Together with a few of Jordan's friends I did all I could to persuade the authorities to commute this sentence to transportation, even resorting to bribery, without success. All our representations came to nothing and the sentence was duly carried out at the appointed hour.

I stayed with Elise all through the day of execution, for she sorely needed consolation. I saw Jordan the previous night and can report that he went to his death bravely. He begged me to prevail upon Elise not to attend the hanging and this I did since she was already distraught and he had sufficient friends there to ensure that he was not entirely unattended. They reported privately to me afterwards that they hung upon his body and that the end was as quick as anyone could hope for.

As the hours went by, Elise grew strangely calm as if she had wept all the tears of which she was capable. My respect for her has grown mightily. None can gainsay that she behaved badly in her elopement with Jordan, but though her life here has been a hard one (and despite his brave end the man was undoubtedly a rascal who treated her poorly) she utters no complaint of him and has conducted herself throughout with great dignity and maturity. I would go so far as to say you would scarcely recognise her as the heedless girl you once knew.

I embark now on the part of my letter which is more difficult to write even than what has gone before and is the reason why I shall find a seaman who will place this into your hands and no other, first ensuring that your husband is still in France. Before I write more, my dearest, I must assure you of my constant love which is as strong now as it ever was. I shall love you until the day I die. Believe me, dearest Charlotte, nothing can alter that.

Naturally I assumed that once Elise had settled her affairs she would return home to London and I offered to give her as much money as she required for the journey. She was vehement in her refusal. It was not through lack of love for you or her father, she insisted, but rather that she could not bear the thought of the kind of marriage her father would demand – marriage, as she described it, to some long-faced Calvinist whose virtue was only matched by his dullness.

I argued with her, but she was adamant. She said she would stay in Dublin and obtain work as an actress at the theatre before running home with her tail between her legs (her words again).

I said to her that I could well imagine what a blow this would deal to her father. Well then, she said to me, if you are so anxious about what will please him, why do you not ask me to marry you?

At first I thought that she jested, but then I saw that she was in earnest, and that she liked the idea of a new land and a new beginning, and the more I thought about it the more it seemed to me that though I shall never feel for her as I feel for you, I have always felt an affection for her even in the worst of times. Since I must (I suppose) marry one day, and since I cannot have you, then it seemed to me that perhaps some order could be achieved out of chaos if, after all, I married Elise, which as you know has always been Gabriel's desire.

I can imagine no other circumstances in which I could contemplate such a step. My heart is yours and I long for you with every breath I take. I am no kind of a husband for anyone, yet I know that if I sail away from Dublin tomorrow (as I must do), leaving Elise to fend for herself in the sorry state in which she finds herself, I shall feel that I have compounded all the wrong I have ever done towards Gabriel. I beg that you will understand my feelings. I am persuaded by the example set by yourself and Gabriel, that many good marriages are based on affection and friendship, which two emotions I feel for Elise. My love, as I have said, is always yours.

We plan to marry tomorrow morning before the ship sails on the early tide. Forgive me, my darling Charlotte. A nearby vessel is leaving for London within the hour and I shall entrust this to one of the crew to bring to you.

He signed the letter 'Always and forever, your Paul', and for some time Charlotte sat as if frozen, her eyes fixed on the signature as if this were the only part that made sense to her, as if the rest were in some foreign tongue. She felt the room sway about her and she clutched the arm of her chair to steady herself.

Her breath was rapid and shallow and she found herself making a strange, mewing sound as if her pain were physical. It was not true! It could not possibly be true – none of it! Never, never, never would he marry Elise –

Elise! At the thought of her the pain seemed to focus into one single point and the tears poured down her cheeks as she wept, not only for herself, but for that enchanting, golden girl whom she had loved as her own child; that wilful, infuriating, lovely and lovable creature who had suffered so much sorrow.

It would be comforting to hate her, but she could not.

That is our curse, she thought angrily, jumping to her feet and pacing distractedly around the room. None of us has any capacity for hate. We all love each other too well – Gabriel, Paul, Elise, myself. It should, in theory, equate to perfect happiness, but instead it means that our loyalties are forever divided and that guilt is our portion when any one of us selfishly disregards the good of the other. If only I could hate!

The anger ebbed away. She subsided into the chair again and sat motionless, consumed by misery, arms wrapped around herself as if for comfort, leaning forward, staring at nothing. She did not know how long she sat there, how long the tears poured down her cheeks.

Somehow, she thought, I must learn to bear it. Somehow I must learn to live with this, so that when Gabriel hears of it and rejoices as he undoubtedly will, he will not be aware that my joy is a lie and that I welcomed the news with tears.

And as she sat there, it seemed to her that from the moment they had embarked on that fishing boat more than seventeen years before, the threads of their lives had been woven together. It was not a new thought, but it had never seemed more apt, the threads never more inextricably combined, the shuttle never more inexorable.

Perhaps one day the pattern would become clear.

21

Gabriel sat on the filthy straw with his back against the cold and slimy wall of the dungeon into which he had been cast. He had repeated every psalm he had ever committed to memory; and would return to them. But for the moment he thought of Charlotte.

He would have liked the chance to write a letter to her, just one last word, but he had no writing materials and could not see to use them if he had, for it was perpetual night down here in the depths of the fort. Tomorrow he would see the daylight again, would take one last ride in the sun, but tomorrow it would be too late.

No trial had been deemed necessary. He had been sentenced once before and had escaped; now the law would take its course without the intervention of advocates or judges. The authorities had even forgone the usual formalities: the *question ordinaire*, which was accompanied by torture, and the *question extraordinaire*, enforced by even more refined torture. They had tried it before and he had not broken, and much to his relief it seemed that it was now considered a waste of time.

They knew he would answer 'No'. He would not accept the Mass, he would not abjure. This they knew, but for his own good he would be given the chance to recant while he lay in agony on the wheel tomorrow, every bone splintered by a hammer-wielding executioner.

He had no idea of time. Was it night or day? It was impossible to tell here in this blackness, and he had forgotten how long ago it was that the last meal had been thrust towards him – if meal it could be called, for it was no more than a hunk of mouldy bread and a cup of water.

He could hear footsteps approaching down the stone passage outside the cell. Had the night gone already? Was the time now?

A key sounded in the lock and the hinges shrieked as the door swung open revealing the jailor, a lamp in his hand. Christ help me, Christ be with me, Gabriel prayed silently, and stood, his manacled hands held before him.

'There's a visitor for you,' the jailor said. 'Fifteen minutes, you can have –'

'A visitor?' Gabriel blinked and turned his eyes from the light.

'It is I, Gabriel. Jules.'

'Jules!' Gabriel attempted to take a step forward but was jerked backwards by the chain around his ankle.

'Can you not loose him?' Jules asked the jailor. 'Lock the door upon us. We can neither of us leave without your knowledge. Here, take this for your pains –'

The jailor eyed the money and did not hesitate for long though he grumbled enough as he took a key from a bunch at his waist and bent to unlock the chains that bound the prisoner.

'I'll be in trouble, do the sergeant find me out in this.' His voice had a whine to it. 'Too good-hearted I am, and that's a fact.'

'The good Lord will bless you for it.' Gabriel tenderly felt his wrists, rubbed raw by the biting iron manacles.

'Leave the light, my good fellow –' Jules put out a hand to stop him as he left.

'I can't see my way to that!'

'Not even for a few more francs?'

'Well –'

Duty wrestled with cupidity once more, but not for many moments. The money changed hands and he left the light behind him, hanging it on a nail beside the door. The two men stood motionless as the key was turned once more.

'You are more than welcome.' Gabriel's voice was low but quite calm. 'What time is it?'

'Close to midnight.'

'I – I do not know at what time I leave in the morning.'

'Eight o'clock.'

'Nothing here happens on time!'

Jules Arnoult drew in his breath.

'Oh, my brother!'

With one accord, as if at a prearranged signal, they embraced, and of the two it was Jules who was the most visibly distressed.

'I have tried everything,' he said, his voice trembling with emotion. 'The fact that you are no longer a French national, that you have made no attempt to proselytise, that the Camisards are within a hand's breadth of negotiating a settlement to include the release of prisoners, that almost twenty years have elapsed since you were in jail before –'

'I knew you would be working on my behalf.' Gabriel drew back a little so that he could look at his brother, but he retained a grasp of his arms as if he clung to human contact while there was yet time. 'I also knew that your efforts would be fruitless.'

'I even tried bribing this jailor, but he would go no further than to allow me in.'

'Be calm, Jules, even as I am.'

'How can you be calm? I blame myself for pressing you to become reconciled with our mother. She would never have wanted this.'

'You did not ask me to come here.'

'It was one element that persuaded you to do so.'

'One among many, none of which are important now. Jules, I desire you to perform yet one more act of kindness.'

'Anything!'

'I want you somehow to go to Charlotte, my wife. Tell her I die unafraid – that I have not for one moment wavered either in my trust in God or my love for her, and that above all things I desire her happiness. Tell her –' He hesitated for a moment before continuing. 'Tell her I understand all and forgive all, just as I hope she has forgiven me.'

'You can trust me to do so.'

'Jules –' Again Gabriel hesitated, looking earnestly and with love into his brother's face. 'How many years we wasted! That I regret more than I can say.'

'I, too.'

'Tomorrow will be hard for you. You will need much fortitude –' He broke off abruptly and looked quizzically, almost with amusement, at the other man. 'They did not send you to make one last attempt to beg me to recant, I trust?'

'No one sent me, and I should not dream of asking you to recant. A man's conscience is between him and his Maker.'

'Hold to that, Jules! The time will surely come when the whole of France believes it. Tell me, did the Huguenots march upon Nîmes in strength as we planned?' He smiled ruefully as Jules shook his head. 'So Roland won after all.' He sighed, and for the first time his shoulders drooped as if this news had saddened him. 'The struggle goes on, then, with peace as distant as ever.'

397

'Cavalier is still here. There is talk that he will accept de Villars's offer, no matter what Roland thinks. You know it was the man Durel who alerted the authorities to your presence? It was an evil act that has done both him and Roland much damage among the Camisards.'

'God have mercy on him.'

'Gabriel –' It was Jules's turn to hesitate and struggle for words. 'One thing I have ensured, and God knows it is little enough –'

Patiently Gabriel waited for him to be able to speak.

'Don't be afraid,' he said after a moment. 'Say what is in your mind. What have you ensured?'

'That your sufferings will last no longer than two hours.' His face twisted and he turned away. 'Six hours it was decreed you would lie upon the wheel, but I made representations to the courts, to the church, to the governor of the prison – everyone I could think of. I tried to make them reduce the time still further, but the Abbé maintains that one hour would give you insufficient opportunity to consider fully the danger you court in the hereafter if you do not abjure. Two hours is the best I could do.'

'And at the end of two hours?'

'You will be strangled.'

'A strange favour, some might think, but I thank you heartily.' Gabriel reached out once more and gripped his brother's shoulder. 'Fortitude,' he said again. 'Be easy in your mind, even as I am. Were not our blessed Saviour's sufferings far worse when he died for us all on the tree? Listen! I think our friend returns.'

The measured steps of the jailor were unmistakable, and the men embraced again. It was Jules who wept, though neither could speak, and it was in silence that they parted. Once more Gabriel was manacled and the door was slammed upon him.

'You'd best get some sleep,' were the jailor's last words to him. 'You'll need your strength, come the morning.'

He did not sleep, but spent the night in prayer. It was before eight when the door opened to admit the Abbé who subjected him to a final exhortation to abjure, clearly distressed at the thought of yet one more soul doomed to outer darkness. Gabriel listened politely, but shook his head at the repeated question.

'No, monsieur,' he said wearily. 'I will not take the Mass.'

Rough hands were ready to seize him, to strip his filthy clothes from him and dress him in a coarse white garment, and when

398

this was done he was hurried from his cell through the never-ending dank corridors out into the hazy sunshine of the early summer morning.

The light hurt his eyes and he blinked dazedly, stumbling as he was pushed towards the cart which was to take him to the place of execution. He had no manacles now, and was able to stand erect holding the side of the cart.

'I am here, Gabriel,' he heard a voice cry. 'God keep you.' And blinking, he turned his head and searched among the watching, gaping crowd and saw that Jules was there only a few feet away from him, and Cavalier, too. He raised a hand briefly in recognition and allowed his gaze to wander over the crowd, wondering what motivated people such as these – mothers, fathers, kind people, no doubt – to stand and jeer at a man going to his death, a man who had done them no harm. Had they risen early that day so that they could be at the fort at the appointed hour?

There were many others along the route taken by the cart. He stood erect, not looking at them but at the way ahead and at the blue sky. Such a beautiful day! The last day he would ever see. A golden day.

He saw Jules keeping pace beside him and called out to him.

'Tell Charlotte, it was a golden day.'

It was brave of Jules to champion him so openly, and brave of Cavalier too, for it seemed to him that there were not many Huguenots on the street that day; and who could blame them? It was the thought of the grand gesture missed that he minded more than anything, the feeling that he had after all done nothing significant to bring about reconciliation.

Arrogant until the end, he thought wryly. What had given him the notion that his life, or his death, was any more significant than those of other men?

'Into thy hands,' he prayed silently. 'Lord be with me and sustain me.'

Astonishingly, he was not afraid; it was no pretence. Even when the cart arrived at the Place de la Cathédrale and he saw there the infamous wheel and the gallows, and the unlighted pyre ready to reduce his broken body to ashes, he was conscious only of calm and of the strength of his beliefs and of the inevitability of his present position. And when once more the Abbé called upon him to abjure before he stepped off the cart, his only response was to turn to the crowd to address them in ringing tones.

'I have lived a Protestant,' he declaimed. 'And as a Protestant I shall die.' And he repeated the words that Jules, a good Catholic, had said to him the night before. 'A man's conscience is between himself and his Maker. May God bless you all and forgive those who have misused not only me but many other souls, more noble and more innocent.'

He did not notice that the crowd had fallen silent, for he looked only inward now, searching for the resolution and the strength that would sustain him for the next two hours. It was left to others to remark and wonder at it, and to speak of it long afterwards.

Could such a man be completely mistaken, they asked each other?

Utter misery is all absorbing. Charlotte, moving like a sleepwalker through the days, realised suddenly that May had turned to June, still without word of Gabriel, and the awareness of passing time and lack of news began to cause her serious concern.

'What can have delayed him?' she asked Nan worriedly. 'From his last letter I had thought him almost on his way home.'

'Madam, why do you not go to Whiteacres?' Nan had for weeks been worried at her pallor and lack of spirits. 'London's no place for you this weather. The master would want you to go.'

'I shall wait until I hear from him. He must surely come soon.'

She was swept by longing for him. Paul was gone for ever and she knew that this would cause pain for the rest of her life; but at the same time there was a dream-like quality about the love they had shared, as if right from its beginning she had been aware that there was no place for it in the real world.

Now she hungered for the comfort of Gabriel's presence, the certainty of his love and the warmth of his companionship. Meantime she did her best to rouse herself from the lacuna of inertia in which she had languished for so long and went to discuss future work with le Bec. Somehow it seemed to bring Gabriel closer.

She was thus engaged when a message came to say that a gentleman had called to see her.

'Perhaps it is the mercer from Bath,' le Bec said. 'The one I spoke of. Would you prefer me to see him, madame? He should be told we can extend him no more credit.'

'No, monsieur.' Her voice was decisive. What would Gabriel say if on his return he found that she had handed over control even of the smallest matters? It was more than high time that she took a grip on life again. Besides, it was a challenge to confront gentlemen who cherished the illusion that because they were doing business with a woman they could get away with all manner of sharp practice. 'No, I shall deal with him.'

The moment she saw the stranger, however, she knew he was not the mercer from Bath. This man was French and addressed her in that language.

'Madame Fabian? I am Jules Arnoult, half-brother to your husband.'

His expression told her all she needed to know, and she caught her breath.

'Come upstairs,' she said and, hurrying, led the way up to the drawing room, conscious of a sick feeling of dread. 'Tell me,' she said, closing the door upon them. 'You have news of Gabriel?'

'I regret that he is dead, madame.'

Blindly she groped for the back of a chair and held it for support.

'When?'

'Ten days ago.'

'How?'

For a moment he hesitated.

'Broken upon the wheel,' he said huskily.

'No!' The word emerged as a long-drawn-out, shuddering cry. She clutched her stomach and bent over as if the pain were more than she could bear. Jules went to her, and taking her by the arm gently urged her to sit down.

'I must get you something – brandy perhaps? Shall I call your woman?'

'Tell me everything – everything –'

'He died bravely, with many messages for you. He told me to assure you that he was unafraid.'

'How could that be? Such a terrible, terrible death!' Charlotte searched his face, seeing the grief there and the kindness. Was he saying these things merely to be kind now, shielding her from the worst of the agony?

He lifted his hands and let them fall again.

'God alone knows how any mortal man could be unafraid,' he said. 'I can only assure you that there was such an air of calm about him that there was not one who saw him who was unaffected by it. Afterwards the crowd dispersed silently. There was no gloating, no exultation. Merely the feeling that here had died a brave man.'

'He told me there was no danger –'

'Nor would there have been, but he was betrayed by an enemy – a fanatic who considered him a traitor to the Huguenot cause.'

'Gabriel, a traitor?'

'He preached peace and reconciliation. To some that is treachery.'

'It seems he preached it without success.'

'His death was a success, in its way. It made all who saw it pause to consider. Even the Abbé who attended him and begged him to abjure seemed to me to have doubt in his eyes when it was all over. He told me he had never seen a man braver or more strong in the faith. I must tell you,' he went on, 'of the messages I was enjoined to bring you. He said – he said that he had never wavered in his trust in God or his love for you. He said that above all things he desired your happiness and that he understood all and forgave all, just as he hoped that you would forgive him.'

She bowed her head and wept then, and Jules went in search of one of the servants to attend her. It was Nan who came and who, with infinite gentleness, herself in tears, helped her mistress from the room.

Charlotte turned on the threshold.

'Pray do not leave, monsieur,' she said earnestly. 'You must need refreshment and we have much to talk of. Give me a little time to compose myself.'

'As long as you wish, madame. Wait – there is yet one more message I have forgotten to deliver. It was said to me on the day of execution as he stood in the cart.'

'Yes?'

'Gabriel said: "Tell Charlotte this is a golden day."'

She looked at him without speaking, the tears running unchecked down her cheeks. Then she nodded, as if this strange message made perfect sense to her, before turning to hurry from the room.

* * *

402

He stayed only a short time, for he had commitments at home and was anxious to return. It was long enough for Charlotte to understand the rapport that had been established between him and Gabriel during the short time they had known each other. There was a steadfast quality about him; a basic honesty which seemed to shine from him.

She liked him, but she was glad when he left. Grief had sapped her energy, had made her unwilling to make the effort to talk or to listen, or to do anything but exist, in a mindless, timeless vacuum.

There were formalities that had to be attended to. The lawyer came with Gabriel's will, which held few surprises. He had left a legacy of a thousand pounds to Simon le Bec and two thousand to Elise; he had left to Madame Colbert the deeds of her house, and apart from a few bequests to charities such as La Soupe and the French Hospital, all the rest was left to Charlotte.

'Will you inform Madame Colbert of her good fortune?' the lawyer asked.

'I should much prefer it if you did.'

The man looked at her in some puzzlement, unaware of the breach in the family.

'Would it not be of some comfort to you to have a relative close to you at this time, even if it is merely a relative by marriage?' he asked.

'If you mean Madame Colbert, no! Oh, she is welcome to her little house – pray don't think I grudge her that. Heaven knows she has wanted to own it outright for years. Well, now she has her wish.'

'And his daughter?'

Charlotte hesitated, took a breath.

'At the moment I have no address for her. The last I heard she was on her way to America. No doubt I shall hear eventually.'

'So for the moment, you are alone?'

'Except for the servants, yes.' Charlotte looked at him directly. 'I am quite alone. I shall go to Whiteacres, our house in Kent, as soon as possible.'

'An excellent idea, if I may say so. Er – it may seem somewhat precipitate to mention this, Mistress Fabian, but should you decide to dispose of this house and business, then I am at your service to advise on the matter. Since your own relatives are in Kent, then it may be more suitable to take up residence there.'

She looked at him without speaking, and he coughed uncomfortably, beginning to assemble his papers. She seemed in a strange mood, he thought – almost as if she were in a trance, unable to see him though her eyes were wide open.

Well, grief took many forms. It had certainly transformed her from a comely young woman to a pale, haggard ghost – but at least she was dry-eyed.

There was nothing quite so trying, in his long experience, as widows who wept.

'Perhaps I should have said I would go to Madame Colbert,' Charlotte said. She was brushing her hair before the mirror in her chamber while Nan pottered in her usual fashion, putting her mistress's discarded gown into the press, folding stockings and kerchiefs and underwear.

'There's no reason you should, if you're not minded.' Nan held no brief for Madame Colbert, even though she had no knowledge of the rift, other than that it existed.

'I am glad she has her house, in spite of all.'

'It was good of the master.'

'He was ever aware of all he owed to her.' Charlotte sighed heavily. 'I've no doubt she's heard the news about Elise and Paul through servants' gossip, but I should have told her directly.'

'Don't you bother with her, madam,' Nan advised robustly. 'You've enough to think of. The sooner you get to Whiteacres and some good country air, the better it will be. You're looking that peaky.'

'Can you wonder at it?' Charlotte frowned at her reflection. 'I must confess I don't feel myself at all. I brought up my breakfast again this morning. That makes four days in a row.'

She was aware out of the corner of her eye that Nan had straightened up and was watching her, suddenly very still.

'Madam,' she said after a moment, her voice sounding strange. 'You don't think – could it be –?'

'Oh, really, Nan! Out with it!' Charlotte was tired, and was mildly irritated by the hesitation.

'A baby, madam. Could it be?'

The hairbrush clattered to the table as Charlotte turned quickly and gazed at her open-mouthed. Could it be? Was it possible?

'I suppose,' she said slowly at last, 'it must be eight weeks or more since my monthly flux. I should have realised! It never occurred to me.'

'You've had that much on your mind. But you've all the signs! Oh, madam!' Nan took a step closer. 'How pleased the master would be, could he but know!'

Charlotte continued to stare as if transfixed, bereft of speech.

A baby! Paul's baby! But only he and she knew that, and he was on his way to America – was probably there by this time. If only he had not married Elise – if only, if only –

She brushed aside such fruitless thoughts, would not allow herself to dwell on them. To all others it would be Gabriel's baby, born posthumously, for who knew or cared that he had left England a few weeks too early for this child to be his? Clearly no such suspicion had entered Nan's head.

Slowly she turned towards the mirror and looked at her reflection.

'You're right,' she said at last. 'I look quite monstrous peaky.'

'We'll have you well in no time at Whiteacres. Oh madam, I'm that pleased. A baby! After so long! Oh, nothing can take away the hurt of the master's loss, that I know, but a baby will be a remembrance, like.'

'Yes.' Silently, staring at herself, Charlotte repeated the miraculous words. A baby! Was she quite certain that the fear had gone? Oh yes, there was no doubt! She knew no fear, but only a dawning excitement, a faint indication that somewhere, beyond the present grief, there was hope and love lying in wait for her. 'Yes – a remembrance,' she said. 'And so much more!'

Still she stared at herself as if stunned, and her voice was faint.

'Oh madam,' Nan said, excited enough for both of them. 'Oh madam!' She looked a little anxiously at her mistress. She was so still, pale. 'You do welcome the little soul, don't you?'

In the mirror, Charlotte smiled at her, a faint flush at last appearing on her cheeks.

'With all my heart,' she said.

There was too much work on hand to go to Whiteacres for a week or two, much as she would have liked to abandon everything. She was looking through some old designs in the hope that they might inspire new ones when Nan gave her the news that Madame Colbert was unwell. One of the kitchen maids had heard it from the footman at the house on the corner where Marthe worked as cook.

'I suppose I should go and enquire for her,' Charlotte said, without enthusiasm.

She bought a posy from a flower-seller, and for the first time since the quarrel she knocked upon Madame Colbert's door. It was opened to her by Berthe, grown fatter and a little more slovenly, who stared at her without attempting to conceal her hostility.

'What do you want here?' she asked rudely.

'To see Madame Colbert, naturally.'

'She's not up to it.'

'Kindly ask her if she will receive me.'

'Berthe!' Faint tones came from an inner room. 'Is that Madame Fabian's voice I hear? Has she news of my darling?'

Taking advantage of Berthe's momentary inattention, Charlotte stepped past her and went unannounced into the room where, despite the warmth of the day, Madame Colbert sat close to a fire, her face grey and drawn.

'What is it, what is it? Is there news of that sweet child?' she asked quaveringly.

She had aged twenty years, Charlotte thought in astonishment. The flesh had fallen from her bones and her hair looked strangely dry and sparse.

'I've no recent news,' Charlotte said. 'I came to see you, madame – to see how you did. I'm sorry to hear you are unwell.' It was impossible to speak other than pleasantly to this old and much diminished Tantine. 'I should have come sooner, perhaps, but as you're no doubt aware, I have had much to trouble me.'

'Ah yes, your husband. He has gone to his rest.' There was a vagueness in her manner and she uttered no condolences, however perfunctory. 'But what of my darling? Berthe told me some tarradiddle that she had gone to America.'

'It was no tarradiddle, madame.'

'And her husband hanged – or was that another? I disremember.'

Distractedly she moved the objects on a table beside her. A pill box, a glass of water, a scent bottle, a pomander, all were pushed about with quick, irritated movements. It was so hot in the room that Charlotte felt she could hardly breathe, yet Madame Colbert broke off this exercise to pull her shawl more tightly about her.

'Elise's husband did hang,' Charlotte told her, 'but she married another – did Berthe tell you that? She married Mr Paul Bellamy.'

'Who? I know no one of that name. I disremember. I have had such pain.'

'Madame,' Charlotte said gently. 'I fear you are ill. Have you seen the physician?'

Berthe, entering at that point carrying a chalky liquid in a small glass, gave a derisive laugh.

'She's well looked after, madame, don't you fret. No call for you to trouble yourself! She would have fared poorly if left to you. Here you are, madame, drink this physic, and we'll soon have you to rights.'

Obediently Madame Colbert drank, pulling a face like a child as she did so. Charlotte chewed her lip, troubled at her decline and troubled, too, by the change in Berthe who had a proprietary, overbearing air.

Charlotte had never liked Tantine – had indeed hated her at one time not so long ago, but no one could hate this confused, ailing old lady. Charlotte leaned forward and took her hand. It felt very light and dry.

'Madame, soon I go to Whiteacres. Do you remember White-acres? The garden and the woods and the pool? Will you not come too so that we may enjoy the country air together? My father could tend you.'

Madame Colbert's face brightened a little and her muddied eyes flickered towards Berthe.

'You expect her to travel in this state?' Berthe demanded. 'Never fear, I shall look after her, as I always have done. Isn't that so, madame?'

She raised her voice as if Madame Colbert were deaf, though as far as Charlotte knew, deafness had never troubled her. 'Doesn't Berthe look after you well?'

'Oh yes, yes.' Madame Colbert hastened to agree. 'I simply don't know what I would do without you.'

'You'll soon be well with me to look after you.'

'Indeed I shall.'

'It must be as you wish, of course.' There was something in the atmosphere that made Charlotte uneasy and she would have liked nothing better than to run from the room, but conscience made her stay. 'I shall not leave for Whiteacres for ten days or so yet. If you change your mind you must let me know.'

It was Berthe who answered.

'I'll make sure she does so, madame. Now, if you don't mind, she ought to rest. She tires very quickly.'

The small, coal-black eyes looked into hers and Charlotte's unease grew. Was she imagining things, or was it evil that gave this room its threatening character? If so, then it emanated from this woman.

As much else had done, she realised. Oh, Tantine was foolish and gullible and insanely possessive where Elise was concerned, but Berthe had played upon all those things, had encouraged Tantine in her spite. Yet what could anyone do? It was clear that the old woman depended and doted on Berthe and, far from making any complaints, she blessed her name at every opportunity.

'That husband of hers,' Madame Colbert said, suddenly returning to the subject of Elise. 'He was always a rascal. He stole my purse.'

'Madame, that was never proved. He always denied it.'

'Berthe saw it in his hand.'

And who, in their right mind, would trust Berthe? Charlotte felt a pang of pity for Peter Jordan. How could anyone know how he had felt, how terrified he had been, when as a boy he had been accused? Perhaps it was not, after all, so unbelievable that a second false accusation could drive him to such rage that he could commit murder.

'You have much to answer for,' she said bitterly, looking towards the maid who stood so stolidly, fat hands folded over her apron, eyes lowered.

'Celestine was such a pretty little thing then – such golden hair, everyone admired it and loved her for her pleasing ways,' Madame Colbert said.

Berthe moved towards her to place a hand on her shoulder.

'Celestine died years ago, madame. You are confused.'

'Yes, well, perhaps. I am so tired.'

'You see?' Berthe looked at Charlotte. 'You'd best leave.'

'Very well.' She bent over Madame Colbert. 'I wish you a swift recovery, madame. And do not forget to let me know if you change your mind about Whiteacres.'

There was no reply beyond a faint snore. Sagging in her chair like a small rag doll, Madame Colbert had fallen asleep.

* * *

Charlotte was thoughtful as she walked back along the street.

Old women grow senile, fall ill, she thought. It was foolish to see anything sinister in that. Clearly she was devoted to Berthe; yet evil was in that room – and Marthe was a herbalist.

Oh, surely she was allowing her imagination to run away with her!

But Tantine had money and was a houseowner now. How ironic, if Gabriel's bequest was only serving to hasten her end! It must not be; she must put events in train, make sure that Tantine was being treated well, that Berthe was not as evil as she feared. The responsibility was hers, and she would not be able to rest if she ignored it.

She was coming to life, she recognised. Her concern for Tantine was surely evidence of it.

Once she reached the square, however, all thoughts of Madame Colbert were banished temporarily from her mind, for emerging from a hackney carriage at her own front door was none other than Madame Belamie, Mrs Bellamy – by whatever name she chose to call herself, Charlotte was delighted to see her. With a cry of joy she hurried over and the two women embraced warmly.

'I have never been more glad to see anyone,' Charlotte said.

'I had to come! You need someone, and who else but me in the absence of your own dear mother? Dearest child, how can I express my sorrow?'

Charlotte's tears flowed afresh in the face of her sympathy, but they were not so bitter as they had been at first. Did she cry for Gabriel or Paul or both? She scarcely knew any more. Both were equally lost to her. She only knew that little by little the grief was becoming, if no less, then containable.

'Oh, how glad I am to see you,' she said again, when later they drank chocolate together in the drawing room. 'But I must not tire you! Perhaps you should rest after that horrid journey.'

'I'm well enough. I slept at Rochester last night.'

Close the mind to Rochester and the sparkling Medway and the ride to the Downs, and the Downs themselves –

'Tell me!' Casually Charlotte looked into the chocolate pot as if she had nothing more on her mind than the amount remaining within. 'Have you heard from Paul?'

'Alas, no – nothing since the astounding news that he was to marry Elise. He said he wrote to you the same evening. We still await word of their arrival. Pray God they are safe!'

'Gabriel would be so pleased to know of the marriage.' Charlotte was proud of the calmness of her voice, the evenness of its tone. 'It was a match he always longed for, for he loved Paul dearly. It seems so strange that he never even knew of her marriage to Peter Jordan.'

'Poor child! How she must have suffered! I, too, am pleased about the marriage. Oh, Elise can be difficult and headstrong, I know, but there is an endearing gaiety about her that I have always admired. Paul wrote most warmly of her courage and spirit, and though I know that to a certain degree it was a marriage of convenience, it was clear he was moved by both. She rose above her misfortunes in a truly remarkable way, he said, and never complained. There is a toughness about her that will serve her well in a new land. If Paul does not love her now, I am inclined to believe he will do so before too long! It is hard to see how any man could resist such dazzling looks.'

Charlotte's hand clenched involuntarily upon the black lustring of her skirt. Close the mind, close the mind. The thought of Elise in Paul's arms was something she could not face, not yet. One day, perhaps; but not yet.

'Shall you come to Whiteacres now?' Mrs Bellamy went on.

'I – am not sure.' Charlotte hesitated a moment. 'My man of business seems to think I should sell all and live there permanently.'

'Perhaps he is right. You have always loved it.'

For a few moments Charlotte did not reply. She got up and went to the window, toying with the blind's cord, looking absently down into the street below as if unsure how to respond.

'There is one item of news I have not told you,' she said. 'Madame, I am *enceinte*.'

'Charlotte!' It was a joyful cry, followed by a sad echo. 'Oh, Charlotte.'

Charlotte turned and looked at her, faintly smiling.

'You once told me there was no joy like it.'

'Did I? I have forgotten it – but I was right.'

'It was on the fishing boat, when Elise was born.'

'So it was! You were just a frightened child. I longed to mother you.'

'I longed to be mothered! Well, we shall see. I shall learn of the joy, perhaps.'

'You will, Charlotte; this I promise.'

'We shall see,' Charlotte said again. She looked down into the street once more, seeing the flower-seller on the corner; the pie-man delivering to the next-door house; a man crying knives to grind; two girls walking in the sunshine without their mantles. Lower down the street, a dray and a carriage were duelling over the right of way.

'I shall call him Gabriel,' she said softly. 'And he will be a silk-man, through and through.'

'Have you thought that it might be a girl?'

'I know that it is not.' Her voice left no room for argument.

Madame Belamie came over to her and embraced her once more.

'You are very brave, and I am proud of you,' she said.

'No – no –'

Confession trembled on her lips, but she said nothing. What purpose would it serve? She would keep her secret, shoulder her own burdens, ask for no help, learn to live with the guilt; for guilt there would always be, she was in no doubt about that. She had no way of knowing how far she and Paul had motivated Gabriel to take that fatal journey.

'The Queen sent her condolences,' she said, apparently at random. 'Or rather, Mistress Hill sent them on her behalf. She assured me that Gabriel did not die in vain, that he did influence the pact that has brought the Camisard rebellion to an end.'

'I am sure she is right.'

'Are you?' A bitter little smile twisted her lips. 'I wonder. You forget I have met one of the worst of the fanatics – Etienne Boyer. Nothing Gabriel ever said influenced him, and I suspect there are many like him. One such was responsible for Gabriel's death.'

'Where there are men, there will always be sin. And redemption.'

Redemption? Like the joy, like the acceptance of Paul's marriage, it was something for the future, something she could not at the moment comprehend. But perhaps acceptance that it existed meant that the guilt would not, after all, weigh her down for ever.

'Look,' she said, indicating the far end of the street with a nod of her head. A hackney carriage and a water cart together with two sedan chairs had joined the first carriage and the dray and from this vantage point it looked for all the world as if they were locked in mortal combat, their drivers gesticulating in fury, a crowd gathering to cheer on the opposing sides.

Charlotte laughed, ruefully and with a hint of affection.

'Freedom Street!' she said.

Madame Belamie smiled at her.

'I take it you will be staying here.'

Charlotte shrugged her shoulders.

'Where else?' she asked. 'It's where we belong, Gabriel and I.'